THE BEST MISTAKE HE EVER MADE

JIM ALLEN

Fulton Books, Inc.
Meadville, PA

Published by Fulton Books 2021

ISBN 978-1-64952-559-8 (paperback)
ISBN 978-1-64952-560-4 (digital)

Printed in the United States of America

CHAPTER 1

Everyone Makes Mistakes

When I answered the phone, my friend Norm said, "I'm going to the horse sale in Seattle, and I wish you'd ride over with me."

I replied, "I'm done with the horse business." I had been out of the business for almost a year, and I enjoyed not paying a training bill every month.

He said, "I'm not buying, I just wanna watch them sell." We were in the business together for more than twenty years and had never gone to a sale because we always bought our horses locally, from friends who owned breeding farms. We had run some nice horses but never made any money to speak of. I thought it might be fun to watch them go through the sales ring, so I told him to pick me up in an hour. Seattle's a little over a two-hour drive from Yakima, and we had fun talking all the way over.

As we were walking in, we ran into a friend who owned a breeding farm near Yakima, and Norm asked him if he had anything in the sale that he liked. He replied, "If you could buy number 67 for four thousand dollars, it would be a good buy." After listening to them, I knew Norm had more in mind than just watching. We found two seats near the front, and I was surprised at how quickly the horses went through. I enjoyed reading the sales book because it listed the dam and the stud of each sales entrant and told how they did both running and producing. While Norm watched the horses go through, I studied the book. There were some nicely bred mares and studs. Most were a couple generations from the really big sires, or they would probably have been sold in Kentucky, California, or Florida. The fact is, the blood was there. Seattle Slew was an example of a horse that was a couple generations from a sire named Bold Ruler. He sold for the bargain price of seventeen thousand dollars and turned out to be one of the best runners and sires of all time. Everyone dreamed of finding another Seattle Slew, but they were few and far between. My cousin's daughter was married to a cousin of one of Slew's owners. I always followed the horse very closely because he was locally owned.

After number 45 went through, I asked Norm if he was ready to leave. He wanted to watch number 67 sell, so I knew he was interested in buying him. He was a big boy, and if he wanted to buy the horse, I certainly didn't care. There were still twenty horses to go, so I started looking more closely at the book. One, in particular, caught my eye. The stud was two generations from Northern Dancer, and the dam was by a nice sire named Round-Table. He was both their first crop, and neither had run, but I loved the breeding.

When number 60 went through, Norm asked me if I made a bid. I told him I didn't, so he told me to be careful because they almost accepted one from me. I told him I may have scratched my nose, and he suggested I scratch between horses.

We had seven horses to go, and each time one went through, I sat like a statue. If they went through fast enough, I didn't even take a breath. When number 66 came in, I thought *Great, just one more, and we can go home.* He was the one that caught my eye in the book, so I was anxious to see what he'd sell for. Somebody close to me was bidding, so I sat perfectly still to make sure they wouldn't take a bid from me. The bidding stopped at two thousand dollars, and I thought, *Somebody may have gotten a good buy.* A lady walked over and handed me a clipboard, so I said, "I don't know what you think you saw, but I didn't buy that horse."

She smiled and said, "The man beside you did. Will you please hand him the board?"

As I handed it to Norm, I asked, "Why did you buy that horse?"

He said excitedly, "Kenny said, if I could buy him for four thousand, it would be a good buy. **I got him for two!**"

"Not trying to burst your bubble, my friend, but number 67 is walking in right now."

"That's not funny," he said with a scowl on his face.

"Look at the number on the tag," I replied. He slumped in his seat, and his smile was gone. He sprang out of his seat like a shot and was headed for the office. We were known for razzing each other, but I really felt bad because it wasn't like losing when gambling for a cup of coffee. When he entered the office, I was right behind him, and a middle-aged lady asked if she could assist him.

Norm said, "I just bought a horse by mistake. Would it be possible to sell him back?"

She replied, "You could run him back through, but you'd have to pay the sales commission, and the buyers would think you saw something wrong with him. You wouldn't get anything for him."

"I'll just keep him," he said with a disgusted look on his face. He was as low as I'd ever seen him, but there wasn't much I could do to make him feel better.

When we walked outside, I said, "It's not all that bad, Norm. I'm glad it's only two thousand dollars."

"I've told you before, **it's not two thousand dollars, Jim!** It costs at least ten thousand to get a horse to its first race, and that's if everything goes perfectly." I was trying to look on the bright side, but I understood his disappointment.

He said, "Let's go back to his stall and see what I bought. Did you hear what Ken's horse sold for?" I told him I was more interested in how he was doing.

When we got back to the horse's stall, we were greeted by a lovely young lady. She had a nice smile on her face and asked very cheerfully, "Are you the guys that bought him?"

Norm said dejectedly, "I did, but I thought I was buying a different horse."

She replied, "I'll tell you right now, you bought a very nice horse. He's perfectly straight and really smart. His bloodlines give him a chance to be any kind of runner, so I think you'll be happy with him."

Norm said, "I just thought I was bidding on a different horse." The disappointment was still evident in his voice.

I said, "He's a pretty horse."

Norm replied, "In this business, pretty is as pretty does."

"I wish you the best of luck," the young lady said as we turned to walk away. *She was nice.*

We went back into the office, and Norm told the lady he'd have somebody pick the horse up the next morning. She said, "That's fine, you have up to three days to pick him up. There'll be people here to watch him and make sure he has hay and water. I'm sorry this happened, but I've seen times when it's worked out well."

"I'm just glad I'm not the first one to do it," Norm said.

She replied, "You'd be surprised at how often it happens."

On our way home, I tried to be supportive, but I couldn't say anything without laughing because I couldn't get his startled look out of my mind. After several unpleasant looks, he laughed and said, "I must have had a pretty shocked look on my face."

I replied, "I wish I had a picture to show you, but I'll buy 20 percent of him, just to tell the story." He tried to talk me out of telling people what happened, but I told him the story would be told whether I bought part of him or not. He then tried to sell me half, but I told him 20 percent was my limit. I handed him four crisp hundred-dollar bills, and we were partners.

I said, "Just so you don't think I'm stupid, I looked at the sales book quite a bit. Four or five horses jumped out at me, and he was one of them. The girl at the stall didn't have to say the things she said because the horse was already sold. "Think about it, Norm, he brought quite a bit for no prior history on the stud or dam. The bloodlines are there, and what I like most, he's bred for the classic distances."

Norm replied, "That worries me too because there aren't many races over a mile and a sixteenth in Washington."

"That is a concern, but I feel good about this. Yakima Meadows allows some training on their track, so maybe we can get someone to leg him up there and save some money." He told me he'd look into it, and it was good to see the color returning to his face.

Norm and I were both retired and single, so we had some time on our hands. The next morning, he called a horse-hauling company to take the horse to Yakima Meadows. He knew a lady who was training a few horses there for a couple of her friends, and she told him she'd get our horse started for fifteen dollars a day. That included feed, so it was a good deal. She had owned and trained a really nice filly in the past, so we knew she was good.

The horses being trained there were mostly running at bush tracks around the state, and the track wasn't well cared for, so you didn't want to have expensive horses trained there.

The trailer hauling the horse arrived at three that afternoon. Pat, the lady training for us, had showed us the stall he'd stay in, and after putting him away, we stayed until Pat came in to feed. He settled in like he had been there all his life. I remembered the girl telling us he was smart and that's at least 50 percent of the battle. I knew of many talented horses that weren't mentally able to run.

We were at the track by seven the next morning, and Pat had already put him on the walker. She explained, "He has a lot of baby fat, so it's easy to see he's had no training. What we'll do today is walk him a half hour. I have a vet coming at noon to float his teeth and check him out, but make sure the trainer in Seattle knows he doesn't have his tattoo."

I replied, "Believe me, we will because we had to scratch a horse one time over that. We were fined for it in addition to missing the race, so we learned our lesson."

She explained, "My plan is to walk him for ten days, and then we'll jog him for ten days. We'll start galloping him slowly after that and have that fat off him before you know it." The horse was a bay, and there was nothing to make you say *wow*, but there was nothing wrong with him either. It was obvious that he'd be big before he finished growing. Pat loved his conformation, but at that point, he just looked like a saddle horse to me. I wasn't accustomed to seeing them before they were almost ready to run.

We were at the barn at six thirty the next morning, and as he walked, Pat said, "I measured him. He's sixteen hands and still has some growin' to do. They don't have to be big to run, but most of the great horses are, and he'll be a big boy."

I asked, "Did you see the book to see his breeding?"

She answered, "I did, and if he runs up to his bloodlines, he could be any kind." She told us she had gone over his legs and he had good bone structure so he should stay sound. It was nice to finally be hearing some positive things after the way we started out.

She asked his name, and Norm said, "He doesn't have one, so we better get on it."

I replied, "We have plenty of time, but the Jockey Club can be slow sometimes, so yes, I think we should."

We went for coffee and started working on the name. I said, "We should have *wrong* in there somewhere."

"I thought you might feel that way. How do you feel about Wrong Way North?"

"We could send it in," I said. We filled out the papers and sent it and a couple more, along with some pictures of him. *We're on our way.*

The next morning, we met at the track and watched two of Pat's horses gallop. Our horse was on the walker and really studied his surroundings. He was feeling good and seemed to dance while walking. After watching him walk for three more days, I said to Norm, "Sleep is more important to me, so I'll start coming out again when he goes to the track."

A week later, we met at the track at 6:00 a.m., and Pat said, "Your horse will be the third horse to go to the track." It was sixty-five degrees with a very soft breeze, and I thought, *It's nice to be back in the business.* I could actually see a few muscles starting to replace the baby fat, and it was easy to see he would be a good-looking big horse. When her second horse came back, Pat told the rider to put him on the walker. She put the tack on ours and left him in his stall while going to pick something up. She was only gone a matter of seconds, but I heard her scream **"Oh no!"** so I ran over to his stall. The horse had somehow gotten his bit hooked to a buckle on his saddle, and Pat was trying to get them apart. She was in hysterics and screamed, **"I can't move it, it's too tight!"**

I very casually said, "Loosen the saddle." She looked at me like a light just came on and reached under him to unhook the buckle. The saddle slid forward, and the horse was able to free himself.

"Thank you, Jim," she said with a long sigh. "If he had flipped with his neck twisted like that, his neck would have snapped. How did you think so fast?" The fear was still evident in her voice.

I said, "I never thought about him getting hurt, so it was just a matter of loosening where the two items hooked together. Bringing the saddle forward seemed the most logical way, so I guess ignorance can be a good thing sometimes."

Pat said, "I should have had him hooked to the wall. I've been in this business too long to do something that stupid."

Norm said, "Don't beat yourself up, Pat, you were only gone for a couple seconds."

"As you can see, that's all it takes sometimes. The good thing is this horse is really smart and calm. I'd say 80 percent would have flipped. Intelligence is almost as important as ability."

Pat's daughter was the rider, and Pat said, "Just a slow jog once around." She legged her up, and we watched them walk onto the track. He was just jogging, but I could see he had a nice way of moving. While they were going around, I told Norm we needed a nickname.

"What did you have in mind?" he asked.

I thought for a second before saying "Charlie."

Norm chuckled and asked, "Why Charlie?"

I replied, "It's as good as any."

"Charlie it is," he said while laughing and shaking his head.

When they were close to us, the sun was shining on him, and I said, "He's losing his winter coat and looking better every day."

When they came off the track, Pat's daughter said, "You guys might have something here because he has a really nice way of goin'. Did you really buy him by mistake and only pay two thousand for him?"

Norm said, "Yes, Jim makes sure everyone knows that."

"Norm, I think you're gonna have the last laugh here," she replied as she was dismounting.

We went for coffee, and I said, "I liked hearing what she had to say."

"She pretty much likes everything she gets on," he replied.

I said, "Still, I love hearing it. This is the time I like most because they're all unbeaten at this point and we can dream all we want to."

"It's easier to dream when you're only paying 20 percent," he kidded.

We were at the track every morning at six thirty. He was just jogging, but we could see a change coming over him. His coat was shining more each day, and much of his fat was replaced by thick muscle. Pat's daughter said, "I think it's time to gallop him because he's becoming a handful."

Pat said, "We'll gallop him a half mile tomorrow and see what kind of stride he has."

The next morning when we arrived at the track, Norm told us the name Wrong Way North had been accepted. "He'll be Wrong Way North in the program but Charlie in our hearts," I replied. When Charlie walked up, I thought, *He's lookin' good, so we just might have some fun with this guy.*

Pat said, "Jog him a half mile and then a nice, easy gallop for a half." The half-mile pole was right in front of us, and when they came around, it was great watching him go from a jog to a gallop. Pat said, "He has a beautiful long stride." When they reached the finish line, we could see he wasn't easy to pull up, and coming back around to us, we could tell he wasn't ready to come off the track. As they were coming off, Charlie pranced like he knew he was good. "I know it's early to say, but this guy could be special," Pat said.

She asked her daughter what she thought, and she answered, "He's better than anything I've been on at this stage."

Pat asked her, "**Even the filly**?"

"Sorry, Mom, but even her."

9

Pat looked at us and said, "She's always thought there's never been anything like that filly." I knew the filly was very special, so I thought, *We might really have something here.*

Norm and I went for coffee after Charlie walked, and Norm said, "That filly made over three hundred thousand."

I replied, "She beat the boys in a big futurity, so we know Charlie's good in the morning, but now we have to see how that translates to racing. We can really dream now." I had owned a couple of morning glories, so I knew not to get too excited until I saw him run. They can have all the talent in the world, but without the fire in their belly, they're not worth much.

After a couple of days, he was starting to take a good hold of the bit and looking better all the time. Pat said, "I wanna breeze him a quarter, and Larry Farmer will be here at eight in the morning. He's a jockey who rides sparingly on the bush tracks but has some ability. If it wasn't for the bottle, he could have a great career. Be here by seven so we can go over the track and make sure it's clear of clods and rocks."

The next morning, we arrived at six thirty and walked around the track, throwing off all the clods and rocks that we could find. Larry showed up right on time, and Pat legged him up while saying "Gallop him to the quarter pole, and breeze him to the wire. He's not fit, so don't ask him for too much." Larry nodded and jogged him around to the finish line. At that point, he put him into a nice gallop. A couple of strides before the quarter pole, I could see Charlie's body lower a little, and in two strides, he was up to full speed. When he passed the finish line, I asked Norm what he caught him in.

Norm was looking at his watch in disbelief and said, "Twenty-two and one, but that's not possible."

"That's exactly what I got," Pat said. "Wow, this big guy is bred for distance, but it looks like he has speed."

Coming off the track, Charlie was blowing a little but strutting like he had just been elected prom king. He was starting to tuck up and was looking more like a racehorse.

"**Who is this?**" Larry wanted to know.

"We call him Charlie," I answered.

He said, "Charlie can go a minute eight and change anytime he wants to, and he has a stride that tells me he can go long. Let me know when he runs so I can bet him."

"What do we have here? A minute nine will win most races," I said to Norm. He just shrugged his shoulders. "**Thank you, Lord**," I whispered as I thought about our good fortune. *What's going on?*

The next morning on the way to the track, Norm said, "I think it's time to get him to Seattle, so who do you think we should send him to?"

"He'll only get one or two starts before the end of the meet, so maybe we should give him to Jim Carlson. He can take him to Portland for a couple races after the Seattle meet."

"I'll call him," Norm said as we were getting out of the car.

Pat was really good about it when we told her we were sending him to Seattle. She said, "If we go much further with him on this track, we could hurt him. If you don't mind me asking, who are you sending him to?"

Norm said, "Jim Carlson because he'll just be getting fit when the meet in Seattle ends, and Jim can take him to Portland until we know if he's good enough for California."

Pat replied, "I expect to see him in California soon. With his breeding and speed, I have high expectations for him. When will you send him over?"

"A van will pick him up in the morning," Norm answered. We both hugged her and thanked her for a very nice job of getting him started.

After Charlie galloped, Norm and I went for coffee in a café that we had adopted as our office. He said, "We have 4,600 in him right now, including the purchase price. If he doesn't shin-buck or get sick, we shouldn't have over eight thousand in him when he runs. Pat has really helped us keep the costs down."

"I've already had enough fun for the amount of money we have in him," I replied.

"It's easy for you to say that because you're only paying 20 percent," he said. He smiled before saying "It's been a lot of fun for me too." He liked razzing me about only buying 20 percent, but I don't think he would sell any more of him, with the reports we were getting.

Jim didn't have a stall right away, so he made arrangements with a training track and told us he'd have a stall at the track in about a week. Charlie was picked up the next day, and both Norm and I were sad as we watched the van pull away. We thanked Pat for all she had done, and she said, "I have very high expectations, so I'll be watching him."

"We owe you," I told her while hoping I could return the favor someday.

The day after Charlie arrived in Seattle, Jim called us and said, "Charlie's sore in the back end. The track vet looked at him and said he's sore because his testicles are too large, so I think we should geld him."

Norm told him to go ahead before asking, "When will it be done, and how long will it set him back?"

"Just a couple days. He should be walking the next day and jogging within three days, if all goes well." He told us the vet could do the surgery the next morning.

Norm said, "Please call and let us know how the surgery goes."

We were having lunch the next day when Jim called, and he said, "Everything went well with the surgery. The vet said there was quite a bit of inflammation from them rubbing together, so it's good that we corrected it right away. I'll call you if there's a problem, but I don't expect one."

I said, "Good or bad, we're on our way." It was good to see Norm was starting to get excited. "You wanna sell 30 percent for six hundred now?" I asked him. He smiled and shook his head. I said, "I didn't really want more, but I wanted to know that you're happy with the way things are going."

"I think he'll be better than the one I thought I was buying," he said with a silly grin on his face.

"Oh, that reminds me, that horse of Ken's sold for 4,800."

I saw Norm at ten the next morning and asked him if he had heard from Jim. He answered, "He hasn't called, and no news is good news." *I'm happy to have Charlie in my life.*

CHAPTER 2

Charlie Runs in the Emerald City and So Much More

Three days later, Jim called and told us Charlie was at the track. He said, "He's really lookin' good and is moving much better. Have you breezed him?"

"The day before we sent him over, he breezed a quarter," Norm answered before putting his phone on speaker.

"That's probably what caused the soreness to show up. Did you time the work?" he wanted to know.

I answered, "Twenty-two and two."

"I'd say that's not correct because that's awfully fast for a horse with his stride."

I said, "Norm and Pat both had the same time."

"We'll see how he does here in about four days," he replied. He promised to call us the day before he worked so we could drive over.

He called three days later and told us he decided to hold off for a few more days. Norm asked him if there was a problem before putting his phone on speaker. "No, not at all, I just don't wanna rush him because the girl that's galloping him thinks he's special. I'll call you the day before he works."

About a week later, Jim called and said, "He'll breeze in the morning." We were on the road the next morning at four thirty and arrived at the track at seven. We told the guard we were going in to get our license, so he let us go in and pointed the way to Jim's barn. When we got there, Jim was up at the track with another horse, but the girl who was galloping him met us. Norm knew her quite well from other horses she had galloped for him.

She wanted to know where Norm got him, so he explained how he purchased him by mistake. "Do you mind me asking what you paid for him?" she asked.

He answered, "Two thousand dollars."

She laughed while saying "You're one lucky son of a gun. I've ridden all the good two-year-olds on this track, and he's better than any of them. I galloped his mother in Southern California, and she would have been a real runner, but she got cast in her stall and tore a tendon the day before her first start. She was picked right on top due to the way she was working, so if she passed on her talent, he could be really good."

Jim walked in and said, "Go up the track because I want you to see him out in the sunshine, under tack."

We were standing by the gap, enjoying the morning, when a beautiful horse pranced up. I turned to Norm and said, "I sure wish that was him."

Jim had walked up behind us and asked, "Are you kidding?"

"Not at all, that horse is gorgeous."

"That horse is your horse," he said. I was stunned because he didn't look at all like the horse we sent over. Jim asked, "Does he have a name?"

I answered, "Wrong Way North, but we call him Charlie." He explained that he asked the rider to gallop him to the quarter pole and let him roll a quarter. I hadn't noticed the rider, but when they jogged away, I could see that, from behind, it looked like a female. A very attractive female, from where I stood. "Please tell me that's a girl riding him," I said to Jim.

He smiled and said, "Yes, she is."

There's nothing worse than thinking a person walking away is an attractive girl and finding out he's a man. I remembered back to a time when I was a young man. I saw a person walking away and thought it was an attractive girl, but when he turned around, I was shocked to see he was a man with a full beard. That'll shake you up a little. We were close to the quarter pole when the rider set Charlie down, and he was so smooth down the lane. Jim checked his stopwatch and said, "Huh, twenty-three flat."

Norm said, "I had him in twenty-two and three."

The clocker called down and asked Jim if that was his horse that worked. "He didn't work. He just got away a little," Jim replied.

"I'd say he got away, I caught the half in forty-five, and the last quarter was twenty-two and two. If it wasn't a work, I won't write it down, but it looks like you have a nice one." ***This is happening way too fast.***

When we got back to the barn, the horse was already back. The rider dismounted, and Jim said, "Guys, this is Vickie Martin, and she'll be riding Charlie." The sun glistened off her perfectly straight and white teeth as she flashed a beautiful smile. I thought, *She's too lovely to be a jockey.* I was taken aback because I hadn't thought that about a woman in over four years. *What is it about this one?* Maybe I was just excited about Charlie and the fact that she was riding him. *She's gorgeous.*

I said, "Hello, Vickie." When I shook her hand, I was a little surprised at how firm her grip was. I hoped I hadn't stared too long, but my first glimpse of that lovely face rocked me all the way to my toes. Norm knew her quite well because she had ridden for him before.

She asked what we caught Charlie in and was a little surprised when Jim told her twenty-two and three. "Wow, he did it so easy. This is the nicest two-year-old I've been on in a long time." As she was walking away, I thought *Yes, that certainly is a female body.* I chuckled while thinking, *At least I haven't forgotten what they look like.*

On our way back to Yakima, Norm said, "This is a much nicer ride back than after the sale."

"No offense, buddy, but I really enjoyed that drive," I replied while laughing.

"Yes, I know you did," he said with an irritated look on his face. It turned out to be a wonderful trip as we talked about how Charlie had grown up.

"We sent a boy over, and he's grown into quite a man," I said as I thought about how he looked going onto the track.

He had three more works, each five days apart, and we drove over for all of them. The whole barn was buzzing about how well he was training. The second work was five furlongs in one minute flat under wraps, and Vickie was beside herself. The third was scheduled for another five-furlong breeze, and we were standing at the gap when Charlie walked up. Actually, he didn't walk, but stomped and pranced. Vickie looked over and said, "He's becoming a beast, guys." She had to use all her riding skills because he was up on his back legs, then his front, and then all four were off the ground. Her beauty certainly didn't hinder her riding.

Jim said, "This is not a rodeo, Vickie."

She laughed and said, "**Please tell him**!" She galloped him around to the five-eighths pole, and when she set him down, he looked magnificent. We were standing right on the turn for home when he came around, and he switched leads so quickly that I almost missed it. He was a fabulous athlete, to say the least.

After he crossed the finish line, the clocker called down, "Wrong Way North, five-eighths in fifty-eight and two." Norm and I were amazed because anything under a minute is great for a sprinter.

Jim asked, "I believe you said one minute flat?"

The clocker replied, "Actually, I meant to say one minute and two seconds flat."

I looked at Jim, and he said, "He's been known to make a wager now and then. Along that line, you guys should stick around for the first race. I have one that Vickie really likes, but one thing I wanna say, if I give you a tip, **never bet more than you can afford to lose!**"

When we got back to the barn, Vickie was smiling from ear to ear. "This guy is for real, but if we don't get him into a race soon, he might hurt himself. You saw him going onto the track. He's way too full of himself."

Jim said, "I could work him another five-eighths and have him really fit or run him. He may not win the first one, but a race would be as good as two or three works. He's fit enough that he won't hurt himself." He pulled out his condition book and said, "There's a five-eighths maiden special weight race on Sunday. That's six days, so if you want to, we can run him there. I'll gallop him two strong miles every day until then so he might be fit enough."

"Sounds good, and we'll stay to watch your horse before leaving today," Norm said.

On our way to the café, Vickie caught up to us and said, "What Jim said about him not being totally fit, don't worry about that. He could beat any maiden on this track if he was only 60 percent fit, so bring your money, boys." She then said, "I believe Jim told you about his horse in the first. He'll win, and Charlie will win much easier."

I said, "I'll bet you get told how pretty you are quite often." I was gazing into her big blue eyes.

She flashed that gorgeous smile while saying "Not often enough, sweetie." *I like that.*

Jim's horse was in a six furlong, ten-thousand-dollar claiming race. His morning line was eight to one, so I bet twenty to win and place on him. There were nine horses in the second race, so I bet two-dollar daily doubles, Jim's horse in the first to all in the second.

While we were waiting for the race, I said, "I've never had a trainer or jockey tell me a horse would win, so either she really knows her horses, or she's much too confident."

"We don't have to wait long to find out," Norm said as the horses were entering the gate. Jim's horse was the three and was nine to one when the gate opened. The three was in third about two lengths off the leader, going into the turn. He pulled to within a length entering the stretch, and two hundred yards from home, he went ahead and began to draw away. He won by four widening lengths, and Norm said, "On that one, she certainly wasn't overconfident."

I collected just over three hundred dollars and still had the double to go. I told Norm to root for the longest shot on the board. We didn't get the longest odds but not the favorite either. The horse was eleven to one, so the double paid 260 dollars.

When we were back at the barn, Jim was looking at Charlie and said, "You gave two thousand for him, and I'll give you twenty, right now."

Norm said, "We're having way too much fun to stop now."

I gave Jim two fifty-dollar bills and said, "Thanks for the tip. Please give one of them to Vickie, and we'll see you on race day."

"Don't be too upset if he doesn't win this time."

"I won't bet any more than I can afford to lose," I promised him.

On the way home, I repeated to Norm, "I've never had a jockey tell me their horse would win, so this is a whole new ballgame."

"Let's just hope she's not batting five hundred in this case," he replied.

I said, "I'm five hundred up, and I'll put it all on Charlie." I was happy to be back in the horse business, so I told Norm I was glad he lost his bearings on the day of the sale.

I laughed when he replied, "**I knew he'd be good all along!**" We enjoyed our drive home while talking about what Charlie might become.

I said, "I was getting depressed, but I'm feeling much better since we bought Charlie. Maybe buying him was more of a blessing than a mistake."

He replied, "It makes me happy that you find Vickie so attractive."

"She really is. I've been trying to figure out why her and why now, but I can't stop looking at her."

He replied, "She reminds me a little of Linda." *That might be it.*

We met for coffee every morning, and in our conversations, Charlie got better every day. By the time we were driving over for the race, we were dreaming that he was the favorite in the Kentucky Derby. As I said before, that's the really fun time with a racehorse because there are far too many disappointments once they start running. We arrived at the track three hours before the races were due to start, and Vickie was at the barn. I asked if I could ask her a question.

"This sounds serious," she said while flashing me a questioning look.

"How long did you ride Charlie before you knew he'd be good?"

"I knew before we got to the end of the shed row. I know that's hard to believe, but the special horses have a different feel."

I thanked her and told her I was happy she was riding for us. *She really is cute*, I thought as she was walking away. I laughed while thinking, *Coming and going*. It really was nice to find a lady attractive for the first time in almost five years, and again, I wondered, *Why her?* I called her back to say "Please don't think I'm a flirt, but my wife worked in dentistry, and I couldn't help noticing you have an almost-perfect smile."

She replied, "Thank you, when I was a girl, my teeth were a little crowded and not very straight. My parents couldn't afford braces, so when I started riding, the first thing I did was get them." She flashed that radiant smile before saying "You're so sweet to notice, and a little flirting never hurt anyone." I know I looked into those big blue eyes longer than I should have, but she was very captivating. Again, I wondered, *After so many years, why now and why her? She may look like Linda looked twenty years ago.*

Norm and I walked up to the café to kill some time, and we ran into a friend that worked for our trainer in Spokane. "Do you have anything in today?" he asked me.

"Yes, we have a first-time starter in the fourth."

He looked in his program before saying "Maiden special weight, you must be high on him."

"Keep it quiet, but we think he'll win."

"Good luck today," he said before going back to work. I knew he'd put a couple of bucks on Charlie, and I hoped it would help him.

When the horses were called for the fourth race, Norm and I walked to the paddock together. When Charlie walked in, he looked like a monster, so I said, "I'd bet him on looks alone."

Jim said, "He's lookin' good, so let's hope he runs up to his looks."

When Vickie came in, she gave us both hugs and told us the race was in the bag. The call came for "Riders up," and my heart was about to jump out of my chest. There's something nerve-racking about running a first-time starter, and this one could be very special.

Jim gave Vickie a leg up and said, "God's speed."

She winked and said, "Bet your money, boys, **he will not lose**!"

I bet two hundred to win on him. There were eight horses in the race, so I said, "Five-dollar exactas, the four on top of all and two-dollar trifectas, the four on top of all with all."

The seller said, "I think you like the four."

I answered, "I own him and have a tendency to bet my heart instead of my head."

"Good luck," he said before punching out a ten-dollar win for himself.

By the time I was outside, the post parade was ending. The race would start on the other side of the track, so as they jogged around to the starting gate, I whispered, "Lord, I know you don't get involved in the outcome of races, but I ask that he runs his best and comes back safely." Charlie was five to one when they entered the gate.

"They're off" rang out over the PA system, and Charlie went right to the front. The first quarter was twenty-one and three, and Charlie was in front by three lengths. The half was forty-three and one, so I thought, *He can't hang on*. He opened up a six-length lead at the top of the lane and drew off to win by eleven. He was just one tick off the track record, so I was in total disbelief. I had watched horses do what he did but didn't think I'd ever own one of them.

We all hurried to the winner's circle, and Jim asked, "**How good will he be when he's dead fit?**" I was speechless. It was what I hoped for but so much better when it actually happened. Vickie was beaming when she brought him into the winner's circle, and after she dismounted, we all walked out together.

She whispered, "You boys have no idea what you have because I wasn't close to the bottom of him. Believe me, you'll have a lot of fun with him." I loved seeing her so excited. She gave both of us nice hugs, and I'm sure I squeezed her tighter than I should have. I went inside to cash my tickets and received over 2,200 dollars. *This is exciting!*

I cashed at the same windowed where I wagered, and the seller said, "You should bet your heart more often."

When I was back at the barn, I gave Jim two hundred-dollar bills and told him to give Vickie one of them. We watched Charlie on the walker, and he was a little tired but looked fantastic. He had been bathed, and his coat glistened in the afternoon sun. His baby fat was gone, and he was massive. *How far will this beautiful horse take us?*

The next day, Jim called and said, "Charlie came out of the race just fine. There are three weeks left in the meet and the last day, there's a never-win-two allowance for two-year-olds, going six furlongs. I'd like to have another week, but I wanna get another race in him before we move him. If it's okay with you, I'll enter him there." We were on speaker, and both told him yes at the same time.

We met for coffee almost every morning. Norm was divorced, and my wife was killed in a car accident with a drunk driver four and a half years earlier. We were good company for each other, and Charlie was some added excitement for us. Norm told me again that he was happy to see me find Vickie so attractive because I hadn't been able to look at a woman since my wife's death. I said, "It's hard to believe this horse, purchased the way he was, could enrich our lives as much as he has. If someone told me this story, I wouldn't believe them." *God is looking over me.*

A couple of days before the race, Jim called and told us he was wrong, thinking the race was too soon. He said, "He's tearing up the barn. I don't like working them this close to a race, but I was afraid he might hurt himself. I breezed him this morning, and he went a half in forty-six and change. Vickie tried to slow him down, but he loves to run, so if she lets him go, he'll always run fast. I hope he kept enough in the tank for day after tomorrow."

I replied, "You gotta do what you gotta do because, if he's too fresh, he'll get rank and run off. I'm sure he'll have plenty left, the way he finished last time." Jim always worried about what might go wrong.

The morning of the race, we arrived in Seattle at eleven thirty and went to the café for lunch. I picked up a program and saw that we were in the eighth race. There were ten horses in the race, and Charlie was number 9. He was the second choice at four to one. The three was the favorite at nine to five because he just missed by a nose three weeks before in the same race. It's tough for horses to break their maiden and then win against winners the next time out, but the good ones get it done.

After lunch, we walked back to the barn, and Jim said, "I know this horse is too good for Portland, but there's a stake for two-year-olds going a mile, in one month. The purse is twelve thousand dollars, and I'd like to run him in that, if you don't mind." Norm told him it would be fine. Jim said, "If he comes back good after this race, I can haul him to Portland for half of what the hauling vans would charge you. That would put him a couple hundred miles closer to California."

"If he comes out of the race in good shape, that would be great," Norm replied.

"Don't be alarmed if he's not on the lead at the start today because we wanna teach him to rate. We think his best distance will be a mile or more with his breeding, and he'll be much tougher coming from off the pace."

"Do you have a place where I can take a nap?" I asked him.

"If you're serious, there's a couch in my tack room. This is moving day, so it's a mess, but you're welcome to sleep on it if you want to." I slept for two hours, and they were calling horses for the sixth race when I woke up. It startled me at first because I thought we were in the fourth. I guess I'd been dreaming about his last race. I shook my head to get fully awake before walking to the front side. The day looked really bright. *When the sun shines in Seattle, it must be a lot like Heaven,* I thought as I soaked in the sunshine. I noticed the girls were working on their tans and wondered if Vickie was responsible for me noticing girls again. *Too bad she's so young.*

When I found Norm, he told me he was a couple bucks ahead, and that could have meant any amount. The sixth race was just finishing up when Norm asked if I wanted to split a pick three, so I asked him what he had in mind. "Put the three clockers' selections in the seventh, to Charlie in the eighth, to all in the last. There are eight horses in the last, so that would cost us twenty-four dollars."

I looked at his program and said, "There's a long shot I wanna add in the seventh, so it would cost us another four dollars each."

"Okay by me," he said. I made the bet just before the seventh race left the gate and the eight-to-five favorite went right to the front. He led every step but the last. The twenty-to-one long shot that I liked nipped him at the wire, and Norm asked, "Where did you come up with that horse?"

"I have a really weird number system that doesn't work all the time, but in cases like this, I throw them in."

He replied, "Whatever, I'm glad we added him. If Vickie's confidence is well-founded about Charlie, we should have a nice pick three."

We were in the paddock for the eighth race when Charlie came in doing his dance. I said, "I don't know if he's the best horse in the race, but he's the best feeling horse for sure." Vickie hugged us when she came in and laughed when I told her I could get used to her hugs.

"You **really are** a flirt," she said before kissing my cheek.

I replied, "I hope it doesn't offend you, but you're the first woman I've flirted with in a very long time."

She whispered, "I don't mind at all because I think you're cute." *Nice, a cute old man.*

"Riders up" rang out, so Jim legged her up. As they walked around the paddock, she looked over and winked at us.

I said, "She either likes us or the horse."

"I'm quite sure it's the horse," Norm replied.

"You just won't let me dream, will ya, old buddy," I said while laughing.

"You don't know how happy it makes me that you're looking," he replied. I knew how much he had worried about me. I absolutely wasn't interested in her romantically, but it was nice to find her so attractive. I loved the feelings she had running through me, for the first time in five years.

I went in and bet at the same window where I bet his first race. "Give me two hundred to win on the nine, and give me three-dollar exactas, the nine on top of all. Give me two-dollar trifectas, the nine on top with all to run second and third, and for my last wager, I'd like five-dollar doubles, the nine to all in the last race." I handed him $339.00. *I've never bet like that before.*

I went out to find a good spot to watch the race, and when they entered the gate, Charlie was three to one. He broke in second, but Vickie eased him back to fourth, three lengths off the lead. They were able to find a spot just off the rail, and a hundred yards from the turn, she guided him between two horses. When they turned for home, she took him to the outside and smacked him twice. Within a hundred yards, he had opened up a five-length lead, and I heard the announcer say "We're watching a budding star, ladies and gentlemen." The time was one minute and eight seconds flat, so I thought back to what Larry said when he breezed him in Yakima. He was absolutely right, and I knew Charlie would be better going longer. **We're really on our way now!**

When Vickie brought into winner's circle, she raised both arms while saying "What a marvelous animal he is."

I said, "That's no animal, that's Charlie."

"Well, excuse me," she said while flashing a smile that made me shiver. **What a marvelous animal indeed!** *Wake up, Jim, she's younger than your daughter.*

As we walked out of the winner's circle, Norm asked Vickie if she was going to Northern California. She told him she was, so he explained that we were letting Jim run him in a stakes race in Portland in four weeks. He told her the mount was hers if she wanted to ride him in California before asking her to find us a trainer she trusted.

"I absolutely wanna ride him, and I'll find a trainer that you can work with," she promised.

A ten-to-one horse won the last race, so I collected 5,200 dollars in total. When we got back to the barn, I handed Jim four hundred-dollar bills and said, "Two for you and two for Vickie."

He said, "You don't have to keep doing this."

"I won't stop doing something that's working so well. How dumb do you think I am?" He smiled and started to speak, but I said, "Don't answer that, I want us to remain friends."

"I really do appreciate it, and so does Vickie," he replied.

I said, "Tell her a hundred is for her beautiful ride, and the other is for her good looks." I almost fell over when I heard a female voice ask why I didn't tell her myself. I turned around, and she was smiling at me. "I'm so sorry," I said as my face turned red.

She stood on her tiptoes and kissed my cheek before saying "I don't know a girl that doesn't like a compliment once in a while." She thanked me for the money before saying "We'll have fun with this guy because **the sky is the limit**! Oh, by the way, you're not too bad yourself." *What a nice thing for her to say to an old guy.*

I thanked her for letting me off the hook, but Norm told her he wished she hadn't. After telling us we were crazy in a fun way, she walked away. I really did do my best to not watch her go. *That's amazing.*

After Charlie was in Portland for ten days, Jim called and said, "I'm glad he's had time to work on this sandy track, because he was blowing quite a bit for a few days. This will really set him up for California. I have to tell you, a guy from California made an offer of a hundred thousand to buy him."

Norm said, "Very tempting but he's been way too much fun."

"I'll tell him," Jim said. When Norm was off the phone, he told me about the offer and told me he wouldn't sell him for twice that.

I said, "Not for ten times that."

"Then we're on the same page?"

I answered, "He's not just a horse now, he's family." We agreed that we were having way too much fun to stop, and I told him they would do a movie about us someday.

Two days before the race, Jim called and told Norm he had to tell him something. "Jim, let me put my phone on speaker," Norm said. All kinds of bad things went through my mind because I'd been in the business long enough to know that more horses get hurt training than they did in races.

I asked, **"What happened?"**

"It's not bad, but I felt I should tell you, the man from California upped his offer to 250,000."

I sat there somewhat in shock and said to Norm, "The decision's yours, but you know how I feel."

Norm didn't think long at all. In one sentence, he replied, "No, thanks, how do we look in the stake?"

Jim laughed before saying "I had to pass that on, but Charlie couldn't be doing better."

Norm replied, "We're glad you told us, Jim, but he could be worth much more if he wins a stake in California. Even more important than that, we're having way too much fun." We agreed that, at our age, money wasn't as important as it once was.

Jim said, "Charlie's bigger and better than he was in Seattle, and he'll win in a gallop. A horse that broke his maiden for forty thousand in Northern California is coming up for the race. They're trying to get some black type, but the way Charlie's training, I don't fear any horse. When you see him, you'll know what I'm talkin' about."

I thanked him for calling before telling him we'd see him on race day. When we hung up, I said, "I've known Jim for several years, and that's the most positive I've ever heard him be about a race. Charlie must be developing fast."

The morning of the race, we left Yakima at eight thirty and enjoyed a splendid drive through the Columbia Gorge. There was a little snow in the mountains, but the roads were clear. We saw beautiful mountains and trees on one side and the Columbia River on the other. My mind drifted back several years to a trip Linda and I took. We were going to Lake Tahoe, and when we passed Goldendale, she started playing an audiobook that was written by a man in Portland. My job had taken me to every location mentioned in the book. We were going down to Biggs Junction when it talked about driving through the Columbia Gorge. *What a great book and story behind the book that was.*

"Are you asleep?" Norm asked.

"I was just thinking about a trip Linda and I took a few years ago."

"Sorry I interrupted that, I miss her too."

When we arrived at Portland Meadows, we went through the back gate and stopped in the café to pick up a program. We were in a two-year-old stake, going one mile. To our surprise, the purse was fifteen thousand dollars. Wrong Way North was the five horse in a field of ten, and his morning line was nine to five. The California horse was five to two. I said, "We may get some odds."

He replied, "That California horse might be really tough, but we wanna be sure Charlie's good enough to send to California. This could be a good test for him."

We were given directions to Jim's barn, and he was in his tack room when we walked up. He said, "I've put two five-furlong works in him and that four-furlong breeze two days ago. Other than that, he's been galloping two miles every day. I can't remember having a horse that loves to run as much as he does. I wanted you to see him first when he came over for the race, but I can't wait. Go outside, and I'll bring him out."

When we saw him, we were amazed, so I said, "I can't believe how he's changed. He must be fifty pounds heavier, and I think he's taller."

He replied, "Sixteen and three-quarter hands, and he may reach seventeen before he's done growing. He has enjoyed his time here." His coat was shining, and he was dappled out all over.

I said, "Thank you for being so understanding about us sending him to California."

"I knew he was too good for this track, but did you notice the purse is three thousand more than I told you?"

I answered, "We did notice, and that may mean the television wagering is helping you." After Jim put him back in his stall, I said, "If he beats this bunch, he should compete in California at some level."

He replied, "I never say a horse will win, but I'll be shocked if he doesn't."

Norm said, "That California horse might be tough."

Jim replied, "I'm not worried because Charlie's the best horse I've ever been around. I'll bet him when he runs in California, and you might bet a few bucks on my horse in the last race today."

I told Norm we should bet a pick four. In the seventh, the favorite was eight to five and had run well in Seattle, so I said, "We could each bet it because there are three singles."

He replied, "There's one in the seventh that I remember from when he ran in Seattle."

He was six to one in the program, so I said, "It would cost twenty dollars to get two in the seventh, ten in the eighth, and one in the last two." We decided to bet it on our own, and I spent forty dollars to bet it twice. The horse Norm liked went off at nine to one and won very easily. I remembered that, in the past, he noted horses that had gotten into trouble and did very well betting them. Again, I thought, *We're on our way.*

We went to the backside café for a quick meal, and the horses were pulling up from the eighth race when we walked out. The winner was twenty-five to one, so Norm said, "With the first two and Jim's in the last two, it'll be a monster pick four."

I was proud, walking across the infield with Charlie. In the paddock, Norm and I were shocked when Vickie walked up. She had paid her way up so she could stay close to Charlie. Jim wanted to surprise us, and neither of us noticed that she was listed in the program because we were too busy thinking about the purse being raised. When she hugged me, I said, "Mmmm, I only came down for that amazing hug." *She feels so much like Linda.*

"Talk, talk, talk, you didn't even know I'd be here." "Riders up" came over the PA system, so I went up to make my bets before the post parade. I bet five-dollar exactas, Charlie on top of all, and put him on top of all with all for two dollars in the trifecta. The last thing I bet was a twenty-dollar daily double, Charlie to Jim's horse in the tenth. They were just finishing the post parade when I walked out to the rail.

Norm walked up and told me it was nice to see me having fun with Vickie. I said, "It's too bad she's younger than my daughter."

Charlie was seven to five when they entered the gate. "They're off" rang out, and the California horse opened up five lengths on the field before the first turn. Charlie sat cool in second, and the California horse was up by ten by the time he was midbackstretch. I said, "Norm, this is perfect, he won't hit the board." By the time he was entering the second turn, Charlie was within four lengths, and when they hit the stretch, Charlie was head-to-head with him. Vickie hand rode him to the wire, and they won by six lengths.

The California horse ran dead last, so Norm asked, "How did you know that horse wouldn't hit the board?"

I answered, "That's why Jim worked Charlie a half. That horse was rank and ran off, saving nothing for the lane."

We went down to the winner's circle, and when Charlie was led in, Vickie said, "I don't believe this guy. I didn't ask him for a thing. I'm not quite sure what you have, but I'll bet there's never been a better horse on this track."

I told her she put a nice ride on him before saying "It must have been tempting to not let the other horse get so far ahead."

"Not at all, I knew he was running off, so I just let Charlie do what he wanted to. He's definitely a route horse because he could have gone around again. I don't know how far this horse will take you, but I hope you'll take me with him." *Those big blue eyes sparkle like diamonds.*

Norm and I both said, "You're his rider as long as you choose to be."

Jim's horse won the last race quite easily, and I collected over nineteen thousand dollars after taxes.

When I got back to the barn, I handed Jim ten hundred-dollar bills, and he said, "This is too much."

"You were a big part of what I hit, and that's a very modest tip. He has turned into quite a horse under your guidance, so wherever he goes from here, you started him on his way."

Vickie walked up to hug both of us and protested when I gave her a thousand dollars. Norm told her he would send her a check for the plane ticket before giving her some hundred-dollar bills.

"You two are way too sweet because I love riding this horse," she whispered while trying not to let the tears cascade down her face. She had us set up with a trainer, and I was sure she had him the whole time. That was great because it meant she knew and trusted him.

Norm told Jim that Charlie would be picked up the next morning before giving him some bills. I didn't know what denomination or how many, but Jim was happy. "Get me your final bill, and I'll send you a check right away," Norm said.

"I'll see you guys again, and best of luck with Charlie," Jim said before we turned to leave.

"Wasn't that great of Vickie to come for the race? She must really think Charlie's special, or it might be because I'm so darn cute and she couldn't stay away," I kidded. He wasn't too high on my theory.

He said, "By the way, Steve Stacy is the trainer."

I replied, "Our friend Bobbi told me to watch him when he moved to California from New York, and I've done well betting on his horses."

He said, "Vickie's excited to get him back and thinks he'll easily be a stakes winner in California."

I replied, "You talked to her more than I did."

He laughed while saying "Of course, she likes me best." *You'd think a guy his age would be smarter than that, but we're both playing second fiddle to Charlie.*

I said, "I'll set up a separate account for betting because I'm up almost twenty-seven thousand just betting on Charlie and the horses Jim has given us. I don't know if Steve will tell us about the horses he likes, but he brings in some with good odds." ***How good is this horse?***

The next morning, we met for coffee and were still high about the race. I said, "I don't know how much more I can take."

He replied, "My friend, you better brace yourself because we're just gettin' started."

Jim called while we were drinking our coffee, and Norm put his phone on speaker. "Charlie came out of the race great, and his legs were ice-cold. They picked him up at six this morning, and I gave the driver his papers, so you're all set. I hope Charlie takes you all the way to the Kentucky Derby."

I said to Norm, "I thought we were dreamers. Maybe we should nominate him to the Kentucky Derby before he turns three."

"We have plenty of time, so let's see how he runs in California first."

"You can't get away from being an accountant long enough to let me dream."

"Believe me, I'm as excited as you are, and I hope he takes us to Louisville as much as you do." *Sounds like he thinks it might happen.*

The next morning, Steve called us and said, "Charlie shipped very well. I usually have a contract signed before I start training, but you came highly recommended by Vickie, so we can take care of that when you get here. There's a 258,000-dollar grade 2 going seven furlongs in three weeks, and I'd like to nominate him to that, if you don't mind."

Norm replied, "Let me wrap my mind around that. Absolutely, you can nominate him, but it's unbelievable how fast this has all happened."

Steve said, "Three weeks may be a little soon, but Vickie thinks he'll win."

I replied, "He ran great the last time he ran on three weeks' rest."

Steve said, "If you can send me five thousand dollars, I'll nominate him as soon as it gets here."

Norm told him the check would be in the mail right away. After saying goodbye, we sat there looking at each other for some time before Norm said, "I've been in this business for over twenty years, and I've always wanted a horse like Charlie. I didn't really think it would happen, but I bought a horse by mistake, and here we are."

"I'm just glad I was smart enough to buy part of him," I replied.

He said, "If you were smart, you would have bought 50 percent that first day."

"I didn't say I was the smartest kid on the block, and I'm happy with my 20 percent. You've put way more into this business than I have, so I'm glad it's coming back to you." *He was a lifesaver for me after Linda's accident.*

A week before the race, Steve called and told us we were in, before saying "I hope you're coming down."

"We'll make flight arrangements today," Norm promised.

Steve said, "We have his papers, but you should be here early to get your California license."

Norm replied, "We'll do that, and if you'll have your contract ready, we'll sign it."

We were flying out of Seattle at 7:00 a.m., so I said, "Not knowing what the pass will be like, we should go over the day before. We've stayed at a motel near the airport many times. We can park our car there and take their shuttle to the airport. Do you want separate rooms?"

"No, just get two beds because we won't be there very long."

We started over at noon, and the roads were great. We rehashed all the events of the last few months before I said, "I'm sorry, buddy, but the best thing is still the look on your face when you realized you bought the wrong horse."

He smacked my arm before saying "Sorry I can't enjoy that with you, old buddy."

I said, "I thought right away that you bought him because of his breeding. With his bloodlines, the sky really is the limit."

He replied, "He sure looks like he has ability, but we'll have a much better idea in a few days."

We were up early the next morning, and it was nice to know we didn't have to find a place to park. We had breakfast at the motel before taking their shuttle to the airport. During the flight, I said, "If he wins the race, we should go to Reno for a couple days."

"The flight's set to go back to Seattle," he informed me rather rudely.

"If we win **this race**, we can afford to change the flight," I said with a big smile on my face. He nodded his head while adjusting his seat for the flight.

I said, "I'm up twenty-seven thousand dollars, and it doesn't seem like I'm betting real money. I've never bet like I have since we bought Charlie."

Norm replied, "I sure hope it continues for both of us. I think Charlie's special." *One thing I know, the funnel is much smaller at the top, so the races will continue to get tougher.*

We landed in Oakland and rented a car to drive to Bay Meadows. There was a nice motel within walking distance, so we rented rooms for two nights. We walked to the backside of the track and explained to the guard that we were going in to get our license. He wanted to know who was training for us, and when I told him it was Steve, he said, "I know him well, go on in."

We went to the office and filled out the papers. The form asked the names of the trainer and any horses we had in training. I almost wrote down Charlie for his name because that was all we ever called him. After getting directions to Steve's barn, we walked back. He was on the phone in his tack room when we walked up, and not wanting to interrupt him, we started walking down the shed row.

We had only gone a few steps when a voice rang out, "**May I help you?**" We turned around, and Steve was giving us an unpleasant look. Norm stepped toward him to shake his hand, and after we introduced ourselves, he said, "Sorry to jump out like that, but there's a lotta money in horseflesh down there."

I replied, "I'm glad you're on top of it, and we're looking forward to working with you."

"I understand you call him Charlie. How did that come about?" He asked.

Norm answered, "I asked Jim the same question, and his answer was 'as good as any,' so I couldn't argue the point."

"Charlie it is then. I have one more question that I have to ask you, but I hope I don't kill this relationship before it gets started. Did you really buy him for two thousand by mistake?"

Norm said, "I don't mind you asking because Jim would make sure you knew anyway. I can't think of many he hasn't told."

We all laughed before Steve said, "If you make another mistake like him, please count me in."

I said, "If you had been in the car going home from the sale, you could have bought him cheap."

"Timing is everything," he replied. *This will be a fun group, but I wanna see Vickie.*

I asked Steve, "What are we running against?"

"It's a good field. There are two coming up from Southern California, and one of them won a grade 3 at Delmar. The other ran fourth in a grade 1 at Hollywood Park, so they'll both be tough, and there are four or five from here that look really solid. At this point, we're just trying to see what we have. Charlie couldn't be doing better, so there will be no excuses if he loses. Vickie says he'll win, but I don't know many jockeys that wouldn't say the same about their horse."

Norm said, "We're happy she's riding Charlie because we both like her very much."

"She has nothing but good things to say about you guys," Steve replied.

I added, "She's easy on the eye, along with being a good rider."

He replied, "My wife and I have loved her since arriving here from New York. I'm really happy that she's decided to stay in California year around." We signed the papers before walking down to Charlie's stall, and he was sleeping when we walked up.

"He seems to be taking everything in stride," I said to Steve.

"He's a really laid-back horse, and that shows a lot of class. Don't worry, he'll be on his game tomorrow, but I'm not sure his game is good enough for the horses he'll be facing down here."

I walked up and scratched Charlie's neck, and he laid his head on my shoulder. "He remembers me," I said excitedly while rubbing my ear against his jaw.

After saying goodbye to Steve, we walked back to the motel. We had separate rooms, so I climbed on my bed and was asleep in a couple of minutes. I dreamed about the race and hoped it would turn out the way it did in my dream. Norm called and asked if I wanted to get some dinner before saying "I saw a pizza restaurant while we were walking over here."

"That would be better than driving, so it sounds good to me." We walked to the restaurant and ordered a large pizza. While we were waiting for our meal, Steve walked in with a very attractive lady and waved when he saw us. I said, "You're welcome to join us if you'd like to."

After they ordered, they walked over, so we stood up. Steve said, "Guys, this is my wife, Sandy. Sandy, this is Jim and Norm, the owners of Charlie."

"Who is Charlie?" she asked with a lovely smile on her very pretty face.

Steve explained, "From this day forward, Wrong Way North will be known as Charlie."

She asked, "Should I ask where Charlie comes from?"

Steve answered, "You could, but you wouldn't know any more than you do now."

"Charlie it is," she said before telling us Steve was really excited about him.

I said, "I sure hope he can run with the horses he'll be running against tomorrow."

"You won't know until he runs against them," she replied. *I like this lady.*

"It was wonderful meeting Sandy," Norm said on the way to the motel.

I said, "She's a real doll, and I'm quite sure she liked me best."

We were both tired, so we said "good night." I went to sleep while watching television and woke up at two in the morning. I turned off the TV before going into the bathroom to get cleaned up and was sound asleep in no time.

I was startled awake by the ringing of my phone, and Norm said, "Good morning."

I shouted, "It will be when morning gets here."

He replied, "Six fifteen, half the day is gone. I'll be down at the breakfast buffet when you come down."

"It'll be about an hour," I told him before trying to shake the cobwebs. I don't think a shower ever felt better, so I let the hot water run over my head for a good five minutes while thinking about how much fun we were having on our adventure. I was a little surprised that Vickie's lovely smile appeared to me right then. I shook my head while thinking, *She's younger than my daughter, for goodness' sake.*

After getting out of the shower, I hustled downstairs. "This is a good-looking breakfast," I said before going through the line. I had scrambled eggs, sausage, and an English muffin while looking out the window. The coffee was really good, so I had another cup, and my mind drifted back to when Linda traveled with me. *I sure wish she could be here to enjoy Charlie with us.* The horses we had back then seemed to yield more disappointments than they did good times, but I was sure this horse was very special.

Norm asked, "Did you fall asleep on me?"

I answered, "I was wishing Linda could enjoy Charlie with us."

"You don't know how much I wish that too. She made me feel like I was part of your family after my divorce."

I said, "She liked you very much, but that's about the only fault I can remember about her." They really had been close friends, and we had him over for meals at least once a week. *Hard to let go of the memories.*

We walked over to the track and showed the guard that we had gotten our license. "Do you have anything going today?" he asked me.

I answered, "Wrong Way North in the two-year-old stake. If he runs like he did up north, he has a chance."

We went into the café to buy a form, and on the front page was written, "**Washington Bred in Deep Water Today**." I looked at Norm and said, "Deep water doesn't say enough." It was good that Charlie couldn't read the form because it picked him right on bottom at thirty to one. Each horse had a sentence about him, and Charlie's was short and sweet: "doesn't belong with these."

Norm had a program open, so I asked what his morning line was. He said, "He's thirty to one here too, so I hope he outruns his odds."

I replied, "I'm betting his money, so I'll hit him hard." *I **hope** he can run with the horses down here.*

Norm said, "I'll put a couple bucks on him too." When he said a couple, he was really saying a bunch. He had always been quiet but was never shy at the betting window.

When we arrived at the barn, Steve said, "I had to take him to the track this morning because he was so full of himself, I was afraid he'd get hurt before the race. Vickie galloped him a mile and came back really excited."

I walked to the café to order a burger and sat down at a table. There were some horsemen sitting behind me, talking about our race. One of them said, "The two horses from down south will be really tough."

One of them snickered before asking, "Why would the owners of Wrong Way North bring him from Portland and put him in this race?" None of them had much respect for Washington breeding. *Do we belong, or will we look stupid?*

Charlie was the four horse in the ninth race. The two Southern California invaders were eight and ten, so I decided to bet early. "I'll have two hundred to win and place on the four and five-dollar daily doubles, the four in the ninth with all in the tenth. I'll have two-dollar exactas, the four on top of all, and five-dollar exacta boxes, four eight and four ten. I'll also have a five-dollar trifecta, the four on top of the eight ten and ten eight." I walked away hoping I hadn't thrown my money away.

I found Norm wandering around by the rail and asked, "Have you been betting?"

"Ya, I sure wish I woulda been with you."

"Charlie will make you money." I told him what I heard in the café and said, "They could be right, but as I said, I think he's special and he'll win."

When the horses were called for the ninth race, we walked into the paddock as Steve was bringing Charlie in. We agreed that he looked fantastic. "I don't know if you can bet a horse on looks, but he sure looks better to me than anything in here," Steve said.

Vickie walked up and said, "You boys look nervous, but believe me, it's in the bag. He's the best horse I've ever been on by the length of the lane." *I love her confidence.*

I whispered, "Best of luck, Vickie." I was already excited when she hugged me, so I squeezed a little harder than I should have. When she winced, I apologized before telling her I was excited about the race.

She had a cute smile on her face when she said, "Settle down, big boy, before you hurt someone." *Mmmm, she feels fantastic. Settle down indeed.*

"Riders up," came over the PA system, so Steve gave her a leg up. I had forgotten to get tickets for them, so I ran inside and bet two separate ten-dollar win tickets. Charlie was sixty to one, the ten was nine to five, and the eight was three to one. When the gate opened, the ten wanted the lead, but Charlie easily got between him and the rail. With some effort, the ten was able to go ahead, but Vickie was smart to make him use some energy while Charlie used none. Charlie was very content to sit in second, a couple lengths back. Going up the backstretch, the ten tried to pull away, but Charlie was his shadow. Turning into the stretch, Charlie caught him, and they were five lengths ahead of the rest of the field. Charlie was on the outside, so Vickie reached back and popped him twice left-handed. When he started to pull away, Vickie put away her whip and hand-rode him to the wire. He won by ten lengths, and the eight went by the ten just before the wire. I was stunned. Norm and I walked to the winner's circle without saying a word because we were both a little bit in shock.

Steve said, "You guys look like you've seen a ghost."

"I think we have," I said while wondering if that really happened.

When Vickie brought him to the winner's circle, she laughed while asking "Are you guys going to a funeral? Cheer up, there was never a doubt." After the picture, she walked over to us and said, "I wasn't close to the bottom of this guy.

Believe me, he's the real deal." I took her hand and kissed it while giving her the ticket. She glanced down at the ticket before looking at the tote board and said, "Thank you so much." *She's fantastic.*

Charlie went to the test barn, and Steve was outside, waiting for him, when I gave him his ticket. "What were the odds?" he asked.

I answered, "Darn it, only sixty to one."

He asked where Norm was, and I answered, "I lost track of him. I hope he shows up pretty quick because he had a wild look in his eyes." Norm came walking back, and Steve asked him where he'd been.

"Cashing my tickets," he said before asking if I cashed mine.

"I still have the daily double to go, so I'll cash them all at the same time."

A seven-to-one horse won the last race, and the return on my wagers was forty-two thousand in total. I told the ticket seller I wanted two thousand in cash and the rest in a check. I walked away, patting the pocket I put the check into, knowing my horse account was nearing seventy thousand dollars. Vickie said we were in for quite a ride, and I believed we were. *I've never dreamed this big.*

We decided to eat dinner at the backside café. The special was T-bone steak for $10.99, so I said to Norm, "I can afford that." He ordered the same thing, and I told him it was my treat.

He whispered, "I made eleven thousand on the race."

I replied, "It's still on me because I did a little better than that." He wanted to know how much I made and was surprised when I told him it was forty-two thousand.

"You were always the one in the group that wouldn't bet five dollars on a horse unless it was yours and a mortal cinch."

I explained, "That was when I was betting my own money. It's much easier spending money that Charlie has given me."

"I love it, so let's hope this unbelievable ride continues. The way he won today, there's more to this horse than you or I would have ever dreamed. Speaking of dreaming, I keep pinching myself to make sure I'm awake. Please tell me I'm awake."

"Yes, we're a couple retired guys that got really lucky."

When he turned his head, I pinched his arm, and he shouted, **"Ouch, that hurt!"**

I said "Good, you're awake." I don't think he ever appreciated my humor the way he should have.

After dinner, we walked back to the motel. I had told the lady at the desk that Charlie was running, so when we walked in, she wanted to know how he ran. I pulled out 120 dollars and handed it to her.

She asked, "What's this?"

"He won, and I put a two-dollar win on him for you." She was shocked that he paid that much. I told her to buy herself something with the money. *I love sharing our good fortune.*

I didn't sleep well because I dreamed about the race all night. He won in every case but not as easily in any of them as he did on the track. The phone rang, and Norm said, "Good morning."

"Are you nuts? What time is it?"

"Five thirty, time for any normal person to be up."

"Well, that answers my question. **You are nuts!**" I shouted.

"Quit crying, and get down here. You have to see this article in the paper."

"Now help me to understand, the article would have changed if you called at seven?"

He said, "Just get down here and meet me at the breakfast buffet."

This almost makes it worth getting up at this time for, I thought when he showed me the article.

> ## Wrong Way North Comes South and Proves He's the Right Horse

It told how few Washington-bred horses competed well against stakes horses in California before saying "He didn't just compete but toyed with the field." The last line was "This is the best Washington bred this reporter has had the pleasure of watching. It looked like there could be much more to come."

Norm had called and changed our flight, so he said, "We'll fly to Reno today at one and go on to Seattle from there day after tomorrow."

"Great, I have my Harrah's player's card, so I'll get us a room. Do you want separate rooms or one with two beds?"

He answered, "I don't spend much time in the room, so one is fine with me." I hadn't been to Reno in about five years, so when the clerk asked if I had stayed with them, I explained that we used my wife's card and told her about the accident. She asked her name and was off the phone for a couple of minutes. When she returned, she told me how sorry she was about the accident, and because of our prior play, she gave us two nights at no charge. Our conversation caused my eyes to tear up and again, I wished Linda were with us to watch Charlie run. *Will this pain ever go away?*

When we stopped by the track, Steve and Vickie were both there. "Charlie's doing great," they said at the same time. Steve said, "There's a grade 2 at Santa Anita in four weeks, and I think he'll fit." Vickie had a couple of horses to gallop, so we thanked her again before she walked away. Steve said, "I'm glad she had to go. Do you wanna pay to fly her down there or use one of the local riders?"

I was just about to speak when Norm said, "Vickie's Charlie's rider, so we'll pay hers and your expenses. Unless she can't get out of prior obligations, she goes where Charlie goes."

"Don't worry about prior obligations, she'll follow Charlie wherever he goes."

I said, "By the way, Steve, we're going to Reno for a couple days. If you don't mind me asking, do you have anything running today or tomorrow?"

"What time will you arrive today?"

I looked at Norm, and he said, "We arrive in Reno at two fifteen."

"That works, I have one in the last race today. He's run one time, and we found out after the race that he had mucus in his lungs. He's doing well now and should be right there." He surprised me when he said, "If you take my word, don't bet more than you can afford to lose."

I asked, "Do all trainers say that?"

He answered, "If they're smart, they do. I sure wish I was going with you guys."

It was good to see Reno again after so many years. We checked in after about twenty minutes in line and dropped our bags off at the room before hurrying down to the sports book. There were nine races, and the fifth had just run. Steve's horse was the three in a field of nine, and the race was a maiden, twenty-thousand-dollar claiming race. *I'll bet early and play for a while.*

I told Norm I wanted to buy some Keno tickets and walked over to the keno area. I played the same numbers every time. First, I got two five spots. One ticket was 1, 3, 5, 7, and 9. On a separate ticket, I got 2, 4, 6, 8, and 10. On a separate ticket, I put the two together for a ten spot, and the last ticket I played was all the fives, five through seventy-five. I had played those numbers for years at an Indian casino near home. They kidded me by calling me Mr. T. because the ticket looked like a *T* when played on one ticket.

I bought five games of each before walking back to the sports book. The winner of the eighth was sixteen to one, so I liked the start of my double. "Did you bet that?" Norm asked.

I answered, "I wheeled to Steve's horse in the daily double." He didn't have it, so I said, "I bet a three-dollar, so I'll sell you one dollar, if you want it."

He said, "I'll take it if you really don't mind." Steve's horse was six to one in the entry sheet, and at post time, his odds were nine to one. Vickie broke him out of the gate on top and was never more than a length in front, until the stretch. She smacked him twice, and he opened up three lengths in the stretch. A horse was closing but never got closer than a length. The daily double paid 280 dollars, so I gave Norm 140 before collecting a little over 1,700 in total.

I said out loud, "Sweet ride, Vickie, you just paid for my trip." *There's something I like about that girl*. I wondered if I might be infatuated with her riding, but whatever, I was glad she was part of our team.

I walked over to the Keno area and had the lady check my tickets. It was a good thing the horse won because my twenty-dollar Keno investment paid just two dollars. I gave the two dollars to the lady before walking away. I went to the blackjack tables, looking for Norm, and he had a rather large stack of chips in front of him. I didn't talk to him because I didn't wanna hear how I changed his luck. I never could understand how my talking to him could break his luck, but he believed it could.

I walked around looking for a slot machine that appealed to me. I enjoyed the penny and nickel machines because they had so many ways to win. The games were certainly more fun than watching the wheel spin. I found a game with unicorns and thought, *As good as the horses have been, I'll try it*. I put a twenty in and played for over an hour. In the end, it took my twenty, but I had enough fun that I didn't mind. It was getting late, so I walked over to where Norm was playing and told him I was hungry. "I am too," he replied. He had the dealer color him up and was over seven hundred dollars ahead. He gave the dealer one of the twenty-five-dollar chips before we walked away. He showed me a slip of paper and said, "The pit boss gave me dinner for two at any restaurant in the house." I asked him if he had a date, and he answered, "**Not a very pretty one**."

"You can insult me as much as you want to as long as you feed me," I said as we walked in search of a seafood restaurant. We were very impressed with the quality of the food, and after dinner, I said, "I'm beat, so I'm going up to the room." He told me he'd be up later, so I took the elevator to the ninth floor. I turned the TV on but fell asleep in no time. I was awakened by the door opening at four thirty. I turned over and went back to sleep, but after a little while, I heard a strange sound. Norm snored and exhaled all his air before being totally silent. I lay there listening for what seemed like an eternity, but he wasn't breathing, so I shouted, "**NORM!**"

"**What?**" he asked with anger in his voice.

I said, "Never mind."

"**Why did you wake me up?**" he asked in the same angry tone.

I said, "I thought you were dead, but I'll talk to you about it in the morning."

The clock said it was eight fifteen, but the room was completely dark. I quietly got up and went into the bathroom before leaving the room without waking him. *What a glorious day,* I thought as I stepped into the elevator. It had nothing to do with the weather because I hadn't looked outside. What Charlie accomplished was just sinking in. I'd seen horses run the way he did on television, but I never thought I'd own one of them. I went to the buffet for breakfast and enjoyed two cups of coffee before going through the food line. *If I die today, I'll die very happy because of Charlie and Vickie.*

I walked by the blackjack tables and didn't see Norm, so I went over to see if anyone was playing the unicorn machines. I found one that was open, so I sat down and put a twenty in the slot. I usually played a hundred credits on penny machines, but since I was ahead, I pressed the three hundred credit button. On the first spin, the screen was almost totally populated with unicorns. While it was counting out the credits, I thought how unlucky the person was who just walked away. It paid 750 dollars. I played it four more times, hitting nothing, so I cashed in and walked over to buy my Keno tickets for five games. Still no Norm, so I went up to the room. It was ten thirty, and he was still asleep. The housekeeper was just two doors away, so I asked her to leave a set of towels and told her everything else would be fine.

She said, "Please leave the other towels in the room." I took the new set of towels to the room after giving her a five-dollar tip. *It's nice, having extra money.*

Norm asked, "What are you doing?"

"The day is half gone," I replied.

"Give me a half hour, and we'll go eat."

I said, "I'll check my Keno tickets and meet you at the blackjack tables." I collected nine dollars, so I gave one to the lady at the counter and kept eight. I started to walk away but turned around and said, "I'll buy those five more times, please." I sat down in the Keno area to watch a few games, and in the first game, the first three numbers were 1, 5, and 7. The 9, along with three of the even numbers, came up, so I ended up with four out of five and seven out of ten. I looked at a booklet to see what it paid. Four out of five paid twenty-four dollars, and three out of five paid one. The best part was, seven out of ten paid 320 dollars. I was on a little bit of a hot streak and having a great time.

Norm walked up and told me he was hungry, and I said, "I walked by a buffet that I think has a cure for that." He told me that sounded good, so we walked over to see what they were serving. I spotted some crawdads and put a bunch on my plate along with a cup of clarified butter.

When Norm sat down, he looked at my plate and said, **"You're eating spiders!"**

I replied, "Mmmm, they're really good." He had never tried them, so I explained, "They taste like lobster, so if you have patience, they make a great meal." He wanted to know why I wasn't eating anything with them. I said, "I had a big breakfast, but I'll have some dessert when I finish these."

After lunch, we went back into the casino. Norm played three-card poker, and I walked around watching people for a while. It was good to see so many of them having fun. I played slots for a while but wasn't hitting anything, so I walked over to Norm and said, "I'm going outside to walk around for a while." He wanted to keep playing, so I went out alone. It was a bit depressing because other than the four big casinos, there wasn't much left. I wondered if the Indian casinos had hurt Reno. It was nice to be outside, breathing the fresh air, so I sat on a bench and reflected on our good fortune. I stayed out longer than I thought, so I was surprised when I noticed it was getting dark. When I got back to the table where Norm was playing, I asked him if he was ready to eat. We both just had a bowl of soup because we ate too much for lunch. We had fun but agreed it would be good to get home.

The next day, we went to the airport an hour early and were glad we did because there were some long lines. After we checked in, I saw a spot to sit down at the end of a bench, next to the wall. I grabbed the seat and laid my head back. After a few seconds, a soft voice whispered, "You look tired." I looked to my left and saw a very attractive elderly lady, sitting in a wheelchair.

"I'm sorry, I guess I didn't notice you sitting there."

"You look tired," she whispered again.

I replied, "I had a good night's sleep, but it's been a long and fast-moving week."

I was surprised when she said, "If you don't mind, I'd love to hear about it."

I smiled while saying "It could be a long story."

"I have time, and I'd love to hear it," she repeated. I was surprised at how comfortable I was talking to someone I just met.

"To tell this properly, I must go back several months." She shifted in her seat and seemed very interested in what I had to say. Her face looked almost angelic. I explained, "It all started when the guy I'm on this trip with called and asked if I wanted to go to a racehorse sale."

"Sounds like you're very good friends," she whispered.

"For about forty years. When we arrived at the sale, one of our friends that owns a breeding farm told Norm that he liked one of the horses he was selling. To make a long story short, Norm bought a different horse by mistake."

She whispered, "**Oh no!**"

"That's what he thought too. I got such a kick out of it that I bought part of the horse, so I wouldn't feel bad telling people the story."

"You really are a good friend," she said with a very soft smile on her slightly wrinkled face.

"Actually, I looked at the horse in the sales book, and I really liked his breeding. Quite by luck, he turned out to be a nice horse."

"What's his name?"

I answered, "Wrong Way North, but we call him Charlie."

"Oh my, I watched him win the stakes race. I thought he was pretty, so I bet five dollars on him to win." She flashed a pretty smile while saying "That paid me three hundred dollars." It was good to see the excitement on her angelic face. She said, "That was some mistake Norm made."

I replied, "It was the best mistake he ever made."

"You know, it may not have been a mistake. I feel that good things happen to good people, and you're a very nice man."

I replied, "That's very kind of you."

"I'm so glad you're both having fun. I've saved all my life for my retirement, but as you can see, I'm confined to this chair." I was about to say I was sorry, but she said, "Please don't feel sorry for me. I have a wonderful family that seem to enjoy being with me and include me in many things they do."

"Anyone would be lucky to spend time with you," I said. The time had slipped away so quickly that I was surprised when they called for us to start boarding. I said, "I'll say something I've never said, I wish my flight had been delayed because it's been wonderful talking to you."

"I've enjoyed it also, and I'll be watching for that horse," she said while running her hand softly down my arm in what I thought was a motherly gesture. *What a wonderful lady*, I thought as I was walking to my gate. When I looked back, the space she was sitting in was empty. I wondered if I had imagined the wonderful conversation. *Is it possible I fell asleep?* She was right about one thing. "Enjoy life while you have your health."

When we were in the air, I said, "You haven't told me why you stopped breathing the other night."

"I have a sleep disorder called sleep apnea. It seems to happen mostly when I'm overly tired. I have a mask to wear at night that will make me breathe, but I can't sleep when I wear it."

I said, "If you could hear what I heard, you'd find a way to wear it. I've heard that, when people die, they exhale all of the air out of their lungs, and that's exactly what you did."

He replied, "We're all gonna go sometime." *When that day comes for me, I'll be able to see Linda.*

CHAPTER 3

Let's Get Out of the Cold Weather

The next morning when we met for coffee, I said, "My heart is down with Charlie, and I'd rather be down in the warmth of California." *I miss Vickie.*

He replied, "There's nothing keeping me here. I picked up the papers to nominate Charlie to the Kentucky Derby, and it would be nice to stay close to him."

I said, "I was gonna talk to you about that. Now we can dream about that too. I was thinking, we could buy a pickup and fifth wheel for not too much if we buy them used. I have enough in my horse account to easily pay half."

"If we buy them, the money will come out of the purse money because it'll be a good write-off."

I said, "Only 20 percent of that is mine, so I'll pay enough that we both own half." He asked me if I wanted any money from the purse account, and I said, "Unless we have to do it for taxes or if you need some, I'd say no. I'm about sixty-five thousand ahead betting on the horses, so I don't need the money."

"I'm good too, and I can figure the taxes with the money in the account. It's nice not having to pay horse bills every month." He promised me we would never pay another month on Charlie.

"Wow, what a blessing Charlie is turning out to be," I said before giving thanks for him in a silent prayer. We were driving out to tell Pat how Charlie was doing, and on the way, we saw a diesel pickup and fifth wheel for sale at a farmhouse. The sign said twenty-one thousand for both. When we pulled in, a man

43

came out of the house that I recognized from Yakima Meadows. I didn't know his name, but I had seen him many times.

He said, "I just saw you two in the winner's circle on TV. That's some horse you have. I've heard the story of how you bought him, and I'm glad it happened to someone from this area."

I replied, "We're very happy with him. We stopped to look at the pickup and trailer, so do you have time to go for a test drive?"

The pickup had 130,000 miles on it, but that's nothing with a diesel. It was very clean and drove like it was brand-new. The trailer was in great condition also, so Norm asked if he would take twenty thousand for the pair.

"I will on one condition, you let me know when that horse will run again."

I replied, "I'll do one better than that. He'll be in a stakes race at Santa Anita in three weeks, and he's improving with every start."

"Now what's his name again?"

I answered, "Wrong Way North." He wrote it down while wishing us good luck, and we made arrangements to pick them up the next morning.

We drove on out to Pat's farm, and she was out working with the horses. She said, "Well how about that, I've watched every race he's run, and he's turned into a real monster."

I replied, "Except when he's in his stall, he still lays his head on my shoulder."

"He always was a joy to work with. This makes the day he had his bit caught on the saddle look pretty big. Jim, I've told many people how calm you were when you told me to loosen the saddle. If not for that, this day may never have come."

I replied, "If I'd known he was in danger, believe me, I wouldn't have been so calm. For as big and powerful as these animals are, they sure are fragile."

"I just lost a yearling to colic. It's hard to imagine they can die from a tummy ache, but it happens. He died from twisted gut because I didn't get to him in time."

"I'm sorry to hear that Pat," I said before asking if it was her horse.

"He was and I'm happy that he was because it's hard to give that kind of news to clients. Have you nominated Charlie to the Kentucky Derby?"

Norm said, "It's probably crazy but we're in the process."

"I think it would be crazy if you didn't. He's bred to go a mile and a half, and I can't believe his speed."

I said, "Vickie says he's push button now, so I expect her to take him back next time." I told her we bought the camper and were going to California for a few months. *I wonder if Vickie's seeing someone.*

44

"You win the Derby for me so I can tell people I trained a Kentucky Derby winner," she said as she was walking us to our car.

Norm replied, "That's a long way off but believe me, if he takes us there, we'll go along for the ride."

We were both anxious to hit the road because going down for coffee wasn't as exciting as it was before Charlie. I said to Norm, "We need to run more often because I enjoy Vickie's hugs."

Norm smiled and nodded in agreement before saying, "It's really nice hearing you say that after all the years you've spent in mourning." I believe I could see a tear in his eye, so I wasn't the only one that had missed Linda all those years. She was always willing to laugh at his attempts at humor and I think he liked that about her.

We got the check and picked up the pickup and trailer. I told Norm we should change the belts and hoses because those are the causes of most breakdowns along the road. We took it into the shop the next day to have the work done. I had no bills and I stopped the newspaper until I notified them. After paying five hundred in advance on my utilities and asking my neighbor to get my mail for a couple months, I was ready to go. We decided to leave at eight the next morning, so I called my daughter in Portland to tell her we were coming through. I asked if they wanted to meet for lunch and we decided to meet at the truck stop in Gresham. I had one more thing to do. I bought some ear plugs to muffle Norm's snoring.

We left town at eight the next morning and I told Norm I made plans to meet Tammy at the truck stop around noon. There was a lot of snow in the mountains, but the roads were bare and dry. We got to Gresham just past noon and Tammy was flashing her car lights. I had told her to look for our pickup and trailer. When they stepped out of the car, I thought how the kids had grown. Cory was fourteen. He walked up to me first and stuck out his hand to shake but I grabbed his hand and pulled him to me for a big hug. "I don't care if you make the major leagues and I meet you on the field with all the other players, you'll get a hug. Your mom told me you scored thirty-six points in a basketball game."

He lowered his head and said sheepishly, "I got lucky." I was surprised at how deep his voice was.

"I'm glad you're humble," I said before asking him to please never lose that. My grandkids had always loved Norm, and Kayti was giving him a big hug. Jenna was eleven and my youngest grandchild. She came over and hugged me before I said, "And you, little girl, I hear you're playing volleyball and basketball with girls two years older than you."

She had a big smile on her face while saying, "I'm the leading scorer on our basketball team."

I said, "Your mom told me and we're both very proud of you." She had no shortage of confidence and she was a very good athlete. Kayti walked over and hugged me. She was five eight and about a hundred and fifteen pounds. I felt guilty when I thought how pretty she was because I didn't know if it was alright for a grandpa to think that. "So, this will be your third part on Leverage," I said in a questioning way.

She was very humble and said, "It'll be such a small part that you probably won't see me."

"You said that last time and I counted nine times you were in that one. That last close up really blew me away."

She said, "Don't expect that this time." She hugged me and kissed my cheek while saying, "I love you Papa." I told her she was my little Kayti Bug.

Tammy said, "I'm glad you weren't late because the kids were driving me crazy, thinking every camper that went by was yours. You need to get down here more because they miss you."

"I miss all of you too, but Charlie needs me now."

She replied, "The newspaper had an article saying how incredible he is. They went on about how he won a stakes race here and went down to California and beat those horses by more than the horses up here."

"He's doing well," I replied before telling her I hoped it would continue. Unless you're involved in the business, you don't know how fragile they can be and that each race can be their last.

We walked toward the restaurant to get some lunch and on the way, Kayti put her arm around me. I said, "You're awfully skinny so I hope you're eating enough." While we were eating, I asked her if she had any more gigs coming up. She didn't have anything going right then but was really enjoying college. I was surprised when she told me she wanted to be a doctor.

I kissed all of them before giving Tammy a check for five thousand dollars. I told her it was from Charlie. "We'll see you when we can," I promised while climbing into the pickup.

It was getting dark when we reached the last truck stop before California, so we pulled in and filled up with fuel. I told Norm he could stay the night if he was tired. "That sounds good. We can get an early start in the morning," he replied. He asked the kid filling the tank if the food in the restaurant was good.

He said, "I eat here all the time. I know it's close to Thanksgiving, but the hot turkey sandwich is the best I've eaten."

I replied, "Turkey it'll be because you can never get too much turkey. Is there a place to park for the night?" He pointed to a place in the back, so I thanked him while giving him a ten-dollar tip. We hooked the trailer up to power before going in to eat. The kid was right about the turkey. It was just like my wife cooked it and everyone loved her turkey dinners. I asked Norm, "Does Steve know we're on our way?"

"I called him last night and he seemed anxious to see us. I know you're in a hurry to see Vickie." I smiled and nodded as I thought about how perfectly she fit Charlie's saddle. I knew I should stop having those thoughts about such a young lady, but she had quite a hold on me. *She's so beautiful that she has to be seeing someone.*

We hit the sack early. The ear plugs didn't keep out all of the noise, but they were an improvement, so I fell asleep in no time. Knock-Knock-Knock! My eyes opened but I thought I was dreaming. Again, I heard the knock, only louder that time. I was half asleep and started to open the door. **"Don't open it,"** Norm shouted.

I shook my head before asking, "Who is it?"

A male voice answered, "Vince."

"I don't know any Vince," I said as I was waking up. I asked him what he wanted.

He asked, "Do you have a phone I can use?"

It was 3:00 a.m., so I said with anger in my voice, "Go to the truck stop and use their phone, **Vince**!"

"I didn't wanna walk that far," he said.

"Vince, have you ever hunted jackrabbits?" I asked with even more anger in my voice.

"No, I haven't, sir," he replied.

"If you do, don't use a shotgun. The last time I did, I used the one I have in my hands and shot one at twenty yards. When I got to him, all that was left was ears and little bunny feet, **Vince**!" I said with a little more emphasis on his name. I heard footsteps running away and thought *maybe it's too far to walk but apparently, it's not too far to run.*

Norm was laughing and asked, "Little bunny feet, Jim?"

I answered, "It sounded good at the time." I reached into the cupboard beside my bed and pulled out my .357 magnum before saying, "This isn't a shotgun, but it tears a pretty big hole." I tried to go back to sleep but never did fully. The next time I looked at my watch, it was five thirty, so I got up and took a shower before stepping outside. No Vince in sight.

It was a cool morning, and I thought how lucky that, out of the huge universe, Charlie found his way into our lives. If I had said no about going to the sale, Norm wouldn't have gone, so someone else would have bought Charlie, and we'd still be going down for coffee every morning. *Good things happen to good people* sounded inside my head one more time. I looked up and thought about how much the lady in the wheelchair looked like an angel. When I stepped back inside the trailer, Norm was sitting up, laughing. "Did you have a funny dream?" I asked.

"Ya, about little bunny feet. I'll never understand where some of the things you say come from."

"Well, I'll tell you, buddy, when I figure it out, you'll be the first to know. One thing I know for sure, if I had asked him to please leave, he would have knocked again."

He asked, "Are you worried that he might report you to the police for threatening him with a gun?"

"A man pounding on your door at three a.m. is not likely to report anything to the police, and what's this about threatening him? I merely told him about my hunting trip. Now get cleaned up, I'm hungry." On the way to the restaurant, I said, "If this breakfast is as good as the turkey, we're in for a treat." We both ate big breakfasts because we wouldn't stop before Bay Meadows and agreed that the breakfast was indeed as good as the dinner.

"How's your horse account doing?" he asked when we were back on the road.

I answered, "I've spent some, including what I paid on the camper, so I have a little over fifty-eight thousand left."

He asked, "How much was in there before you started betting Charlie?"

I laughed and answered, "Before Charlie, I was losing, so there was no horse account." We pulled into the back of the track at four thirty, and I asked the guard if there was a place where we could park for the night. We met him the last time we were there, so he pointed out an area for temporary parking.

I said, "Let's go get something to eat at the café." When we walked in, Vickie was sitting with a couple of other jockeys. When she saw us, she came over to give us both nice hugs. "Oh, how I've missed those hugs," I said.

She smiled and said, "Steve said you were coming." She smacked my arm playfully when I told her I was just breathing hard.

While trying not to laugh, I said, "We don't wanna take you away from your friends, but you're welcome to sit with us if you want to."

She replied, "Oh, them, they're not friends, just the characters I ride with."

She said it loud enough that they heard her, and one of them said, "We love you too, Vickie."

She walked over to pick up the drink she left at the table, and I wondered if she might be putting on a show for us, the way her hips were swaying. "Good to see you, guys," she said as she was sitting down. Norm asked her how Charlie was doing. "If you can believe it, he's getting bigger and better every day. I don't wanna sound overconfident, but I think he'll win the race in Southern California. I'll talk to Steve about this, but I'll run it by you guys now. I wanna use that race to teach him to rate." She took a deep breath before continuing, "I know it sounds crazy to use a three-hundred-thousand-dollar race to teach a horse, but... I guess I'm getting ahead of myself. That's if you want me to ride him down there?"

Norm replied, "Where Charlie goes, you go if you choose to, because the five of us are a team."

"That means so much to me," she said while using her index finger to remove a tear from her eye. I smiled as I thought about how pretty she was. *It's so nice to be back.*

I told her to hold still and kissed under her right eye before saying "Nothing sweeter than a teardrop from a beautiful woman."

"**You're such a flirt,**" she said while laughing.

I whispered, "Please forgive me, but you're the first lady I've flirted with in a very long time."

She placed her hand on mine while saying "It makes me happy that I can help you, and I kinda like to flirt a little bit." It was obvious that she knew about Linda's accident, and I could tell her words were sincere. I really didn't know why she appealed to me so much, but there was no doubt that she did. *Slow down, Jim.*

Norm said, "On to a crazy subject, we nominated Charlie to the Kentucky Derby." We were both surprised when she jumped out of her chair and gave him a big hug.

"Get a room," we heard from her jockey friends.

She waved them off before saying to Norm, "That's been a lifelong dream of mine."

I said, "I wanted to nominate him, so I should get a hug too." After about an hour, I said, "I'm beat from the trip, so I think I'll turn in."

"Me too," Norm said. Vickie went back to the table with her friends, and we saw her whisper something to them. They all gave her high fives and seemed genuinely excited for her.

When we were outside, I said, "I think we made her night, but you might have told her to hug me."

He told me to stop crying before saying "The kiss you gave her was enough. She's really sweet."

"Now tell me, was there a little more sway in her hips than normal when she picked up her drink?"

He replied, "I think there was in your mind, and that makes me happy for you."

After a good night's sleep, we headed for the track and stopped by the café for a sweet roll and coffee. When we arrived at the barn, Steve had a smile on his face and said, "You guys made Vickie happy last night. She was worried you might have a local rider ride him, so she was willing to pay for her own flight."

"Both hers and your expenses will be covered," Norm said. Steve let us know that he would drive, so Norm said, "We'll pay for your meals and mileage. We'll get your room also, and if Sandy wants to go, we'll buy her meals."

"That's nice, but she won't be able to make it, and I'll stay at the track," he said before telling us Charlie would work in about ten minutes.

I said, "I'm pretty good with a rake and pitchfork if there are any stalls to be mucked. I've cleaned a few in my time and received the biology lesson that goes with it."

Rather puzzled, he asked, "**Biology lesson?**"

"The filly's stalls are the wettest around the edges and the boys in the middle."

"Oh, that biology lesson," he said while laughing. "You're not expected to work while you're here."

"We'll be here awhile, so we may as well do something other than get in the way." I thought again, *This will be a fun ride.* I hoped Charlie would stay as sound as Pat seemed to think he would. I said, "I thought we told you that Vickie will ride wherever Charlie goes."

"She just needed to hear it from you guys," he replied. We followed Charlie to the track, and Vickie jogged him to the finish line before putting him into a fairly brisk gallop. The five-eighths pole was a little to our left, and when he reached it, I could see his body lower. As they came by us, he was in full stride and went all the way around the turn without moving a foot off the rail.

I said, "He's some athlete." When they went by the finish line, Vickie let him gallop out fast."

The clocker came over the intercom and asked, "Do you want the five-furlong time or the mile?"

Steve said, "The five-eighths will be fine."

"Fifty-nine and one and off the record, he galloped out in one thirty-seven flat. I want you to school those boys down south."

"We'll do our best," Steve promised. Norm and I were excited to be back with the team. I guess God knew I needed a boost, and that's why Charlie literally fell into our laps. I had never been depressed because I had Linda to keep me happy from the time I was a teenager. *I'm glad I can spend some time around Vickie.*

When Vickie came back, she said, "Unbelievable, and after that, he wouldn't even blow out a candle. I can't wait for the race to get here."

Steve asked, "Are we peaking too soon?"

She told us he always felt that good. I thought back to when we had him gelded. As much as he had grown, he may have gotten too big in his neck area, and that could have thrown off his center of gravity, changing everything. *That was pretty darn profound for someone who knows almost nothing about horses.* My daydream was interrupted by Steve handing me a shank and asking if I wanted to take Charlie to his stall.

"Suuuure," I said with a frightened look on my face.

"If you're not comfortable with it, I'll take him."

"I'd love to. I've moved horses around before but never one like Charlie," I replied.

"He's easy to work with."

I hooked the shank to his halter before unhooking him from the walker. I patted his cheek and scratched his neck before starting to walk toward his stall. After we had gone four or five steps, he stopped me in my tracks. He threw his head into the air while taking two steps back. My first thought was to pull, but luckily, something that my first trainer said to me came back. "I don't care how big or strong you are, if you get in a fight with a horse, you **will** lose. Go with the horse, and get him under control."

I shook the shank twice and took a step toward him while saying, "Easy big guy."

"Good job," Steve said, and I was glad he was watching me.

I whispered, "What caused him to do that?"

I said it a little louder than I intended to so Steve replied, "I'll show you what caused it." He pointed to a very small trickle of water, caused by a hose being left on.

"**That little bit of water**?" I asked with doubt in my voice.

He explained, "It's normally not there, and they're creatures of habit." We showed Charlie the water was nothing to worry about, and I took him to his stall. Steve said, "I liked the way you handled that."

I explained to him how much I enjoyed working with the horses on the weekends when I first got into the business. "My first trainer enjoyed teaching me and told me to go with the horses rather than try to pull them to me. A young girl that I knew was running a horse and asked me to paddock him for her. I was nervous but had downed a couple beers, so I thought, no problem. The horse was as big as Charlie and really full of himself. He got up on his back legs and started going back. Like today, my first thought was to pull him to me, but thank God, what she told me came back through the haze caused by the beer. I got him under control, but I've always been haunted by how stupid I would have looked, being dragged around the paddock."

He said, "Probably, nobody said it, but I guarantee, several people there admired your ability with horses."

"Better than skin burns from being dragged on the ground," I replied.

I said, "We need to get our trailer off the track's property." Steve took us to an RV park about a mile away. After signing some papers, we picked up the camper. I noticed a grocery store on the way over, so I said, "Let's get some groceries and act like this is a real home." We bought two really good-looking T-bone steaks along with some nice potatoes to bake. "Tonight, we christen the trailer," I said. Norm grabbed a bottle of wine, but I said, "None for me, thank you. Steak, potato, and diet cola for me."

"Someday you'll have a drink with me again," he replied.

"If we win the Kentucky Derby, I'll drink a whole bottle with you," I promised. I stopped drinking right after Linda's accident because the other driver was drunk, and I couldn't stand the thought of inflicting the pain I felt on someone else. *I hope someday this pain will go away*, I thought as I was climbing into the truck. I hoped the tear in my eye wouldn't trickle down my face.

About five years before, I went through a couple of rounds of chemotherapy, and they really messed up my emotions. Thinking about the chemo made me flash back to one series of treatments. I mentioned, the lady in the wheelchair was angelic. The nurses in the infusion department are all that way. They know people are worried and do all they can to put them at ease. My doctor's name is Dr. Boyd. He's a brilliant doctor and flies around the cancer center a hundred miles an hour all the time. I got to laughing with the nurses about how fast he moved, and a couple of them shared cute stories with me. The first was shared by Joyce. A very elderly lady told her she really liked him and called him Humming Boyd because of the way he flew around. The second story was shared by Rita. Another elderly lady called him the Mad Scientist because of the way he could do so many things at the same time. His memory and knowledge were incredible, plus he was fun to be around. My last story about him is, two nights before my appointment with him, my feet woke me up because they were ice-cold. That was the only time it happened, but he wanted to know about any changes. I also wanted to know if the chemo in my system would harm my wife if we had unprotected sex. I grabbed a paper towel and wrote "cold feet." Below that, I wrote "Talk about sex." I set it down on the examination bed before he came in so I wouldn't forget. I should have mentioned, he sees everything. He hadn't been in the room three seconds before he saw the small note. I laughed so hard when he asked me, **"You're having cold feet about talking to me about sex?"** I was quick to tell him they were separate issues. He wasn't worried about the cold feet and told me I should maybe wait a week before having sex.

I said, "I'm not dead yet, Doc, I'll get some condoms."

He kind of stuttered. "Th-th-th-that would be all right." I told you before, God really blesses me. Even when he gave me cancer, it was one that was very manageable and had **no pain**. I have CLL, an adult form of leukemia. It's really no worse than sugar diabetes or some of the other ailments that adults get, but the word *cancer* makes it seem worse.

While we were getting the groceries out of the truck, two guys about our age stepped out of the trailer beside us. They shook our hands and said, "Welcome, hope you're stayin' a while." One of them said, "I'm Earl, and this here's Hank."

I said, "I'm Jim, and he's Norm." We chatted for a while, and they were from Montana, so I asked what brought them down.

"The weather, as we speak, it's five below where we come from, and here it's sixty-five above. That's quite a difference." He wanted to know why we were there.

Norm told him we had a horse running there, and he said, "Please let us know when he runs so we can watch him."

Earl asked his name, so I said, "Wrong Way North, but we call him Charlie."

"Shoot, he's not just a horse, he's a champion," Hank said.

I laughed before saying "Thanks, but he hasn't proven to be a champion yet."

"I've seen the chart on him. Four wins out of four races, and none of them was a claiming race. Believe me, that would make him a champion in Montana."

"Well, thank you, we just hope it continues." I then told them I was hungry before saying "good night."

We arrived at the track about six thirty the next morning, and Charlie was just walking because he worked the day before. I was watching him on the walker when Steve walked up and said, "This horse amazes me. As fast as he runs in races and workouts, there's not a pimple on him. I'll leave in the morning with him for Santa Anita, and I have a gallop boy to exercise him down there. He's really looking forward to galloping him because he was shocked that a Washington bred was able to destroy the horses in that stake, the way he did."

Norm said, "Sounds like everything's under control." I cleaned four stalls and really enjoyed being on the backside again. It's hard to explain, but there's something very soothing about working with horses.

Steve said, "Vickie asked me to tell you, she likes her horse in the third today. It's a maiden twenty-thousand-dollar race for fillies. She didn't get out of the gate last time, so Vickie just let her get some experience. If I or Vickie gives you a tip, please keep it between you and Norm."

I replied, "My mama taught me a long time ago not to bite the hand that feeds me."

Norm and I ate lunch at the backside café and picked up a program to look at the filly Steve told us about. She was the three in a field of nine, and her morning line was fifteen to one. I told Norm what Vickie said about her last race. He looked at the fourth and said, "This is a horse I put in my memory bank. He got bumped hard last time and was closing late."

There were eight horses in the first and nine in the second, so I said, "For seventy-two dollars, we could wheel the first and second to the three in the third and the four in the fourth. Thirty-six dollars each would cover the pick four. Bet it right now so we don't forget." We had split bets for years but never had the information we were getting since Charlie, so we usually lost.

While we were eating lunch, three guys sat down at a table right behind us and started talking about Steve taking Charlie down for the stakes race. Charlie still had a lot to prove because none of them gave him much of a chance. I thought, *It's nice to not be known and be able to hear the trainer's thoughts.*

The first race had finished before we walked over. The winner paid $16.80, so I said, "That's a good start."

"We still have to worry about the last two races," he replied. The second race went to the third favorite, who was nine to two, but the really good thing was, the favorite was four to five. That would knock a lot of players out of the pick four. We walked over to stand outside the paddock, and as the horses came around, Vickie winked at us. There were a couple of college-age guys standing behind us who had downed a few drinks. They thought she was winking at them and agreed that she was very pretty. *It's not just me that thinks that.*

I bet seventy-seven dollars to win and place and wheeled her on top with three-dollar exactas. I then wheeled her on top with all to run second and third in the trifecta. I bet a ten-dollar double with her to the four in the fourth and thought how cute the seventy-seven to win and place was. As an afterthought, I bet twenty-dollar win tickets for Steve and Vickie. When the horses were in the gate, the three was thirteen to one, and she broke like a shot. I said to Norm, "The gate work has paid off." She opened up four lengths within an eighth of a mile, but by the time they entered the turn, the favorite had closed to within two lengths.

Norm said, "Looks like we're in trouble."

I replied, "Looks like good riding to me because Vickie hasn't asked her for a thing." When they hit the stretch, the favorite pulled alongside, but Vickie popped her filly twice, and they opened up three lengths in a heartbeat. That was the winning margin, and a twenty-to-one horse passed the favorite right at the wire. When we walked over by the winner's circle, I mentioned to Norm, "I love the way she false-paces. She teases the horses behind her and says 'See ya later.'"

"It was pretty to watch," he agreed before saying "She teases me when I'm behind her."

I told him he was no good, but knew I was guilty of the same thoughts. I was carrying a lot of cash with me, so I counted out five one-hundred-dollar bills for her because I knew, no matter what happened in the last race, I was hitting big.

The daily double and pick four would just be good bonuses. After Vickie left the jubilant people in the winner's circle, I told her "Good ride" while grabbing her hand and giving her the money.

She kissed my cheek and whispered, "I can ride pretty darn well when I want to." She had a sexy look on her face, so I wondered if there was a double meaning in there, but I thought it best let her walk away. *Was she trying to tell me something? I think she enjoys teasing me more than I do her.*

Norm asked, "How much did you give her?" I held up five fingers, so he said, "Darn, I can't let you get ahead of me."

After getting my mind off the conversation with Vickie, I said, "If your memory bank serves you well, five hundred won't put a dent in what we win." The will-pay on Norm's horse was 24,600 dollars. The double was five hundred and eighty-six on a two-dollar wager. The horse went off at nine to one but ran like he should have been one to nine. He broke in third and had the lead by the stretch. From there, he improved his position, as the saying goes. We collected 19,600 dollars after taxes on the pick four alone. I said to Norm, "Thanks to your memory bank, I have to find a Chase bank." He told me he knew where one was located. I gave Steve five hundred dollars and both of them their twenty-dollar win tickets. It felt good to share the wealth and was more than I could have thought about before Charlie. *What a blessing he is.*

Steve asked, "Will you make out all right on this?"

"Let me put it this way, if I was tipping for a meal, you'd think I was a poor tipper. Since Charlie, it's like I'm not betting real money. I was the smallest player in our group and was laughed at because I only bet five dollars to win and place on one of our horses that we were sure would win. When the money's coming out of the budget, it's much harder to part with. I've never seen a roll continue the way this one has."

"I don't expect money every time I give you a tip, but check out the three in the last race tomorrow. The trainer's a friend of mine. They had one of the horse's testicles removed because he's too well-bred to geld, and my friend said, since the surgery, he's been tearing up the track." *Reminds me of AP Indy.*

I said, "I really do appreciate it, Steve, and giving you part of the win is just spreading the wealth a little. I'm very happy to do it." I silently thanked God for the blessing he sent me in the form of Charlie and for sending a young lady who had me thinking about female companionship again. *It's too bad it can't be her, but she's just too darn young for me.*

I kept two thousand out of my bank deposit, and my horse account was over 120,000 dollars. When I told Norm, he said, "That's more than you have in purse money."

"It's easier to bet now that it's play money," I replied while laughing.

That night, Earl popped his head out when we pulled in. "We're having a poker game tonight if you boys wanna join us."

I asked, "What's the game?"

"Dealer's choice with three-quarter bumps each time around."

I said, "Doesn't sound like we'd be risking our rent money." I looked at Norm, and he nodded, so I asked, "What time?"

"Seven thirty at the recreation center." I told him we'd be there.

I made spaghetti noodles with a white clam sauce for dinner. I added some peas, and when I set it on the table, Norm said, "Mama would be proud."

"Meet Jack and Dan," Earl said when we walked in. They were retired and a little older than the four of us. Their mamas had raised them right, and we would soon find out that they were both good poker players.

The player to my right had the first deal, so he called High Chicago. Norm said, "You'll have to explain that one."

Before anyone could speak, I said, "Seven-card stud with the high spade in the hole taking half the pot."

Earl said, "That country boy's done this before."

I explained, "We used to play about three nights a week before it started causing everyone family problems." The first hand, my two hole cards were both queens, and one of them was the spade. I was the first to bet, so I threw a dime into the pot, and everyone called. The third card was dealt, and a third queen came up. The ace and king of spades were not up, so I figured one of the others had one of them in the hole.

Dan, to my left, said, "Fifteen cents." Everyone stayed in, and the next time around, I was dealt the king of spades, up.

Earl said, "I'll bet you wish that was in the hole."

I replied, "No, I'd probably bet it and be crushed by the ace." The next time around, Hank got the ace of spades up, so I said, "Now I wish that king was in the hole." I knew my queen was best but thought I'd continue the conversation from the card before. The ace was high, so Hank had the first bet. He threw in a quarter, and Norm dropped out. When it came to me, I bumped it a quarter, and Dan, to my left, bumped it another quarter. "That's the last raise," I said while wishing it wasn't. I looked at Dan's up cards. He had a jack and six of hearts, so I figured him to be drawing for a flush. The next time around, I was dealt the ten of hearts, and I could see a little disappointment on his face. His card was the three of hearts, and his lips curled just a little, letting me know he hit his flush. We got the three bumps again with four players still in. The last cards were down, so I peeked at mine. It was the king of diamonds, giving me queens full. Hank had the high hand showing with a pair of aces, so he threw a quarter into the pot. When it came to me, I raised a quarter, and Dan raised it for the third bump. We all called, so Dan showed his flush, Jack turned up the jack of spades, and Hank had two pairs, aces and deuces. I said, "This is no way to meet new friends." I turned over the boat with the queen under.

Jack said, "I was afraid one of you had the queen, but I had to stay since it was the only card in the deck that could beat me." *Been there before.*

Dan said, "I couldn't see a full house at all." It was well hidden because I didn't even have a pair showing. I introduced them to Black Mariah, which was the same game as Chicago except, if the queen of spades came faceup, the hand started over. We played spit in the ocean, threes and nines wild, and some games I hadn't heard of. We played for four hours, and I was thirty dollars up at the end of the night. I was the biggest winner, so no one lost very much, but we all had a great time. We all said we wanted to do it again.

The walk back to the trailer was nice. The sky was clear, and the stars were bright as I looked up and whispered, "Love you, sweetie." I told Norm that Steve gave us a horse for the next day, and it looked like a good one. *Will I ever stop missing her?*

The next morning arrived with a little rain, and when we arrived at the track, Steve was loading things into his horse trailer. I said, "Let me look in there. Cool, a sleeping quarters for you too."

"I've spent many a lonely night in that trailer," he whined.

I replied, "Probably, if you asked please, Sandy would go in there with you."

He laughed while saying "She's not one for roughing it. Her idea of camping out is an inexpensive motel."

Charlie was the last thing to go on, so I said, "Careful with that cargo, big guy."

"Believe me, I'm aware that he's precious cargo. Good luck with that horse in the last today."

I said to Norm, "I can't believe how much a part of my life Charlie has become. I hope he never breaks down because I don't think I could survive it." While we were cleaning stalls, I said, "I'm gonna bet that horse early so I don't forget."

"If you want to, we could go to the casino down the road to bet," he suggested.

When we arrived at the casino sports book, we picked up an entry sheet. The three was twenty to one, so I told Norm I would do something different. "I'll wheel him top and bottom in the exacta because a trainer once told me horses sometimes take time to realize they won't hurt, being creatures of habit." I decided to bet early and bet fifty to win and place plus a four-dollar exacta wheel with the three to run first or second. "Now I don't have to worry about forgetting to bet if I get on a hot streak," I said. Norm made his bets early too before going out to play blackjack.

I bought my Keno tickets for five games and started looking for a machine that appealed to me. I found a unicorn machine that wasn't being played and lost forty dollars in less than ten minutes. *I hope this doesn't mean the horses will be bad today.* I walked to another machine and inserted a twenty. On the first spin, I won thirty dollars. *That's more like it.* I played for two hours before I lost the twenty I started with. I really didn't mind losing a little, but I wanted to have fun while doing it, and that machine was fun. I found Norm at the same table and it didn't look like his luck was good. I asked if he wanted to go to lunch, and he was glad to leave the table. I said, "Let me check my Keno tickets first." I was pleasantly surprised when the machine said I had 356 dollars coming, so I told Norm lunch was on me.

He replied, "You really get lucky at Keno sometimes. You do know it's the longest odds in a casino, don't you?"

I asked, "Would you rather buy your own lunch?"

"**No**, I guess the odds aren't that bad." After an hour in the buffet, we walked to the sports book. The ninth race was still over an hour away, so he said, "Let's play let it ride for a while." We played for an hour, and we both did all right. Norm won forty dollars, and I lost fifteen. When we walked into the sports book, the post parade for the ninth race was coming onto the track. Norm said, "The three is beautiful."

I replied, "Steve said he's very well-bred." The race was a mile maiden special weight for three-year-olds, and the three was thirty to one when they left the gate. He broke dead last, a couple lengths behind the pack, so I said, "This may not be one of Steve's better tips." By the time they were out of the first turn, he was up to the pack, and his rider took him to the outside. He was in third place going into the final turn, but the leader had opened up a three-length lead. Coming into the stretch, the three was in second and had dead aim on the leader. I said "**Go, go, no!**" It was a photo finish, and Norm wanted to know why I said no. "Look at the other horse. He's seventy to one, and I have the three on top and bottom. I hope he did win for you, but I got excited when they passed by the odds board."

The photo sign came down, and the three was the winner, so Norm said, "I hope you don't mind if I cheer now."

"Not at all, I'm happy for you, but I wouldn't be as happy if I didn't have fifty to win on him. I can't get over the information we're getting from Steve and Vickie." *Better than picking them out of the form.*

He said, "Only betting the horses we hear about is a real plus too." I collected just over 9,900 dollars and put away five hundred for Steve before going back into the casino.

I told Norm I'd try some blackjack, and he said, "Watch the way I bet, and I'll show you how to make money at this game." I told him I knew how to play, and he said, "Yes, you're a good player, but I'll show you how to bet according to the table." *I'll try it.*

The first hand, we bet five dollars each. Norm was dealt a blackjack, and I had twenty. The dealer had eighteen, so we both won. The next hand, Norm bet ten, so I bet the same. I was dealt a blackjack, and Norm hit eighteen. The dealer had seventeen, so we won again. It went on like that for several hands, so we were up to betting twenty-five dollars a hand and were both up over two hundred dollars. New dealer was called, and I gave our dealer ten dollars on her way out. Norm cut back to five-dollar bets, so I did the same. After losing three hands in a row, I thought, *Time for me to go.* I was colored up to 340 dollars. After cashing the chips, I started walking around, and the time flew by as I admired the art and artifacts. It was getting late, so I walked over to get Norm. He was glad I pulled him away because he hadn't done well since the new dealer arrived. He asked, "Shall we eat dinner out or get something at home?"

"Home sounds good to me," I answered. The lights were off in Earl's trailer when we pulled in, so I said, "They must be out raising heck."

The next morning, we were at the barn at seven. I didn't like not seeing Charlie, so we cleaned some stalls and decided to go down to Santa Anita that day. After hooking our trailer up to the truck, we were on the road by nine. We were able to avoid the rush-hour traffic, so we made good time and arrived at the track before three. I showed the guard our license and asked him where we could park the trailer. He pointed to a parking space before giving us directions to the stakes barn.

Charlie looked at home in his stall, and Steve was dozing off. I gave him the five hundred dollars when I walked up, and he asked, "Still a bad tipper?"

"Not quite up to par," I replied before thanking him for the tout.

I told him he was really adding to my horse account, and he said, "I'll give you one down here for day after tomorrow." I bit hook, line, and sinker and asked what race. "The stake," he said with a grin on his face. I told him he was really cute before he said, "The rider is superimpressed with him, but when people ask about him, he tells them he's just another horse from up north. He'll gallop Charlie in the morning at about seven."

We invited Steve to dinner, but he told us Sandy sent some food. When we walked into the café, I said, "Wow, this place is nice for a backside café." Norm was looking all around, and I could tell he was impressed also.

We ordered the special before sitting down, and two guys sitting at the table beside us were talking about our race. One of them said, "The horse coming in from New York looks really tough. He ran second by a neck in a grade 1 at Belmont." They both thought Charlie ran well in the stake up north but couldn't wager on a Washington bred in that field. The guy who spoke first said he talked to the boy riding Charlie, and he wasn't all that impressed. After dinner, we walked back to the trailer and hit the sack. I said "good night" to Linda before falling asleep. *Can't wait to see Vickie.*

The next morning when we arrived at the track, Steve had Charlie's tack on him, and the rider was just walking up. Steve said, "Gallop him a good mile, but don't make it a two-minute lick." We followed him to the track, and I thought it was great, watching our horse gallop on the Santa Anita track. It was a thrill I never even dreamed of before Charlie. They jogged around to the finish line before settling into a nice gallop. There were no horses working at that time, so the gallop was uneventful, but coming off the track, he stood up on his back legs. When he came down, he jumped and had all four hooves off the ground. He then started the dance I liked so much.

The rider said, "That was exciting, he's really on top of it." I was amazed at how the riders could stay a step ahead and not get bucked off.

When the rider dismounted, Steve said, "Jason, this is Jim and Norm." We shook his hand and thanked him for riding for us.

He replied, "It's my pleasure. I'm not blowing smoke, this is the nicest horse I've been on, at least this year."

I told him I loved it when he let us know he would bet him. I gave him a hundred dollars and told him it was for telling people he was just another horse from the north. When he walked away, we told Steve about the guys in the café who were saying Jason told them Charlie was just another Washington bred.

Steve said, "He likes to gamble, and we should get fifteen or twenty to one. Charlie couldn't be doing better, so I might even make a wager."

I smiled before saying "I know where you can find five hundred bucks." We both had a good chuckle before I told him we would watch Charlie if he wanted to go to breakfast.

"That sounds good, and if you don't mind, I'll also take a shower. Do you feel comfortable taking him from the walker to his stall?" I told him I would and offered to let him use our shower, but he was fine with the showers provided for horsemen.

After twenty minutes, I put Charlie away without a problem. I was a little concerned because of the way he acted, coming off the track.

Norm said, "The forms should be out by now, so if you don't mind staying, I'll go get one." When he brought it back, he showed me the front page. In big letters, it was written, **"Wrong Way North May Be Too Far South."** It had us picked seventh out of nine at fifteen to one, and beside his name, it was written, "Not ready for these." We stayed around the barn for a couple of hours until Steve came back. He apologized for being gone so long, but we were happy to help him get away.

It was interesting watching everybody speeding here and there, doing all kinds of things. Unless you've seen it, you can't possibly know how much care the horses get. I saw a man burning a horse's hooves with a paper sack and asked Steve if it was legal. "I think it is. I've never heard it's illegal, and he isn't trying to hide it. Lots of things go on that are right on the fringe because there's a shortage of horses, and if they cracked down on everything, we might not be able to run." He explained that he wouldn't do anything to put the horses or jockey in danger to win races, before saying "My wife and Vickie are really close friends, so I'd be in trouble at home if I did something that could harm her."

I said. "You're very lucky with the woman you married, so enjoy every minute because things can change in a heartbeat." *I certainly know about that.*

It was five thirty. Norm had taken a nap, and while shaking his head, he asked, "How long have I been asleep?"

I answered, "Too many interesting things goin' on to watch you sleep."

Steve laughed and said, "It's hard to believe you guys are friends."

Norm replied, "He's kind of a jerk, but I've learned to ignore a good many of his faults."

I said, "Steve, our earlier conversation got me thinking about plugging in lazy horses. What are your thoughts about it?"

He answered, "Some people think it's easier on the horses than whipping them too much. When you plug a horse in, you scare him, and the track's fear is he'll jump into the path of other horses. It's really tough because horses can also shy away from the whip. The penalty for plugging them in is so severe that I wouldn't do it." I told him I'd heard pros and cons and wondered what he thought. "You do bring up some interesting points," he said. I asked him if he knew people who did it, and he answered, "That's something you don't talk about."

"Let's go to a nice dinner," I suggested to Norm. "If you can get away, Steve, I'll buy." He couldn't leave but told us about a place a mile from the track that catered to horsemen. The name of the restaurant was Slim's Fine Food and was said to have the best steaks in LA. We wished him a good night and went in search of Slim's.

When we walked in the door, a man greeted us by saying "Howdy, I'm Slim." Believe me, he was nothing like his name. He was about six two, and I'd say he probably weighed 350 anyway. It was perfect that he was out front because anyone could easily tell he enjoyed the food. I had always heard you couldn't trust a skinny chef, and I totally trusted Slim. The food was even better than we hoped it would be. *We'll bring Vickie here.*

After we finished eating, we both enjoyed looking at many win pictures on all the walls. A person could spend hours looking at racing history. George Royal, now that was a name from the past, and Silky Sullivan was maybe the greatest closer of all time. I had watched a documentary about him, and it was unbelievable how far back he would get and still win. His trainer said he was beating all his other horses so badly in workouts that he would give the others a head start. Silky thought that was the way he should run. All three pictures of Affirmed winning the Triple Crown were there, and many more. They were all autographed by the owners, and I was sure they were steady customers. I was a little startled when Slim walked up behind me and asked if I liked the races. I answered, "I've been involved in racing for many years, and we have Charlie going in the stakes race tomorrow."

He looked a little puzzled before saying, "I'm not familiar with Charlie, and I've looked that race over pretty well."

I explained, "Habits are hard to break. Charlie is Wrong Way North's nickname."

"That horse intrigues me. You just don't see Washington-bred horses in these races, but from what I can see, he fits. The guys down here run him down, but believe me, you have their attention. Do you think he can beat this bunch?"

"You got another spot on your wall for a picture?" I asked.

"I like that confidence, so I'll bet him a little. Your jockey's a real looker."

I replied, "I hear ya there." He asked if I flirted with her, and I answered, "Every chance I get, but she's very professional and younger than my daughter. Neither of those things keeps me from admiring her feminine charms, however." We both laughed when I told him she was gorgeous, coming and going.

Norm introduced himself and told him the food was great before promising to come back. Slim whispered, "Good luck tomorrow, guys, but don't tell anyone I said that." We thanked him before walking out.

When we were outside, I said, "Slim is a nice guy and thinks Charlie has a good chance, but his customers live down here, so he can't say too much." Walking to the pickup, rubbing my stomach, I said, **That was good food**. Let's bring Vickie here if she can get away after the race."

He asked, "Do I detect a little crush on her?"

"If she was a little older, I could go for her, but with the difference in our ages, I just enjoy being around her. Believe me, I've had some less-than-innocent thoughts about her."

He said, "You and me both. I don't know how a guy could look at her and not have those thoughts."

I replied, "Let's keep it business because things are going too well to rock the boat." *I **think** he agrees with me, but she is a foxy little rascal.*

CHAPTER 4

More Than a Pretty Face

The next morning, we arrived at the track at eight, and I told Steve he was right about the food at Slim's. He hadn't eaten there but had heard really good things. I said, "Add us to the people saying good things." He had a program, and our morning line was twelve to one. I said, "The odds maker here likes us a little more than the racing form."

He replied, "Let's hope they think more of us when the race is over."

It surprised me when Vickie walked up, so I said, "You got up before breakfast, little lady. You got a compliment at dinner last night." She wanted to know from whom, so I said, "From the owner of the restaurant where we had dinner." With a big smile on her face, she asked me what I told him. I said very casually, "I told him you're maybe a little above average." She smacked my arm playfully and told me I was mean. "Actually, I told him you're one of the most beautiful women I've ever met, and I can't keep my eyes off you."

She smacked my arm again before saying, "**You did not**!"

I said, "You have my word that I told him one of those two things, so you decide which one it was."

She gave me a look that I didn't recognize while saying "You really are mean."

Charlie had a muzzle over his mouth and nose, so he knew it was race day. We were in the eighth out of nine races, and the time seemed to drag by. Maybe it was because we were running at Santa Anita. Vickie went across sometime before, Norm was napping, and Steve and I sat looking at each other.

We both started to laugh before he said, "All this buildup for less than two minutes of racing."

I replied, "It reminds me of when I wrestled in high school. I always wished I was smaller so I could wrestle sooner because the waiting was always the toughest part."

"Not much different here. You always want these kinds of horses, but the feature races almost always run late. Before I forget, Vickie and I decided this will be a good race to bring him from a little further back because there are three horses that seem to need the lead."

It seemed like an eternity, but they finally called the horses over for our race. "What a beautiful place," I whispered as we walked over with Charlie. I had seen it on TV thousands of times, but TV did it no justice at all. It's possible, I was looking at the history along with the mountains as we walked to the paddock. Charlie was the two in a field of nine, and he was twenty to one when we reached the paddock. Everything seemed to be spinning. I saw professional athletes I recognized, and there was a very pretty young lady I recognized from the movies. I said to Norm, "This is a long way from Yakima Meadows."

He said, "**I love it**."

Vickie walked up and told us we looked like we had seen ghosts. I said, "I'm sure I saw ghosts of the legendary horses on our walkover."

She replied, "Soon, he'll be one of the horses they talk about." She gave us the wink that I had learned to look for, and it had a very soothing effect on me. She asked Steve, "Any directions?"

"Toward the finish line," he answered. People in the paddock must have thought we lost our minds when we burst out laughing.

I said, "Steve, if that was designed to relax us, I wanna thank you." Lest I be judged for the bet I made, we must remember that I was wagering with Charlie's money. I put five hundred on him to win and bought ten-dollar exactas, Charlie on top of the field. I bet another twenty-dollar exacta, Charlie over the favorite. I bet three-dollar trifectas, Charlie on top with all of the others to run second and third. My last wager was a ten-dollar double, Charlie with all in the last race. As I was walking outside, I thought how far that was from the days I only bet five dollars to win if I thought the horse was a mortal cinch. ***One more time, Charlie!***

When the horses entered the gate, Charlie was twenty to one. "They're off" rang out, and Charlie broke on top like a shot. Vickie didn't stand up, but I could see her bringing him back. If he had been rank, she would have had to fight him, but he came back like the champion we would later find out he was. She settled him behind three horses that were fighting for the lead and had him on the rail, two lengths behind the leaders. The four, a forty-to-one long shot, came up and settled beside them when they entered the backstretch. I said, "**Go by, idiot!**" When he stayed there, I said to Norm, "We have some race riding going on." When they were halfway up the backstretch, I saw Vickie pull Charlie back, and the four went back with them. "That goes beyond race riding," I said. When they were five lengths behind the leaders, she reached back and smacked him once. He went forward like a shot, and when he had just cleared the four, she swung him to the right and was out. I hoped it wouldn't take too much out of him. To top it off, the rider of the four jerked the head of his horse up when Vickie came out and then went back to riding. I knew an inquiry would be called. By the middle of the turn, Charlie was even with two of the three front runners, but the leader had pulled ahead by two lengths. Vickie popped him twice and put away her whip. There was a dead silence over the crowd as he went from two lengths back to five in front, and his final margin of victory was eight widening lengths. The two-to-one favorite closed to be second.

When Vickie brought him into the winner's circle, she raised both arms while saying "**He had a lot left!**" *I didn't know he could run that fast.*

The people from Southern California must have thought we just came off a hog farm because we were jumping around like he had never won instead of never lost. We were high-fiving each other and having way too much fun. We hadn't noticed, the claim of foul was on the board, but it only took a minute for the announcer to say "There will be no change in the order of finish." After the picture, a lady with a TV crew came in to interview us.

She talked to Steve first, and he told her he knew the horse would run well but wasn't sure his best was good enough. He said, "He answered that question emphatically."

Next, Norm had the microphone and said, "I just wanna thank Steve and Vickie for putting us in this position."

When I had the floor, I said, "We have as much faith in Steve as anyone could have, and Vickie has always had total faith in the horse. One more thing I'd like to say, please, she did a great job, getting out of the trap the rider of the four set for her." I turned to her and said, "Great ride, young lady."

When Vickie was handed the microphone, she thanked Steve and us for putting our faith in her. She then got serious. "I believe in race riding. That's part of the game, but when I went back to go around the horse, he went back with me, and that went beyond race riding to almost race fixing. When you think more about keeping another horse from winning than winning yourself, it's wrong." I thought, *This is a very articulate speaker, along with her athleticism.* I reckon there wasn't a whole lot I didn't like about her. I reminded myself that she was younger than my daughter. *Who cares, **she's gorgeous and sooo athletic!** Knock it off.*

When we were back at the barn, we asked Steve if he wanted to go to dinner with us at Slim's. He replied, "Charlie looks good enough to travel, so I think I'll get him out of here. I don't like what happened on the track."

I had some cash in my pocket, so I gave him a thousand dollars while telling him how much we appreciated him. He looked at me and started to say something, but I lifted my hand and said, "A really poor tipper this time."

"I assume you're doing the same for Vickie and you can still say that?"

"Thanks to you two and Charlie, that's correct." Norm had stayed to collect his tickets, so when he walked back, I told him I needed to collect and asked if the last race had run.

"Yes, the winner was ten to one, but I didn't have the double, so I didn't notice what it paid. Did you have the double?"

I answered, "Five times. Ask Vickie if she wants to go to Slim's for dinner, and I'll buy."

I didn't get the breakdown, but I collected 53,200 dollars. I asked the cashier to give me a check for fifty thousand and the rest in cash. I gave him two hundred dollars before heading to the barn. Vickie was there, so I gave her ten one-hundred-dollar bills while saying "This win was all you, beautiful lady."

She said, "It'll do me no good to argue, but Charlie's the reason we won. Thank you very much for the money, sweetie."

I explained, "That was good thinking outside the box when you escaped that trap."

"It's just instinct from many years of riding."

"That's exactly what I'm talking about," I replied. "Did Norm invite you to dinner?"

"He sure did, and going out with two fine-looking gentlemen like you two would be my pleasure." She looked deeply into my eyes while asking "Will you tell me which of the two things you said at dinner?"

I kissed her cheek and whispered, "You know you don't have to ask. You're absolutely gorgeous." I said to Norm, "We might be a little long in the tooth for her." He told me to speak for myself as he was wrapping his arm around her.

She smiled at me and said, "You're the only one that thinks you're old." She kissed my cheek while putting her other arm around my waist. *What a wonderful young lady.*

We stayed at the track until Steve was ready to go, and we both told him how much we appreciated his dedication.

As he started to drive away, I said, "Godspeed, my friend." He smiled, waved, and was gone. I turned to Vickie and said, "When people watch those interviews, they have no idea what jockeys and trainers go through. On top of long hours, you riders risk your lives every day."

"Believe me, there's much risk of injury for trainers too. Crawling under those animals is no walk in the park. Some of the studs would just as soon rip your arm off as look at you, and fillies can be worse."

I said, "I helped a vet suture a mare in Yakima, and I was actually scared."

"I don't blame them for getting upset about that," she said with a grimace.

I replied, "You'd know more than me." We both laughed while wincing from the pain that the thought brought both of us.

When we entered Slim's, he walked over to Vickie and said, "Fabulous ride, little lady. Give the big guy a hug."

She thanked him and, as usual, told him it was all Charlie.

He replied, "If you can get him through that door, he'll get a hug too." He turned to me and said, "Because of your confidence last night, I put three hundred on his nose, so to all three of you, dinner and drinks are on me." I asked if he wanted a picture, and he said, "You bet, it may not be out front you understand, but I have a great spot for it in my office."

I replied, "I've been a salesman my whole life, so I totally understand."

When we were seated at a table, Vickie said, "When he hugged me, I could smell that he'd been drinking."

I replied, "When he whispered, I could too. He's been celebrating Charlie because he thought we could win and made a lot of money on him."

She asked, "Why would he want it kept quiet?"

"The same reason Steve left town tonight and a jockey forgot about winning, to keep Charlie from winning. It seems we're not welcome in this town. Slim has to think about his business, so actually, I was surprised that he was as friendly as he was. It's bad enough when a horse comes here from Northern California, but add to that, he's a Washington bred, we've ruffled a few feathers."

"Have you guys stopped to think what this has done for Charlie's graded stakes money?" she asked.

I answered, "I'm not an accountant like Norm, but I'd say about 330,000."

"As an accountant, I'd say exactly that," Norm said.

She asked, "**Do you know what that means?**"

I answered, "Yes, it means I don't have to pay any more training bills."

"I don't know which of you two is the craziest. It means he has probably qualified for the Kentucky Derby," she said while laughing.

I said, "Well, there's that too."

She shook her head while saying "You guys are just too much fun."

Norm replied, "We're living a fairy-tale life right now, and our biggest fear is we'll wake up to find this has all been a dream."

She said, "If you wake up, leave me alone so I can continue to dream." She really surprised me when she covered my hand with hers and said, "Jim told me in Seattle about your wife, and I'm terribly sorry for your loss."

I brought her hand to my lips and kissed it while thanking her for her kind words. I said, "I've been miserable for several years, but you're helping me to cope. Please know that I'm not hitting on you, but it makes me feel really good to have you as a very special friend."

She said, "If you ever need to talk, I'm a good listener." *I can't be alone with her.*

"Norm has been a great help to me also, but he hasn't made me start taking notice of women the way you have."

She was almost in tears when she said, "That's some compliment. I'm happy for any relief I might bring you because you mean a lot to me too."

Our meals arrived, keeping us from saying more. The meal was great, and the company, even better. Vickie was due to fly out at nine the next morning, so we walked her to her car and tried to outdo each other when we hugged her.

"You two are a lot of fun to be with," she said before getting into her car. I thought, *That's a real lady to treat two old guys so nicely. Why, after all the women I've met since the accident, does this one appeal to me so much?*

The next morning, the paper said, "Horsemen around Here Can't Wait for Him to Find His Way North." The article was very complimentary of both Charlie and Vickie. It ended by saying the writer was ashamed that the incident happened in LA. Norm said, "It's too bad things like that have to happen, but we're not running for two-thousand-dollar purses anymore."

We headed back at eight thirty, and I said, "It was nice getting to know Vickie better."

Norm replied, "She enjoyed it too, and Slim couldn't have been a nicer guy." I told him I hoped he didn't lose business for treating us so well, and he asked, "Did you taste that food? Believe me, Jim, they'll get over it. I'm tickled that he put three hundred on Charlie and made a quick seven grand." After several miles, he said, "I'm glad the rider wasn't able to hurt Charlie or Vickie. I can't imagine what he was trying to do."

I replied, "The writer in the *LA Times* said much the same thing. I'm sure the rider will get days, and it could be worse, if it's determined he was trying to fix the race."

He replied, "That would be a mess I wouldn't wanna be associated with."

It felt good to be home even though our home went with us. Earl came over to help us set up the trailer and said, "That horse is a beast." He told us he opened an account on the horse channel so he could wager. He was all smiles when he said "I put ten to win and place on him, and that'll pay for a lotta poker nights." *Nice guys.*

We went to bed early and arrived at the track at seven the next morning. Steve said, "Charlie will go to the track tomorrow. I can't believe how quickly he bounces back. Jim really built a base under him, so I called to thank him. He's really excited for you guys, and it seems everyone around Portland Meadows is mad at that jockey for trying to keep Charlie from winning. The rider could be barred for life if they determine race fixing was involved."

I replied "I would hate for anyone to lose their livelihood, but race fixing was my first thought. That could have ended both Charlie's and Vickie's careers, and on top of that, it's a real black eye to the sport if it comes back that he was trying to change the outcome of the race."

Steve said, "That'll get the gambling commission involved, and none of us wants that to happen. On a happier note, there's a grade 2 for two-year-olds going a mile and a quarter on the grass in fourteen days. That's a quick turnaround, but he's doing so well that I think he'll be fine. The purse is 250,000, and his share of that would assure him a spot in the derby. After the race, I'll turn him out and let him enjoy being a horse for about six weeks."

After cleaning some stalls, Norm asked me if I wanted to go up to the lake for a few days.

"What lake is that?"

"**Tahoe**, have you heard of it?"

"Never so rudely, but thanks for asking. When do we leave?"

He told me we could leave the next morning, and Steve said, "Here's something to maybe help you tomorrow. I have the 10 going in the ninth race. He's recovered from a flapper operation and has been doing great in his workouts. He's running in a ten-thousand-dollar race, so if the surgery was successful, he'll run away from the field. As long as he's been off, he might have some odds." I thanked him before heading to the café to grab a sandwich.

Earl invited us to play poker that night, and we told him we could play for a couple of hours. Charlie was the main topic of conversation. Hank wanted to know when he would run next, so I told him it would be fourteen days.

Norm told them we were going to the lake the next morning, and Earl said, "You boys must have some money left from his last race." He was happy when I told him I bet him really well. They were certainly turning out to be a fun bunch, and the poker games helped pass time between races.

We arrived at the hotel in plenty of time for the race. Our room was on the eleventh floor, and we had just thrown our bags on the bed when a loud alarm made us jump. I said, "If I'm not mistaken, that's a fire alarm. We could tie all the blankets, sheets, and pillowcase together, but they wouldn't reach eleven floors."

He told me he noticed the exit on our way in, so we put our hands on the door to see if it was hot. No problem, so we opened the door and started for the exit. We were about halfway when a voice came over the PA system, telling us not to be alarmed because it was a problem with their alarm system. I said, "It's a little late to say 'Don't be alarmed.'" I hadn't noticed, but several people were out in the hall with us. They all started to laugh nervously while agreeing with me. I said, "I'll bet whoever said 'Don't be alarmed' isn't on the eleventh floor."

The elevators had started working again, so we stepped in and headed to the casino. Norm asked, "You think we should get down and kiss the floor?"

I answered, "It's been a long time since I've been with a woman, but I'm not that hard up."

"I don't know how Linda put up with you for so long," he said while shaking his head.

When we walked into the sports book, the fourth race was running, so I said, "I think I'll bet now so I don't start winning and forget about the race." Norm told me he would also. We went to separate windows, and I said, "Bay Meadows ninth race, I'll have fifty to win and place on the ten. Just a minute, here's my player's card." He swiped it and told me the wager would show. "Same race, I'll have three-dollar exactas, the ten on top of all, and one-dollar trifectas, the ten on top, with all to run second and third." I thanked him as he was handing me my player's card.

Norm went to play blackjack, and I bought my Keno tickets before going in search of a slot machine. I played for two hours at a machine on twenty dollars because, every time I was close to going broke, I hit something. I thought, *This is like our poker games, lots of fun for a small investment.* When the twenty ran out, I looked at my watch and hurried over to see if the race had run. The horses were pulling up from the ninth race when I walked in, but the results were not yet posted.

I asked Norm if the horse won, and he answered, "By about twelve lengths."

I replied, "That's what Steve said should happen, so it sounds like the operation was successful."

"What operation? You didn't say anything about an operation."

I asked, "Would you have bet as much if you had known about the operation?"

"I don't know."

I said, "Just collect your money, and be happy I forgot that detail." He went off at seven to one, so my total was just over a thousand dollars. I said to myself, "Thank you, Steve, you just paid for my trip." I put away a hundred for him before playing slots for about an hour. I was losing, so I went over to ask Norm if he wanted to go to dinner. He wasn't at any of the tables, so I walked up and down the rows of slots. He was playing a penny machine, and like always, he was playing the minimum of forty cents. When I walked up, he told me how much fun he was having, so I said, "Think how much fun it would be if you were playing some money."

He replied, "Don't you worry about what I play."

I laughed while thinking back to a time that he, my cousin Mel, and I went to Lake Tahoe. Mel and I left him at a slot machine where he was playing one quarter a spin. We made plans to meet across the street for lunch in an hour, and we looked for him for at least thirty minutes after the hour had passed. We couldn't find him, so we went back to the casino where we left him. He was still at the same machine, playing one quarter. Mel and I couldn't stop laughing. We had a great time that entire trip because we were all born in February and it was our birthday bash. *Some wonderful memories.*

He printed out his ticket and showed me it was twenty dollars and twenty cents. "That's the twenty I started with," he said with a big smile on his face.

I replied, "I'm happy for you, and since you won, you can buy dinner." We went to the buffet, and they had my crawdads, so I was happier than a frog during a fly infestation.

After dinner, Norm said he would play some cards, but I went to the room. I was tired from the trip and was asleep in no time. When the door opened, I woke up and asked him if he won. He answered, "I didn't lose all I made on the horse."

The next thing I knew, it was 8:00 a.m., and Norm was snoring away. I slipped into the bathroom to get cleaned up, and after my shower, I opened the door quietly. I had a breakfast sandwich and a cup of coffee before buying my Keno tickets for five games. I found a unicorn machine and sat down. I was playing two dollars, and on the third spin, the unicorns came running. I won 160 dollars on that spin and played it for about thirty minutes before cashing eighty-five dollars. I walked by the tables, but Norm wasn't in sight. I checked my Keno tickets and had twelve dollars coming, so I gave the girl two and put the ten in my pocket. I turned to walk away but noticed how comfortable the chairs looked. I turned around and said, "I'll play those again, please." She printed out the tickets, and I handed her twenty dollars before taking a seat.

The first game, I didn't hit a thing, but the second game produced two dollars. *Good, I don't have to throw the tickets away.* The third game, the first two numbers were 5 and 75, and the third was 15. I didn't get excited because I'd seen many games stop right there. The next three numbers missed me completely, but 25 and 35 were next. Two more misses and then 65. *Eighty bucks,* I thought. That was good because four numbers remained to be called and one more would win me $1,500. The next number was 35, and the girl at the desk was startled when I shouted, "**Yes**!" The next number was 45, and I watched in disbelief as the entire line filled in. The girl braced for the cheer she was sure would come, but I just sat there in shock. I had played those numbers hundreds of times, hoping for that result, but I never thought it would happen.

I snapped back to reality when Norm asked, "Are you doin' all right?" Being in shock, I just pointed at the board. "I don't play, so I don't know what I'm looking at."

"Do you see the line of fives from top to bottom?"

"I see it, but what does it mean?" he asked.

"Twenty-five thousand dollars," I replied. He didn't believe me, and I think I really was a little bit in shock. Norm looked at the girl selling the tickets, and she smiled while nodding to him.

"You're not kidding, are you?" he asked me.

"I'm glad to say I'm not this time." It took almost a half hour for the game to be declared official because four people in sports coats checked the balls in the tubes.

Finally, the fourth man walked over and shook my hand while saying "You just won twenty-five thousand dollars." I was glad to hear him say it because I thought something was wrong and was hoping at least seven were correct. Norm was sitting beside me when they asked for my social security card and asked how much to take out for taxes.

I answered, "Twenty-five percent, and I'd like all but two thousand in a check, please." It took him about twenty minutes to get the check and money. When he returned, he gave me my social security card before counting out twenty hundred-dollar bills. He then handed me a check for the balance. I handed him a hundred while thanking him and gave the girl who sold me the tickets three hundred. I handed Norm a thousand, and he started to protest, but I told him to keep it.

"I'll just say 'Thank you,'" he said while putting the bills in his pocket.

Norm was hungry, so we went in search of a place to eat. I said, "It'll be on me."

He replied, "You better believe it." I let him pick the restaurant, and he decided on the Burger Barn, in the food court. They gave us the meat on a bun, and we added our condiments. It turned out to be fun and a really good burger. We agreed that we would come back because, no matter how many fantastic meals you eat, sometimes, nothing beats a good burger.

After lunch, a very fashionably dressed man walked up to me and shook my hand before handing me a voucher. "My name is Tom Baker, president of operations, and I'd like to thank you for staying with us. Congratulations to you on your big win. The voucher I handed you gives you dinner for two in any restaurant in this hotel, and if I may, I'll recommend the steak house on the top floor. We'd also like to upgrade you to one of our finest suites and extend your stay another three or four nights, if you'd like to stay."

"Thank you, but the room we have is perfect," I replied. I didn't want to go through the trouble of moving. I said, "We did get a fright when we checked in. The fire alarm went off, but I've worked with equipment my entire career and know that all equipment is faulty sometimes."

"Actually, a young man was angry about losing money, so he set off the alarm. We'd never say that over the PA system, so we say a faulty system."

"Has that happened before?"

"More than I like to think about. I know this is something people say all the time, but you look familiar."

"I don't know, my wife and I were here years ago, so maybe our paths crossed then."

He said, "I'm thinking horses."

I replied, "We just won a stake at Santa Anita and were interviewed on television."

"Wrong Way North, wow, what a horse. I hope you don't mind me asking, but rumor has it you bought him by mistake for two thousand dollars?"

"Rumor has it right, and I don't mind you asking at all. My friend Norm is the one who bought him, and I bought part of him to make him feel better. I'm sure glad I did because you wouldn't believe the good fortune we've had with him." I laughed while saying "We both pinch ourselves to make sure we're not dreaming."

"I love stories like that," Tom said before asking if we were wealthy before buying him.

"We're both retired with comfortable pensions, but by no means are we wealthy."

"That's my kind of story," he said. I couldn't believe how quickly we bonded, and it felt like I'd known him for years. "When will your horse run again?" he asked.

"In thirteen days, we're running him a mile and a quarter on the grass. He hasn't run on grass but has trained really well on it."

"I'll watch for him, and if you need anything, don't hesitate to ask. The upgrade still goes if you want it." We shook hands, and I thanked him one more time. He started to walk away but turned around and asked, "Have you heard the latest news about the jockey that tried to keep your horse from winning? It looks like the gambling commission may get involved because some race tampering may have occurred."

I had thought about it quite a bit since that day, so I said, "I don't think anything like that happened. I think the jockey was doing some race riding and got carried away. Why would someone pay the kid to cause our horse to lose so they could make money on the race when Charlie was twenty-five to one? It would make more sense to bet him if they were worried about him."

He asked, "Did you say Charlie?"

"That's just a nickname we have for him."

"Then Charlie he'll be to me, if you don't mind."

"I'd be pleased if you called him that, and about the jockey, if you hear something while we're here, please call me." I gave him my cell phone number, and as he walked away, I thought, *What a personable man.*

When I found Norm, I told him about my conversation with Tom. He was very pleased about the dinner until I told him I might have a date. "If I have to get a wig, I guess I will," he said. *I'm glad I can't see that.*

"Norm, you're not even a good-lookin' man, so please, don't ever let me see you as a woman. Vickie has just made me start looking at women again, and the thought of you as a woman might make me switch teams."

He said, "If I had any feelings, you woulda just hurt them." My whole body convulsed as I tried really hard not to visualize him as a woman.

Norm went to a blackjack table, and I started walking around, watching people. A woman very nicely dressed was jumping up and down, so her husband came over and hugged her. She was excited about winning sixty dollars. They looked like they certainly didn't need sixty dollars, and it was good to see that, at that moment, what was happening outside the casino meant nothing. That's what I had always loved about going to casinos. I always had a responsible job, and it was nice to be totally irresponsible sometimes. Walk through the doors, and leave your troubles outside. A dear friend who was a partner in a couple of racehorses said that about being irresponsible years before, and I never forgot it. She was a grade school teacher. She was very proper and always perfectly dressed but really loved to have fun. We went to Reno with her and her late husband a few times, and we always had a great time.

My daydream was interrupted by Tom tapping my shoulder and saying "I just saw Charlie and your trainer on the horse channel."

"What's goin' on?"

"Steve announced that Charlie will be in the race you told me about. They also asked him about the ongoing investigation, and he said pretty much the same thing you said. My wife and I need to get away, so we might come down to the Bay Area for a couple days, and we'd love to watch your horse run."

"If you make it, call me, and I'll take you through the backside. If you'd like to see the behind-the-scenes action, I'd love to show both of you around."

"We'd appreciate that," he said. He told me to enjoy my stay, before going back to work.

The afternoon passed far too quickly. I didn't win anymore, but I didn't lose much. I had fun watching people enjoying themselves. I walked around looking for Norm and found him at a blackjack table. He had a rather large stack of black chips that I estimated to be over 1,500 dollars. "This playing on house money really does work," he said. I told him I was ready for dinner, but he wasn't hungry, so I walked away. I didn't feel like playing, so I walked outside to look at the lake. I thought, *If only Linda could be here with me.* She really loved the water, and the lake was exceptionally pretty.

The ringing of my cell phone startled me. Vickie was calling, and her first question was "Are you winning?" *She's so cute.*

"Steve gave us a horse, and I hit him, so I'm up a little for the trip." *I won't tell her about the big win.*

"I called to give you a horse in the fourth race tomorrow. It's a maiden special weight, and Steve is really high on him. I've worked him, and we think he'll be a graded stakes winner. If you bet him, well you know the rest."

"I promise, I won't bet any more than I can afford to lose."

She said, "I don't hear any machines."

"I'm outside enjoying the lake, and it's unusually beautiful tonight."

"I wish I was there to see it with you," she said before telling me I sounded down.

"I was thinking about how much Linda would love the tranquil water, and it bothered me, but it's all part of the healing process. I want you to know that talking to you really does help me."

She surprised me when she said "I wish I was there with you." She seemed almost embarrassed and told me she meant it as a friend. I knew what she was saying, but it was nice to hear. *Why does that little rascal appeal to me so much?*

I said, "I'm so happy that you called. Every morning, I get excited while driving to the track. I've always thought I was anxious to see Charlie, but lately, I find myself thinking of you. Don't get me wrong, I'm not trying to get anything started, but I love the feelings you've brought back into my life." I thanked her for calling, one more time, before we hung up. *It would be nice if she was here to see the sun sitting over the water with me.* Again, I thought about how pretty she was. I then went back to wishing Linda were with me and knew I had no room in my life for a woman right then, even if she wasn't young enough to be my daughter. *Why is life so complicated?* I wondered as visions of both Linda and Vickie danced through my mind.

It was getting dark, so I walked back inside. Norm was cashing in and told me he was about to come looking for me. After he cashed his chips, we went to dinner at the steak house on the top floor. Everything was so elegant, and we both ordered their barbecued beef ribs. The meat and sauce were outstanding and just fell off the bones. "This is good Southern cooking," Norm said. They were served with a really nice baked potato and scones with kernels of corn, but what really topped it off was a beautiful cheese and potato soup. It had the texture of fine silk in my mouth. Norm tapped his stomach three times before saying "**Tom was right**!"

I said, "Tom and his wife are coming down for Charlie's race, and if Steve doesn't mind, I'll take them to the barn." I left a fifty-dollar tip and paid for the meal with the voucher.

After dinner, we went down to play for a while, and I was taken by surprise when a woman who was very well dressed and quite attractive asked me to buy her a drink. I could tell she had been drinking, so I said, "You don't have to buy drinks. If you sit at a machine, they'll give you one."

She looked a little angry while saying "**I'm not a prostitute!**" I was about to say I, at no time, said anything about a prostitute, but she stomped away. I stood there dumbfounded. *I was trying to help her. Don't waste your time trying to figure out how women think.* I walked over to where Norm was sitting. He was the only one playing, and the dealer was a very pretty young lady of about twenty-two or twenty-three. I proceeded to tell them about upsetting the lady.

"She was hitting on you," Norm said very casually. I told him I didn't think that was the case.

The dealer asked, "If I wanted to go out with you, would I have to come out and ask?"

I asked, "Do you wanna go out with me?"

"No, I was just wondering what a girl would have to do to make it happen."

I said, "I must be gettin' old."

She replied, "You're not old."

"Then you are asking me out?"

"No, I'm married, but I do think either of you would be fun," she said while laughing.

I couldn't walk away after that, so I said, "My job was hiring salesmen, and you would make a great salesperson." I handed her a hundred for some chips and played for forty-five minutes. I was up fifty dollars when they changed dealers, so I gave her a twenty-five-dollar chip and said, "You tell your husband I said he's a very lucky guy."

"He tells me all the time," she said while flashing a warm smile. *She's gorgeous. Mmmm, it's nice to think that after so long.*

I played awhile with the new dealer but left after losing twenty dollars. I told Norm I was going up to the room, and he told me he'd be up in a while. I thought about my conversation with Vickie and hoped I hadn't said too much. *I need to back up and think about this. She's way too young, and I'm not over losing Linda, so don't set yourself up for that terrible pain again.*

"Turn the TV off" woke me at three thirty. The sound was down, so it hadn't kept me awake, but Norm wasn't so kind.

"I assume you didn't notice I was sleeping?"

He said, "Oh, so sorry, that dealer was cute."

"And sweet too, but what I'm thinking right now, she'll be just as cute and sweet in the morning." I didn't hear his response but knew it wasn't nice. It was nine when I woke up, and I not so quietly took a really long, hot shower. When I opened the door, steam rolled out into the room.

"You trying to kill me?" he asked while coughing and spitting steam.

"I'm so sorry," I said before telling him I'd see him downstairs.

The last thing I heard before closing the door was "**I'm awake now!**" I laughed all the way to the elevator while thinking about how great paybacks could be. We had decided to stay a couple of extra days since it was offered. We could wash a couple of sets of underclothes and pairs of socks in the bathroom and hang them on the shower curtain. That would get us by just fine. Norm came down about a half hour later and scowled at me, but it soon turned to a smile. He said, "I guess I deserved that."

"Deserved what? Let's go eat," I said before informing him that it was his turn to buy. There was no response, but he had his wallet out when we walked up to the buffet register. It was nice to not be in a hurry. We stayed in the dining area for over an hour, browsing and eating small portions of several foods. I told Norm that Linda always did that at buffets, but my plate was usually full before I was halfway through the line.

He replied, "I always thought she was too good for you."

"I always thought she was lucky to have me," I told him, but I knew he was right.

After breakfast, I bought my Keno tickets before looking for a slot machine. I played for over an hour and lost forty dollars, but I had a lotta fun. When I walked into the sports book, the first race was about an hour away, so I decided to bet early. Her horse was the four in a field of eight, and the race was going six furlongs. His morning line was eight to one, so I bet fifty to win and place. I then bet three-dollar exactas with him on top of all. My last bet was a one-dollar trifecta with the four on top of all with all.

When I checked my Keno tickets, I only had two dollars coming, so I told the girl to keep them. I walked away, thinking, *Today's not my day so far, but the horse will bail me out.* I decided to go outside and walk around for a while. It was cold, but the sun was shining, and the lake was beautiful. I decided a fast walk would help cut some calories. I walked a little too far, so when I turned around, the hotel seemed a long way away. When I got back, I was tired but exhilarated from the brisk walk.

I arrived at the sports book just as the horses for the fourth were entering the gate. Vickie's horse was six to one, and when they broke, the one went right to the front. The four was third, about three lengths behind the leader. In the middle of the backstretch, Vickie shook the reins, and the horse started to roll. They were even with the second-place horse going into the turn, but when her horse switched leads, she stood straight up. I could see that she was pulling with everything her little body had to offer, and she was somehow able to hold his head up. They didn't go down, but I could tell it was bad because the horse couldn't put any weight on his left front leg. Steve ran out to check him before the horse ambulance took him away. It was good that he was able to hobble onto the trailer, but I knew he was finished in the first start of his very promising career.

Norm and I sat down and just looked at each other. When the silence broke, he said, "That could have been Charlie."

"Absolutely, he wasn't doing anything he hasn't done dozens of times in workouts. It could have been a rock, a clod, or just a bad step when he changed leads."

Norm said, "It can happen at any time, so the horses and jockeys put their lives on the line every time they run. If Vickie hadn't held him up, they might have both been killed."

Tom walked up and said, "I thought I might find you two here. I have a feed into my office, and I was watching because I knew your trainer had that horse in the race. Do you know the owners?"

I answered, "I've seen them in the mornings but never met them. Steve says they're wonderful people." In a low voice, I said, "I'm sorry, Tom, have you met Norm?"

"I think briefly," he said before shaking his hand. "Give everybody involved my best, and tell them how sorry I am. My wife would love to see the backside on the day your horse runs, if you still don't mind."

"Call me, and I'll meet you at the back gate," I said. He told us he was sorry, before walking away.

Norm said, "He seems like a nice guy." We couldn't possibly have known at that moment that the owners of the colt's terrible loss would later heap huge dividends on us. Neither of us felt like playing, so we went out by the lake. We sat on a bench, saying nothing for about ten minutes, but Norm finally said, "I can't stop thinking that could have been Charlie."

I replied, "Praise God, it wasn't. Charlie could have an aneurysm or a heart attack and die, or he could get cast in his stall and hurt himself. He could have flipped in his stall and broken his neck in Yakima that day. A star could fall out of the sky and hit earth, but I believe things happen the way they're intended to. I told you before that I pray for a safe return every time one of my horses goes to the track. Let's enjoy Charlie every day we have him and thank God for him."

Norm called Steve and put his phone on speaker. Steve was very quiet, so Norm asked, "Can you talk?" He didn't want to bother him if the owners were there.

"Yes, I can talk." I asked if the horse had to be put down, and he answered, "No, but it'll end his career, and **that was a nice horse**! By the way, I asked Vickie to tell you about him, so if you lost money, it's my fault."

"We didn't bet any more than we could afford to lose," I promised.

"Thanks for that, Jim, I always worry about it."

Norm said, "The money's not at all important. We'll let you go, but please kiss Charlie for me."

He replied, "Charlie's fine, but I know how these things scare owners."

We sat out until it was too cold, and when we went inside, we still didn't feel like betting, so we walked around the casino, before going through some stores. *I'd love to buy something for Vickie.*

At six thirty, we decided to have dinner, but neither of us was very hungry, so we both ordered a sandwich. After eating, we went up to the room and talked about checking out the next morning. We decided to wait and see how we felt.

The next morning, Norm said, "That's the most sleep I've ever gotten while staying in a hotel with a casino." We decided to stay a day or two longer because we wouldn't feel much different at home.

At lunchtime, I was a hundred dollars down, so I decided it wasn't my day. When I found Norm, he told me he was up a little and asked, "Do you wanna see if your spiders are being served?" I was way ahead for the trip, so I told him I'd buy. They did have my crawdads, and Norm tried a few. He agreed that they were good but way too much work. We stayed in the dining area for a half hour, and when we left, I decided to buy my Keno tickets and sit down to watch the games. I didn't win, but I passed some time while not losing much. The rest of the day, I played really small because I couldn't get my mind off that horse walking on three legs. I was happy they didn't put him down and wondered if he was well enough bred to be a stallion prospect. *We'll have to talk to Steve when we get back.*

We went up to the room early, and the next morning, we got an early start down the mountain. The traffic was light, so we were able to get to the track in the early afternoon. We didn't know if we should go in or wait until morning but decided one night wouldn't change much.

We went to the café for a sandwich and found Steve and Vickie sitting at a table. We asked if we could join them, and after getting our meal, we sat down. I told Vickie how sorry I was, and she started to cry. I said, "If you cry, I will, young lady."

A small smile crossed her lips as she whispered, "It was so needless."

"It always is, but the job you did keeping him from going down was borderline miraculous. It may have saved both your lives."

She stood up and leaned over to kiss my cheek before saying "You don't know how much I needed to hear you say that. You're so special to me."

"You've helped me so much," I said while wishing I could hold her in my arms. *Am I falling for this young girl?*

I asked Steve if the colt would make it, and he answered, "He'll live, but he has a badly bowed tendon, so he won't make it as a racehorse." I asked if he was well-enough bred to be a stud, and he said, "The breeding is good, but there are too many studs to try to make one out of an unraced horse."

Before leaving, Vickie hugged Norm before hugging me. She told me she hoped I'd always be there for her when something like that happened. I noticed that my heart rate was elevated and thought, *Settle down, Jim, she's just a kid. My goodness, this won't be easy.*

I whispered to her, "I hope I didn't say too much when we talked on the phone, but I was down, and speaking to you lifted my spirits. Thank you for being there for me."

She whispered, "The reason I didn't respond was what you said made me emotional. I'm so glad I can ease your pain, and I love our conversations, so don't ever apologize for anything you say."

We ate dinner at home that night, and Earl knocked on the door to ask, "You boys seen what's been goin' on about that jockey thing?" I told him we hadn't, so he said, "If you wanna see it, I taped it." We were tired but thought, since he took the time to tape it, we should watch it. Nothing was said that we didn't expect. After talking to several trainers, they decided they couldn't prove any race fixing had gone on.

I said, "The gambling commission goes a little overboard, but that's better than making it look like it's being covered up. When it all blows over, I'm sure the jockey will get days, but that'll be all."

Earl had a puzzled look on his face and asked, "What do you mean, get days?"

I answered, "That means he'll be suspended for some racing dates. I don't know how many, but with all the hoopla, it won't be a slap on the wrist."

We thanked the guys for taping it for us before going back to our trailer. Norm and I agreed the penalty would be severe because both Vickie and Charlie could have been killed. *Please, God, don't let anything happen to her. She really has helped me want to go on living, and I thank You so much for bringing her and Charlie into my life. She's gorgeous.*

CHAPTER 5

Charlie's Value Skyrockets

After getting cleaned up and eating a bowl of cereal, we arrived at the barn just as Charlie was walking onto the track. Steve said, "He'll work six today, then one more work, and he'll gallop up to the race." When Charlie reached the three-quarter pole, he was willing, but the first quarter was twenty-three flat.

I said, "That's slow for him."

He replied, "I told Vickie to work on going out a little slower and having a stronger finish." The half was forty-eight flat, and I saw Vickie shake the reins. Charlie picked it up, so the six-furlong time was one eleven and one. The last eighth was eleven and one, but the really impressive thing was, he galloped out a mile in one thirty-eight flat.

When they came in, Vickie said, "Push button." She told Steve he did a perfect job of getting him ready, before saying "He's a totally different horse than the one that first arrived, and believe me, he was great then." I loved seeing her so excited. *Is there anything I don't love about her? Don't set yourself up to be hurt, and don't make yourself look stupid.*

Norm and I each cleaned three stalls before going to lunch in the backside café. Some of the people we were able to listen to before recognized us after the last interview. It was nice to see how they had changed. Charlie was no longer just a Washington horse because many people had adopted him as their own. They'd nod or say "good luck with Charlie." I thought it was great that his nickname had gotten around. The problem was, we were no longer able to sit quietly and hear their thoughts.

I told Norm I saw a par 3 golf course up the road a couple of miles and asked if he wanted to play. "Have you ever seen me play golf?" he asked.

"I have to say, I haven't."

"I'll play if we don't keep score," he suggested.

I said, "Now that's my kinda golf." We drove to the course and each rented a set of clubs. There were very few people on the course, so we had time to discuss our shots. We talked about the fact that the ground in Yakima was probably covered with snow, and that alone made it a lot more fun. Surprisingly, we both made a few good shots. We agreed that the Senior PGA had nothing to fear from either of us, but we pretty much kept the ball in play. At the end of the round, I estimated my score to be around 40. That was 13-over par, but only 4 over bogey golf. I was satisfied with that, after not playing for so many years.

The day of the race finally arrived, and Charlie was as good as he could possibly be. I didn't know how he'd run on grass, but I wasn't at all worried about the distance. I said my silent prayer, asking God to look over Charlie and Vickie. Tom, from Lake Tahoe, called me at eight thirty and told me they would be at the track around noon.

Steve was happy when I told him the couple would come through the back gate. He said, "Show them around as much as you want to because that's how we get new people into the business. I especially like it when the man and wife are here."

"He's a very nice guy and told me his wife grew up on a farm or a ranch. He looks athletic, and I've found that former jocks really like the horses."

I walked to the back gate at noon, and the guard was very receptive when I told him the situation. All the people working there were very nice when it came to bringing new people to look things over. They must have had employee meetings about bringing new, potential horse buyers in. *Not a whole lot different than selling coffee.*

At twelve exactly, a beautiful Kelly-green pickup drove up. The driver's-side window rolled down, and Tom asked me where he could park. I pointed to a spot before walking back to open the passenger-side door. When his wife stepped out, I was **very** pleasantly surprised. Actually, I was a little starstruck because she was gorgeous while not being overdressed. Her body was what the manufacturer had in mind when they designed the jeans she was wearing. Her top was plaid and fitted to her body to attract attention but not at all pretentious. She was wearing a beautiful pair of cowboy boots, and what occurred to me was ***this is some cowgirl!***

I hoped I hadn't stared too long, but she was very gracious, and I could tell Tom didn't have to coax her to go to the track. *Don't stare, Jim. You're acting like you've never seen a pretty woman.*

Her first words were spoken in a delightful Southern drawl. "I pretty much grew up on horseback."

I replied, "I never rode them much, but I absolutely fell in love with them the first time I went to the races." I laughed while saying "Hello, Tom, I didn't mean to ignore you." *She's amazing.*

With a very proud look on his face, he said, "Most people do when they meet her."

"Without offending you, Tom, I have no trouble at all, believing that."

She walked over and kissed her husband's lips lightly before saying "Well, aren't you sweet." I could see they had a very special relationship, and for a moment, my thoughts drifted back to my wife.

Before I could fall into a daydream, Tom said, "I didn't introduce you. Jim, this is my wife, Liz." With a beautiful smile, she told me how happy she was to meet me and how much she appreciated the hospitality. I had to take a deep breath because my first glimpse of her had literally taken my breath away. *She's gorgeous.*

While trying to regain my composure, I said, "Tom was very good to us at the hotel, so I'm glad you could make it."

She replied, "He told me you hit an 8 spot playing Keno, and that's hard to do."

"I've been playing those same numbers for years and had never even hit 7 before that game."

Tom laughed while saying "You had to do it in my casino."

"Sorry, Tom, it just happened to be my day."

"I'm very pleased you won that, Jim, because our Keno sales have been up since then. It's funny how word spreads about a nice win. Keno is a profit pit for us because not only are the odds in our favor, but many people buy their tickets and play something else at the same time."

"I usually do that, but I did happen to see that game," I replied while hoping my face wasn't flushed from the sudden impact of watching Liz step out of the truck. *She's amazing, to say the least.*

On the way to the barn, she asked me if I was married. I said, "I was for forty years before my wife was killed in a car accident." I could tell it made her sad, but without being offensive, she changed the subject. It was fun walking with them because men and women took notice of her. She carried herself like royalty, and I couldn't remember having met a more ravishing woman. It made me appreciate Vickie one more time for helping me to notice. *I would have noticed her, even without Vickie.*

I said, "Steve and Norm, this is Tom and Liz." Norm always did like the pretty girls. In fact, when I wanted to find him playing blackjack, I always looked for the best-looking dealer, and it was amazing how many times I found him that way. They exchanged pleasantries, and I could see that Steve was impressed with both of them. Tom told Steve he bet horses many times because he was the trainer.

"That's very kind," Steve said before telling him he and his wife loved going to his casino when they could get away. He told him they loved how clean they kept it.

Tom very proudly replied, "Liz is the one that keeps the place looking so good." I could see that she took great pride in helping her husband, and again, I hoped my finding her so attractive didn't show on my face. I believe I could have counted on my fingers the number of women in my life who impressed me the way she did. Well, maybe a couple of toes, but she was right at the top.

We walked down the shed row, and Steve told them the names of every horse along the way. When we arrived at Charlie's stall, it was obvious that Liz knew about horses. She said, "I'll bet he knows it's race day when you put that muzzle on him."

Steve replied, "It doesn't take them long to pick up on it. I'd take him out of his stall if he wasn't running, but I pretty much leave them alone on race day."

She asked, "Just out of curiosity, if a person wanted to get into the horse business, what would be the best way to buy one?"

"I'd think the safest way to get into the business would be to claim your first horse. You pretty much get what you pay for that way. Sometimes you can run them up the claiming ladder because some trainers try to sneak them through. You might get a good buy, but usually, when they put them in for a tag, that's pretty much what they're worth. One other way you may wanna try, send Norm to a sale, and tell him the number of the horse you want him to buy." I could see a look of horror on Norm's face as Steve continued, "If you get really lucky, he'll buy the wrong horse, and you'll be set for life."

We all exploded into laughter when Norm said "That may have been pushing it a little, Steve."

"It made my day," Liz said in that gorgeous accent. "I hope you don't mind, Norm, but Tommy told me about it, and that's a great story. Back on the ranch, we called that stepping into a pile of poop and having it turn to pure gold."

I couldn't help myself. I said, "The look on his face was worth more than any amount of gold when he realized he purchased the wrong horse." She wanted to know how I became his partner, so I explained, "On the way home from the sale, I told him I'd buy 20 percent to get that pathetic look off his face." Norm failed to see the humor in what I said, but I continued, "He suggested I buy half, but I didn't want more than 20 percent."

Tom said, "I'll bet you wish you had taken him up on 50 percent now."

I became a little more serious while saying "Not many times in life does a friend like Norm come along, so I couldn't be happier if I owned all of Charlie. I wouldn't have nearly as much fun without him, and if not for his brain cramp, we wouldn't own any of him."

Norm said, "I knew being nice wouldn't last long with you."

Tom handed Steve his business card while saying "The next time something comes along that you think could be good, please call me." A smile swept across Liz's face. *What a smile that is!*

I said, "You bought us a really nice dinner when we were at your casino, so I'd like to reciprocate."

Tom replied, "That's an impressive word."

I said, "Just don't ask me to spell it. There are some really nice restaurants on the other side, if you would like to try one."

Liz suggested, "Going along with the theme of the day, let's eat at the café back here."

I invited Steve to lunch, but he said, "You know me, I can't leave Charlie alone on race day." When we turned to walk away, I saw him steal a glance at her tight-fitting jeans, and a very slight smile crossed his lips. *Vickie has him looking too!*

On our way to the café, we ran into Vickie, so I introduced her to Tom and Liz. She looked at Liz and said, "You're one pretty cowgirl, lady."

"And you are a very pretty jockey," Liz said in return.

I couldn't resist. "You are one gorgeous partner," I said to Norm. "I always wondered how it would feel to say that."

Liz said, "If you weren't living together, it would seem a little more innocent."

We all had a good laugh when Norm said **"I promise, it's innocent!"**

"He doesn't love me," I said as we were approaching the café.

The aroma of barbecued ribs smacked us in the face when we walked in, and Liz said, "That tops off a really lovely morning." The ribs were the lunch special, so all but Vickie ordered them. She ordered an apple, and Liz told her she had some discipline.

Vickie replied, "It's easy to see that you watch your diet very closely. **Jim**, I don't wanna hear anything about Norm's figure."

"You're no fun, Vickie," I said, but I couldn't help thinking she would be. *I'm really waking up.*

Vickie had a mount in the second race, so she couldn't stay long. I asked her if we should wager on him, and she answered, "We're still trying to work some things out with him, but I do like my filly in the seventh." *Never got touts like this before Charlie.*

As she was walking away, I wished her good luck before saying to the others, "I just got my pick three."

Liz smiled at me and asked, "Why did you watch her so closely until she was out the door?"

I stuttered, "Jus-just to make sure the door didn't hit her." My mind was spinning because, if she picked up on that, I hoped she couldn't tell what I was thinking about her.

She said, "**I see**. Now, what's that pick three?" She was trying really hard not to laugh.

"I'll put her horse in the seventh, with Charlie in the eighth, to all in the last race," I said while hoping my face wasn't too red. I explained, "Since there are ten horses in the last race, a one-dollar pick three will cost ten dollars. That way, if the first two win, I sit back, relax, and root for a long shot in the last."

She looked at Tom, and he said, "I'll get it." He turned to me before saying "I've never known how to figure the pick three, four, and six."

"Just multiply the number of horses you wager in each race. For example, let's say you're betting a pick three and you like two horses in all three races. It would be two times two is four. Then it would be four times two equals eight. The last leg would be eight times two, so the total bet would be sixteen dollars. The more horses you wager in each race, the more it costs. The nice thing here, there are two singles, so it's one times one times ten. That's why the total is ten dollars on a one-dollar wager."

"Thank you, I never did really look into that, and might I say, you explained it very well."

Liz had a personality to match her gorgeous looks, and that doesn't always hold true. She patted my hand and said, "It's easy to see Vickie cares for you, and she **does** have a very nice behind."

While blushing, I replied, "I like her very much. She has become a wonderful friend."

Her smile broadened, and again she said, "**I see.**"

The ribs were better than they smelled, and I was just diving into mine when my phone rang. Kayti was calling, so I said, "Excuse me, I have to take this." I asked, "How's my favorite girl in the whole world?" I could see it made Liz take notice. "I love you too, bigger than the sky," I said to Kayti. She told me she got another spot on *Leverage*, and I said, "I'm out of town, so if I'm not home before it comes on, please tape it for me. I love you too, sweet girl."

"Sounds serious," Liz said after I hung up.

I replied, "That's not the half of it. That was my granddaughter."

She tapped Tom's hand while saying "**You'll wanna remember this one!**"

I laughed and said, "Nothing like that. She called to tell me she has another small part on *Leverage*."

She asked, "Are you talking about the series on TNT?"

"Yes, she's had small parts on the show a few times before."

Liz said, "I have it set in my DVR so I never miss an episode."

"I do too, but I may not be home before my DVR is full, so Kayti will tape it for me."

Liz wanted to know if Kayti had met all the actors and actresses. I told her she had, so she asked, "What does she say about them?"

"She really likes all of them because they joke around all the time." She asked who her favorite was, and I said, "I don't mean to sound like a politician, but she told me she likes all of them." She asked me who I liked best. "Like Kayti, I like all of them, but if you were to pin me down, I'd probably say Parker. She's really funny, but I like MMA, so I like watching Elliott fight."

"I like Parker too, she's a hoot. Talking about MMA, did you see the episode when Elliot fought the California Kid?"

I answered, "That was the first show Kayti was in, and she played Nurse Gail."

"Jim, I saw her. She's lovely."

I thanked her before saying, "So far, she's had really small parts."

"Have you had bigger parts than that?"

I answered, "I have in my dreams. I'm very proud of her, but I don't like to brag about her too much."

She told me the pride showed in my face before saying "It's quite all right to brag about your granddaughter."

I could tell I was gonna love her, as well as Tom, so I said, "Tom, I hope you'll forgive me for what I'm about to say. Liz, you're very sweet and down to earth for someone as beautiful as you are."

She replied, "That's very nice, sugar, but we're all God's creations."

Tom said, "You're forgiven, and I'm pretty darn happy with the way God created her."

She asked, "See why I love him so much?"

I answered, "If you hadn't pointed out that I live with a man, I'd tell you I love him too."

She laughed while saying "I think I'm gonna like you, and the look on your face told me you're interested in more than friendship with Vickie."

"She's beautiful but younger than Kayti's mom. I couldn't have a relationship with anyone right now because I still have too much love in my heart for Linda, but what you said about her behind, I may have noticed. I will say, she's pulled me from a very dark place by being the friend that she is." *How could she tell I was interested in Vickie? Do women have a sixth sense when it comes to matters of the heart?*

Their delightful presence made the day pass very quickly. We stayed on the backside until after the sixth race, and when we reached the other side, I bet a ten-dollar pick three, Vickie's horse in the seventh, to Charlie in the eighth, to all in the ninth. "An even hundred dollars," the seller said before asking me if I thought Charlie could handle the grass.

"We'll find out together. Steve told me he works well on the surface, and Vickie loves him, as usual, so I'm thinking he should win."

In the seventh, Vickie's horse was eight to one when they left the gate. The race was six furlongs, and he broke second, a couple of lengths behind the eight. They stayed in second all the way to the turn as Vickie kept him on the rail. Coming out of the turn, they were within half a length of the leader. The lead horse drifted out just a little, allowing them to shoot through the gap. Her horse was full of run and drew off to win by three open lengths. I had bet a hundred on his nose, so I was pretty excited. *Am I excited about the bet or watching her ride?* I turned to Tom and said, "She was right about that one, so let's hope Charlie does his part."

In the paddock, I remembered the movie star at Santa Anita, but believe me, she had nothing on Liz. That's not an exaggeration. Liz was an absolute knockout and so very down to earth. I would have expected a woman who looked like her to be at least a little arrogant, but she couldn't have been more pleasant. Her accent just added to her beauty. Again, I silently thanked Vickie for helping me take notice. I felt like a man who hadn't eaten for a week, but it wasn't food I was hungry for. As I told Liz, I wasn't over Linda, but I was starting to believe that life could go on.

When Vickie walked into the paddock, Steve said, "I never tell you how to ride, but I couldn't see any speed in here."

She replied, "I saw the same thing, so I thought I'd send him."

"If somebody goes with you, take him back," he said while sounding like he was asking kindly.

She promised she would, and I could see they had a wonderful relationship. Charlie was the five out of eight horses, and when I went in to bet, he was four to one. There were two horses that shared favoritism at three to one, so I put three hundred to win on Charlie and bet ten-dollar exactas with him on top of all. The last thing I bet was a two-dollar trifecta with him on top and the rest to run second and third.

He was seven to two when they left the gate. Nothing went with them, so they had eight lengths on the field before they reached the first turn. *Easy, Vickie.*

Norm said, "Not too fast, Vickie." When the first quarter time was twenty-three flat, he said, "We're okay, he gallops faster than that." Going up the backside, Vickie showed what makes a good jockey great. She slowed him down, and the half was forty-eight flat. He hardly ever worked that slow, so I knew we were in great shape.

I looked at Liz and said, "If the three quarters is more than one minute and twelve seconds, he'll win by ten."

Two horses had come to within a length of him when they entered the lane, and Tom said, "They're catching him."

The six-furlong time was one thirteen, and the mile had picked up to one thirty-seven flat. I said, "Watch him now." Vickie popped him twice, and he opened up six in less than a hundred yards and was drawing away at the wire.

Liz said, "You know this horse." The second-place horse was three to one, and the third was seven to one. Tom and Liz went into the winner's circle with us, and she told Steve she couldn't believe how much she enjoyed the race.

Steve showed a little salesmanship when he said "It's much more exciting when it's your own horse." I heard her tell him to keep his eyes open for a horse, and he promised to find them a good one.

Vickie brought him into the winner's circle and wanted to know if anybody had any doubts about the distance or running on grass. "Now you're gettin' cocky," I said.

She replied, "If you were up here feeling what I feel, you'd be cocky too." She told us she still hadn't found the bottom of him, but I couldn't get past being up there feeling what she was feeling. I wished she hadn't worded it that way. *She's way too sweet for me to be having these thoughts.*

Tom said, "This is a day Liz will remember for a long time."

I replied, "I'm glad you made it. Liz is about as special as my wife was."

"I can't tell you how sorry I am about your wife," he said while placing his hand on my shoulder.

I said, "We had forty really good years, and lots of people can't say that."

"I hope Liz and I have that long together," he said while rubbing my back. *Nice guy.*

"I pray that you do," I replied before asking him if he bet the pick three.

"I sure did, in fact I spent twenty dollars and bet it twice. Did you bet it more than once?"

"Ten times, I've made more wagering on Charlie than I have on my percentage of the purses. Now that I'm betting money that he's won for me, it's much easier to part with. I almost feel bad when I tell people what I'm betting because, before Charlie, I wasn't a big gambler at all."

"Believe me, Jim, you're not a big gambler. I see people playing ten thousand a hand playing blackjack, and they do the same at the craps table. We have one man that comes in every year from LA to bet a million on the Super Bowl."

"Does he win?" I asked with a startled look on my face.

"Sometimes yes, sometimes no, and his facial expression never changes either way."

I said, "I'd say that man has money."

Tom explained, "He owns a big company in San Francisco. Forgive me for not mentioning the name, but I don't give out that kind of information. He's put millions into horses and has never won the big dance."

I asked, "Are you talking about the Kentucky Derby?"

"Yes, the derby is correct."

"The reason Vickie was so happy about the mile and a quarter is that's our goal, and this win guarantees we'll get in, if he stays sound."

When the ninth race was about to start, I told Liz to think long shot. She told me it was already on her mind. The favorite led every step but the last, before a fifteen-to-one horse nipped him at the wire. I said, "We don't have any really big long shots, but none of the three were favorites. Did anyone see the will-pays?" We all agreed that we were too excited about Charlie to notice. We were very happy when it paid 1,250 dollars. I asked Norm if he had it, and he also bet it ten times.

Tom and Liz were happy about the day, so she said, "Jim and Norm, when you guys come back, let's all get together." She then made me laugh when she said "You two are hoots."

What a lovely couple, I thought as I walked them to their pickup. Charlie was responsible for our meeting them, as well as all the other things he had done for us. ***Please don't wake up!***

As Liz was climbing into the pickup, she looked at me and said, "Your sense of humor reminds me of someone I knew a long time ago. I'm glad you hit that 8 spot so we could meet. Don't kid yourself, sugar, you're interested in more than friendship with Vickie." *I wish we were closer to the same age.*

After saying goodbye, I walked back to the barn. Steve said, "That was a nice couple, and I think they're both interested in buying a horse."

While we were talking, Vickie came back, so I gave them both five hundred dollars before saying "Great job by both of you."

Vickie was excited about him going a mile and a quarter so easily but said, "He won't get an easy lead in the derby, but the good thing is how manageable he's becoming." She made me smile when she said "He refuses to lose."

I replied, "I enjoyed that year too." Steve wanted to know what we were talking about, so I said, "The first league title the Mariners won, they were several games behind the Angels late in the season but kept finding ways to win games. They came all the way back to win the pennant, and their motto was 'Refuse to lose.' I'm not sure if it was the last league game against the Angels or a play-off game with the Yankees, but I can still see Edgar hitting that double and Griffey scoring from first to win the game. The third-base coach would have had to tackle him to stop him. That may be the single biggest moment in Seattle sports."

Vickie said, "I couldn't agree more."

I asked, "Were you as lovely then as you are now?"

She winked at me before asking "**Where have you been all my life?**"

Norm shook his head before saying "I was watching the game with Linda and Jim. We were all hugging each other when Griffey scored, and just so you know, I liked hugging Linda much the best."

Vickie laughed and said, "I think thou protests too much."

I replied, "He does seem to worry about his sexuality, but since Liz pointed out that we live together, he likes women more than you can imagine."

Vickie said, **"Uh-huh!"** We invited them to dinner, but they both had plans, so we agreed to meet at the track the next morning. *She must be seeing someone.*

When we arrived at the barn the next morning, Steve had a serious look on his face and told us he needed to talk to us about Charlie. My heart skipped several beats before I asked, **"What on earth happened?"**

"Nothing bad, but you were offered three million dollars for him. That mile and a quarter really got people's attention."

Norm said, "He's not for sale, no matter what is offered." Steve told us he hoped we'd say that, but he would understand if we sold him. "Charlie's family," Norm explained.

Steve said, "Vickie has been worried sick, but she would understand if you sold him."

I replied, "Tell her this, she'll be the first female jockey in history to win the Kentucky Derby, and I'll kiss her on the mouth after the picture's taken. I guess I should ask her if she's dating someone before I say too much more."

Steve laughed and promised to tell her about the kiss, before saying "Sandy and I know her quite well, and she hasn't mentioned seeing anyone. I hope you keep joking around with her because she seems happier than I've seen her in a long time. I've been thinking, if we wanna run Charlie in the derby, we better just give him a month off."

I replied, "He seems to thrive on running, so I think a month should be long enough, but you're the boss."

Norm said, "That'll give us time to go back to Yakima to tie up some loose ends.*" I can't believe we're about to run in the Kentucky Derby. This journey just keeps getting better, so it has to have been scripted by God. I wonder if Vickie is part of His plan. No, if she was, she'd be closer to my age. My goodness, she's beautiful.*

CHAPTER 6

The Lure of California

We checked out of the RV park after saying "so long" to Hank and Earl, and the further we drove into Oregon, the more snow we encountered. The truck handled it like a dream; in fact, it handled better pulling the trailer. It was 11:00 p.m. when we reached Yakima, and Norm dropped me off at my house before going to his apartment. I slept until ten thirty the next morning because it felt so good to be in my old bed.

At noon, I called Norm and invited him to lunch. We ordered steaks at the Cottage Inn, and the owner came over to sit with us. He seemed to enjoy the stories we told him about our adventures and said, "I've watched all of Charlie's races on the horse channel. Norm, have you ever made a better mistake?"

He answered, "Not one that comes to mind."

After much thought, I told Norm I was selling my house. He wanted to know why, so I explained, "I don't need it, and I don't wanna worry about it when we're out of town."

I listed the house with a realtor I'd known for years, and he told me he'd take care of everything. I felt good about selling the house because I only held on to it because it was my last tie to Linda. As much as it hurt, it was time to let go. *Our marriage was more than a house. Thank you, Vickie.*

We missed being able to play golf, but it was too cold in Yakima that year. A restaurant in town offered off track betting, so we played for a couple of days. It reminded us of how badly we did before Charlie, so after the second day of losing, we decided not to go back. We both wanted to be in the warm weather and fun we left in California. I called Phil, the realtor, and told him we were leaving sooner than expected. He told me not to worry because he had everything under control. He had a company that handled estate sales to liquidate all my belongings. He told me to remove all my personal items, and the rest would be sold. He had my cell number, so I asked him to call me with any viable offer.

The next day, I used the pickup to remove everything I wouldn't want sold. I took a load to the dump, and I stored about half a pickup load in my daughter's garage. I gave her a couple thousand dollars and told her, if the items were too much in the way, I'd have them moved. I had a car that was three years old and was paid off, so I gave it to her. I had my mail forwarded to the RV park in California, and I was ready to go. *I'm coming back, Vickie, so I hope you're not seeing someone.*

Norm had finished everything he needed to take care of, so I called my daughter in Portland to tell her we were coming through. We left town in the early afternoon, and the roads were good, so we made it to Portland around five. Their traffic was horrible, so it took a little longer to get to their house. Tammy had dinner ready for us when we arrived, and the kids were excited to see both of us. She had an outside electrical hookup, so we would be comfortable. We sat inside talking to them until late. Kayti told me she wasn't sure when the episode of *Leverage* would show, so I said, "Try to remember to tape it for me." She promised that she would.

The next morning, we were up early. The house was dark, so we unhooked the power and headed for I-5 South. We were on the road at six thirty, so the traffic was much better than the evening before. "Are you up for any adventures on the way down?" Norm asked.

"Let's play it by ear. Just getting out of the cold weather makes me happy." We hadn't been on the road a half hour when I blurted out, **"Lincoln City!"**

It startled him, so he asked, **"What about Lincoln City?"**

"You asked about adventures, and I know there's an ocean there, plus it just so happens they also have two nice casinos."

We stopped at the casino on the way in and played for a couple of hours. Neither of us hit a thing, so Norm said, "Let's go to the beach."

As we were driving, I said, "I lost two hundred dollars, and it wasn't fun at all."

"I wish I'd only lost two hundred. I expected you to give me a couple hundred and tell me to play on house money."

I replied, "If I had done that, it would have had to be money from Jim's house."

"That would have been fine," he said while trying not to laugh.

We pulled into the casino on the beach, and I asked the guy at the door if there was a place we could park and plug into power. He wanted to know if we were playing, so I said, "As soon as we get parked." There was a spot right on the end, facing the ocean. Norm was driving, so he backed in, and I said, "For a bean counter, you're gettin' pretty darn good at this."

"I can't spend my entire life trying to save you money on your taxes," he replied. It was the seventh of January, so taxes were on his mind.

I asked, "Will it be difficult to do the taxes if we leave our money in the account?"

He answered, "I ran a two-hundred-million-dollar business for twenty-three years, so believe me, I ran into much bigger problems than that."

I said, "I think I brought everything you'll need to figure them. Now, let's go win our money back from the last place."

When we walked in, I bought my Keno tickets for five games. The girl at the counter asked if I had a player's card, and I told her I was from out of state so I wouldn't be there enough to use the card. I sat down at a machine and lost twenty dollars without hitting a thing. *It's crazy to keep playing.*

While looking for another machine, I walked past a board on the wall that showed the Keno numbers. I was pleasantly surprised when I looked at it, and thought, *That's the top row!* My eyes were not what they once were, so I walked up closer. It was the top row, and I hit all five of the odd numbers and three out of five of the even. I checked to make sure it was within the five games I played and it was the fourth game on my tickets. "**Yes!**" I said out loud, and a lady beside me asked if I had the top row. When I told her I had a 5 spot and eight out of ten, she was happy for me. Gamblers love to share in the excitement when others hit something big. *I wish Vickie was here.*

I called her and said, "Please don't read too much into this, but I miss you terribly."

She laughed before saying "I was just thinking how much I miss your sense of humor. When will you be back?"

After telling her we were on our way, I walked to the Keno area to look at a game booklet. Some casinos pay differently, and it was like the casino I played at in Toppenish. I won 2,320 dollars. The good thing was, no taxes. At $1,500 to one, I'd have to pay taxes, and the eight out of ten paid $1,500, but with the dollar taken out for the wager, it was $1,499 to one. I had to wait until after the next game to collect, so I sat down. I hit four out of five that game, and when I collected, the total was 2,408 dollars. My numbers were running, so I bought each ticket fifty times. The girl counted out 2,208 dollars after the wager, so I handed her the eight dollars plus one of the hundreds. She was happy, I was happy, and Norm was happy when I gave him three hundred dollars and said, "Now you can play on house money."

I knew he wanted to ask me where I won, but I had no time for chitchat. I thought, *It's time to make money.* Your mood certainly changes after you make a nice score. The first machine I went to, I played for over an hour on twenty dollars. I was down to two dollars in the machine, so I played both dollars on one spin and would go away happy even if I lost. I wasn't sure what I hit, but it put me into a bonus round. Since I played two dollars, it said all bonus spins would pay four times the amount. I had ten free spins coming, and on the first spin, I won another ten free spins. The bonus games played for fifteen minutes, and when it went back to the regular screen, I had 530 dollars. I never walk away after hitting something, so I decided to play the thirty dollars. I played for another hour before the machine was down to five hundred. After collecting the money, I said out loud, "That's the kind of machine that keeps me coming back." It wasn't just because I walked away ahead, but it was a lot of fun getting there.

When I found Norm, he wanted to know if I was winning. I told him I was, and he pointed to a nice stack of black chips while saying "The table finally turned my way."

I said, "I was gonna ask if you wanted to eat, but you won't leave if you're on a run."

He grumbled a little before saying "You stopped the run when you walked up, so let's go." He was colored up to 1,650 dollars and gave the fifty to the dealer.

As we were walking away, I said, "Someday, I might develop some feelings, and you'll surely hurt them." He gave me back three hundred dollars and told me he was starting to believe in playing on house money. I put two hundred in my pocket while saying "Dinner's on me, my friend."

I asked one of the security people for directions to the best restaurant in the house, and his directions took us past the Keno area. I looked at the board and saw I had thirty-five games left to play. The game that was on the board showed me I won a dollar on two tickets, so I said, "I won't have to throw those tickets away."

Norm wanted to know what I was talking about, so I said, "I played two hundred on Keno, and I know I get back at least two dollars."

He replied, "That sounds like some of my investments."

"The difference is, if I don't hit another dollar, I'm still two thousand up playing Keno."

He said, "I meant to ask where you won. I can't believe how much you've been winning, playing Keno. The odds are so much in favor of the house, so what's your secret?"

"I always play the same numbers and let the board come to me. Like every-thing else, Keno has been better since Charlie. What you're really asking me is, why have I been so richly blessed? I've been asking myself that for several months, and one thing I know for sure: this entire journey has lifted me from a very dark place, so I'm glad you asked me to go to the sale with you. I feel much better than I have since Linda's accident, so thank you for always being there for me." *He's a good buddy.*

We enjoyed a nice meal while going over all the things that had happened to us on our incredible journey. The bill was fifty-three dollars, and the girl waiting on us told us she'd collect at the table. I handed her a hundred and told her to keep the change. It was nice to see her face light up when she said "It's my little boy's birthday, and the gratuity will buy him a nice gift." Norm handed her another twenty while wishing her boy a happy birthday.

When we walked to the trailer, the wind was blowing in from the beach, and there was a lot of moisture in the air. I was glad there was a retaining wall on the ocean side of us. Norm said, "This is why there was a spot open facing the ocean." The retaining wall was only about two-thirds as high as the trailer, so when we were inside, the trailer was rocking. Norm said, "I've never gotten seasick on dry land."

After being inside for about an hour, we heard a loud crash that sounded awfully close. We weren't going outside to check on it with so many objects flying around, so I said, "Let's hunker down and ride it out." After turning in for the night, I said, "This rocking motion is nice. So as long as we stay on the ground and nothing comes through the windows or walls, we'll be okay." I didn't get a very good night's sleep because I could hear things hitting not only our trailer but also, it seemed, every trailer around us. It settled down about two in the morning, so I was finally able to fall asleep.

Norm woke up at six and not so quietly took a long shower. It was dark out-side, but he went out to assess the damage. After taking my shower, I joined him.

The passenger-side window of our pickup was gone, and the seat was covered with glass. Norm walked up and said, "That seems to be the only damage we sustained, but you'll have to see the seaside of this casino." We walked around to that side and saw that several windows were broken out. There were lawn chairs, ice chests, and other items scattered all around. Norm said, "I talked to some people that were on the beach when the storm rolled in. They said it hit so quickly that people left everything and headed for cover."

I replied, "Those items became missiles, and one of them found our window."

We walked up the beach, and it was amazing, the damage we saw. There were more broken windows than we could count. We saw lounge chairs and ice chests on top of the buildings and on the balconies of all the floors. I said, "That's a lotta power."

Norm replied, "I heard the winds topped out at eighty-six miles an hour."

"That's eleven miles over hurricane force," I replied. We looked out at the beach and saw refuse scattered all over the place. He asked me if I'd been in a hurricane, and I said, "You won't believe me, but I delivered milk in three hurricanes, three weeks in a row, and all on Tuesday."

He laughed while saying "It's gettin' a little deep."

"I wouldn't believe it either if I hadn't lived it." He asked where I was, and I answered, "I was in Kennewick all three times." He was surprised to hear Kennewick received that much rain, and I said, "There was no rain, just ninety-plus-mile-an-hour winds."

"If there was no rain, they weren't hurricanes," he replied while laughing.

"Okay, I'll play your silly game, hurricane-force winds. When we were on the ground, we weren't moved, but when jumping out of our trucks, the wind moved us a couple feet. There were six of us delivering, and we all thought it was kind of fun. It was interesting, comparing stories when we were in the office. We all worried about flying objects, but no one was hit by anything. We decided it was something we could tell our grandkids someday."

Since we had the parking space, we decided to stay another day. There were a lot of glass company cars up and down the beach, so I asked one of the representatives if they worked on car windows. He looked at our pickup and called to see if they had one in stock. They brought it out and put it in that day. He told us he'd file the insurance claim for us if we would pay the deductible. *That's great service.*

We had fun playing in the casino the rest of the day. We didn't win, but we played a long time on a small amount of money. When I checked my Keno tickets from the night before, I only had nine dollars coming, so I told the lady to keep them.

Before dark, we walked up and down the beach, and it was amazing how quickly things were being put back together. Many of the local people were cleaning the beach, so we pitched in and helped for a while. It reminded me of how everyone helped their neighbors in Yakima after Mount Saint Helens blew her top. What an unbelievable mess it was, but it was good to see everyone come together.

The next morning, we were back on the road, and I said, "Charlie will be back in training in about a week."

He replied, "The time has really flown by, so I hope he's been off long enough to do him some good."

I said, "This is one time in horses' careers that trainers push them the hardest because they only get one shot at the Kentucky Derby. It's the most prestigious race in the world, and we've qualified, so let's pray he stays sound. It's hard for me to believe we could be in the race."

"We have four months to go, so yes, now is the time to pray he stays safe."

It seemed like no time before we were back on I-5. We stopped for fuel before entering California and decided to stay at the Indian casino where we played before. That would get us to the RV park early the next day. It was almost dinnertime when we hooked up the trailer, so I said, "Let's play for an hour, and the one that wins the most can buy." Norm went to a blackjack table, and I bought my Keno tickets before playing a couple of machines. I didn't hit a thing playing the slots, and when I checked my Keno tickets, I had a dollar coming. I gave that to the girl selling the tickets and told Norm I was down eighty bucks. He was down forty-five, so I said, "You buy because you lost the least."

He replied, "The deal was who won the most, so we'll pay separately."

It seemed to me that it was like splitting hairs, but we paid separately. I said, "You sure are cheap."

He replied, "You bet I am, I pay 80 percent of Charlie's bills." *That's cute, Norman.*

We played a while after dinner, but it wasn't our night, so we went to the trailer early. I asked him if he told Steve we were on our way. He told him we'd be there before Charlie was back in training.

The next morning, we were on the road early, so it was just before noon when we pulled into the RV park. We hadn't called, so we hoped a spot would be available. Earl and Hank's trailer was still there, but the spot beside them was occupied. We were able to get a space a couple of rows away and had everything set up before going to the track.

No one was at the barn, so I said, "Nothing to do but play golf." We brought our clubs back, so we didn't have to rent them. I kept my score in my head, and 34 is what I counted. That was 7-over par, but I was happy it was under bogey. I asked Norm if he kept his score.

He said, "No, and if we start that, I'll stop playing." *Sounds like a child who would take his toys and go home.*

We were back at the barn at five thirty, and Steve seemed happy to see us. "Charlie's doin' great, and the farm manager told me he's been running the fence line every day. We turned him out to let him rest, but he's getting as much work as he would be in training. It's doin' him a world of good mentally because they need to get away from the track sometimes. We're bringing him back a couple days early because there's an un-graded stake going a mile in three weeks. If he's lost as little as we think he has, I'll put him in there."

I said, "That sounds great because we've missed seeing him run." I looked up and down the stalls while thinking *It's nice to be back.*

The next morning, we were at the barn at seven, and we both cleaned a couple of stalls. I loved when Vickie hugged me and told me how happy she was to see me. I said, "It's too darn cold in Yakima."

"Oh, you're here for the weather. Darn, I thought it was me."

"We both cried ourselves to sleep every night over you," I said while trying not to laugh.

"It was me and the weather then?"

I said, "Mostly you." She was looking at me very closely, and I was getting a little nervous, having her look at me like she was. "What are you lookin' at?" I finally asked her while hoping nothing was hanging out of my nose.

"I was trying to see if your nose is growing."

Norm said, "You know we love you, Vickie." She told us we really had been missed. She was getting more comfortable with us, and she had a delightful sense of humor, but what I still liked most was watching her walk away. *Mmmm, that's nice.*

She turned back to me and said, "I almost forgot, you promised me a kiss on the lips if I win the derby."

I could feel myself getting red and said, "I was kidding with Steve."

As she was turning back around, she said, "Just as I thought, **all bark and no bite!**"

I laughed before saying "If you win the derby, I just might nibble a little." She looked over her shoulder to wink at me, and I was sure she had a little more sway in those lovely hips. I had missed that sense of humor more than I realized. *She knows how cute her butt is, and she loves teasing me.*

The next morning, we were at the barn when Charlie arrived. When he backed out of the van, he knew where he was, and for several seconds, he didn't have all four hooves on the ground at the same time. I asked Steve, "Do ya think he's happy to be back?"

"He looks as good as he did before we turned him out," he replied. He put him on the walker, but it could hardly be called a walker, because he was running and taking the walker arm with him. He started raring, so Steve said, "Okay, that's enough. That's when it's dangerous. I've seen some good horses get their legs over a walker arm and end promising careers, so we'll hand walk him for a few days." I thought again about how happy I was to be back, and it really did feel like we had come home.

The groom walked him around the grounds, and I felt sorry for him because, actually, Charlie was leading him. He said, "He really feels good." Steve promised to send him to the track the next morning before telling us he wanted to see us in his tack room. *That sounds rather ominous.*

Norm asked him if something was wrong, and he said, "Not now, but there's something I need to tell you. I wanted you to see Charlie before we talked because we almost lost him a couple weeks ago."

I asked, "Are you saying he got out of the paddock?"

"I'm saying, he almost died." We just sat there looking at him, and he continued, "He had a bad case of colic. I know that doesn't sound bad if he was a human, but horses can't regurgitate, so to fight the pain, they get down and roll. In many cases, they get what is called twisted gut, and it can be deadly to them. He was in a pretty advanced stage when the people at the farm found him. His eyes had rolled back in his head, and he was in terrible pain, so the manager gave him a shot containing pain medication and a muscle relaxant before calling their vet. His vet was there within minutes, and when he arrived, Charlie was standing up, and his eyes were bright. The vet said the muscle relaxant allowed his intestine to relax and correct itself."

I asked, "Is he all right now?"

"They did an MRI, and there was no damage, so there will be no aftereffects, but he was virtually minutes away from death."

"Are they sure it won't happen again?" I asked.

"You can never be sure of that, but he has no more chance than if it wouldn't have happened."

Norm said, "I'm glad you let us see him before telling us."

Steve replied, "He looked like he does now just hours after it happened."

I said, "Don't think I'm trying to do your job for you, but did they run a blood panel on him?"

Steve smiled and said, "You've paid attention to a trainer somewhere. Yes, the stress threw his blood off, but he's been given medication to correct it. The vet said it's perfect now, but that was an educated question."

I explained, "I had two partners that were vets, and I was interested, so I asked many questions. One of them was an instructor at WSU at one time, and he enjoyed teaching me. If he was doing a surgery when I stopped by his office, he'd tell me to grab a gown and get back there. After getting used to the blood, it was very educational."

He asked, "You both knew about twisted gut?" We smiled and nodded. *I like working with him.*

Vickie told me she was really high on her mount in the second race, so I said, "I'll take a look at it, and I do appreciate you keeping me posted on the horses you like. I wasn't kidding when I said I missed you."

She told me she missed me too. I wished again that she was closer to my age, but if she were, she wouldn't have been riding, and we wouldn't have met. At least she had me thinking about women after so many years. I was as confused as I was when I was a teenager, and I hoped she couldn't tell how interested I was. *Can she see what Liz saw the day I met her?*

We cleaned stalls until almost noon, and I told Norm I was happy to be back, before telling him about the horse Vickie gave us. He wanted to know why she gave me the touts instead of him, so I said, "Because I'm much younger, and she knows I won't forget." He called me a name that I'll not mention, but it wasn't very nice.

The second race had eight horses and was a six-furlong, forty-thousand-dollar maiden race for three-year-old fillies. Her filly was the 1 and was six to one in the program.

Norm and I had lunch at the café, and three people came up to tell us it was nice to see us. It was good to think how Charlie had turned them around because we weren't very well liked when we first arrived. During lunch, I said, "After what Steve told us, we need to put insurance on Charlie." He told me he hadn't looked into horse insurance. I had purchased some several years before, so I explained, "About ten years ago, the cost was 7.5 percent of the amount they're insured for."

He said, "We turned down three million for him."

"That would be too much, but one million would be reasonable."

He said, "That'll be seventy-five thousand a year, so I'll get it done right away. It'll come out of the purse money because it's deductible."

The horses were coming onto the track for the first race, so I didn't think I could walk across in time to bet the double. I bet in the café and bet five-dollar doubles, all in the first to the one in the second. Norm also made his bet before we started across. We watched the race from the infield, and I could see the 4 won, but I didn't know the odds until we reached the other side. He went off at seven to one, but the best thing was, he was fourth in wagering, and the favorite was six to five. Norm asked if I had it, and I told him I wheeled to her horse. He put five horses with the 1, but the 4 wasn't one of them, so I said, "That's why I wheel. I have a five-dollar, so I'll sell you one dollar for ten bucks." He told me he'd take it. We helped each other that way many times in the past, but before Charlie, it usually helped the one selling the ticket.

We were standing outside the paddock when the horses walked around. Vickie was looking for us, and when she saw us, she winked, so I knew all was well. I went inside and bet fifty to win and place for me and twenty to win for her. I wheeled the one on top in the exacta for three dollars, but I didn't bet the trifecta. Since it was a new year, I wanted to start out slowly. She was the first one in the gate, and that, sometimes, is the problem with being in the one hole. It's not too bad if all the others enter smoothly, but the 5 was giving them problems. Her filly stood in the gateway too long, and as it happens many times, she wasn't ready when the gate opened. They were four lengths behind the field at the break, but Vickie didn't try to rush her up and leave her race on the backside. She settled her on the rail while making steady progress. They stayed on the rail going into the turn and were able to pass three horses on the inside. She looked like a great artist as a seam opened up coming out of the turn, and she shot through. I was thinking, *Whether she wins or not, this ride is beautiful.* With two hundred yards to go, she moved into second and was closing on the leader. When they crossed the wire, her filly had her nose in front. A photo was called, but I was confident that she won. When the photo sign came down, the 1 was on top, and a fifteen-to-one filly ran second. "This is a good start to Charlie's three-year-old year," I said to Norm.

He replied, "It's good to be back." We both knew we'd be getting many more valuable touts.

After Vickie celebrated with the owners in the winner's circle, I shook her hand. She and I were the only ones in the crowd who knew the ticket I bought for her was in her hand. "**Thank you,**" she said while looking into my eyes. *I love those blue eyes.*

"**Thank you**, it's really good to be back," I told her before kissing her cheek. The filly paid $17.80, and the exacta paid eighty-nine dollars for a two-dollar bet. The double paid 130 dollars for a two-dollar bet, so I gave Norm sixty-five and put just over $1,200 in my pocket. *She's helping me in so many ways.*

We settled into a routine of playing nine holes of golf almost every afternoon, and one day I said, "We'd be inside freezing in Yakima, so weather alone makes it good to be here. The only thing warmer than this weather is Vickie's lovely smile." We had no reason to return to Yakima for a very long time, so we went to a post office and rented post office boxes. After making arrangements to have our mail sent to them, I said, "We're California residents."

Two days before Charlie's race, Steve said, "I didn't tell you, I claimed a horse for Tom and Liz. It's a three-year-old colt, or I should say he was a colt. He had the same problem Charlie did, so we gelded him, and I think he'll be a good one."

I asked, "Is he still a maiden?"

"Yes, that was his third start. He ran second his first time out but went backwards from there. I watched him walk off the track after his second start, and I could see he was sore in the back end, so I explained to Tom that I'd geld him right away. He'll run tomorrow and Charlie the next day. Tom and Liz are coming down and will stay the night so they can watch both races. I wanna thank you for getting me their business."

"Your reputation did the work, Steve. All I did was win twenty-five thousand in his casino."

"I'll bet you hated that," he said. After laughing, I told him Liz was kinda nice to look at.

"Huh, I didn't notice," he lied.

"I sure wish Vickie was here so she could see your nose growing. Did I mention Vickie is also very lovely?" A female voice asked whom I was talking about, and I turned around to see Vickie. "How do you sneak up on us like that? I was telling Steve I think Liz is lovely."

She told me she enjoyed sneaking up on us, before saying "Liz is the most beautiful woman I've ever met."

I said, "I know a jockey that'll give her a run for her money."

"I wish that was true," she whispered as she looked deeply into my eyes. *Why does she have to have those gorgeous blue eyes?* I told her they were coming down for the races before inviting her to dinner with us.

After she went back to work, Steve said, "That was smooth. Yes, you've mentioned that you find Vickie attractive, and I agree with you."

I replied, "I'm gonna tell Sandy."

He said, "She tells me how pretty she is all the time. Women say that about each other quite often."

I asked, "Would you like to say that about me, Steve?"

He lowered his head and raised his eyebrows while saying "**No!**"

"You and Norm worry way too much about your sexuality."

He replied, "The answer is still **no!**" *He's as bad as Norm about not caring about my feelings.*

Charlie galloped a strong mile, so I said, "He looks to me like he's right back where he was before being turned out."

Steve replied, "The farm manager couldn't get over how much he ran the fence every day. We'll find out day after tomorrow if he's all the way back."

After cleaning Charlie's stall, I asked Steve if I should bring him in. "Go get him, he's walked long enough." I checked the ground to see if there was any running water, and it was clear, but Charlie was moving around a little. I had heard of some horrific injuries people suffered with horses on walkers, so I waited until he settled down. When he relaxed a little, I walked in while making sure to stay in front of him. I put the shank on him while scratching his neck, and that made him very docile, so I walked him to his stall without incident. Steve said, "I noticed you were very careful walking up to him, and I was glad to see it."

I explained, "I knew a lady in Yakima who was kicked in the face, going in to take a horse off the walker. It really broke her up, and she had two or three surgeries to correct the injuries. I also know, the closer they get to a race, the tougher they are to handle."

"Ya, Charlie's on top of it right now," he said before telling me I did a good job.

I asked him to show us Tom's horse, so he took him out of his stall and let us get a good look at him. He was just under sixteen hands and stocky, so I said, "He looks like he has speed."

He replied, "I don't know if he'll ever go a rout of ground, but there are some good sprint races here." I asked how far he was going in his upcoming race, and he answered, "It's a maiden sixty thousand, going six furlongs, and he should fit well in there."

I said, "Northern Dancer was built like him, and he could go a mile and a half, so maybe they'll get lucky."

He replied, "Let's break his maiden before worrying about where he belongs."

We ate lunch at the café before going out to play golf. The afternoon was nice, but I could see some threatening clouds in the distance. We finished our round just before it started to rain, and it was coming down pretty hard. I said, "I'm sure the track is a mess."

Norm replied, "Except for Portland, which is beach sand, Charlie has never run on a wet track, so let's hope it clears up before his race." We stopped by the track to see how the horses were running, and there had been some long shots since the track had gotten wet. Norm said, "Some horses run better on off tracks."

I replied, "The key is figuring out the right horse before the race, and add to that, there are several kinds of muddy tracks."

Norm said, "Ya, I'd rather bet horses on a fast track." Steve told us they would seal the track as soon as the last race ran. "Has Tom's horse run on a muddy track?" Norm asked him.

"No, but he's bred for it, so let's hope he runs to his breeding."

When we got back to the trailer park, we stopped by Earl's trailer. They were not in, so I left a note, telling them the number of the space we were in. About eight, Earl knocked on our door. We invited him in, but he said, "I can only say 'Welcome back' because Hank's in the hospital." We asked if it was serious, and he said, "He's had some chest pains, but they don't think it's too serious. They'll keep him overnight for observation."

Norm told him to give him our best, and I told him to tell him we couldn't play poker without him. "I'll pass that along, and welcome back," he replied.

We got a good night's sleep, had a quick meal at the café, and arrived at the barn about seven. The rain had stopped during the night, and since the track was sealed, it was in pretty good shape. Charlie galloped a mile very willingly, and he just glided over it. When they came off, Vickie said, "A wet track won't bother this guy." I asked if the track would be considered muddy, and she answered, "No, but it's off enough to tell he can handle most any track." I very casually asked her if she had always been so beautiful. A smile lit up her face as she whispered, "I really missed you, and it's so good to have you back." *She's fun.*

I asked Steve what time Tom and Liz would arrive, and he answered, "Pretty soon, I hope, because they have to get their license." Before leaving, Vickie told us she liked her horse in the fourth.

"Is that Tom's horse?" I asked.

"I should have known Steve would tell you about him."

I said, "It sounded so much better passing through your lips. Have I mentioned how much I love your smile?"

She shook her head and laughed before saying "He's going up in class, so you should get some odds. He's superfast, and guys would be better off without those things anyway."

I doubled over and groaned like I was in pain before asking "Where did all that beauty come from?" She did a double take before asking if I was talking about Tom's horse. I said, "I was talking about his rider."

"**You're such a flirt today!** You said I've helped you, and I want you to know, you've helped me because I used to be too serious around male owners." *I am in a flirty mood today.*

"You do understand, I'm not like most men," I said while biting my lip so I wouldn't laugh.

She replied, "Seems I've heard that one before." She laughed and tossed her beautiful dark hair, so I could tell she enjoyed our flirting as much as I did. She was the primary reason I wanted to stay in California for a long while. I knew I was too old for her, but I couldn't wait to see her each morning. *If only she was a little older.*

Norm and I cleaned a couple of stalls before lunch, and when we walked into the café, we saw Tom and Liz sitting at a table. Liz jumped up when she saw us, and when she jumped, one of her legs went up behind her.

"You were a cheerleader," I observed. She asked how I knew, and I said, "The way you lifted your leg when you jumped. I spent a lotta time watching cheerleaders."

Tom stood up and shook my hand while saying "You and me both, my friend."

Liz said, "You were supposed to be watching the games."

I looked at Tom and asked, "Is that how it works?"

He answered, "I can see where she might think that." Norm shook Tom's hand and hugged Liz.

Liz asked me, "Why is Norm always so quiet?"

I answered, "If you get him going, he perks up."

I asked if she mentioned she was from Texas, and she answered, "I sure did, sugar."

I said, "Norm comes from your neck of the woods." They were raised across state lines but only a couple hundred miles apart. They exchanged pleasantries about their years growing up, before I said, "Norm and I talked about the humidity in that area. He told me they had swamp coolers when he was growing up, and I don't think I could do that."

She asked him, "How did you get by without air-conditioning?"

His answer was "We didn't have a choice, and no one I knew had air-conditioning."

I said, "We had a swamp cooler growing up but not that terrible humidity."

Norm replied, "It's not so bad once you get used to it."

I asked Tom, "What's this I hear about you buying a horse?"

He replied, "I have you to thank for that."

"We should wait until after the race to see if you'll be cussing me or thanking me."

He said, "Steve likes him, and I have a lot of faith in him."

"I'll certainly be rooting for him and wager a few bucks. Have you picked up your license?"

"We were hoping you would help us with that," he replied.

As soon as we finished eating, we went to the office and filled out the papers. I hadn't asked the horse's name, and where it asked the names of horses he had in training, he wrote *Slimsfinefood*. I said, "That's a very nice restaurant in Los Angeles that caters to horsemen. Their food is fantastic."

He chuckled while saying "At least I know where the name comes from." After they gave him his license, we walked back to the barn, and Tom told Steve the license was taken care of.

I said, "Steve, I didn't ask you the horse's name. If his running is as good as Slim's food, they're in for quite a ride."

After the second race, we walked across, and when we were seated, Liz asked me if I was betting the third. I said, "I don't know anything in the race, so I'll sit this one out." The favorite started out at four to five, but I looked at the board, and he was one to five. They were jumping all over him, so I said, "What we could do is put the five in this race, to the four in your race, to all in the fifth. That pick three would cost nine dollars so I'll do that, except I'll spend eighteen dollars and bet a two-dollar pick three."

Liz laughed while saying "You're a hoot. At first you weren't gonna bet at all, and then you talked yourself into betting twice."

I asked, "Do you think only women change their minds?" She laughed, and Tom gave me two thumbs up. *They're sure a fun couple.*

He walked in with me and bet the same thing I bet. As we were walking out, he told me he appreciated me making Liz feel so comfortable. I said, "My pleasure, Tom, your wife is a delightful lady, and she's amazingly down to earth for someone as beautiful as she is." *She makes me miss Linda.*

The five went off at even money and won quite easily, so I said, "Now it's up to Slim."

When we walked to the paddock, I looked at Liz and noticed she was getting quite pale. I told her to take some long, slow breaths, so she took several, and the color returned to her face. I said, "The first time I had a horse run, I kinda went into shock, and things went on around me that I didn't remember till the next day."

When Vickie walked in, she went right to Liz and hugged her before shaking Tom's hand. As she started to walk away, I asked for my hug, and she said, "Charlie runs tomorrow, sweetie." She then winking at me and blew me a kiss. *Wow, slow down.*

That seemed to help Liz as she laughed and said, "You two are so cute together."

She asked me to help her bet the trifecta, so I explained, "Since there are eight horses in his race, you can put Slim on top with the rest to run second and third for forty-two dollars. Let's get our tickets before it's too late, and I'll go more into detail after we bet." I let her stand in front of me so I could listen, and she said it perfectly. She also bet a hundred dollars on him to win and thanked me as she walked by. I bet the same trifecta that she did, plus I wheeled him on top with three-dollar exactas. I then bet thirty to win and place on him.

When the horses entered the gate, Slim was sixteen to one, and true to his looks, he broke right on top. After he was three lengths in front, I could see Vickie bringing him back a little. I said to Liz, "This girl can ride."

Turning for home, a horse pulled up to his flank, and she shouted, **"We're gonna get beat!"**

I smiled at her and said, "That's just good rating on the front end." When they turned for home, Vickie threw a cross, and they were gone. She wrapped up on him with a hundred yards to go, and they still won by three very easy lengths. *Wow, that surgery really helped him. Life is so good.*

"How did you know?" Liz asked me.

I explained, "Horses need to be rated on the front end, as well as coming from off the pace. I call it false pacing, and Vickie does it exceptionally well."

Liz smiled and said, "You seem to like her a lot, and she certainly is a beautiful woman."

I replied, "She's a very special lady, as well as a great rider." She surprised me when she asked if I agreed that she was beautiful. I explained, "I do, but she's younger than my oldest daughter, so I try not to think about it."

She surprised me when she whispered, "You're awfully sweet, sugar, but one day soon you'll realize, she's more than a friend." I smiled as I wondered how women were able to pick up on that.

It was a party in the winner's circle. Liz was hugging everybody, and that was fine with me. Tom even hugged me, and I asked, "What day is it, Tom?" He smiled and shrugged his shoulders, so I laughed and said, "You'll remember later." He gave me a puzzled look, so I explained how I went into shock the first time I had a horse run.

He said, "I don't think that's the case, but I'll tell ya later." When Vickie brought Slim in, Liz tried to hug her while she was on the horse.

Steve took hold of her arm and gently brought her back while saying "I don't want you to get hurt." *Nice to see her this excited.*

While laughing, Vickie looked at Liz and said, "It makes me feel good to see you this excited." Liz just nodded, and I'm not sure she even heard what Vickie said. After the picture, Vickie gave both Liz and Tom big hugs. She looked at me and said, "All right." She walked over and hugged Norm, Steve, and then me.

I laughed and said, "I love watching you ride." Slim paid $34.80 to win and $12.60 to place. The two-dollar exacta paid 264 dollars, and the one-dollar trifecta paid $1,353. I told Liz she'd have to collect the trifecta at the IRS window, and she wanted to know if they withheld taxes. I told her they would if she wanted them to. I stood behind her while she collected, and she had them take 30 percent out, so I thought, *They must really make good money.* I had them take 20 percent out of mine, and I collected just over two thousand.

When I caught up to Liz, I said, "Let's root for a long shot in the next race." A ten to one horse won, and the one-dollar pick three paid eight hundred and sixty dollars. I said to Liz, "It's income-tax time again." After taxes, I received almost $1,300 on the pick three, so my horse account was on the move. *How much longer can this go on?*

We went to a very nice restaurant for dinner. Vickie, Steve, and Sandy joined the four of us, and Tom told us many times how much they enjoyed being owners. The purse was $18,200 after the commissions, so I said, "Slim is over 50 percent paid for after one race, and if he wins next time, he'll be in the black."

Vickie replied, "He had a lot left, so he'll be tough right back." *She really knows her horses.*

Norm said, "I'll call this a business meeting and pay it out of Charlie's purse money." The dinner and drinks cost over three hundred dollars, so I was glad we could write it off. Norm told Tom to keep records of miles, meals, and rooms. Tom smiled and thanked him, but we would find out later that he was an accountant. He was too nice a guy to tell him at the time. We agreed to meet for breakfast at the backside café the next morning.

The morning was sunny and beautiful, so I said, "The track will be fast by race time."

Tom and Liz were in the café when we walked in, and Liz asked, "Did I make a fool of myself last night?"

I answered, "Not at all."

She said, "I was too excited to contain myself."

Norm replied, "When you stop getting excited, it's time to get out of the business because there are some bad times along the way!"

She said, "Right now, this whole thing is a hoot."

We were in the seventh race, and having Tom and Liz there was a big help to us. We joked and told stories to pass the time, and I enjoyed hearing Norm tell Liz about his days of riding in the rodeo. She asked him if he rode bulls, and he answered, "I know I don't look too bright, but believe me, I'm not that foolish." He stopped short of saying stupid because she could have relatives or friends who rode bulls, since she was from Texas.

"**It's very foolish**," she said before telling us about her brother smashing his face into the back of a bull's head. "He had several surgeries to fix his face, and to top it off, the bull tried to kill him when he was on the ground.

Norm said, "Horses wanna buck you off, but they never come after you on the ground. That's one reason I liked watching bulls from outside the fence." She was delightful, and it was easy to see that Norm found her to be quite intelligent. We enjoyed a nice breakfast before walking to the barn. Steve told them Slim was doing very well, and he would look for an allowance, never-win-two race for him.

We split a couple of small bets to help pass the time, and when the race before our race was about to run, Tom asked me to split a pick three.

I explained, "Since Charlie's the prohibitive favorite, I won't bet it. If we get three favorites, we could hit all three and still lose money. With Slim, we knew he'd have odds, so the bet made sense."

The five-to-two favorite won the seventh race. We went down to the paddock to see Charlie, and when Vickie came in, she was full of confidence. She winked at us before taking him onto the track. I said, "If Charlie's below even money, I won't bet him." He was even money with two minutes to post, but when the board changed, he went up to seven to five. I hurried in and bet five hundred to win on him, and when the gate opened, he was eight to five. His first stride out of the gate, his front feet broke out from under him, and his head looked like it went all the way to the ground. Vickie was up on his neck, and only her tremendous athletic ability kept her from going over his head. Both of her feet were out of the irons, and by the time she was back in the saddle, they were at least fifteen lengths behind the field. She let him settle, but he never did run. Vickie didn't pull him up but never asked him for a thing.

Liz told us how sorry she was, and I said, "There was nothing that could have been done."

Norm added, "I just hope he's not injured."

I said, "I know it's not a leg problem, or she would have pulled him up." They didn't go far past the wire and were first to come back. I was standing beside Steve and said, "Look, Steve, he's bleeding from his nose." When they were within talking distance, I asked Vickie if his nose hit the ground. She told me she thought it did but was so busy trying to stay on that she couldn't be sure.

Steve took a rag out of his pocket and started to wipe away the dirt, but Charlie jerked his head back sharply. Steve said, "He hit the ground hard."

We called a vet to have him scoped, and when he arrived, we told him what happened. He said, "I could scope him, but we know there's blood in his lungs, and there's no way to tell if the blood is coming from the lungs or back to his lungs from his nose. If you want me to, I can put him on Lasix just from seeing blood in his nose."

Steve said, "Let's wait since he did hit the ground hard, and he's never bled before." He didn't charge us for the call because he had made a lot of money betting on Charlie.

The next morning when we arrived at the barn, Charlie was on the walker and was really full of himself. Steve said, "That race took nothing out of him, so I'm very confident his lungs didn't bleed. I'll suggest something that may sound extreme. I wanna work him a mile tomorrow." Norm and I just looked at each other, so he said, "I'll tell Vickie to pull him up if he starts to labor. Well, say something, guys."

When I was able to speak, I said, "You've never worked him a mile, and now you want to, two days after a race. Steve, I don't question your ability, but you have to admit it sounds strange."

"Look at him, that race took nothing out of him and was nothing more than a glorified gallop. If he did bleed from his lungs, we must know now, and if he did, the Kentucky Derby may be out."

"You're the boss," I said while hoping we could go to Louisville. *Lots of injuries before the derby.*

Norm said, "Go ahead, it just took us by surprise."

I was cleaning Charlie's stall while he was on the walker when Steve came over to me and said, "What I'm saying is radical, but we need to find out if his lungs bled, and Vickie will know within half a mile."

I replied, "Really, Steve, we have complete faith in you, so if this is your decision, don't second-guess yourself."

When we finished cleaning the stalls, we told Steve we'd see him the next morning, and there was a genuine look of concern on his face.

We went to the golf course to play nine holes, and we were both very quiet. Finally, Norm asked me if I agreed with what Steve was doing. I said, "It's like being a passenger in an airplane."

"Now that one you'll have to explain."

"You may not like the way the pilot is flying the plane, but you know he wants to get to his destination as much as any of the passengers. We may not understand what Steve is doing, but one thing we do know, he wants Charlie to run at Churchill as much as we do."

"That's a different way of saying it, but you're right. I don't know if you noticed, but I made some good shots today."

I told him I noticed, but I lied. I wanted to be positive about Charlie, but I was worried, even though I knew how much Vickie loved him. I was sure she'd take care of him, and I hoped he hadn't bled because we all wanted to be in Louisville, the first Saturday in May.

When we arrived at the barn, Steve had Charlie's tack on him. Vickie walked up and, in a somber voice, said, "Good morning." *She's worried too.*

Steve legged her up while saying "Remember what I said, if he starts to labor, back off on him."

She replied, "I promise all of you that I'll take care of him because I truly do love this guy."

Steve called up to the tower and said, "Wrong Way North, working a mile."

There was a pause before the clocker asked, "I believe you said 'Wrong Way North working a mile'?"

Steve replied, "That's correct." The tension hung in the air as Vickie jogged him to within a hundred yards of the finish line. She put him into a gallop there and set him down at the wire. Like the pro he was, he started running right on schedule, and when they were close to us, Steve said, "Quiet, so I can hear him breathe. That's what we wanted to hear." He cornered perfectly, hugging the rail all the way around. Vickie shook the reins in the lane, and he picked it up. When they crossed the line, he was going strong, and it took half a mile to pull him up.

The clocker said, "One thirty-six flat."

Because the clocker was a friend, Steve said, "We had to know if he bled."

The clocker replied, "With that work, I'd say he's just fine." He told Steve the work wouldn't show.

When they came in, Vickie raised both arms like she had just won the derby, and said, "Absolutely perfect." I could see the relief on her face because her lifelong dream had been on the line.

Steve put his ear against Charlie's chest and said, "Yes, he's perfect. If he had bled, there would have still been some broken blood vessels, and he would have bled again. We had to know, so we can go on. To give him a chance in the derby, we need to teach him to run a mile and a quarter, and there's no time to waste." He had won going a mile and a quarter on the lawn, but we knew the derby would be a much different pace, and Churchill could be very demanding.

Steve said, "The Northern Cal Derby runs in sixteen days. It's a grade 2, three-hundred-thousand-dollar race, and we'll win it. Thanks, Jim." I asked him what he was thanking me for, and he said, "For telling me not to doubt myself. I've never trained a horse like Charlie, so I've second-guessed myself many times. He'll take me to my first Kentucky Derby, and we'll win it. I've never had anything even close to this guy."

I said, "*Shhhhh*, I'm sure I can hear some inspirational music coming from somewhere."

He laughed while saying "You just couldn't give me my moment." I told him he inspired me.

A heavy burden had been lifted, so we all breathed a sigh of relief. I silently thanked God again and thought, *This whole journey has been a wonderful blessing. I don't understand why we've been so richly blessed, but please know that we are thankful.*

Charlie had so few problems as a two-year-old, but as a three-year-old, he had almost died, fallen on his face, and lost his first race. *I hope bad things stop at three.*

After the stalls were cleaned, we decided to play golf. As we walked past Steve, I shook his hand and said, "You were right and stood your ground. You're the boss, so stay on course."

"Thank you and Norm for having faith in me. I was somewhat apprehensive because I've never had a horse with 50 percent of his ability." Norm told him how glad he was that we knew he hadn't bled from his lungs and promised to never doubt him again. It was nice to see the confident look back on Steve's face.

I was interested in actually seeing some of Norm's shots that time. He shot first and his ball was pin high but ten yards to the right of the green. My shot was three feet short of the pin, on the green and right in line. Norm chose his pitching wedge and chipped to within a foot of the cup, so he made par. He really was getting better and ended up shooting bogey golf for the first time. After we finished the round, he said, "Let's keep score next time."

I replied, "I have your score if you want it."

"Go ahead and tell me."

I told him he shot thirty-six, and he asked if that was good. I said, "I think you're really improving and the walking is good for us, so let's play as often as we can." He told me he thought it was a good plan before taking a deep breath, filling his lungs with fresh air.

We decided to stop by the backside café for dinner and smelled the aroma of hickory wood smoking as we walked in. Norm said, "It would be hard to eat anything but barbecue after smelling that." Steve and Vickie were eating, and they asked how we were doing.

I said, "I've been trying to stay ahead of Norm on the golf course."

She replied, "Sounds like he's improving."

Norm said, "We think we'll start keeping score."

Steve told him not to ruin a good thing before he asked us to join them. We both chose the barbecue beef sandwich and took the order number to the table. Steve said, "We were just talking about a first-time starter I have going in the third tomorrow. He's a four-year-old, so obviously, he's had problems, but I think he should run really well. The race is three-year-olds and up, maiden special weight. He's not a world-beater, but he's a nice colt."

I replied, "Steve, there's one thing I know for a fact. I won't wager any more than I can afford to lose."

"You're learning, my boy," he said as Vickie laughed out loud.

When our meal came, Vickie said, "That looks so good."

I replied, "I'll split it with ya."

"I have to lose two pounds for a race tomorrow."

"Sounds like you got in light, huh?"

"We did, but I don't think he'll win. He could surprise me, but this will be the third time I've ridden him, and the last two were very disappointing. He's in the last race if you wanna look at him, but I don't recommend you bet him."

I asked, "The one in the third is the one you like?"

She answered, "Very much." I told her I'd bet that one, before taking a bite of my sandwich and offering to let her taste it on my lips. She leaned toward me, so I scooted back quickly, and she said, "Just as I thought, you're all talk." *She's adorable.*

I said, "You weren't supposed to call my bluff, little lady." She playfully ruffled my hair and laughed again on her way to the door. ***That doorway has never looked better!***

It was raining lightly when we got up the next morning, and the forecast was for more rain. On the way to the track, I said, "I hope this horse can run in the mud."

When we talked to Steve, he said, "I scratched him because I've put too much time into him to have him reinjure himself on a slick track his first time out."

We cleaned stalls and played golf for the next three days, and on the fourth day, Steve said, "That four-year-old is back in today, and he's still doing great."

"What race?" I asked.

"He's in the fourth. It's still a maiden special weight, but this time, it's only going five and a half furlongs. I don't expect him to get the lead, but he shouldn't be too far back."

There were nine horses in the race, and he was the only four-year-old. His morning line was ten to one, and we were in the paddock when the horses came in. Steve was leading the 5, who was as big as Charlie is and a beautiful roan. I told Norm I liked betting gray horses because they were easy to see.

Vickie winked when she rode him around to us. He was nineteen to one, so I bet thirty to win and place plus a two-dollar wheel in the daily double. I also bet twenty-dollar wins for both Steve and Vickie. He went off at twenty to one and broke in third place. He easily secured a spot on the rail, and she had him settled in third around the turn for home. Coming out of the turn, she took him to the outside and caught the leader with a hundred yards to go. He put his head in front and stayed there to the wire. The margin of victory was a neck, and when Vickie took him into the winner's circle, she told the owner he ran a little green, so he had a lot of room to improve. The owner asked if she could feel anything from the injury, and she answered, "He's as good as new." A fifteen-to-one horse won the next race, so the double paid 1,142 dollars. *This little lady is making me a lotta money.*

Vickie and Steve were happy with the tickets I bought for them. Steve said, "Sandy's very fond of you two because she's getting to do a lotta shopping."

I told Norm I had to go to the bank, so we went to the trailer to get some money that I had hidden in a safe spot. After the deposit, my account was a little over 122,000 dollars. I couldn't believe how much Charlie had changed our lives. Because of my horse account, I wasn't touching my Social Security or pension. When the house sold, I deposited the money into the account that my Social Security and pension were being directly deposited to, so that account was looking good also. Charlie truly was a gift from God, and other than missing Linda, things couldn't have been better. *If only she could be here for this journey.*

That evening, we went to the barn to help feed and enjoy some leisure time with the horses. We stopped by the café for dinner and Vickie was there. She came over to sit with us and told us how much she appreciated us putting our faith in her. She whispered, "You could get many better-known riders than me for the derby."

I said, "We know you and how dedicated you are. That, plus Steve wants you, is all that matters."

I asked her if everything was all right, and she answered, "So many good things have been happening since the three of you came into my life, and I'm a little worried it might all go away."

"Vickie, that's normal when things happen as quickly as this whole thing has, but you can rest assured that Norm and I absolutely don't want any other rider. Please relax and enjoy the experience with us." *If she was Linda, I would hold her in my arms and tell her everything would be all right.*

She hugged me and said, "Thank you so much. I was just feeling a little insecure."

I whispered, "You feel pretty darn good to me." I loved the way she laughed when I told her that.

Norm had been sitting quietly but spoke up, "Vickie, you're a huge part of our success, but believe me, we know what you're going through. We really do pinch ourselves to make sure this is not a dream."

She hugged him and said, "Thank you both so much."

The days passed quickly up to Charlie's race. The sun was shining, and the track was fast. The form had him picked at eight to one, and the caption beside his name said, "If we can throw out his last race, he fits with these."

Norm said, "I'm glad Steve worked him that mile, or I might be afraid to bet him."

I replied, "That was a gutsy move, so I'll get him a nice wager." The program had Charlie at six to one. The race was going a mile and an eighth, and Charlie was in the 2 hole. The favorite was a grade 1 stakes winner from Southern California. I bet five hundred to win on Charlie, plus I wheeled him on top in the exacta and trifecta. I also bet a twenty-dollar exacta, Charlie on top of the favorite. My last wagers were two-hundred-dollar win tickets for both Steve and Vickie.

When the gate opened, Charlie was nine to one, and the favorite was eight to five. The favorite went right to the front while Charlie broke in the middle of the pack. Vickie had him on the rail and maintained her position to the first turn. There were two horses side by side, a length in front of them, and going around the turn to the backside, the inside horse went a little wide, taking the other horse with him. Vickie shook the reins, and Charlie was through like a shot. He was in third, a length behind the second-place horse, and the leader was in front by two lengths. Vickie was in no hurry, so she stayed on the rail, saving ground through the final turn. The second-place horse hugged the rail, so she took Charlie to the outside and popped him twice. He exploded and went by both horses with two hundred yards to go. He began to draw away, and his margin of victory was four lengths. The favorite was second, six lengths in front of the rest of the field. When they came into the winner's circle, Vickie said, "He absolutely has no problem with bleeding, and I stayed in the irons this time."

I shook her hand and gave her the ticket. When she thanked me, I said, "You and Steve are the reason Charlie's as good as he is, and I'm looking forward to my kiss after the derby." *I love when she looks at me that way.* **Could she be interested in me?**

When I gave Steve his ticket, he said, "Wow, you must have done really well."

I tried not to grin when I said "Pretty good. You and Vickie are the reason we're going to the Kentucky Derby." We were all very excited, and Charlie was hungry, as usual.

On my way to collect, my cell phone rang, and I saw it was Tom. "That'll silence a few doubters," he said. I asked how he was doing, and he said, "Probably not as good as you but not bad."

"Did you hit him?"

He answered, "Two hundred to win and place."

"Good for you, and how about Liz?"

"Two hundred to win and place because she told me to bet for her what I bet for myself."

I replied, "I'd say she made a good decision."

Tom said, "When you two come back up, the suite is yours for as long as you wanna stay."

I replied, "You know us, that could be sooner than later." I collected just over eight thousand and said, **"This is gettin' to be fun!"**

Norm asked how I did, so I told him and asked how much he bet. "Just a little more than that," he said while smiling really big. That meant a lot more and could have been any amount. *Maybe he'll stop playing forty cents when he plays the slots.*

When we were back at the barn, Charlie was just finishing his walk, so Steve asked me to put him in his stall. I expected him to be tired, but just after we left the walker, he stood up on his back legs. I had worked with him enough that it didn't bother me because I knew he was just having fun. He danced all the way to his stall, and I took him inside before scratching his neck. I said, "I sure wish you knew how much you mean to us."

When I walked out of his stall, Steve said, "You're gonna spoil him."

"Good, he has sure spoiled me," I replied before smacking him on the back. *I'm almost too excited.*

He said, "I think we can all relate to that."

I told him Tom called me right after the race to congratulate us, and he said, "I'm glad you mentioned that because his horse is running in three days, and I need to call him."

Vickie had joined us, and I handed Steve my phone after I put it on speaker. I said, "Hit star 69, and you'll have him."

"This is Tom, president of operations."

Steve said, "I hope you don't mind, I have you on speakerphone."

"You have me at a disadvantage," Tom said before asking who was calling.

"Steve, Jim, Norm, and Vickie," he answered.

Tom replied, "Four of my favorite people."

Steve said, "Your horse is running in three days."

Tom said, "Jim, tell me if I do this right. How far, for how much, and what's our post position?"

"I'd say you have that down pretty well, but now you ask Vickie if he'll win."

Steve asked, "Does this make Jim assistant trainer?"

Vickie said, "Nothing like puttin' me on the spot."

We all laughed when Steve said "My life used to be so much easier, but not nearly as much fun."

Tom said, "Oh, darn, I have some people coming in from corporate in three days, so I guess I'll watch it from here."

"If you can't come down, we'll come up," I replied while shooting a glance at Norm.

Norm said, "Sounds good to me because I just came into some money."

Tom replied, "Let me make the reservation for you, and you'll get the suite I offered you last time." Vickie asked him if she would get a suite when she came up, and he said, "Sweetie, you'll be treated like a royal princess, I promise you."

She said, "You may have to get another rider because I wanna come with them."

He replied, "No no no, anytime, but then **you're my rider.**"

124

He couldn't see the smile that lit up her lovely face as she said "That means so much to me, Tom."

Tom said, "Liz would kill me if anyone but you rode Slimsfinefood." Again, Vickie told him how much that meant to her. I couldn't help thinking how pretty her face was when she smiled and how timely the things Tom was telling her were. After we hung up, Steve thanked me again for helping him get Tom as a client.

I replied, "For some reason, he thinks I know something about this business, but he couldn't be more mistaken."

Steve said, "I don't know why you act like you know far less than you do. Somewhere along the line, you've worked closely with a trainer."

"There's only room for one chief, Steve, and that's you. I appreciate you and every trainer I've had, taking the time to teach me, but I could never do what you guys do. Seven days a week is not my thing, no matter how much I love these animals."

Vickie said, "With all the praises floating around, I almost forgot why I came here. There's a Texas Hold'em tournament tonight to benefit disabled jockeys. The buy in is five hundred dollars, and 20 percent of the prize money goes to the charity."

Norm said, "Count us in." We each handed her five hundred dollars and asked her to sign us up.

"I love you guys," she said before walking away.

The guys shook their heads when I asked, "Is it just me or does she look fantastic, walkin' away?"

While shaking his head, Norm said, "She seems to have her confidence back."

I replied, "I don't think that has anything to do with the way she looks walkin' away, **but maybe**." They both told me I was sick.

The tournament would start at nine, so after talking to Norm, I called Tom to tell him we would be up the next day. I said, "The length of our stay is yet to be determined."

He laughed while saying "As long as you wanna stay, the room is yours."

Norm and I were seated at the same table, and one of the jockeys across me went all-in the first hand, after the first two cards. I had a pair of queens, so I called, but everyone else folded. When we turned our cards over, I was puzzled because he had the poorest hand in poker, a two and seven of different suites. I got another queen on the flop, so the hand was over.

He laughed and said, "It's past my bedtime."

I shook his hand and said, "Sleep well, my friend, and thank you for donating to the cause." After half of the players were eliminated, I was dealt a pair of aces for my first two cards, so I pushed all-in.

The table folded around to Norm, and he called me while saying "Sorry, buddy." When we turned our cards over, he had a pair of kings, so his head dropped when he saw my two aces. On the flop, a king and an ace came up. I was thinking, *I wish this was someone other than Norm.* The next card did nothing for either of us, but sadly, I, as so many players before me, drowned on the river when the fourth king in the deck came up. I shook his hand before taking a seat in the stands to watch them.

They made it a big thing when the final table came together. Norm played really well, plus he was getting good cards. He was down to playing heads up with one of the trainers, and they played four hands back and forth, but on the fifth hand, Norm again was dealt a pair of kings. He pushed all-in, and the trainer called. Norm turned over the king of spades and diamonds. The trainer turned over the king and queen of hearts. The flop was the nine and ten of hearts and the ten of diamonds. Norm had two pairs, and the trainer had a possible straight flush. The turn didn't help either of them, but Norm was sunk when the river produced the jack of hearts. Everyone stood and cheered both of them while Vickie awarded the prize money. Norm won $3,500 for second, and a loud roar went up when he said "Put it all in the jockey fund." Vickie stood on her tiptoes to kiss his cheek.

On our way home, I said, "We have to take swimming lessons, old buddy."

"Why would you say that?"

I explained, "We both drowned on the river."

He laughed while saying "I had a great time."

"Sure you did, you got to kiss Vickie."

He laughed and said, "She likes me best."

The next morning, before going to the lake, we stopped to see how Charlie came out of the race. He looked super, and we asked Steve if he had anything he liked other than Tom's horse. He didn't but told us he'd call if he heard something.

There was still quite a bit of snow on the pass and a good amount around the lake. The sun shining on the tranquil water was gorgeous so for a moment, I thought about how Linda would have loved the sight. When we went to the front desk, we found that Tom had made our reservation. Our room was a beautiful suite with separate bedrooms and bathrooms. I said, "This could become a habit."

Norm replied, "I stayed in some suites when I was CFO of the hospital but none that compared to this." A bottle of champagne on ice was sitting on the table. He said, "If Tom's horse wins, we might just open that." *I'll have a drink with him sometime.*

We went downstairs and right to the buffet. I noticed they had my spiders, and to top it off, they had hot and sour soup. I said, "It doesn't get any better than this."

He replied, "Those crawdads will be the end of you." We stayed in the dining area for about forty-five minutes and sampled several foods before going into the casino. When Norm sat down to play blackjack, I looked at all of the tables and smiled as I noticed he picked the one with the best-looking dealer again. That made me think about Vickie's feminine charms, one more time. I wasn't in love with her, but everything made me think about her. I laughed out loud when I thought, *She's a kick.*

I went to the Keno area and bought my numbers for five games before walking in search of a unicorn machine. I had just sat down at one of them when my cell phone startled me. Vickie was calling and asked, "How you doin', sexy?"

I said, "You never talk like that when we're together."

She replied, "I feel much safer on the phone."

"I'm flattered that, at my age, I can put fear in the heart of women as pretty as you. I don't know what's going on with me, Vickie, but everything that happens makes me think of you."

She whispered, "I love hearing you say that because you're on my mind all the time. I know you're dealing with the loss of your wife, but please know, I'll always be here if you need someone to talk to."

I asked what she called about, and she said, "I'm riding a filly in the last race today that should do well. She's only run once and was the favorite due to the way she'd been working. She had the lead but stopped badly because, for whatever reason, she hadn't been sutured." She asked if I hadn't talked about suturing a mare.

"I told you I was half scared to death, helping a vet suture one of my trainer's fillies."

"Speaking as a woman, I don't blame her a bit," she said with a cute laugh.

I replied, "I didn't say I blamed her. I said it scared the daylights out of me." She was laughing when we hung up, and I thought, *She wouldn't laugh if she was in that stall with us.*

When I swung by the sports book, the seventh out of nine races was running, so I picked up a program and looked at the ninth. Vickie was on the 5, and her morning line was five to one. I wheeled the eighth race to her in the late double before going in search of Norm. Tom and Liz were talking to him when I walked up, so I told them about Vickie's call before saying "If you wanna bet the double, we need to get over there."

They were able to make their wagers, and Liz said to me, "I told them to put all in this race to the five in the next. Did I do it right?"

"Like you've been doing it all your life," I replied. Since we had a little time, I explained that the filly hadn't been sutured before her first race. Liz asked what that meant, so I looked at her and then Tom. I stammered while wondering what to say.

Liz said, "Sweetie, you're blushing."

"I'll let Tom explain this one."

Tom said, "Thanks a lot, I've never heard of it."

I took him by the arm, and we walked about ten feet away. After I explained it, he said, "Ouch, is that true?"

"Unfortunately, it is."

He asked, "How do they breed when they're done racing?"

I replied, "That's a very good question. As far as I know, they reverse the surgery with another surgery, but I've never been involved in that part."

The one horse won the eighth race at seven to one, and when the horses entered the gate for the ninth, the 5 was seven to one. I thought, *I like betting horses when they're the same odds.* That was just one of my many quirks and a good reason that, before Charlie, I seldom walked out of the races ahead. I put a hundred to win and place on her and wheeled her on top in the exacta.

"There they go," the announcer said, and like a shot, the 5 was that many lengths in front. I said, "She stopped before, so let's hope the surgery did the trick." She didn't stop, and Vickie never touched her. She won by seven lengths, and I thought, *Both horses were seven to one, and the filly won by seven lengths. That's triple sevens, and we're in a casino, so this must be my lucky day.*

After the race, Tom said, "Liz was happy that you didn't explain the surgery to her, and I think it bothered her when I did. The only word out of her mouth was **ouch**."

"That seems to be a common thing you hear when you explain that surgery, and I wasn't comfortable explaining it to a woman."

The five paid $16.80 to win and $7.40 to place. Both the exacta and double required nothing to be taken out for taxes, so I collected just under 1,700 dollars. I thought, *Vickie, you just paid for another trip.* I put away three hundred dollars for her and thought, *I wish she was here so we could enjoy some time by the lake.*

Liz said, "Now I have some money to bet on Slim. I sure hope he wins again."

I explained, "It's hard to go from beating maidens to beating winners on the first try, but Steve thinks he has a good chance, so he must really like him."

Norm and I played up until dinnertime, and neither of us won much, but we didn't lose too much. Tom called my cell phone and told me he and Liz wanted to take us to dinner. We went to the steak house on the top floor, and Tom signed for the meal.

I left sixty dollars for the tip, and Tom said, "That's too much, Jim."

I replied, "When I win, your employees will also because I enjoy sharing my good fortune."

Liz, in that beautiful Southern drawl, said, "You'll not go to hell treating people like that, sugarplum. *" I love some of the things she says.*

Norm and I were getting pretty close to both of them, and from what I could see around the casino, all the employees absolutely loved them.

After dinner, we thanked them for being such wonderful hosts. Norm went to play cards, but I bought my Keno tickets for ten games and took them up to the room. I spent at least thirty minutes looking around the room and left the TV on when I went to bed. I don't remember falling asleep, but I woke up when Norm came in at four thirty. I asked him if there was anything exciting to talk about, and he answered, "I lost a couple hundred playing cards, but with Vickie's tout, I'm still up for the trip."

The next morning, we slept until ten thirty and only woke up then because the housekeeper knocked on the door. I stayed in bed and told her to come in. When she put her head inside, she looked a little embarrassed and said, "I'm so sorry."

I replied, "We should be up by this time. If you'll just leave a set of towels, we'll be fine." She left them and apologized again before walking out. Since we both had bathrooms, it didn't take long to get ready.

We walked to the sports book and picked up an entry sheet. Slim was in the third race. It was an allowance; never win two, going six furlongs. He was in the 10 post, and his morning line was twelve to one. The 4 was the favorite at two to one because he broke his maiden at Santa Anita in a maiden special weight. We took the sheet with us to the buffet and enjoyed our coffee for fifteen minutes before going through the line.

Norm said, "We're getting the hang of this buffet dining."

I replied, "Some diets actually recommend that you eat at buffets when eating out."

He chuckled while saying "I don't think they recommend eating as much as we do."

"We do our best," I said while rubbing my stomach.

I went to the Keno area to check my tickets and got back ninety-six dollars. I bought my tickets for five games and tipped the girl five dollars. It was eleven thirty, so Slim's race was a couple of hours away. I found a unicorn machine that wasn't being played, and on the second spin, I said, "Look at the little ponies." I was just playing one dollar, so it paid seventy-six dollars. I played the machine for an hour before printing my ticket. I made sixteen dollars and had a wonderful time. After cashing the ticket, I checked my Keno games and only had three dollars coming back, so I told the girl to keep them. *This is relaxing.*

When we walked into the sports book, Tom and Liz were sitting with four guys who were dressed in expensive suits. Tom told us they were from corporate headquarters, and one of them asked if I was the one who hit the 8 spot. I told him I was, and he asked, "Do you know how rare that is?"

"I know that I've played those same numbers for several years, and before that, I hadn't even hit seven out of eight. I've hit six out of eight several times but wasn't able to get over that hurdle." They all shook my hand and congratulated me, so I said, "I hope you'll believe me, it has turned out to be better than I could have hoped because the win led to a wonderful friendship with Tom and Liz."

The one who looked the most important said, "We're here to honor them for having the longest average employee retention."

I replied, "From the few times I've been with them around their employees, it's obvious that he and Liz are deeply loved." One of the guys asked Tom if he was paying me for the remarks, so I said, "Sorry, Tom, I overdid it." I told him I'd give him a discount, and they all seemed to get a kick out of it.

Slim's race was five minutes away, so I said, "Time to get serious." I put a hundred to win and place on him and wheeled him on top with three-dollar exactas and one-dollar trifectas. I bet twenty-dollar win tickets for Steve and Vickie before sitting at a table. When the horses entered the gate, Slim was eleven to one. Liz asked if we minded her sitting with us, so we both asked her to please sit down.

When the gate opened, Slim wasn't quite set. I expected him to go out on top, but he broke about fifth. With Slim being on the outside, it was important not to be too wide going into the turn, but she shouldn't burn him out on the backside either. Liz asked, "Are we in trouble?"

I explained, "Things don't always go the way you want them to at the start, so it's good to have a plan B." She used just enough of him to find a seam to the rail, behind the third-place horse. Going into the turn, a little opening came along the rail, so she shook the reins, and Slim went through. He was in second, two lengths behind the favorite, when Vickie took him to the outside. He got up in time to win by half a length, so I looked at Liz and said, "To answer your question, you're not in trouble."

I could see she was quite relieved, and while laughing, she said, "It sure took you long enough to answer."

"I will say, Slim got a really good education today. He learned to get dirt in his face and how to come from behind."

She frowned and asked, "Did he really need to learn to get dirt in his face?"

I explained, "When they work, they're usually alone or with one or maybe two horses, so they don't get much dirt until they're in races. Some horses back up when they feel it because it hurts. Slim acted like a real veteran, so I'd say you have a very nice horse." I pointed out the time of one minute and eight seconds flat, before saying, "That's fast."

She asked, "Could he run with Charlie?" She seemed pleased when I told her the time would put him right there. I knew he couldn't because, even though the time was close to what Charlie would run, Charlie's class would be too much for him. That's something horsemen have marveled at for years. It doesn't seem like class should make a difference, but any trainer will tell you it does.

When the prices were posted, Slim paid $24.60 to win and $9.40 to place, so I collected just over 2,100 dollars. Steve and Vickie both received 246 dollars for their tickets.

Tom bet two hundred to win and place and said, "It worked with Charlie, so I thought, why not?" Liz did the same. I told Tom his part of the purse was more than enough to pay for Slim, and he said, "Steve thinks he'll be a very good sprinter."

After congratulations all around, we told the managers how much we enjoyed meeting them. Just before leaving, I said, "In the excitement, I almost forgot, congratulations on your award, Tom."

I bought my keno tickets for five games and put them in my pocket while looking for a slot machine. I thought about how nice a day it was for our friends and hoped there would be many more. No doubt, that was a great claim, so I was getting more confidence in Steve's horsemanship all the time. *I'm glad Vickie picked him for us.*

I sat down at a machine that had Cleopatra and people dressed from that era on the screen, and after a couple of spins, I went into a bonus game. I was playing two dollars, so I did very well. I was up 236 dollars after the bonus round and played the game until dinnertime. When I printed the ticket, I had 260 dollars. *I wonder if Vickie is on a date right now.*

Norm was playing blackjack when I found him. I asked him if he wanted to go to dinner, so he cashed in, and we headed for the buffet. I told him I needed to check my Keno tickets as we walked by the counter, and I had fourteen dollars coming back. I gave the girl two and put the other twelve in my pocket. When I rejoined Norm, he said, "It looks like you won."

I answered, "If betting twenty and collecting fourteen is winning, I sure did."

He replied, "At least you didn't throw the tickets away." I felt the same way.

After dinner, I told him I was going up to the room, but he wanted to stay down and play cards. I turned the TV on and changed the channel to ESPN. They were talking about the incident with the jockey in the Santa Anita race, and I wondered, **What now?** It seemed that Vickie was involved in an incident with the rider's older brother in Seattle several years before. They were riding in traffic, and Vickie swung out in front of him, causing his horse to clip heels and go down. He had been confined to a wheelchair since the accident. The announcer said, "Vickie has agreed to an interview in the morning, and it has come down that the rider will never ride in this country again. The racing commission said there's no way that vengeance on the track would ever be tolerated."

I went down to tell Norm what was happening, and he said, "I thought we were through with that."

I replied, "We'll have to watch the interview tomorrow."

He was a little grumpy and said, "If you haven't noticed, I'm ahead, **so let me continue!**"

I replied, "If your luck changes, it's not because I came down."

He said, "Just hope it doesn't change." I walked away thinking how funny it would be if it did.

When I got back to the room, my cell phone rang, and the caller ID showed me it was Vickie. I answered as quickly as I could, and very softly, she asked, "May I please talk to you, Jim?"

I replied, "Absolutely, I just heard about it on ESPN, and, sweetie, you can call me anytime about anything. *She's done so much for me.*

She told me she didn't see the other horse when she swung out and cried, "He has spent all these years in that chair because of me."

I didn't know if I should speak or just listen because she was sobbing so hard, and I could tell she had been for a while. I asked, "Is this why you're so passionate about helping injured jockeys?"

She sobbed, "Yes, if there was any way I could change places with him, I would."

"Vickie, that could have just as easily been you. Riders make decisions in less than a second, and the decisions can't always be right. That accident didn't give his brother the right to seek revenge. If I was there, I'd let you cry on my shoulder. I love you so much. **Excuse me,** I meant to say, you're such a lovely person." *Where did that come from?*

She surprised me by whispering "I wish you were here with me." She couldn't see how that moved me. My emotions were raging, and I really did want to hold and console her. *Slow down, Jim.*

I said, "You've become such a big part of my life that I hurt when you do. Please don't take this the wrong way, but talking to you has brought back feelings I thought would never return after my wife died. When I said 'I love you,' I didn't mean I'm in love with you, but I love having you in my life."

"Jim, I understand that you're confused about the feelings we have for each other because I'm very confused also. I know you still have feelings for your wife, but I love our relationship and hope we'll always be close." *I'm so glad she feels that way.*

We talked for over an hour before I told her she needed to get some sleep so she would be alert for the interview. I whispered, "Just tell her what you told me, and I'm sure you'll feel better."

After we hung up, I thought again, *I wish I could hold her in my arms and let her cry on my shoulder.* I shook my head while thinking ***This is just a friendship, Jim!*** It was starting to feel like so much more, and I didn't know what to do about it. *Is she as interested in me as I am in her? Could she possibly be, with our age difference? I've already lived my life, so I should leave her alone and let her enjoy hers. A little confused, maybe?*

I woke up at seven the next morning and realized I hadn't heard Norm come in. His bed was empty and hadn't been slept in, so I took a quick shower and hurried downstairs. He was still at the same table where he was playing the night before, so I asked, "Do you still have the money you won on Tom's horse?"

He answered, "That and then some." He had a rather large stack of chips in front of him. I told him I was going up to the room to watch Vickie's interview, so he had the dealer color him up. I had never seen thousand-dollar chips up close, but she counted out six of them plus eight hundred-dollar chips and eighty dollars in green and red chips. Norm gave her one of the hundred-dollar chips while thanking her. He gave me one of the thousand-dollar chips and said, "That's for all the times you've given me money."

As we were walking to the elevator, Norm's phone rang, and he said, "Let me put this on speaker."

I recognized Tom's voice right away when he said "If you and Jim continue to win, you might put me out of business. You're quite a blackjack player, Norm." When Norm asked him how he knew, he explained, "I've been watching you for two hours. It's obvious that you don't count cards but you use great fundamentals." Norm told him he always waited until the table came to him to raise his wagers and never took a card if the dealer might break. Tom said, "If everyone played as well as you do, the casino might be in trouble."

Norm replied, "Believe me, I lose my share."

Tom said, "I'll always root for you, but don't tell anyone." I asked him if he had been watching ESPN. "No, I've been watching Norm." I explained that Vickie would be interviewed soon, and he said, "Not about Slim, I hope." I told him it was about the incident at Santa Anita, and he said, "Just a minute." He came back in about thirty seconds and said, "An escort will bring you to my office because it's about to start."

"As you speak," I replied, as a man in a sports coat was walking toward us. His office was as nice as the suite we were staying in. The interview was just starting when we walked in, and the lady doing the interview started by thanking Vickie for taking time out of her busy day.

Vickie said, "It's haunted me through all these years. I just don't understand why I didn't see him. I hate that he's been in that chair all this time."

The lady replied, "I think I can help you to understand. If you don't mind, we have footage of the accident. I'm sure it's not easy for you to watch, but I think it would be good for you to see it in slow motion."

Vickie replied, "I really do have trouble watching it, but if you have the film, go ahead and show it." She first showed it in regular speed, and I saw Vickie turn her head away just before the horse clipped her horse's heels.

The interviewer said, "I thought I might see you turn away. Have you ever watched the tape?"

Vickie whispered, "No, I can't watch it."

"Vickie, that's why you've blamed yourself all these years. It would do you a world of good to watch the film in slow motion." Vickie told her she'd watch it, and it clearly showed her look under her right arm. They went through the next few seconds, frame by frame, and it showed that, when Vickie pulled out, the other horse wasn't there. A tenth of a second after Vickie made her move, the other rider came out and didn't see her because he was looking behind. The lady said, "It just happened, Vickie, and neither of you were to blame."

"But they took my horse down," Vickie said while sobbing tears of relief.

"We knew that, so we went to the stewards in Seattle and showed them what you just watched. They said, if they had seen it frame by frame, it would have been different." Vickie was sobbing, so the interviewer walked over and hugged her.

Vickie kept saying "Thank you so much." I had to work really hard to hold back tears of my own because, without me really knowing it, she had become a huge part of my life. What started out as joking and having fun was starting to feel like so much more. *She's too young for you, Jim, so you're setting yourself up for another heartache.*

"We have a surprise for you, Vickie," the lady said while pointing at a TV screen.

A man in a wheelchair was on the screen and said, "Vickie, I didn't know that you've been carrying this around all this time." He told her he knew she wasn't there when he turned to see if someone was coming but knew she was there when he turned back around. He said, "We both started out at the exact, same time, so please know that I've never blamed you." He told her he had told his brother many times that it wasn't her fault, before saying "I'm the one that told him to come forward when he told me what he did. Regrettably, in my country, vengeance for family is a common practice. Please accept my apology on his behalf because he really is a good kid. He was becoming a very good rider, so it's a shame this had to happen. Thank you so much for setting up your fund for injured jockeys."

Vickie wanted to know if the rider might get a second chance, and the lady said, "We asked the racing commission that question, and the answer was **'Absolutely no!'** They told us they considered criminal charges but decided to drop the issue if he would leave the country and agree not to return." After hugging Vickie, she said, "We'd like to end this interview with a big 'Thank you' for the work you're doing for injured jockeys." She faced the camera and said, "Let's all wish her good luck in getting Wrong Way North to the Kentucky Derby." My heart was breaking, and I hoped the interview would help her to heal. *It seems we both have some healing to do.*

When they were off the air, I called her cell phone, and she answered right away. "You did a marvelous job," I whispered. She told me a heavy burden had been lifted off her, so I said, "Everything happens for a reason. Maybe without this you wouldn't have done so much for injured jockeys. You're such a lovely person."

She whispered, "That fund brings me so much relief."

I replied, "I'm sure you don't really know how much good you're doing. I feel very proud to call you my friend." After a long pause, she told me she felt the same about me. I thought she hung up rather abruptly, but she was probably crying. *I hope I haven't said too much.*

Tom said, "That's some jockey we have."

I replied, "She's a lovely lady too."

He asked, "How long are you guys staying?"

Norm answered, "No more than one more day, unless my hot streak continues."

He said, "Please stay as long as you want to." We thanked him for the beautiful suite and having us up to his office.

I said, "One thing I have to know, Tom, have you ever had sex on this desk?"

With a big smile on his face, he said, "I can't answer that." *I'm sure he nodded his head.*

I said, "Don't ever get too predictable, and don't think we'll take it easy on you."

He laughed and told us he wouldn't have it any other way, before saying "You know, Liz is right, you two are hoots."

We played the rest of the morning, but much to our dislike, we returned some of their money. We ate lunch at the buffet, and afterward, we went out for an exhilarating walk. It was good to see the golf we were playing had gotten us into pretty fair shape. We marveled at one of God's fine creations as the sun was glistening off the snow and the lake. I said a silent prayer, giving thanks for all that had happened to us during the past year, and asked God to help Vickie through her trying time. *I better back off a little before we both get hurt.*

When we were inside the casino, I decided to go up and take a nap, but Norm, the one who had been up all night, went right to the tables. I thought, *He must be going on pure adrenaline.*

It was four thirty in the afternoon when I woke up, and after getting cleaned up, I headed downstairs. Norm was still playing blackjack, so I bought my Keno numbers for five games before walking over to a let-it-ride table. The first game, I checked my cards and had a pair of jacks, so I placed them facedown while saying "Let it ride." The dealer's first card was a jack, so I was very pleased with the start. Her next card was also a jack, so I just shook my head as I turned over my two jacks. I couldn't believe how lucky I had been since we bought Charlie. *This just doesn't happen, so I really might be dreaming.*

After hitting nothing the next five hands, I decided to walk away. The cards were so bad that I only lost five dollars a hand, so I gave the dealer a fifty-dollar tip before putting away my profit of 725 dollars. The Keno games I played were over, so I checked my tickets. I had eighty-six dollars coming, so I played the games five more times, gave the girl six dollars, and still doubled my money. I believe that in gambling you go through hot and cold streaks. *Lady Luck does have her mood swings.*

I walked around looking at the machines, but my heart wasn't into playing like it was the first couple of days. I walked over to where Norm was playing blackjack with the cute dealer we played with on our previous trip. There was an open seat, so I sat down and bought a hundred dollars in five-dollar chips. I started out playing five dollars a hand, and at first, I was getting good hands, but hers were better. The fourth hand, she dealt me a blackjack, so the next hand, I put out ten dollars and was dealt another blackjack. *Maybe Norm's right.* I won six hands in a row, and when I lost, I went down to five until I won a hand. I was up eighty bucks when they changed dealers, so I gave our dealer ten dollars on her way out. I played five dollars a hand three more times, which I lost, so I walked away.

At six fifteen, I walked back and asked Norm if he was hungry. He wasn't, so I decided to go up to the room and call my niece Jamie. She worked for Comcast Sports and answered, "Hello, this is Jamie with Comcast sports." *She's so sweet.*

I identified myself before saying, "I called to tell you, unless Charlie gets hurt, he'll be in the Kentucky Derby, and it would be nice if you could make the race. We'll give you an interview if you can."

She replied, "It's so nice to hear from you. If you don't mind, I'll see if I can work it into my schedule."

I went back down to see if Norm was ready for dinner, and he wasn't hungry, so I told him I'd grab a sandwich to take up to the room. I went to the Burger Barn and ordered a burger and a salad to go. I was watching ESPN while eating when Vickie's interview showed again. I listened more intently that time because I didn't have all the emotions running through me. ESPN said some nice things about her personally and about what she was doing for injured jockeys. *Darn it, I wish she was closer to my age.*

Norm came up at eight thirty, and I told him he looked like death warmed over. He said, "I feel the same way." He climbed onto his bed with his clothes on and was asleep before his head could settle into his pillow. I watched TV until ten before drifting off to sleep.

I heard a knock on the door and wondered who would knock in the middle of the night. I heard the knock again, and a voice said, "Housekeeping."

It was ten thirty, so I shook my head a couple of times before saying "Just a minute, please." Through the door, I asked her to leave a set of towels. *I was sound asleep.*

She replied, "I'll leave them by the door." I put my jeans on and opened the door to pick them up. Norm was still sleeping, so I got cleaned up quietly and went downstairs. I walked to the Keno area and bought my numbers for five games. I didn't feel like walking around, so I sat down to watch the games. They only produced two dollars, so I told the girl to keep them.

I wasn't really into gambling, so I walked out by the lake. It was another beautiful day with the sun shining on the snow and water, so my mind drifted back to the times Linda and I came up. We didn't gamble much, so we spent a lot of time outside. We visited the house from the show *Bonanza* and the cowboy cemetery a few times. The area around the lake is so beautiful that we loved walking around and holding hands. *I miss her so much.*

Tom walked up and tapped my shoulder while saying "You look deep in thought."

That woke me up, and I replied, "I was thinking about the times Linda and I came up here on vacation."

"I'm sorry to disturb that," he said with a look of concern in his eyes.

"That's okay, I need to learn to live in the present."

He sat down and told me how much fun he was having since meeting us before asking, "By the way, where's Norm?"

I answered, "He stayed up gambling for two nights, so he's catching up on his sleep. I hope his bladder hasn't exploded because I didn't hear him get up last night."

He asked, "Shall we go up and make sure he's all right?"

"Sure, but let's go by the tables first. Just look for the table with the prettiest dealer because, if he's playing, that's where we'll find him." The dealer was gorgeous, and sure enough, he was there.

Tom laughed out loud while saying "You know him pretty well."

His laughter filled the room when I said "He's just an old pervert."

Tom asked, "Norm, I have one question, did your bladder explode?"

"Almost, why didn't you wake me up?" he asked me.

The dealer said, "Tom, you guys are terrible."

I replied, "No, it's just a normal bodily function."

Norm said, "Luckily, I woke up when you left. How long did I sleep?"

"Over twelve hours," I answered.

The dealer said, "That's really good. I don't think my bladder would last that long." We all started to laugh, and she asked Tom, "Where did you meet these crazy guys?"

"Now, Liz says they're hoots, and I think we should go with that."

"Hoots it is," she said.

I asked Norm if he had eaten, and his answer was "Not since lunch, yesterday."

The dealer told us she knew he was at the tables for a long time, so I said, "When it comes to playing cards, he's like the Energizer Bunny."

The dealer replied, "The Eveready Bunny, huh, now that brings a few things to mind."

Tom cleared his throat and asked, "Now who's being bad?"

"You misunderstood me totally," she said. We all laughed and let her get out of it gracefully.

After Tom went back to work, I stopped to buy my Keno tickets on our way to the buffet. We were getting ready to eat, and I could see the 1, 3, 5, and 7 were on the top line. I didn't count the numbers that had been called but could see there weren't many left. "Norm, think 9," I said. It just so happened, the last number to be called was 9, and I startled him when I pumped my fist and yelled "**YES!**"

He asked, "Did the 9 hit?" I told him it did, so he said, "Some of it's mine because I thought 9 really hard."

I told him I'd buy lunch, but he reminded me we had already paid. I said, "That's too bad." I then told him I'd buy dinner.

After lunch, I collected my tickets. Norm was playing blackjack, so I decided to play with him for a while. We played for two hours, and I lost eighty bucks but had a lot of fun.

I told him I'd see him later and went in search of a slot machine. I walked past a unicorn machine before walking back. I should have kept walking because I lost forty dollars in a very short time. I walked over to the sports book, and the eighth race was coming up at Golden Gate. Vickie was riding the 6, and the race was five minutes away. Her horse was thirty to one. She hadn't mentioned the horse, but they're surprised sometimes, so I put ten to win and place on him. There was a reason she hadn't mentioned him; he ran sixth out of eight. *I've been doing great betting the horses they give us, so don't get back into old habits that have proven costly.*

I spotted a *Star Wars* machine that had an open seat and sat down. It wasn't paying much, but often so I played on twenty dollars for over an hour. I cashed in thirty dollars ahead after having a lot of fun. I found Norm and said, "I'll buy dinner at the top-floor steak house if you're hungry." At dinner, we decided to go home the next morning.

We had fun and made some money, but it was time to go back to reality. I called and told the lady at the front desk that we'd be checking out the next morning. Five minutes later, Tom called to say "I hear you're leaving us."

I replied, "Somebody needs to keep an eye on Slim."

"You do that," he said before asking if we enjoyed our stay. I told him we couldn't wait to come back. *I can't believe how much he does for us.*

The trip back was beautiful, and there were many signs that spring was on the way. While driving, I told Norm how impressed I was with people who weren't afraid to take chances and told him about how the company I worked for was started. "In about 1895, two teenage brothers started walking from Ellensburg. First, they went to Walla Walla and worked there for two or three years. They then walked to Portland and started delivering teas and spices, house to house.

The company has been in existence for over a hundred years, and I've always been proud to tell people I worked for them."

"Where did you hear that?" he wanted to know.

"From the founder's son. Ellensburg was part of my sales area, so he talked to me about it every time we were together. He was one of the finest men I've ever met. He passed away some time ago but will be remembered for many years to come."

He asked, "How long did you work there?"

"Thirty-seven years, and I can't believe how quickly they passed."

We entered Sacramento at eleven thirty and were at the track by midafternoon. Steve was just getting there after his midday break and said, "Amazing how much went on while you boys were gone." I told him Tom kept us up on everything, and he said, "His horse ran really well, considering the break."

Norm replied, "Tom and Liz couldn't have been happier."

I said, "Liz asked if Slim could run with Charlie."

"What did you say?"

"Knowing they would never meet in a race, I told her, maybe going six furlongs."

Steve replied, "Even if it was three furlongs, he couldn't beat him."

"I know, it goes back to the difference in class issue." He told me he was glad I told her that before promising they would never meet. I said, "Tom and Liz have become good friends, so I would never want to hurt their feelings."

He asked, "How did you think Vickie handled herself in the interview?"

"She was very professional and kept her composure under extremely trying conditions, so I couldn't have been prouder of her. It's too bad she's carried that guilt for so long." Steve told us he and Sandy were the only ones around who had previously known about it.

I gave Steve the money that I put away for him, and he told us Charlie would work five the next morning. He said to me, "He'll be worked by the jockey that you find so attractive." I smiled and nodded while thinking, *She really is!*

I told Norm we had time for nine holes if he wanted to play.

"Will we keep score?" he asked.

I told him we'd decide after a couple of holes, so we grabbed our clubs and were there by four thirty. "We may play a couple holes in the dark," I said. We both took bogey on the first hole, and I shot par while he got a bogey on the second. I was away on the third hole, and my drive was flag high but fifteen feet to the right of the cup. Norm hit his shot very high, and the direction was perfect. I said, "If your distance is correct, you'll like this." The ball hit about five feet in front of the hole and started rolling right at the flag. We both held our breath, and when the ball stopped, I said, "I can see the ball, so it's not a hole in one, but it's darn close." His ball stopped two inches from the center of the cup, so I said, "If that had fallen in, I'd never hear the end of it."

"Now you'll hear about the one that got away," he told me while swatting me with his club.

I said, "I can live with that." He tapped his ball in for birdie, and my putt had the right distance but stopped an inch to the left of the hole.

"We'll keep score," he said. Going into the last hole, I was up by one, and both our shots were on the green. I was twelve feet from the pin and away. My putt was right in line but stopped three inches short. *I thought that was in.*

Norm had a nine-foot putt and looked it over really well. The sun was down, but we could see pretty well. His putt was going right at the hole, but an inch before the hole, it broke just a little to the right. It stopped two inches past the hole, so I said, "If you had been just a tiny bit firmer, it was in." I ended up 3-over par, and he was 4-over, so we agreed it was a fun round.

The next morning, we were in the backside café at six thirty and were both eating biscuits and gravy. Right in the middle of enjoying our breakfast, Vickie walked in and said, "Look at the two little piglets, eating biscuits and gravy."

I replied, "Mmmm, they're as good as they look."

She said, "You don't know how much I'd love to taste them, but if I had one taste, I'd eat both your breakfasts." I told her I wished I had her willpower, and she whispered, "That doesn't pertain to everything." I smiled and told her she was cute. I was doing my best to keep things professional, but she wasn't making it easy.

She bought an apple and sat down with us. I handed her the money that I kept for her, and Norm gave her some. She hugged both of us before saying, "You guys are way too good to me because letting me ride Charlie is more than I ever dreamed of."

I replied, "I'll tell you something, little lady, I bet a horse I liked up there, and it wasn't on the board, but since I've been betting only Charlie and the horses you and Steve have given me, I've made an obscene amount of money. I'm very happy to share it with both of you." I tapped her nose with my index finger while saying "On top of that, you're so darn good-looking."

"We would tell you anyway," she said before asking "What—what did you say?" I told her she would have to forgive me because I was only kidding.

I nodded when she asked me if I was afraid of her. Norm said, "I'm not kidding, and I'm not afraid to say, you're downright gorgeous."

She replied, "You guys need to go away more often because it's so nice when you get back." She then told us we were both crazy.

I said, "No, Liz says we're hoots."

"Hoots it'll be," she said before asking how Tom and Liz were doing.

"They're both very proud of their jockey, and they both said you were incredible in your interview. Believe me, Norm and I second that." She looked a little sad, but we could tell she was dealing with the situation. I whispered, "The offer to cry on my shoulder will always be there."

She thanked me for talking to her on the phone, before saying "I've talked with the injured jockey a couple times since we were on TV, and his brother asked him to apologize."

I said, "We've all done things we wish could be taken back. It's too bad he can no longer ride in this country, but your job is too dangerous to allow that kind of mindset to exist."

She whispered, "I suppose you're right, but I still wish he hadn't been banished for life." I told her she was way too sweet, but I didn't want her to change.

As she stood up to return to work, I asked, "Do you have any idea what he intended to do?"

She answered, "You won't like this, but his plan was to dive in and put me over the rail in the turn."

"That could have killed you and Charlie, so he should absolutely never ride again."

She whispered, "I know, but I still feel sorry for him." *I wish I could ravish her right now.*

"You're so lovely, and I hope you never change," I said before kissing her cheek while imagining it being her lips. *Wow, I need a cold shower.*

We walked back to the barn with her, and she walked to Charlie's stall to rub his nose while asking "How's my big boy today?" *It's wonderful seeing the love between them, but I wish it was me.*

Steve legged her up while saying "Work him five. I'd say go easy, but we both know that won't happen." The sun was bright, and the track looked fast. Steve said to the timer, "Wrong Way North working five furlongs." Charlie started jogging and bucked a couple of times to let Vickie know he was in charge. Entering the backstretch, he was in a pretty serious gallop, and when they reached the five-eighths pole, she shook his reins. He was in full stride in a second, and they were a blur going by us. I loved to watch him switch leads or at least to know he did. He leaned into the turn and didn't move an inch off the rail, all the way around. He switched back to his right lead just out of the turn, and I swear, he sprouted wings on his way to the finish line. Vickie sat up, but Charlie kept going. She was just getting him pulled up when they went by us, so she looked over and shook her head.

The clocker called down, "Off the record, he worked in fifty-seven and three. He so-called galloped out six in one minute and eight seconds flat, and the mile was one thirty-four and three." He laughed while saying "The form will show he worked five in one minute flat."

He asked if we were taking him to the Santa Anita Derby, and Steve said, "We haven't talked about it, but we don't need the graded money, so I think we'll find a softer spot for him."

The clocker said, "Wherever he goes, my money goes with him. You guys are doing Northern California proud."

Steve said to us, "I didn't want you to hear about my plan that way, but he asked, and he's done us many favors."

Norm replied, "You're the boss, and actually, I like your idea of saving his best for the Kentucky Derby."

When Vickie came back, she didn't know the time but knew it was fast. To her surprise, Steve said, "Just right."

She wanted to know how fast, and when Steve told her "fifty-seven and three," I could tell she was surprised. "He did it so easily. I wish the Kentucky Derby was today because nobody would have beaten him, and **I mean nobody**!"

When Charlie was on the walker, Steve said, "It's five weeks before the first Saturday in May, and there's a grade 3 on the grass next week. I believe we could win the Santa Anita Derby, but I don't wanna push him that hard before the Triple Crown races. Charlie can gallop and win the grade 3, and we'll go into Kentucky under the radar because he hasn't been in a grade 1. We can all make some money, betting him in the derby."

Vickie said, "I like not having a target on our backs." She blushed when I told her I'd been watching her from behind for a long time. "You're a big talker," she said while winking at me. I smiled as I wondered if she knew how good she looked walking away. ***Do girls think about that?***

While trying not to laugh, Steve said, "I'll turn him out for a week after his next race." We all told him we liked his plan, and again, the music was playing somewhere.

I told Vickie to get ready because she had a big kiss coming after the derby.

She winked while saying "I can handle you just fine, lover boy, and after that last remark, you better not be all talk." *She's so cute.*

I loved our interaction and loved the way she made me feel. I was so glad that our conversation on the phone didn't change things. One more time, I reminded myself that she was younger than my daughter, but she seemed to be enjoying our flirting as much as I was. I know I've said these things, before but the feelings were getting stronger. As I thanked God, I couldn't help wondering if Vickie was part of His blessings from the start. *She's too young for me.*

Norm and I played golf every day the next week. Neither of us had been able to shoot par, but we were getting closer. We were out playing the day before Charlie's race, and Tom called to ask, "Is Charlie okay?"

I answered, "He couldn't be better." He told me many people were saying he was ducking grade 1 company and was surprised when I told him we were.

"I don't understand, I thought you were going to Kentucky."

"We are if he stays sound, and the plan is to not push him more than we need to before then."

"I'm glad he's okay," he said before telling us to keep him posted. We agreed that he might be more nervous than we were.

Race day was warm, and there wasn't a cloud in the sky. I thanked God for the day and asked him to take care of Charlie and Vickie. I didn't wanna take the upcoming race for granted, but my mind was totally focused on the derby.

While eating at the café, we picked up a form and program. On the cover of the form, in big letters, it was written, "Nobody Knows Why Wrong Way North Keeps Ducking Grade 1 Company." One of the guys we had gotten to know asked me if that angered me. "Not at all, he needs to run but has enough earnings, so he doesn't have to face grade 1 horses. Believe me, he'll fire his best shot in Kentucky."

Charlie was picked right on top at eight to five, but his caption said, "Soundness is the only concern." There were two horses coming up from Santa Anita that had second and third billing, so I said to Norm, "There must be many people that think he's unsound because we haven't scared anyone."

We went to the barn but stayed away from Charlie because Steve told us he really had his game face on. I took a nap in the tack room and was awakened by my phone. Tom asked if I was as nervous as he was, so I said, "Tom, I've never said this before and may never say it again. Unless Charlie falls down or Vickie falls off, they'll win by as far as she wants him to."

He asked, "Are you serious?"

I explained, "After today, he'll not be the favorite in Kentucky because he'll go in having not won a grade 1, so we can all make some money."

He said, "Good luck, Liz and I'll be rooting for him."

I was glad when the horses were called over for the race, and when we walked into the paddock, I noticed that Charlie was three to one. I looked at Norm and said, "His health really is an issue."

"Either that or the Washington-bred thing," he replied. As always, Vickie winked when they walked by, and when they were on the track, I went up to make my wager. I bet at the same window I had been going to because I had become friends with the guy who sold me the tickets. I said, "Five thousand to win on the two please."

He looked at me kind of funny and said, "I've never seen you bet that much."

I explained, "Many people seem to think Charlie has health issues, but that says I don't agree." As I walked away, I heard him punch out a ticket for himself.

When the gate opened, Charlie was three to one, and Vickie took hold of him to let him settle comfortably on the rail. One of the horses from Southern California went right to the front, and Charlie was running very easily in third. The six pulled up beside them and settled, so I wondered if we had some race riding going on. Vickie was very content to be where she was. Going into the final turn, the leader was out by three, but I knew Vickie wasn't at all concerned. Coming out of the turn for home, the second-place horse drifted out just enough for Charlie to go through. She shook the reins, and he flew through so fast that he was almost on the leader before she swung him to the outside. She never showed him the whip, but he drew off to win by seven. I looked at the board, and he was still three to one. *That's the easiest fifteen thousand I'll ever make.*

The people were standing and cheering even after the pictures were taken, and I was so proud of him. "We're on our way," I whispered while trying not to laugh out loud. ***Next stop, Louisville, Kentucky!***

Walking out of the winner's circle, I shook Vickie's hand, and she could feel there were several bills in my hand. She said, "Thank you, but I should be paying you and Norm because I'm about to realize my lifelong dream of riding in the **Kentucky Derby.**" *She's so excited.*

"Think bigger, you'll be the first woman in history to win the Kentucky Derby, and the kiss you give me after the race will be payment enough."

She kissed my cheek and said, "Thank you so much." I just smiled because I had already said more than I should have. She winked and said, "Practice puckering up, sweetie pie, because you'll owe me that kiss in Kentucky."

I said, "In your words, it's in the bag." She went to the jockeys' room for her shower, and I tried hard not to visualize that lovely sight. I knew I was waking up after so many years of being turned out to pasture, and she was the reason, so I was very much in her debt. *Don't start something you're not ready to finish.*

On the walker, Charlie looked like he hadn't run. I had collected my wager, so I gave Steve a thousand dollars. Norm walked up and handed him some bills before telling me he put two thousand on Charlie. He wanted to know if I bet more, so I said, "A little more than that."

"Come on, how much?"

"All right, five thousand."

Steve heard us and said, "Don't you two get too much into gambling."

I replied, "Only with Charlie. The work he had a few days ago would have won this race, so I'll put ten K on him in the derby."

He replied, "That work would have put him in the thick of things in Kentucky. He'll get a much-deserved week off and should go to Kentucky just like he is now." *We really are on our way to Louisville!*

I asked Norm if it was really happening, and he answered, "Unless we wake up before the first Saturday in May, we're on our way."

I said, "I'm so glad you invited me to the sale and told me to be careful or they would take a bid from me. I can't help believing this entire journey was scripted by God because He knew I was getting depressed." Norm laughed when I said, "It does surprise me that He sent a heathen like you to do his bidding." *He's been a great friend for a long time.*

CHAPTER 7

Almost Time to Run for the Roses

Steve said, "That last race gives him just short of a million in graded earnings, so if he stays sound, the sky's the limit."

"Not a bad two-thousand-dollar investment," I replied.

Norm said, "Not an investment, a mistake."

I replied, "I can just see this in a movie. No one would believe it."

Norm's reply was "How could they? I can't believe it, and I've been here from the start."

On our way home, we decided to take our time and drive to Louisville. I said, "I haven't seen much of the country, so it would be fun to go by the Grand Canyon and see many of the sights along the way. We have a month, and I'd like to be in Louisville to enjoy the festivities of derby week." He agreed that it would be a nice adventure, so we decided to leave as soon as we could get things squared away.

We told Earl and Hank about the trip, and they told us to have fun and win the derby. They both bet the race earlier that day, and Hank said, "The odds aren't as good as they used to be."

I replied, "I didn't expect to get three to one, but his odds will be much better in the derby." Earl asked if I thought he could win, so I said, "Anything can happen when twenty horses are running, but he has enough tactical speed to avoid most of the problems. All in all, I think he has a very good chance. We'll be back in a couple months and should have plenty of money for our poker games."

We hooked up to the truck before going to bed so we could leave early the next morning. After a good night's sleep, we stopped by the track to let Steve and

Vickie know we were going. I said, "You both have our cell numbers if you need us, and we'll see you in Kentucky."

Vickie asked me, "When do I get to go?"

I replied, "You'll be in our hearts every mile."

"Talk, talk, talk," she said before hugging me.

"All kidding aside, you **will** be missed," I said before kissing her cheek. "No kiss for you, Steve, but you'll be missed also." I was surprised that I was so eager to get back on the road because I knew we would miss Vickie, Charlie, and Steve. *Why did I think of Vickie first? It'll be good to get away and let my head clear.*

We took I-5 south to Santa Clarita before heading east on Highway 40. After reaching the Grand Canyon, we pulled into an RV park before dark. They told us a bus would come through and give us a tour of the canyon if we wanted to take it. We met the bus at seven the next morning, and they showed us many really beautiful views of the canyon. *One of God's most beautiful works of art.*

I whispered, "Lord, you really outdid yourself here." They asked if we wanted to ride donkeys along the ridge, but we both told them we'd enjoy the beauty from a distance. We stopped at a barbecue restaurant for lunch. I was a little concerned about cleanliness, but actually, there was dust everywhere we went, and the food turned out to be very good. We got back to our trailer at five thirty, and both of us took another shower. We had been in dust all day, and it was awfully hot for that time of year. Tom called and asked about Slim, so I said, "Sorry, I forgot to tell you we were leaving. We'll arrive in Louisville for derby week."

"I envy you two," he replied.

I told him I'd let him know how Charlie was doing before the race. The next morning, I said to Norm, "We're close to Vegas if you wanna go in."

"If you don't mind not going, I'd like to get on the road."

We stayed on Highway 40 all the way across Arizona. The landscape was so different from what we have in Washington. Where we have millions of evergreen trees, they have millions and millions of rocks and rock formations. We saw roadrunners along the way, and let me tell ya, those things are fast. We stopped at a Mexican restaurant along the highway for lunch, and before nightfall, we entered New Mexico. We found an RV park close to Albuquerque and stopped for the night. We plugged into power without disconnecting the pickup because there was a small grocery store within walking distance. They had a very nice meat department, so we both picked out the steak we wanted along with a couple of large potatoes. *Nice to be back on the road. I miss Vickie.*

The next day, I said, "We shouldn't get to Kentucky too soon." We decided to stop at the next Indian casino we came to and only drove about twenty miles before we spotted one. We asked them if they had a place to hook up for the night. They pointed us to a place in the back and told us, as long as we gambled, there would be no charge. We missed breakfast, so we went to one of their restaurants for a quick meal. After eating, I bought my Keno tickets for five games and put them in my pocket while looking for a slot machine. *Funny how most of the places have much the same machines.* I sat down at a unicorn machine and started playing two hundred credits. On the second spin, the screen was almost completely populated with unicorns, and it rattled off "340 dollars." I played it a few more times, and the same thing happened. I was up to 680 dollars and cashed out when I was down to $670. Norm was playing three-card poker, and there were a couple of empty seats, so I sat down. He told me he was losing, so I pulled out a hundred and handed it to him before walking over to check my Keno tickets. Thirteen dollars showed on the screen, so I gave the girl three dollars and put the ten in my pocket. I spent the next hour looking at the art and artifacts on the walls.

After two more days, I hadn't won anymore, but I didn't give much back. Norm lost a couple of hundreds and said, "Playing on house money didn't work this time, but the hundred was appreciated."

The next morning, we headed east on Highway 40, and when we entered Amarillo, we decided to stop for the night. We talked about the bigtime poker players who had come from the area. Amarillo Slim and Texas Dolly were a couple that came to mind. I said, "Those guys had quite a life."

Norm asked, "Can you imagine playing poker for a living?"

"It sounds like fun, but I'd think there would be a lotta stress unless you had unlimited resources."

The next day, we drove through Little Rock, Arkansas, on our way to the home of Elvis, Memphis, Tennessee. We found an RV park twenty miles short of there and decided to stay the night. We wanted to arrive early the next morning so we could spend the day sightseeing.

We took the tour of Graceland, and I said, "I'm just a hunk a burnin' love." Norm wasn't nice at all when he told me I had fizzled out. We walked the streets and saw the tiny recording studio where Elvis recorded his first record for his mama. We spent the entire day walking around town, wondering if Elvis walked where we were walking.

I did a couple of verses of an Elvis song, and Norm said, "That's good, maybe you should take it on the road."

I replied, "Way too many people do Elvis." I did my Tiny Tim and said, "Maybe I could take that one on the road."

He frowned while saying "You might wanna leave that one home." *Not a nice man sometimes.*

The next day, we drove to Nashville and bought tickets for that night's Grand Old Opry. It was mind-boggling, sitting in front of the stage that Hank Williams performed on. I said to Norm, "Hank didn't seem to be a happy man."

He replied, "He drank a lot, so that could be why he was unhappy."

I said, "I've heard he didn't like the limelight, so it must have been **some change** for that country boy." Norm wanted to know if I did Hank, and I told him it didn't even sound good in the shower.

The next day, we drove to Louisville, and I was a little in awe, looking up at the twin spires. The track had a spot where we could hook up through the race. We spent quite a bit of time looking around town and visited the gym where the young Cassius Clay started his boxing career. He really brought boxing back from the depths. The Louisville Lip, he was called, and he was fun to watch in his younger days. He was known for picking the round he would knock his opponent out, and it was amazing how many times he was right.

Norm said, "He was fast for a man his size."

He laughed when I said, "Almost as fast as me." I surprised him when I broke out my Ali voice and said, "I'm gonna hit him with left and hit him with a right and Smoky Joe Frazier gone plum outta sight. The referee just stands with a frown 'cause he can't start countin' till Joe comes down. If you come to the fight, get a seat by the door 'cause it'll be over by round number 4. If he don't call me Muhammad Ali, I may take him out in round number 3. If he don't do what I want him to do, I'll finish him off in round number 2. If the first fight, he still think he won, I'll knock him out in round number 1. He may not even make it through the weigh-in, he's so chicken and frail, he may pass out right on the scale."

"That one I like," he said.

I explained, "I did a full routine of Ali at a company function when I worked for Carnation. I was out alone delivering milk at four in the morning, so I had a lotta time to fool around with different voices."

Three days before the race, Steve arrived with Charlie. He also brought Slim for an ungraded stake going five furlongs, two days before the derby. I went to

Charlie's stall when he was settled in, and he laid his head on my shoulder. I scratched his neck and said, "You only get one chance at this, buddy." He snuggled a little closer as if to say "It's on me now, so you just relax." I rubbed his jaw briskly while saying "I love ya, big guy."

My cell phone rang, and when I answered, a sweet female voice asked, "Is this Uncle Jim?"

I replied, "Well, I'm an uncle. Who's calling?"

"Your niece Jamie."

I said, "Oh, hi, sweetie."

"Is Charlie okay?" she asked.

"I was just hugging him, and he seemed fine."

She asked if I was kidding, and I told her I wasn't, so she said, "It's unbelievable that a horse, three days from running in the Kentucky Derby, would snuggle with you."

"They totally change when they walk onto the track."

She told me she could be there by Friday if we could still give her the interview, so I asked, "Do you want it before or after the race?"

"Would you consider both?"

I answered, "For you I certainly would."

She said, "I'll see ya then." *That cute little rascal isn't very talkative*, I thought before putting my phone back into my pocket. Her mom, Wendy, and Linda were always very close, so Wendy really took it hard when Linda was killed. Linda was a great wife and mother, and oh, how I wished I could stop missing her so much. I knew God was using Vickie to help me get to that point, so I wasn't about to rush things. She was way too sweet for me to try something that might make me look like a dumb old man. Just being around her was enough for a while.

We invited Steve to dinner, but he told us there was no way he would leave the horses because, if anything happened to them, Vickie would wring his neck. I told him we would bring something back for him, and he said, "A hot sandwich would be nice." I started to walk away but turned around and asked if Tom and Liz would make Slim's race. "Tom told me there's no way he can get away during Kentucky Derby week, so he's counting on you and Norm to root Slim home."

The backside café was nice but not as fancy as I thought it would be. They had a Western steak special. I wasn't sure what a Western steak was, but I ordered one for myself and one to go. The steak was very good but, it seemed like any other steak to me. If they wanted to call it Western, I didn't care. Steve was surprised when I brought him the steak dinner and tried to pay me, but I said, "No, just win the race."

"He's ready," he said before telling me he was thinking about making a wager.

Two days before the derby, Slim was in the third race. He was the one horse, and his morning line was ten to one. The big crowd had not yet arrived, so we had no problem getting into the paddock. When he came in, he was on fire so the groom had a real problem holding him while Steve saddled him. I hadn't seen Vickie, so I was very pleased when she walked over and hugged Norm first and then me. She stepped back and said, "You two will never know how much Charlie means to me."

I replied, "**Not to mention Jim and Norm!**"

"Didn't I mention that?" she asked with a wink and very lovely smile.

Slim strutted onto the track, and when I looked at the board, he was fourteen to one. My big bet would be Charlie, so I just bet fifty to win and place on Slim. He was seventeen to one when the gate opened and Vickie got him out, right on top. *Better break than last time.* She kept a firm hold on him, so he was never more than a length in front, all the way around the turn. What a great ride Vickie put on him, and just as the favorite looked like he would take the lead, she hit Slim three quick smacks. He dug in and stayed a length in front all the way to the wire. I swear, they could have gone another mile, and he would have still won. Coming into the winner's circle, Vickie said, "He's improving every time out."

Just after the picture was taken, my phone rang, and Tom wanted to talk to Steve. Nothing worse than a one-sided phone call. "Ya, he did—I think he is. We'll see you when we get back."

When Vickie dismounted, Steve handed her the phone. "He sure did—I believe he is—thank you for putting him in my hands." She hung up.

I looked at the tote board, and he paid thirty-seven dollars and twenty cents to win and $13.80 to place, so I got back just over a thousand dollars. "That won't cover what I plan to bet on Charlie, but it's a step in the right direction," I said to Norm. I gave Steve a hundred dollars and said, "I'm saving my big bet for Charlie."

He thanked me before saying "Charlie will definitely have odds."

After Vickie showered, I gave her a hundred and told her I loved the ride she put on Slim. She kissed my cheek and told me again how much she appreciated us giving her the opportunity. I must have squeezed her a little too tight when I told her she made it possible, but she felt so good in my arms that I didn't wanna let go.

I apologized after she said "Easy, big guy, you could hurt someone." She then told me she was kidding.

I kissed her very quickly on the lips and said, "Just warming up for Charlie's win."

"You better not be all talk this time," she said before kissing me back in a way that surprised me.

"You just win the Derby," I told her before thinking *That's the sweetest kiss I've had since Linda's accident. I really do like this lady, and she'll be mine someday.* ***Like that might happen!***

When we were at Charlie's stall, a camera team from a major network asked if they could interview us. Norm said he was camera shy and asked if I'd do the interview. They had us sitting on one side, and a young man doing the interview was across us.

He said, "My first question will start with a statement. Your horse has never run in a Grade 1, so why should I bet him in the Derby?"

I answered, "First of all, your statement is correct, and to answer your question, I think it would be foolish to bet him, from a handicapper's perspective."

"My second question is, will you bet him, and if so, why?"

I answered, "Yes, I've always been guilty of betting with my heart when one of my horses runs."

He said, "Your honesty is quite refreshing. My last question is, when so many big named riders are available, why are you riding Vickie?"

While trying to hold my temper, I said, "I wish the question before had been your last because you insulted our trainer, our rider, and all of us at the same time."

"I certainly didn't mean to," he replied.

While feeling myself starting to relax, I said, "Vickie has been an intricate part of this horse's success from the start, and there has never been another rider we've even considered."

He replied, "Please accept my apology, sir."

"I do forgive you, and I'm sorry for getting upset, but Vickie is a very important part of our team." He thanked me and set out in search of another owner to interview. I'm sure he hoped for a less volatile one. *My nerves are really on edge.*

As soon as the interview was over, my phone rang, and a female voice whispered, "I think I'm falling in love."

My reply was "Good, with whom?"

"You, you big dummy," Vickie said before telling me she loved what I said.

"You know that Norm and I feel you're a huge part of our success, and quite frankly, we wouldn't want anyone but you riding for us."

"I just wanted to thank you," she said in a low voice.

"Does that mean you're no longer in love with me?"

She laughed before saying "I'll catch ya later." *Gotta keep it business.*

We went to bed early that night, and Norm asked, "Do you think we belong in this race?"

"I really do because the only time he's lost is when he fell down. One of the things in his favor is his speed in a twenty-horse field, and I think he can stay in front of the traffic problems."

"We'll see in a couple days," he said. I drifted off to sleep, thinking about the race. "They're off in the Kentucky Derby." Charlie took the lead right out of the gate and was ahead by ten, turning for home. "Go, Charlie, go, go, go!"

"Jim, are you okY?" I was still half asleep and asked him what he wanted. He said, "I thought you were gonna fall out of your bed. You must have been having a bad dream."

I replied, "On the contrary, Charlie was ten lengths ahead in the lane."

"Did he win?" he asked with great expectation in his voice.

"I don't know because some goofy guy woke me up before he reached the finish line." I didn't dream the rest of the night, but when I was awake, I could see him bounding home on top. It had been the best run of fun and excitement anybody could ever hope for.

Norm was getting out of the shower, and I said through the door, "No matter where Charlie finishes tomorrow, he's been so much more than we could have hoped for."

"I was thinking the same thing in the shower. All the years of disappointment in this business have led us to this point. Let's cherish every moment we have with Charlie, no matter what happens in this race, because he's the best thing that's ever happened to us. It sure beats freezing in Yakima and going down for coffee every morning. Even if he runs dead last, I'll be happy because it's a big honor to run in the most prestigious race in the world."

I said, "Believe me, Norm, this guy will not run last, and that I promise you. I can't believe it's almost time to run for the roses." *Vickie and this race are too much excitement for a guy my age.*

We had breakfast at the backside café, and there were two horsemen sitting at a table beside us. They didn't know us, so it was fun listening to them. One of them asked the other what he thought about the Washington bred. "If he had shown he could beat grade 1 horses, I think he'd be a real threat, but it looks like they've been ducking the top horses."

The first guy said, "I think he'll run better than people think. Call me crazy if you want to, but I put twenty dollars on him to win. He'll have huge odds."

The other guy told him he enjoyed the interview, before saying "The questions reporters ask are completely stupid sometimes."

The first guy replied, "The major races don't come around that often, and with some of the reporters, they are the only exposure they have to horse racing. The owner handled it really well by letting him know he was out of line, respectfully."

As we were walking back to the barn, Norm told me he was proud of the way I handled the interview. "He was a nice kid, and I think it's like the guy said in the café, he doesn't work with horse racing enough to know what to ask. He has no idea how much owners love their horses and riders. Let's just hope Charlie makes him understand why we're doing things the way we are. I'll tell you right now, if Charlie wasn't ours, I wouldn't bet him." We were almost to the barn when he asked me if I was betting much on him. "Ten thousand to win," I replied.

He laughed and told me I was crazy, before saying "You just said you wouldn't even bet him if he wasn't ours."

"That's correct, if he wasn't ours, I'd have no way of knowing how good he is." I smiled as I thought, *I might bet him because of the way Vickie fits his saddle. As athletic as she is, she has to be amazing.*

Vickie was at the barn when we arrived, and she said, "It's about time you guys got out of bed."

I laughed and said, "It's so nice to sleep in and dream about our jockey."

She shook her head while saying **"You're such a big talker!"**

I said, "My niece works for Comcast Sports, and she'll be here sometime this afternoon. I hope we can get together to give her an interview." Steve wanted to know if they could set up at the barn, and I said, "I'm sure they can."

Vickie told me to call her cell phone when they were ready, before coming over to hug me. She whispered, "I really did appreciate the way you defended me."

I looked down and asked, "Are you cold?" Her eyes were big, and she wanted to know why I asked. She seemed relieved when I told her she was shivering. She told me she was excited about the race before kissing my cheek and telling me she had all kinds of feelings running through her. *Me too!*

"You will be the first female rider to win the derby," I promised her before telling her to practice puckering up. She slapped my shoulder and was shaking her head as she walked away. I thought, *Even the slap felt good.* I wondered if there was any way Charlie could possibly know how much he had done for me. *I'd ask Vickie out if she wasn't so darn young.*

Steve said, "Charlie galloped this morning, and he's razor-sharp, so if he doesn't win, it's because he doesn't fit with these. In my opinion, he's at least as good as any three-year-old running, and now all we have to do is show the world."

I asked, "Why do I hear inspirational music when you say things like that?" He told me he didn't know but wanted me to keep the thought. "You **will** win your first derby," I promised him.

My cell phone rang, and Jamie said, "Uncle Jim, we're pulling into the back of the track." I told her I'd meet her there, and when the gate opened, a Comcast van pulled in. A tiny arm waved out of the driver's-side window, and when I walked up, Jamie stepped out to hug me. She thanked me for the interview before telling me how much she was looking forward to the race.

"I'm very happy you could come out," I told her before calling Vickie to tell her the interview was about to start. She was there in two minutes. Jamie sat on one side, and the four of us sat across her. She told us how much she appreciated us taking time out of our day to talk to her, and I was very impressed by how well she handled herself.

"First, I'll ask Steve, have you had a horse in the derby before?"

"I have not," he answered. She then asked how he thought Charlie would run. "He couldn't be doing better, so I think he's primed to run a huge race."

She kinda surprised me when she asked him, "Do you think he's good enough?"

Steve thought for a couple of seconds before saying "Yes, I believe he is."

"Vickie, you're one of the reasons I wanted to be here. What would it mean to you to be the first female in history to win this coveted race?"

Vickie thought for a few seconds before saying "I like your directness. I don't mean to take so long answering, but it makes me somewhat emotional. First of all, every jockey that rides anywhere dreams about winning this race. To be the first woman to win it is more than I can comprehend. It would be fabulous, historical—I'm sorry, I just can't put it into words. It means so much to me."

Jamie said. My last question for you is "Do you think he's good enough?"

"There's no doubt in my mind that he's at least as good as anything in the race, and right now, he's training like a monster."

Jamie said, "Let's take a little break." When the cameras were off, she took a drink from her water bottle before telling Vickie she was sorry for putting her on the spot. She said, "You don't know how much I'm pulling for you and every woman in our office wanted me to tell you how much it would mean to them, for you to win this race." I could tell she was concerned when she said "Please, I don't mean to put added pressure on you."

Vickie told her how much her words meant, before saying "Don't worry about the pressure. When the gate opens, it'll be just like any other race. I set out to win every time I ride, so I'll be focused on riding the best I can. If I win, I'll be so excited afterward, but not until afterward."

We went back on the air, and Jamie asked, "Norm, my question for you is, how did you acquire this horse?"

Norm laughed while saying "Somehow I thought it might be."

He explained how we bought him, before Jamie said "I have an advantage over most people because I've heard so much about the purchase from my family. For those who don't know, Norm's partner, Jim, is my uncle." She asked Norm, "At what point did you realize the mistake you made wasn't that bad?"

"Wow, that's a fantastic question. It's really hard to set a time, but my first thought would be his first race. However, we were hearing great things about him from the first week we started training him in Yakima. I'm not helping you much, but I can't put an exact time on it. What I'll say, he has been the most wonderful thing that could happen to a retired man and has made my life complete."

She said, "That was a better answer than I could have hoped for." She looked at me a little apprehensively before looking into the camera and saying, "Jim is my grandpa's brother, and they both enjoy teasing a little."

I said, "Jamie, I'm nothing like my brother. I'm much thinner."

She laughed before saying "He told me you'd say that. When did you decide to buy part of the horse?"

"On our drive back to Yakima after the sale. Norm had such a pathetic look on his face that I had to help him." After laughing, I said, "In all honesty, I spent quite a bit of time reading the sales book while the horses were going through. Two or three of them jumped out at me because of their bloodlines. Charlie—forgive me, his nickname is Charlie—was one of the first horses that appealed to me. I told Norm it may not be such a bad thing."

"Norm said Charlie is one of the best things that has happened to him. Do you feel the same way?" she asked me.

I answered, "Next to God, family, and country, he's absolutely the best. Like Norm said, he's made my life complete, and I do believe he's a special gift from God."

"One more question, do you think he'll win?"

Without hesitation, I said, "Yes, I do. A pretty girl like you should have a dozen roses, and I expect Charlie to win those for you. A dozen will also go to the first female in history to win the Kentucky Derby." I winked at her before asking "Jamie, have you ever seen a jockey as lovely as ours?"

Vickie reached over and slapped my arm before Jamie smiled and said, "I don't believe I have."

Vickie, in her modest way, said, "Thank you both." *Someday little girl, someday.*

Jamie said, "I wanna thank all of you for your thoughtful answers." When the cameras were off, she asked if we were still on for the interview after the race.

I said, "Win, lose, or draw, I'll be there." All the others said they would also, and we all told her how wonderful her interview was. I invited her to dinner, but she had a lot of work to do before the race. I said, "If he wins, be sure to get in the winner's circle and have your picture taken with us."

She replied, "I will, but I'm sure I'll see you before that." We all thanked her one more time before I told her she might put a few dollars on Charlie.

Norm, Vickie, and I went to a nice restaurant that night. Vickie ate very small portions of her food while saying "I'm so excited about tomorrow, but please don't think I'll ride any differently than any other race."

I said, "Vickie, you are Charlie and he is you. He wouldn't be here without you."

She replied, "He could win with any rider."

Norm said, "As long as you're healthy and want to ride him, we'll not find out." She touched his hand and thanked him.

We had fun talking about his past races and different ways she could ride him in the derby. "He's very versatile so with twenty horses, I plan to use his natural speed to be in front of most of the traffic, if he breaks well. I'm glad we drew the 8 post." She was very businesslike when she continued, "The 1 and 2 seem to need the lead and with their draw, they'll surely fire out if they can. My plan A is to sit a couple lengths behind them for a good portion of the race." *I enjoy listening to her describe her strategy.* **What don't I like about her?**

At eight thirty, we decided to call it a night. Norm and I received nice hugs before walking her to her car. I told her she meant the world to me, and she kissed my cheek very softly before climbing into her car. *Her eyes are such a beautiful blue.*

I woke up at six thirty to a wonderful, sunny day and asked God to protect Charlie and Vickie during the race. As always, I stopped short of asking for the win, but asked him to let Charlie run his best. Norm started to move around, so I was looking at him when his eyes opened. "You're starting to sleep later," I said.

He got up and kind of made up his bed while saying "I'll take the first shower if that's okay."

"Leave me some hot water" was the last thing he heard before closing the door. I started some coffee and heated a sweet roll while humming "My Old Kentucky Home." I probably would have been singing, but I didn't know the words. I stepped outside to enjoy the morning sun as one of the exercise riders was walking by. He told me he'd be rooting for us, so I thanked him before walking back inside. He would probably root for one of the local horses, but it was a nice thing for him to say. *I wonder if Vickie is nervous right now.* I smiled as I thought about the frightened look she gave me when I asked her if she was cold. It was obvious that she was excited about something.

Knowing Tom was an early riser, I called him and said, "Charlie couldn't be doin' better."

He asked, "Has Vickie mentioned how she plans to ride the race?"

"As a matter of fact, we talked about it quite a bit last night at dinner. She hopes to be in third, behind the 1 and 2, if things work out, and try to stay out of traffic, if at all possible."

"Are you gonna bet him?" he asked and was shocked when I told him I'd bet ten thousand on him to win. "Are you crazy?" he asked.

I went over how my horse account was separate and how it wouldn't hurt me, before saying "If things work out the way I hope they will, he'll never get these odds again." He told me he noticed he was listed at thirty to one in the form, so I said, "I won't tell you he'll win, but he's much, much better than thirty to one." He told me they were having a big party in the sports book, and he made sure Charlie's picture was front and center. I said, "Enjoy the race, and root hard, my friend." He wished us good luck before saying goodbye.

It was seven fifteen so after my shower, Norm and I decided to go to the café for breakfast. We both ordered big breakfasts, knowing we wouldn't eat again before the race. The place was totally focused on the derby, but after the interviews, we were a little more recognizable, so I'm sure we missed out on some of the people's thoughts. After breakfast, we walked to the barn, and I said to Steve, "We'll keep watch on Charlie while you take a shower and have breakfast." Charlie was beautiful even with his muzzle on. He was unimpressed with all the hustling going on around him, so I said to Norm, "If he's this cool, we should be too."

"Sounds good to me," he said before asking if I'd stay with Charlie while he went to the café to buy a program. I leaned my chair back against Charlie's stall and sat on the back legs. I was just starting to doze off when Norm returned with the program.

He looked disappointed when he said "Charlie's thirty to one in here too."

I asked, "What race is he in?"

"What do you mean?"

I said, "What I mean is, it's the Kentucky Derby, and only twenty horses in the world can be in the race. How many horses around this world would love to be thirty to one in there?"

"You always have to be so logical," he said while sounding like an agitated wife.

"Actually, I'm completely in awe of everything that's going on."

The races would start at 11:00 a.m., but our race wouldn't run until 5:00 p.m., so I leaned back against the stall and fell asleep. The call to post for the first race woke me, and I shouted, "I have to make sure Charlie's where he was when I fell asleep!" I had such a startled look that the others laughed out loud.

"Bad dream?" Norm wanted to know.

"I thought I had abandoned my post. Steve said Vickie would kill him if he lost Charlie, so what's to say she wouldn't do the same to me?"

"She would," Steve said while continuing to laugh.

I replied, "She couldn't be tough enough to whip both of us."

Still laughing, he said, "I wouldn't bet on it. Did you hear the party in the infield last night?"

I replied, "I wear earplugs to drown out Norm's snoring, so I didn't hear a thing." I turned to Norm and said, "I'm going out to survey the damage."

He replied, "Wait up, I'll go with you." After looking around, he said, "It looks like the aftermath of a nuclear bomb."

I said, "To me, it looks like a rock festival."

He wanted to know if I went to Woodstock, so I explained, "I've never been to New York, but I went to two of them in southwestern Washington." He asked what they were like, and I said, "They were all about peace and love. Believe me, Norm, there was a lotta love goin' around. Both men and women took baths in the river. Many walked through the crowd topless, and some were naked."

"Did you do that?" he asked.

"I walked around topless. We had pictures at one time, showing signs of drugs for sale, so I guess the police didn't wanna go in as long as things were peaceful."

He asked, "Did anyone fight?"

"I saw one guy acting tough and start to get into one, but four or five guys threw him back and told him there would be none of that. Believe me, he agreed right away. Linda and I went to both of them together and had a great time."

He sighed while saying "Just redneck cowboys where I grew up."

I said, "I like cowboys, and I **really** like cowgirls."

He laughed and said, "I'm gonna tell Vickie enough is enough. She's really rekindled your appreciation of women."

We walked through the crowd, and almost everyone looked very tired and hung over. They were mostly young kids looking for a party, and believe me, they found one. A young girl darted from one tent to another without clothing, so I said, "I stand corrected, this is not like a rock festival, it is one, and just so you know, **I appreciated her**."

He said, "I'm glad we came out here because I've never seen a rock festival."

"Are you saying there were no hippies in Oklahoma?"

"If there were, they kept to themselves."

I asked, "Didn't kids give the peace sign?"

"They gave half of it many times."

We were both laughing when we reached the barn, so Steve asked, "See something you liked?"

I answered, "Some very interesting things that took me back a whole bunch of years."

He said, "We all had our wild times when we were younger."

Norm replied, "Not me." We didn't know whether to believe him or not, so we left it alone so we wouldn't hurt his feelings.

The horses were being called to post for the sixth race, and I was glad the day was passing quickly. We were in the eleventh, so we still had a while to go, but talking about other things like the party helped to relieve some tensions. "I'm going to the café," I said before asking if anyone wanted anything.

Both Norm and Steve said, "Coffee sounds good." I bought all of us coffee and sweet rolls. We laughed and joked with one another until the horses were called over for the tenth race.

Steve said, "We're on deck." Even though Charlie had been wearing a muzzle, Steve rinsed his mouth and throat. "Can't have him sucking a straw down his windpipe," he said. While he flexed all four of his legs, Charlie was patient, but I could tell he knew it was race day. I wondered if he knew what race day it was. I was shivering, but it wasn't cold. *I can't believe this is about to happen!*

After the tenth, we met Steve going out of the holding barn, and he asked me if I wanted to lead him over.

"Too much on the line," I replied. My stomach was in knots, and my top lip was twitching.

He glanced at Norm, and he said, "**Don't even ask!**"

We were very proud to be walking alongside Steve and Charlie on our journey to the paddock. The closer we got, the louder the roar became. It reminded me of being in the Kingdome after Seattle scored a touchdown. It was like a roar that had a life of its own, but Charlie acted like it was just another day. *I love him so much.*

I said, "That's class, I can't believe this is really gonna happen." Norm just took a deep breath. I couldn't believe the people around the paddock. They were pushing, trying to get a better look at the best three-year-olds in the world. Anticipation hung in the air like a dense fog, and my heart was in my throat. ***Almost not worth it!***

We were in the center of the paddock when Vickie came in. She hugged Norm before hugging me, then stepped back before saying "You'll never know what this means to me." I told her we were lucky to have her riding for us. ***Can't wait for them to leave the gate.***

Charlie was thirty-five to one. The favorite was five to two and was in the 13 post. I started telling myself how foolish it would be to bet ten thousand dollars, and I had almost talked myself out of it when I saw Vickie ride by. She winked, and I thought, *I can't change my mind.* She was like a beautiful angel appearing from the fog, and it wasn't until that moment that I realized just how much I had missed her.

I remembered that most of the money I had to bet came from that gorgeous lady, and with her confident wink, there was no way I could change my mind. Even if I lost all the money I had won, meeting Vickie and enjoying the adventures we had lived along the way would make it all worthwhile.

Every horse in the field looked like a world champion, so just having a horse running against them was something that I never thought would happen. *Is it possible that I'll wake up when the horses cross the finish line? Lord, please keep Vickie and Charlie safe, and let him run his best. I know I shouldn't ask for the win, but any help would be appreciated in this race.*

Norm startled me when he smacked my back and said, "Whatever happens, I'm glad we're going through this together." *I am too, my friend, and I'm glad we're giving Vickie a shot at making history. Someday, little lady, someday.*

CHAPTER 8

Vickie Realizes Her Dream

As the horses walked onto the track to "My Old Kentucky Home," I hurried inside to make my bet. Charlie was still thirty-five to one, and I wondered if my wager would change his odds. "Ten thousand to win on the eight," I said before betting two separate hundred-dollar win tickets. One was for Vickie and one for Steve. It was a madhouse outside, so I walked over to where I could see a TV and anchored myself. Somehow, Norm found me in the mess, and I asked, "How did you see me?"

"I didn't, I saw the television."

"They're off in the Kentucky Derby" rang out over the crowd noise. The 1 and 2 were dueling for the lead at a reasonable pace, and Charlie was third, two lengths back. He had a beautiful spot on the rail, in front of the pushing and shoving that was going on behind him. Up the backstretch, all but the really late runners were jockeying for position. A couple of the middle runners were trying to get into contention but were being shuffled to the outside.

I said so Norm could hear, "Patience, Vickie." Just before they entered the turn for home, Vickie shook his reins so they wouldn't be swallowed up by the charging hoard. Charlie hugged the rail all the way around the turn, but the 2 was dropping back, so Vickie swung him to the outside, entering the lane. With a quarter of a mile to go, he pulled alongside the leader and was nose to nose with him. Out of the corner of my eye, I saw the 13 moving fast and said to Norm, "This race will be talked about forever." The three horses were in a straight line across the track, and about a hundred yards from the wire, the 13 put his head in front.

I grimaced and said, "At least get second, Charlie." A chill went up my back when he dug down and put his head back in front. His winning margin was a neck, and I said, "Vickie was right, he simply refuses to lose." The photo sign was on the board, but I knew it had to be for second. It was down in a matter of seconds, and 8, 13, 6, and 15 were posted. I shouted, "**Norm, it really happened!**"

"It sure did, let's get to the winner's circle."

I slapped each leg while hoping they wouldn't fail me as we started walking slowly toward the winner's circle.

Jamie appeared out of nowhere like a guardian angel and said, "You were right, Uncle Jim." I asked her if it was a dream, and she promised it wasn't. I put my arm around her as we walked into the winner's circle, and when Charlie walked in, he was bleeding from the outside of his right rear leg.

I asked Vickie what happened, and she said, "The 13 stepped on him during the gallop out, but I'm sure he'll be fine." Her beautiful face was glowing like a gorgeous sunset as I thought, *If only I was a few years younger.*

I replied, "I'm looking at a jockey who's awfully fine." She laughed while telling me I was a terrible flirt. We had a wonderful time getting our pictures taken, and no one had to tell us to smile. They took us to a podium for the trophy presentation, and Jamie nodded when I asked her to go with us.

A young lady was doing the interview, and her first question was to Steve. "This is your first Kentucky Derby, and it was a winning one, so please tell us what you're thinking right now."

He said, "I was amazed when he dug down and came back in the lane." She congratulated him before going on to Vickie.

Vickie was sobbing, so the lady asked if she could answer a question. Vickie nodded, so she said, "This is a lot of emotion. Would you mind telling us where it's coming from?"

"This is the most exciting day of my life. Steve had a wonderful plan, and it came together beautifully. We were being ridiculed for supposedly ducking grade 1 horses, but we had plenty of graded money, so why should we push him any harder than we had to?"

The lady said, "Steve had the last laugh."

When she went to Norm, his answer was short and sweet, "I couldn't be happier."

Jamie was before me and had her Comcast badge on, but the lady showed class when she ignored it. She asked her for her thoughts, and Jamie said, "This is unbelievable. This is my first Kentucky Derby, and my uncle's horse won! I'm so happy for them."

I had plenty of time to think before she came to me, so when she put the microphone in front of my face, I blurted out, "**Refuse to lose!**"

The lady said, "Pardon me."

I explained, "A couple months ago, Vickie said this horse refuses to lose, and that was the Seattle Mariner motto, the first year they won the pennant. You saw when the favorite pulled alongside him, he simply refused to let him go by."

"I love it," she said before thanking us for the interview.

On our way off the podium, Jamie asked us if we wanted her interview then or when everyone had settled down. Steve said, "I'd appreciate you waiting a little while." He wanted to see what damage had been done to Charlie's leg. I went inside to cash my tickets and collected over 360,000 dollars, so I asked them to give me a check. I also cashed both hundred-dollar tickets, and they each received a little over $3,600. *We'll never get odds like this again, but who cares,* **we won the Kentucky Derby!** You only get one chance, and Charlie made the most of it.

My phone rang as I was walking outside. Tom was calling to congratulate us, and I asked if he bet him. "After talking to you, I put a thousand on him to win, and that paid for Slim. The question is, did you bet what you said you would?"

"I almost talked myself out of it three times, but I just collected a check for 360,000 dollars."

After I was off the phone, Norm said, "Until now, you've won more betting on him than your 20 percent of the purse money. Is that still true?"

I asked, "What did I tell you I'd bet?"

"I fully expected you to change your mind."

I said, "I was thinking about it until Vickie winked, and I decided I had to bet it."

He asked, "Will you give her some money?"

"I got them each hundred-dollar win tickets."

"I just got them twenty dollar wins." He laughed while saying "You just have to stay ahead of me."

"They each earned 120,000-dollar commission, and you own 80 percent of the horse, so I think they're pretty happy with what you've done for them."

When we arrived at the barn, there were some long faces. "What's goin' on?" I asked. Charlie's adrenaline was wearing off a little, and he wasn't putting much weight on the leg.

The vet explained, "The cut is not a problem, but I'm sure he has a bone bruise." I asked if it could end his career. "No, but it may knock him out of the Triple Crown chase. We'll know more in the morning."

Vickie was devastated when she heard the news. I gave them both the money from their wagers before saying "He's a gelding, so he'll run many more times, if he stays sound."

Vickie said, "Yes, we must think of the horse." It didn't take long for the mood to improve.

After getting Vickie alone, I kissed her a little longer than I should have before saying "You'll have to forgive me, but I had to kiss the first lady in history to win the Kentucky Derby. You have no idea how long I've looked forward to that kiss."

She said, "Please don't apologize, you gave me extra incentive to win the race." I really can't describe the look she was giving me, but she certainly wasn't upset. Her face was a little flushed, and I was just about to tell her how much she meant to me when the ringing of my phone brought us both some needed relief. *It must remain business*, I thought before answering my phone. I never understood when people said, "It just happened," but I was definitely caught up in the moment.

Jamie asked if she could interview us, so I said, "Come on back."

Vickie looked up at me with what I decided was desire in her eyes and whispered, "Saved by the bell." I hugged her and told her I loved the way she rode Charlie. *Keep it business.*

Jamie was very disappointed to find out about the injury, but she did a professional job. We all applauded when she mentioned that Vickie was the first female winner of the race. She whispered in my ear, "Should I mention the injury?"

I answered, "Ask Steve how he came out of the race."

She went back to her microphone to ask the question, and Steve said, "His leg was injured during the gallop out at the end of the race."

"Is it a life-threatening injury?" she asked.

Steve replied, "It's not, in fact, we're hoping to go on to the Preakness."

She said, "I didn't know the highs and lows of this game could be so extreme."

He explained, "They're athletes, and you know how fragile they can be." The interview ended with Vickie thanking all of us for letting her ride. She also thanked Jamie for her kind words. I admired how Vickie handled herself with so much class in every situation. I sincerely hoped that I'd find something I didn't like about her because she was much too young for me. *Mmmm, that kiss certainly wasn't one-sided!*

The next morning, Charlie was lame in his right back leg, and there was quite a bit of swelling. "Does this mean he's out of the Preakness?" I asked Steve.

"No, but it doesn't look good. I'll keep him at Churchill for a day or two to see if the swelling goes down." The next day, he was improving a little but not enough to take a chance, so Steve told us he'd take him home the next morning.

I said, "If he's ready to run, I'd like for him to run in the Longacre Mile." He promised that he'd be ready long before that.

I wanted Jamie to break the news, so I called her to explain that he was off the Triple Crown path. I said, "He has a bone bruise from being stepped on during the gallop out of the derby, but he should be back in training in about a month or so." She thanked me for giving her the first shot at the story before telling me how sorry she was. "It may work out for the best. Since he's a gelding, we plan to run him for a long time, and the Triple Crown is very grueling." *Try to look on the bright side.*

I had a sad feeling when the van took Charlie to the airport because it was like that segment of my life had ended. Norm told me he felt the same. We had planned to go to Maryland and then on to New York, so I asked him if he wanted to do some traveling or go back to California. He told me he spent quite a bit of time on the East Coast while traveling for the hospital and offered to show me around.

When we were on the road, I asked if he wanted to stop before New York. New York was one of his favorite destinations when he was CFO of the hospital, so he had told me stories about how much he liked the state. I'd only heard bad things like 9/11, muggings in Central Park, problems on the subway, and so on. He said, "You shouldn't go only by what you hear. There are many beautiful places and really good people throughout the state."

We decided to go to New York first, and I said, "It would be fun if Vickie could go with us."

He replied, "I sure wish you'd tell her the things you've been telling me." I wasn't over Linda, but it was nice to feel the feelings that Vickie had brought back to me. The look she gave me after the kiss in Kentucky told me she wasn't thinking about our age difference. Still, I wasn't ready for a romance with a lady I deeply admired, and I wouldn't be until I was sure I could commit myself to her. *I'm not at all interested in a one-night stand.*

We drove for ten hours the first day before stopping for the night at an RV park. We had dinner at a small diner that was within walking distance. The food selection and prices were very good, and after we finished eating, the waitress told us she'd be our cashier. I gave her a twenty and told her to keep the change. Norm did the same, and our meals were both nine dollars, so she was elated.

We slept until seven the next morning and decided to go to the same café for breakfast. When we walked out, we both said we wouldn't need lunch.

After we were on the road for several hours, Norm's cell phone rang. He put it on speaker, and it was Steve calling to tell us Charlie shipped really well. Other than some swelling, he was improving nicely.

"How long will it take him to heal?" I asked.

He told us he earned some time off before saying "If you really wanna go to the Longacre Mile, we'll have more-than-enough time to get him ready."

"It may be crazy to take a derby winner there, but it's our home," I said, and Norm agreed with me.

"That's where we'll go then, but he'll get one or two races before the Mile. In a couple days, he'll go to the farm to enjoy a few weeks of just being a horse, because they need to get away sometimes."

He wanted to know when we'd be back, and Norm said, "Whenever a strong wind blows in that direction."

"Liz has you two pegged, you really are hoots." I laughed while telling him it sounded much better coming from her mouth. "Have fun, and I look forward to seeing you when you get back." He said before we asked him to keep us posted.

I pulled the check from betting Charlie out of my wallet and said, "I need to deposit this."

He looked at it and replied, "Until now, I didn't really believe you bet that much."

I said, "We'll never get those odds again."

"I just remember you only putting five and five on a horse when you thought it was a cinch, but I'm very happy for you."

I explained, "That was when I was betting my money, but the money in my horse account is all Charlie." I thanked God one more time for the wonderful adventure he sent our way. If only Linda had been with us, it couldn't have been better. *I'm glad Vickie enjoys joking with me.*

Norm laughed when I asked if there was a Chase bank in New York. "Does the name Chase Manhattan ring a bell? The bank started in New York. It was one of the banks that the hospital used and was the primary reason I spent time there."

I got a little bit of a thrill when we crossed the state line into New York and wondered out loud, "Where to now."

He said, "Leave it to me." We pulled into a small town where we saw a Chase bank. I deposited the check and kept five thousand out in cash.

Norm asked my balance, so I answered, "Five hundred and thirty-two thousand."

"That's still more than your share of the purse money. You have just over four hundred thousand in there."

"**I'm almost a millionaire**," I said in a loud voice.

He replied, "You'll have to pay taxes, but you're getting close." He just couldn't stop being an accountant long enough to let me have fun. I remembered the account I put the money from selling my house into, so I was, in fact, a millionaire. The funny thing was, I didn't feel a bit different.

We spotted an RV park and decided to spend the night. There wasn't a restaurant in walking distance, so we disconnected the pickup and went in search of a nice place to eat. We pulled into a family restaurant and found a stack of newspapers that hadn't been thrown away. One that was a day old had an article about another year without a Triple Crown winner. It told how Wrong Way North was injured during the gallop out of the Derby. The reporter wrote, "It just shows how difficult the Triple Crown is to achieve, so my heart goes out to the horse's connections. He's owned by a couple retired guys who have had fun along their journey to the derby." I showed the paper to Norm, and he read it after we ordered.

When we were back at the trailer, we walked around the park a couple of times to help our food settle. We talked longer than normal because it was hard, knowing we lost a chance at the Triple Crown. I said, "All the effort in getting to this point was wiped away by a freakish accident."

Norm replied, "Let's not forget, we won the derby with a two-thousand-dollar mistake."

"That's true, but I can't help thinking about the ones that get away. Vickie had a chance to be the first female to win the Triple Crown, but that chance was wiped away also."

When we were back on the road, I asked where we were going first. He told me Central Park, so I said, "I've seen it on TV, and it looks really big."

"It looks much bigger when you're there," he replied. The closest RV park we could find to the park was twenty miles. The manager told us it was good we arrived when we did because, in a couple of weeks, everything would start filling up for the Belmont Stakes. I told him we hoped to be in the race and explained about Charlie. He was happy about the derby and sorry he wasn't able to go on.

I sighed while saying "One thing I've learned in life, as in poker, you must play the hand your dealt." I then told him how fortunate we were to have traveled our journey. We rented the space for two weeks, and that would free it up for the Belmont crowd.

We went to a park and ride because Norm said we'd never get a parking spot close to Central Park. We walked around for two hours but didn't see the whole park. I saw a couple that reminded me of times Linda and I spent on park benches. There wasn't a day that went by that I didn't remember something about our life together. I came to realize that it was good because I didn't want to forget the good times.

Norm brought me back when he asked if I wanted to ride the subway. It was a brisk walk to where we went downstairs, and I told Norm it felt eerie going underground. "Millions of people do it every day," he replied.

We bought our tickets and went through the turn stiles just like they do in the movies. I looked around at all the people, and I heard languages I'd never heard, so I said, "It's no wonder the terrorists target New York. We could be standing beside one and not have a clue who he was." When we stopped downtown, we got off, and after walking up the stairs, I said, "It's a wonder anyone ever sees the sun around here." My neck was getting stiff from looking up at the skyscrapers. We walked over to Wall Street, and I told Norm I lost some money when the market crashed.

"I wish I lost the amount you did," he said.

I replied, "Luckily, 90 percent of my 401(K) was in guaranteed funds."

He said, "Many people lost almost all of their retirement and had to continue working."

"Our company had a meeting on how to divide our money, and I told them I gambled enough with my horses, so I wanted to be safe with my retirement. Even though we lost some money on the horses, they kept me from losing on my 401(K), so in that regard, I was ahead on our horses even before Charlie." *He's sure adding to my retirement.*

We walked around for an hour before I saw a sign advertising New York pizza. I said, "We have to try some. A friend of mine from Baker City, Oregon, moved there from New York and raved about the pizza in his hometown." We went in and ordered a large pizza to split. Bill, my friend, was absolutely right when he talked about how much better the crust was. It had a delightful texture.

When we went outside, we could see the sun was lower in the sky, and we had trouble seeing it through the buildings. I said, "Let's get back before dark." We took the subway to Central Park and the bus to where we parked the truck. The sun was down when we walked into our trailer, and I told him I was glad we made it home before dark.

He said, "You've watched too many movies."

We were ready to go by seven the next morning and drove to a family restaurant for breakfast. I spotted a newspaper machine and bought one. After we ordered, Norm asked for the sports page, so while he was reading that, I was browsing. "Unbelievable," I said. Norm wanted to know what happened. "Where did we meet the bus to go back to our pickup from Central Park? What end of the park and what time?"

He said, "About four thirty at the east end."

"Listen to this, 'A man and wife from Maine were robbed at gunpoint at the east end of Central Park. The incident occurred at 5:30 p.m. The man suffered a flesh wound, and the woman was struck in the face with a blunt object. They are both in the hospital, in stable condition.' That could have been us if we were there an hour later."

"It's a big park, and nothing says he would have targeted us. It's one thing to go after a man and woman but quite another to take on two men."

I replied, "I don't think we'd scare away too many guys."

He said, "I can look mean."

"Ya, if it was a little puppy doing the robbery."

We asked the waitress how to get to Foxwood Casino and were both surprised when she told us it was in Connecticut. Norm told me he'd rather go to Atlantic City. I had always wanted to go there, so we were on the road right after breakfast.

I took out my Harrah's card and called them. They checked my points and were very happy to give us two nights complimentary at Harrah's on the Boardwalk. It was early afternoon when we arrived, and East Coast or West Coast, the casinos look pretty much the same. Still, I was glad to finally get to Atlantic City. I bought my Keno tickets for five games, and Norm went in search of a pretty dealer to play some blackjack. I sat down at a unicorn machine and played for twenty minutes without winning so I went to the sports book to look at Golden Gate. I saw that Slim was running in twelve minutes, so I tried to call Steve, but he didn't answer. The race was an open allowance because he had used up all his conditions. *Tougher race.*

When I called Tom, he asked, "Where have you been? I've been trying to reach you because both Vickie and Steve like him in here."

I thanked him and said, "I need to tell Norm." Before I left, I bet two hundred to win and place.

I found Norm at a blackjack table, but he didn't wanna stop playing, so he gave me a hundred and asked me to bet fifty to win and place for him. Slim broke right on top, but a horse was only three-quarters of a length behind him. Vickie sat chilly, and when they turned for home, she smacked him three times. He pulled away to a four-length victory, and I thought, *This horse is improving every race.* The time was 108.2 was, so I expected him to be in a graded stake soon. He paid $10.80 to win and $5.60 to place, so I collected just over $1,600 for myself and a little over four hundred for Norm.

Tom called and said, "He's gettin' better all the time. I sure like working with Steve and Vickie because they're both very dedicated." I reminded him that she was also kind of easy on the eye.

"Jim, I'm a married man, so I haven't noticed," he lied.

I said, "Tom, if Vickie was there, she would look to see if your nose is growing."

We were both laughing when he asked, "Where are you guys?"

I answered, "Harrah's in Atlantic City." He wanted to know how we were being treated, so I told him the service was great.

"Did you hit Slim hard enough to pay for your stay?"

"I had two hundred to win and place, so that should cover it."

I just hung up with Tom, and my phone rang again. Vickie asked, "Jim, did you bet Slim?"

"I put a little on him, but I didn't go crazy because I wasn't sure how much you liked him." She apologized for not telling us, so I told her there was no way she could offend me. I said, "We're running all over the country, so it's been tough for us to call you."

She said, "Slim ran great, and I wasn't close to the bottom of him."

"Will he be in a stake next? Wait a minute, I haven't told you today how gorgeous you are."

She giggled while saying "There's a six-and-a-half-furlong stake going in three weeks. I'm sure it'll come up tough, but he's really gettin' better. I called to tell you about a first-time starter in the fourth race tomorrow. He's a four-year-old, and Steve was really high on him when he was three, but he suffered a slight bow in his left front. He's been off for eight months and is completely healed now. He's training up a storm, but I think most of his good works have been hidden, so he could have some odds. Oh, by the way, you don't look so bad yourself. I'll see you when you get back."

I asked, "Before you hang up, how is Charlie?"

She replied, "He's really good. Steve said, if he has time to get a work in him, he might go for the Belmont."

"Do you think he will?"

"I really don't think so, but one never knows."

I said, "The race I want is the Longacre Mile."

"Steve put that on his schedule, and the city of Seattle will go crazy if the Kentucky Derby winner runs in that race."

"They're great sports fans. I want you to know that I expect a kiss just like the one after the derby every time Charlie wins a race," I said while laughing.

"Mmmm, I think we need to run him more often," she whispered.

"Please don't think I'm an old geezer hitting on a young girl," I said before telling her I missed her.

She replied, "If I gave you a funny look after that kiss, it was only because it surprised me. You know how to kiss, sweetie, and I'm not as young as you seem to think I am. I can take care of myself just fine, so please stop worrying about our age difference."

"You're a good friend, and I wouldn't want to jeopardize that."

She replied, "Please, don't give that another thought because I love flirting as much as you do." It surprised me when she told me she wasn't a young girl. It was a business arrangement, but it was getting harder to tell myself that all the time. *I'd stop flirting with her, but she's too much fun.*

I thanked her for calling before saying "I'll see you in my dreams, sweet girl." She laughed and told me I was a big talker when I was two thousand miles away. "There's one thing I know for sure. You get more beautiful with every mile we travel."

175

She whispered, "Mmmm, I think you need to travel more." I had to take a deep breath, and again I wondered, after so many years without looking at women, why does she appeal to me so much? *I'll never stop loving Linda, but Vickie has added so much to my life. She's a cute young lady.*

I caught her just before she hung up and said, "I wanted to tell you, I love…" I stopped there for a few seconds while clearing my throat. "Excuse me, I was trying to say I love the touts you've been giving us, but I had a catch in my throat."

She laughed while saying "That catch in your throat could give a girl a heart attack."

"I'm sure this girl has a very strong heart. I have my eyes closed, so smile really big. Mmmm, you're so beautiful."

She asked, "Do you flirt with all the girls like this?"

"Only you, and before you, I had no desire to flirt with any girl, since losing my wife."

"May I make one request?"

"Anything," I replied.

She said, "Please don't stop because I'm having more fun than I've had in a long time." The line was blank, and she was gone. *I'm glad she doesn't mind me flirting with her. I wonder if it could ever be more.*

His dealer was very pretty, and I said, "I thought I'd find you here."

Norm asked, "Why would you say that?"

I looked at the dealer and smiled while saying "No reason." I pulled out a hundred and said to the dealer, "All in fives, please."

I told Norm about the horse Vickie gave us, and he said, "Good, these cards sure aren't being good to me."

I replied, "I'll change your luck." The first hand, she dealt me a blackjack, and the second and third were the same, so I bumped my bet up to fifteen dollars. She dealt me a twelve, and she had a five showing, so I stayed pat. Norm had fifteen, and he stayed. The dealer turned over a queen, and her next card was an eight, so we both won. *This could be good.* I bumped my bet to twenty-five dollars. She dealt me a twenty, and Norm had a jack showing. The dealer had a seven, so we both stayed, and she turned over a king.

We both had twenty, so Norm said, "You were right about the table turning."

I won six more hands in a row, and all of them were twenty-five-dollar wagers. I lost the next hand and said, "Time to go." After giving the dealer a twenty-five-dollar chip, I cashed out just short of three hundred dollars.

176

I found a slot machine that looked good, and on the second spin, I won a hundred dollars. It was six thirty, so I was getting a little hungry. I had a 118 dollars in the machine, so I decided to play three games at five dollars a spin. On the first spin, I went into the bonus games and had ten free games at five times the amount won. I played in the bonus for twenty minutes because, every time I was about out of games, I'd win five more. At the end of the bonus round, I was up 1,200 dollars. I played two more times at five dollars but didn't hit, so I printed the ticket and walked away. When I got back to Norm, he had a nice stack of chips in front of him and said, "You should have stayed, the dealer kept breaking."

I showed him the 1,200-dollar ticket while saying "I did all right."

"I guess you did," he said. I told him I was hungry. The dealer was a guy, and Norm asked him to color him up. He cashed out 1,460 dollars, and he gave the dealer ten dollars before we walked away.

I said, "If that had been a pretty girl, the tip would have been at least fifty dollars."

He replied, "Maybe." We both went to the cashier's cage to cash in.

I figured in my head, with the horse, blackjack, and slot machine, I was up a little over three thousand dollars, so I told Norm my run was still alive and kickin'.

"Let's hope it doesn't stop," he said as we were walking to the buffet. They had a nice selection of foods, so we spent an hour browsing and eating small portions of several dishes. We were learning to not overeat, and it was nice to take our time. We had both retired from jobs that kept us on the move, so it was nice to be lazy sometimes.

After we finished eating, Norm went to the casino, and I went up to the room. I remembered how Linda and went to the room early and spent our days sightseeing and playing. We started going to the room early because the casinos were always much smokier at night. We agreed that a good night's sleep was too important to stay out late. I fell asleep with the TV on, and Norm woke me when he came in at three. He told me he had been winning for a while but went into a losing streak.

I asked if he was still ahead, and he answered, "Ya, but I lost more than I should have. Maybe I'll learn to come to the room early, like you do."

I replied, "I do it to stay out of the smoke, but since you smoke, it's not an issue with you."

He replied, "It even gets too smoky for me sometimes." After getting cleaned up, he climbed into bed, and I was sound asleep just minutes after he stopped walking around.

The sun coming through the window woke me at six. Norm was still sleeping, so I very quietly took my shower. When I went out of the bathroom, he was still asleep, so I left the room. I bought my Keno numbers for five games before going out on the boardwalk. It was 7:10 a.m., and the place was alive. People were walking, jogging, skateboarding, roller skating and riding bikes. I couldn't believe how many people were doing so many different things so early. I was just sitting on a bench, watching them, and it made me tired. The water was very calm and looked more like a lake than an ocean. I watched an older man catch a fish off the dock. I couldn't tell what kind of fish it was, but it was quite large, and he seemed excited. People gathered around to congratulate him, so it must have been something special.

I thought about my last conversation with Vickie, and I was happy that she enjoyed our flirting as much as I did. With our age difference, there was no way we would ever be more than friends, but I loved being around her. She was fun and lifted my spirits, but I needed to back off a little for her sake. *I'm sure guys her own age are showing interest in her. I'd like to call her right now, but I won't.*

It was almost nine, so I walked back to the casino and checked my Keno tickets. I had eleven dollars coming, so I gave the girl a dollar before putting the ten in my pocket. I went to the sports book and picked up a Golden Gate entry sheet. Vickie's horse was number 5 in a field of ten, and his morning line was fifteen to one. The race was a maiden forty-thousand-dollar claimer for three-year-olds and up, going six furlongs. I bet two hundred to win and place and wheeled him on top in the exacta and trifecta.

I found a unicorn machine and was able to play on twenty dollars for over an hour. When the twenty was gone, I went in search of Norm, knowing I had been treated to more than twenty dollars' worth of fun. He was playing blackjack, and I asked him if he wanted to eat. He wasn't hungry, so I told him not to forget to bet the horse.

I walked around looking for something to eat and ended up in their food court. I ordered a breakfast sandwich and hash browns before walking to an espresso stand inside the court. I bought an unflavored latte and found a table in the center of the court. I enjoyed watching the people. They were moving really fast, and from what I could see, most people in Vegas were much more relaxed. I looked at my watch and saw it was almost noon. *It's lunchtime, and I just ate breakfast.* I went to the sports book, and Golden Gate's first race was a few hours away. I walked by Norm again and reminded him about the fourth race.

"I'm okay," he said. He had plenty of time, but I didn't want him to forget.

After walking around for some time, I bought my Keno tickets and decided to sit down and watch the games. I didn't hit anything the first game, but I fell asleep and was startled when I felt someone squeezing my arm. I was looking through a dense fog, and as it cleared, I could see Norm looking at me. "Did you bet the horse?" he asked very excitedly.

"Yes, I bet him early," I said before asking if the race had run.

"It sure did, and her horse won by five lengths."

"She thought he'd win easily," I said before asking if he had good odds.

"Seventeen to one, and the second-place horse was thirteen to one. With a big smile, he said, "The place paid nineteen dollars." I asked if he bet the exacta and trifecta. He answered, "I got there a little late, so I just bet a hundred to win and place."

"Did the third-place horse have odds?"

He answered, "I didn't notice. It didn't affect me because I just had win and place." The trifecta would be good no matter what the third-place horse paid.

When I stood up, I had to grab on to the seat. He asked if I was all right, and I answered, "I stood up too quickly, and I was a little dizzy." When I got my land legs back, I checked my Keno tickets. The machine said it was three dollars, so I told the girl to keep them. Knowing the trifecta would be big, I took my tickets to the IRS window. After 20 percent was taken out for taxes, I was given 8,860 dollars. I gave the man who cashed the tickets sixty dollars and put away three hundred each for Vickie and Steve. *She's amazing.*

The rest of the day was uneventful as I'd win some and lose some. I spent a lot of time watching people and saw a man angry with his wife for losing too much. He said, "You know you have a budget for each day. If you lose everything the first day, our trip will be ruined." It reminded me of how Linda would get overly excited the first day we arrived in Vegas. She asked me to keep her on her budget. *I wish she could be with us having fun.* The man was right to react the way he did, and I was sure she'd thank him later. It's easy to get overly excited when you first arrive at a casino.

I saw Norm at a three-card poker table and sat down beside him. I watched him play for a few minutes, but I wasn't a fan of the game, so I didn't play. I told him I was going out on the boardwalk for a while. I sat down on a bench and enjoyed watching the people. It was even busier than the morning was. I was thinking about all the modes of transportation when my phone rang. The caller ID said it was Steve, so I asked, "How ya doin'?"

He said, "Obviously, you know it's me." I told him he was on the caller ID, and I was surprised when he told me he hated them.

I said, "I'll ask who it is, if it'll make you feel better."

"Don't be a jerk, you're already gonna tell me I'm crazy." I asked him what was goin' on, and he said, "Charlie's doing so well that I'm running him in the Belmont. The vet said the bruise is healed, and I can't tell that he was cut. The Preakness is in two days, so that gives us three weeks to get him ready. He hasn't lost a thing in conditioning, but I wanna get his mind toughened up after being turned out."

"Can you still enter him?" I asked.

"Oh ya, the nominations are just starting."

"When will you nominate him?"

He answered, "I called back today. We need a twenty-five-thousand-dollar entry fee paid at Belmont Park, so can Norm pay that?"

"We'll do it tomorrow," I promised.

He said, "Thanks, did you bet the four-year-old?"

"I hit him good, so I have some money for you and Vickie. I guess I'll pay you when I see you in New York." I laughed and asked, "Is she as pretty as I remember?"

He replied, "She's a pretty lady." *I'd like to ask her out, but she would probably laugh at me, so I'll just enjoy being around her. Thank you, Lord, for sending her to help fill that terrible hole in my heart.*

PHOTOS

Excitement at the auction was too much! "You bought the wrong horse!"

On the track at Portland Meadows

Lots and lots of Winner's Circles!

The Kentucky Derby at Churchill Downs

Tiny Vickie, 1st Lady
Jockey to win the Derby

Clockwise: Unicorn slot machine, Pai Gow poker, Blackjack, Sportsbook on the horses, Keno ticket- the "Jim special."

Harrah's at Lake Tahoe

Liz with a special hat for
the Kentucky Derby party

Santa Anita and Belmont

Harrah's Las Vegas

Winning by a Length

Jamie, Sportcaster for Comcast

Kayti, modeling at the Bellevue Square Bridal Show

CHAPTER 9

The One That Got Away

When I found Norm, I said, "You won't believe what Steve just told me." He looked startled, so I quickly said, "It's not bad, he's running Charlie in the Belmont."

"You're right, I don't believe you."

I explained, "Vickie sounded like he might but said she'd be surprised if he actually did. The vet said he's completely over the cut and bruise."

He said, "We'll need to find something to do for the next three weeks." When we went to dinner, I could see he was really tired, so I told him I was going to the room right after dinner and he should also. He said, "I'll be up in a while. You're right, I'm tired."

It was eight thirty when I entered the room, and I turned the TV to ESPN. Just as I turned it on, across the bottom of the screen, it was written, "Breaking news, Wrong Way North to run in the Belmont Stakes. It hasn't been confirmed, but it looks like the Kentucky Derby winner will run in the third leg of the Triple Crown. We'll give more details as they come in."

My cell phone rang, and I could see that Jamie was calling me. "Uncle Jim, would you mind if I ask you a couple questions?"

"Ask as many as you want to, sweetie."

"Is it true, Charlie will run in the Belmont?"

"It sure looks like he's going to."

"Does that mean he's over his injury?"

"If he wasn't, Steve wouldn't run him. I answered it that way because Norm and I have been traveling the eastern part of the country since the Derby, so I just learned about it today. I wasn't trying to be smart with the answer."

"Where are you?" she asked very cheerfully.

I answered, "We're in Atlantic City." She told me she always wanted to go there, so I said, "Other than it's on the ocean, it's a lot like Vegas. The casinos all look pretty much the same."

"Are you winning?" she asked.

"We are, but only because Steve gave us a couple horses to bet. Neither of us has done very well at the tables or slots."

She told me she'd like to come back for the race but wasn't sure her budget would allow it. She told me she'd let me know, before hanging up.

I was just about asleep when Norm came in and said, "I haven't been able to stop thinking about Charlie running so soon."

I replied, "I was surprised too, even though Vickie kind of alluded to it. Even she didn't really think it would happen." He asked if I thought Steve would take a chance of running him too soon. "No, he wouldn't risk hurting him. I'd say the bruise wasn't as bad as the vet thought in Kentucky. Charlie has always been sound, so maybe he heals more quickly than other horses. One thing I promise you, **Steve will never put Charlie in danger!**"

We checked out the next day, and Norm asked what I wanted to do. I said, "The Preakness is tomorrow, and I'd like to bet the race. How long would it take to drive to Pimlico racetrack?"

"We'd be on the road the whole time, but we can bet it at Belmont." I told him I wanted to bet the horse that ran third in the Derby. "The horse that beat him is in there," he reminded me.

"He's a come-from-behind horse, and the other is pure speed. I've watched the Triple Crown races for years, and Pimlico has always favored speed."

He said, "We need to pay the nomination fee at Belmont so we can do it tomorrow and stay for the race." I told him not to listen to me about the race but to bet what he liked. "The way your luck has been running, I wouldn't bet against you right now," he said while smacking my back. *It has been amazing.*

It was nice getting back to the trailer because we loved the feel of our own beds. *I'm anxious to see Vickie.*

Jamie called and told us she wouldn't be able to make the race but would have someone from the area interview us if we didn't mind. We told her anyone she sent would be welcome.

We went to a small café for dinner, and I bought a paper. I gave Norm all, but the sports page and on the front page of the sports section, it was written, "**Wrong Way North to Run in the Belmont**. An injury sustained at the end of the Kentucky Derby made it impossible for him to run in the Preakness, but apparently, he's doing very well now. I think the Preakness would be an easier race for him with his tactical speed, so if he wins the Belmont, we'll always wonder if he might have won the Triple Crown."

I showed Norm the article and said, "I certainly wanna win the Belmont, but what will we do to not think about the one that got away?"

He said, "Let's just be happy with every race he wins."

I shook my head while saying "Vickie could have been the first female to win the Triple Crown, and I can only imagine the smile on her face if that would have happened."

Norm simplified things again by saying "It is what it is."

The next morning, we ate breakfast at the same café, and after we ordered, a man at the counter said, "Pardon me for asking, are you two the owners of Wrong Way North?" I nodded. "He ran an unbelievable race in the derby. He must have some heart because I thought he'd be third with a hundred yards to go. He really dug down for that something extra."

I replied, "Vickie always says he refuses to lose, and he's been such a blessing to us. It's hard to believe that our adventures started with a two-thousand-dollar mistake."

A guy listening to the conversation instantly made me angry by saying "Some people think he's dodging the Preakness."

Trying hard to keep my composure, I asked, "Do you realize these horses get one chance in their lives at this opportunity? We shed real tears the night he won the derby because we knew the Triple Crown chase was almost certainly over."

He said, "Please pardon me, I didn't mean to make you angry."

"I'm not mad, but people don't know how much of our heart and soul goes into these horses. Believe me, we'd give anything to be running in the Preakness, and I know the horse is as disappointed as we are. We had to think about possibly ending his career if we tried to go on."

The first guy said, "I heard he was stepped on. Was it during that three-horse stretch run?"

I replied, "No, it was during the gallop out."

"Do you mean it was after the race?"

"Well, it was past the finish line, but the gallop out is part of the race. Some people think it could be the most dangerous part. The reason it can be dangerous is they're changing their stride in a very short distance. You don't hear about many of the injuries, I suspect. We're just happy that he has bounced back as quickly as he has." They were surprised when we told them we just found out he would be in the Belmont. As we were leaving, we all shook hands, and they told us they'd root for Charlie.

At the backside of Belmont Park, we showed our California license and told the guard we were going in to pay the Belmont nomination fees for Wrong Way North.

The guard said, "You don't know how happy we are that he'll be running. You may not know this, but he's become somewhat of a folk hero because he's owned by a couple working stiffs."

I laughed while saying "You must have watched me walk from the pickup, to use those words." He laughed and told me it was just a figure of speech. I told him I loved hearing it before saying "We pinch ourselves and each other to make sure we're not dreaming."

He said, "It's one of the greatest stories I've heard around the race track. You may be surprised by how excited people are that he's running."

"We're excited about it too," I replied. He was a little surprised when we told him we just learned the day before that he was running.

"I would have thought you'd be involved the whole time," he replied.

Norm said, "We gave Steve complete control, and so far, it's worked for us."

When we were in the office, the manager asked why we were there so far ahead of the race. I said, "We weren't expecting to be in the race, so we've been traveling around in our trailer, enjoying the country."

"Are you staying in New York through the race?" he asked. We told him we were, so he said, "You're welcome to park out back at no charge."

We had time to move the trailer before the race, so we moved in. The office gave us a sign saying "Belmont Participant" to put in the window. We were very happy with the spot they gave us. It was in a nice, secluded area under a huge maple tree.

I said, "Norm, I've heard parking in New York is expensive, but twenty-five thousand for this spot seems a little excessive."

He laughed before saying "Let's hope we get six hundred thousand back on our investment."

We went over to the frontside to look around, and the third race had just run at Pimlico. They showed the odds for the Preakness and Cornish Memories was seven to two. The second-place horse in the derby was favored at nine to five. Cornish Memories had drawn the three post, and that should serve his speed well. I decided to bet early to avoid the lines when the race was closer. I told the seller I wanted a thousand to win on number 3, and he recognized me. He told me how much he wished Charlie was in the race, before telling me how happy he was that he was running in the Belmont.

When I walked outside, I noticed that the odds hadn't changed and thought, *I might put more on him if the odds stay there.*

As the race drew closer, I kept thinking I should put more on him. His odds went up to four to one, so I thought someone might know something that I didn't. I looked at a form to see what I was missing, and no horse in the race had his speed except one that hadn't gone past six and a half furlongs. In those races, he was close to the front, but I couldn't see him carrying his speed a mile and three-sixteenths. I decided not to bet more, thinking about the sprinter maybe causing him a problem. Believe me, it wasn't the first time I overthought a race.

Cornish Memories was still four to one when the gate opened. I was hoping he'd get the early lead, but the sprinter went right to the front, and Cornish settled in second, three lengths behind him. I started to get worried when the position hadn't changed entering the turn for home because I knew the favorite would be closing late. The rider turned Cornish Memories loose entering the stretch, and he went by the leader quite easily. He opened up three lengths with about two hundred yards to go, but as I knew he would, the favorite was rolling. He was unable to catch Cornish Memories, so I said to Norm, "The rider put a nice ride on the winner. According to the form, that's the first time Cornish has settled behind a horse, so that'll make him double tough in the Belmont."

He replied, "We can't worry about that now." He laughed while saying "The reason he won this race is you bet him. Your winning streak is still alive, so promise me one thing." I asked what that might be, and he answered, "You'll only bet Charlie in the Belmont." I told him that was a safe bet.

There was a little grocery store close to the track, so we bought some items to make Reuben sandwiches for dinner. It was nice eating at home, and we put some chairs outside after dinner to enjoy the evening breeze. "Charlie will run in the Belmont," I said.

Norm replied, "He'll win."

Steve called and asked if we paid the fee and was happy to hear we did. He said, "Charlie would have won that race today." We both agreed with him before he said "That's why the Triple Crown is so tough. Charlie's perfectly fit, so instead of any more works, he'll have good, long gallops every day. I don't think the mile and a half will be a problem for him. There's a small stake going seven furlongs on the undercard for Slim, but I'm sorry to say, Tom and Liz can't make the race."

Steve wanted to know where we were staying, so Norm told him the track gave us a parking spot through the race.

The next three days, we didn't take out the pickup. We ate some nice meals around the track and lay around, getting lots of rest. We went across to watch a race now and then but didn't make any wagers.

Norm asked me if we should go in search of Foxwood, but I wasn't ready to go to another casino.

We were eating breakfast at the backside café, and people were talking about the Belmont. One person said he was sorry Charlie had gotten hurt because he thought he had a good chance of winning the Triple Crown. It was nice that not everyone knew us because we could hear things we wouldn't if they knew we were Charlie's owners. Sometimes, that can backfire, and you hear things that aren't very nice. An older guy sitting halfway across the café said, "If they hadn't chickened out of the Preakness, we might be going into the Belmont with a chance."

Norm kicked me under the table and said, "Settle down, it's not worth it."

I smiled and replied, "I know, everyone has the right to his opinion, even if it's stupid."

I didn't have to be angry long because a guy to my left stood up and said, "If you don't have anything better than that to say, it would be best you keep your mouth **shut!**" I hadn't noticed, but the one defending Charlie was a really big man, and one look at his face told me he was ready to fight. The mouthy guy saw the same thing and went back to drinking his coffee. I was glad a fight didn't break out, but at the same time, I was happy that Charlie could inspire that kind of passion in people.

After we finished breakfast, we followed the man outside who defended Charlie. I walked up to him, told him my name, and thanked him for coming to Charlie's defense. "**Who is Charlie?**" he asked with a hint of anger still in his voice.

I said, "I come in peace, Charlie's the nickname we gave Wrong Way North."

He looked at me for what seemed like a long time, so I was relieved when a smile spread across his face. "You were on TV after the derby. You're one of his owners, and you're the other," he said to Norm. He took hold of my hand and said, "I'm Clint." For a moment, I thought he might take my hand with him. He shook Norm's hand, and I could see the pain in his eyes. Clint turned to me and said, "Somebody puts that old guy in his place every couple weeks. I'm surprised you didn't get mad."

I explained, "We've been able to sit in these backside cafés across the country without being recognized, so we've heard a lot of bad as he was just getting started in California to a lot of good as his career progressed. It's really fun to hear what people have to say when they don't know we're the owners. To answer your question about me not getting mad, he was getting to me, but before I could get mad, you looked at him in a way that made me feel sorry for him."

"I shouldn't have gotten so upset, but I have to tell you, the race Charlie—if you don't mind me calling him Charlie—ran in the derby was the gutsiest race I've ever seen. I grew up on the track just like my daddy and his daddy before him. The way he battled between two horses coming down the lane was like nothing I'd ever seen. Most horses in the middle like that would be intimidated. He actually lost the lead for an instant, and when he pinned those ears and came back, I had shivers up and down my back. My dad has cancer, so he wasn't able to make the race, but he has tapes of all the Kentucky Derbies and Belmonts since they invented DVDs. I went over and watched the race with him, and after your horse won, with tears running down his face, he said, 'I've looked for that horse my whole life.'"

"That certainly explains your anger in the café. Do you think your dad would like a win picture from the race?"

"He'd love that," he said as his eyes filled with tears. Charlie had that effect on many people.

I said, "If you'll write down your name and address, I'll have one mailed to you, and you can give it to him. Write down your dad's name plus how many years in the business, and we'll make it nice."

He said, "I've heard good things about you two, but this surpasses anything I could have ever imagined." We told him we'd be around through the race and would see him before we left.

I called Churchill and asked to speak to someone about the pictures. I told him I'd like it put in the nicest frame he could find. "This could cost a couple hundred dollars," he said.

I replied, "For the first time in my life, cost is no object." His dad's name was also Clint, and his last name was Collins. I explained to him, "I'd like a small gold-plated plaque saying 'Thank you, Clint Collins, for your sixty-seven years of service to our industry, from Jim and Norm.'"

"Are you talking about the Clint Collins that trains in New York?" he asked. I told him I was and explained how I met his son. "Does he have cancer?" he asked.

I answered, "His boy said he does, but he didn't say if it's terminal."

"Don't worry about the cost. If you don't mind, I'll add 'your friends at Churchill Downs' to the inscription, and we'll cover the cost."

"That would please us no end," I said.

"I'll put a rush on it, and it'll go out tomorrow," he said. I told him we would be glad to share in the cost, but he said, "After what Clint's done for our industry, we'd be happy to pay for it. We're all so excited to hear Wrong Way North is doing well and will be in the Belmont."

I replied, "We're still in shock over it. We've been traveling the East Coast since the derby and were just informed by Steve two days ago."

He said, "I'm not supposed to be partial, but I'll be rooting for him."

"I won't tell a soul," I promised before thanking him for all his help.

I went away feeling good and thought, *This Clint must be a really nice guy for him to react the way he did.* Norm was walking around the parking area for some exercise, and I asked him what he wanted to do the rest of the day. "I'd be happy just to stay here," he answered.

We hung around the track and watched a few races. We were having a great time in our little slice of the Big Apple, so I told Norm I wouldn't mind staying there right through the race. "Let's take it day to day," he suggested.

I got in the habit of taking a nap during the day, and one day, I dreamed about Linda and Vickie laughing while looking at a racing form. I was a little surprised when I realized that I missed both of them. For a guy my age, I was certainly confused. I was sure Linda would have liked her if they had met, and they did look quite a bit alike.

Three days later in the café, Clint walked up carrying a package. He had a funny look on his face, but it certainly wasn't the look of anger that I saw the first time I saw him. He asked if he could sit with us, so I pulled out a chair for him while asking "Is everything all right with your dad?"

"He's doing well and will be much better when I give him this." He opened the package and took out Charlie's picture.

I said, "**Excuse me!**" I slid it closer and said, "This is the first time I've seen the picture." We were all impressed with the frame and the inscription.

Clint said, "This must have cost a bundle."

I replied, "I know about how much it cost, but as soon as I said it was for your dad, they said if they could add 'your friends from Churchill Downs,' they'd cover the cost. I think your dad has made quite an impression in this sport."

"There's one more thing I wanna share with you. I didn't think to mention when I talked to you before, but your trainer is the same Steve Stacy that my dad gave his first job at the racetrack." I was speechless, so I just sat there staring at him. Clint said, "Well, you can say something."

I shook my head and said, "That's unbelievable. I knew Steve came from the East Coast, but to meet the way we did is nothing short of amazing."

I stammered a little more, so Norm rescued me by saying "I think he's trying to say it really is a small world."

I said, "Yes, but I would have said it much more eloquently."

Norm replied, "I'm sure you would have if you had gotten your mouth to work. Please don't use those big words because they sound stupid coming from a backwoods boy like you." There was a huge explosion of laughter all around us. I was so engrossed in the picture and conversation that I hadn't noticed we were drawing a crowd. At least thirty people shook our hands and told us their names, but there was no way we could remember all of them.

One of them said, "Once a New Yorker, always a New Yorker. Steve is the reason I rooted for your horse."

A young guy a little way back, said, "Heck, I put ten on him to win because of Steve."

I said, "I'm glad someone other than the two of us had enough faith to lay down a few bucks."

The same young man told us he knew that many owners didn't bet their horses because they were afraid of jinxing them. I replied, "If my betting him would have jinxed him, he wouldn't have won a race up to now." Every one of them told us how happy they were that he was healthy and in the Belmont. One of them asked if we thought he could win going a mile and a half. I explained, "I don't think the distance will be a problem, and Steve thinks he'll have no problem with fitness, so I believe he's ready to answer all questions."

I was a little surprised when the guy who angered Clint the day we met him came up and told us he was sorry. He said, "Every year I want a Triple Crown winner so badly. Please forgive me because it was disappointment talking." I shook his hand and thanked him for explaining himself. I agreed that I had rooted for one for years also. He shook Clint's hand and told him he was sorry he upset him. "I know what you're going through with your dad, and I didn't mean to add to your grief," he said. Clint told him, for reasons he didn't understand, Charlie was giving his dad the will to live. I had to go outside to hide the tears that were filling my eyes. I didn't know Charlie was loved so much, and I was surprised that it hit me as hard as it did. *Everything makes me emotional since chemo.*

After I went back inside, Clint asked if we'd like to go with him to give the picture to his dad. We both told him we'd love to, so he called him to tell him we were coming over.

They lived in a small brick house about ten blocks from the track. When we walked inside, Clint Sr. was sitting in his easy chair. He got up quite easily and shook our hands while saying "Excuse the mess, I haven't done my chores."

I loved that he called housework his chores. I said, "From what I hear, you've kept up on your chores for many years. Tell me about Steve working for you."

His face lit up when he said, "You'll never know how happy I was when I saw Steve's horse win the derby. He went to work for me walking hots the day after he graduated high school. I knew, the day he started, he was special. He didn't wanna go to college because, from that first day, his heart was with the horses. I'll tell you, horses get along with him as well as anybody I've seen."

He asked how we started with Steve and I explained, "We really like Vickie and told her when Charlie went to California we wanted her to ride him. Norm had been friends with her for some time, so he told her how important it was to him to be able to trust the trainer. He asked her to keep her eyes open for us, and she's the one that picked him. We're sure glad she did."

He said, "You'll never be sorry you chose him."

I smiled while saying "I only keep him around because he has a pretty wife."

He laughed out loud while saying "I've known Sandy since she was a little girl. She lived right over there." He was pointing at a small brick house across the street.

"It really is a small world," I said while shaking my head.

"Do you guys have any idea what you have?" Clint Sr. asked.

I answered, "I know how happy we are, but I'd love to hear what you have to say."

"This guy is a once-in-a-lifetime horse. I've trained for sixty-seven years and was never fortunate enough to get one. I cried at the end of the derby because, when three horses come down the lane head-to-head, the outside horse almost always has the advantage. A big part of that is the outside horse usually has the momentum, and in this case, he did." A tear trickled out of his left eye when he said, "With a hundred yards to go, your horse was beaten. The only one in the world that didn't have him beaten was him." With partially broken speech, he said, "When he pinned his ears and came back, I levitated out of my chair. My whole life I looked for a horse like him, but I wasn't lucky enough to get one. If I couldn't have him, I was glad Steve did. I had horses as fast as him and as all-around athletic as him but never with that heart."

Clint Jr. said, "If you guys ever stop talking, I'll give him his gift."

I said to Senior, "He kinda speaks his mind."

Senior replied, "He gets that from me." When he opened the package, tears ran down his face. He wiped away the tears and said, "I hate when that happens."

"Does it make you wanna punch someone to prove you're a man?" I asked.

"How did you know?"

"Did it start with your chemotherapy?" I asked.

"It sure did," he said before asking again how I knew.

I answered, "I've taken chemo a few times, and I hate what it does to me emotionally, but we're alive."

He smiled while nodding and said, "Without it, I wouldn't have seen your horse and my old groom win the derby."

"Without it, Norm would have Charlie by himself," I replied. We shook hands again, and I told him how much I appreciated the way Churchill handled the picture and inscription. I told him he was very respected in the industry.

"I've put my heart and soul into this sport, so that's nice to hear. Look right here," he said as he pointed to Charlie's ears being pinned to his head. "Look at his eyes, they're on fire. His mind is saying 'You won't beat me today.' I'll bet he was a handful when he got back to the barn."

I replied, "Steve said it took him a little longer to cool out, and he wanted to tear down the walker enough that they hand-walked him."

Clint said, "He was saying 'Look at me, and don't forget what I did for you today.' The best in any sport know they're the best. He knows how good he is, and the good thing is, as long as he stays sound, he'll keep proving it."

"Wow, you made me love him even more," I said as I wiped away a couple of tears of my own. You can't explain to someone how much you love the horses. They just have to live it.

Before we left, I told him I could stay and talk to him all day, and Norm said, "I thought you were going to."

Senior chuckled while saying "Your friend's quiet."

"Not when he's asleep, his snoring rattles the walls."

Senior laughed and said, "I'm guilty of that myself."

"Norm says I'm guilty of it too, but it never bothers me." We said goodbye and promised we'd see each other before we left town. On our way to the truck, Junior told us how much we had done for his dad. I replied, "I would have promised to bring Steve by, but it's hard to get him to leave the horses. I'll talk to him when he gets here." Before we reached the track, Clint mentioned that he sure hoped Steve would see his dad. "Was there a problem?" I asked.

"No, not a problem, but when trainers go out on their own, there are, many times, hurt feelings. If Steve has some, they're not shared by Dad." I told him I'd find out for him. He said, "I'll come by the barn and see him because he was like a big brother to me when I was younger. I'm so happy he's training Charlie."

It was dinnertime when we got back to the track, so I told Clint I'd buy his dinner if he had time. Going to the house threw him behind, so he had to excuse himself. We decided to go looking for someplace different to eat and saw a Mongolian barbecue restaurant. I asked Norm if he had tried it. He hadn't, so I told him he was in for a treat. On the way in, I said, "It was one of these restaurants where I first tried hot and sour soup."

He replied, "Knowing how much you like it, I'll try some." He winced at the first bite, but after letting the soup find his taste buds, he said, "It's good." We spent over an hour enjoying every aspect of the dinner. He was especially impressed, watching them cook the food at the end of the line. He put on the same spices that

I used, even though I told him it would make it hot. At the end of dinner, he said, "I'd love to come back, but I wouldn't make it quite so hot next time."

I replied, "I worked up to that hot, and sometimes I make it too hot."

"Was tonight one of the times it was too hot?"

"No, it was perfect tonight. It's even hotter on the way out," I said while laughing. He didn't sound sincere when he told me he could hardly wait.

The race was a week away, and I was starting to get a little nervous. Steve was due to arrive in two days, and I told Norm it seemed like we'd been home for a long time. He looked at me for a second before saying "We're over two thousand miles from home. I'm enjoying staying here, but if you wanna go someplace, let's go."

I said, "It has been nice getting rested up."

He asked, "What would you think about a Broadway play?"

"Is my feminine side showing?"

He said, "We're in New York, and you may never get another chance to go to a Broadway play."

"I'll go because you go places with me, but don't you dare tell Earl and Hank back home." We called and were able to get tickets to *The Lion King* for the next night. They told us they just had two cancellations, or it would have been sold out.

Luckily, we both packed suits. We drove to a park and ride to make sure we wouldn't have a problem with parking. All the way there, I told him how much of a sacrifice I was making for him. He said, "If you stop complaining, **you might like it!**" When we arrived, the show was due to start in thirty minutes. I was mad about the price of food and drinks. Norm said, "You better go to the bathroom because it's tough once the play starts."

"**I'm okay**," I said. All the way to our seats, I was mad that I had agreed to come, but when we sat down, I looked around and thought, *The building's beautiful anyway.* When the show started, I was completely mesmerized. The production was fantastic, and the outfits were out of this world. I couldn't take my eyes off the stage, but after a while, a familiar feeling came over me. I felt like my bladder might burst, but I didn't wanna miss a minute of the play.

I told Norm my problem, and he said, "You better go now because, if you wait until intermission, you won't believe the lines."

I reluctantly went up after saying "Remember everything so you can tell me when I get back."

I truly believe that some of the world's best conversations are standing in front of urinals. The guy beside me said, "Must be your first play too." I told him it was, and he said, "My wife told me to pee before it started, but I was so angry about being here that I told her no just to spite her."

I said, "My situation is almost the same, but it's a friend instead of a wife." We agreed we had to get back so we wouldn't miss too much. We ran to wash our hands and get back to our seats. On our way, I said, "You know we'll hear about this, don't you?"

"Believe me, I know," he said while shaking his head.

I got back to my seat just in time for intermission and saw the people going up. I said, "Norm, I'm glad I listened to you."

He replied, "If you had listened the first time, you wouldn't have missed a really good part of the show." *Sounds like an angry wife.*

"On the positive side, my bladder's intact, and you'll tell me what I missed."

At the end, they were given several curtain calls but not enough, I thought. I was totally impressed with the whole production, so I told Norm I could see why people went to them. He told me he was hooked the first time he went to one. I said, "I didn't say I was hooked, Norm, but it was quite good." He just rolled his eyes.

The next morning, we went to the backside café for breakfast, and the place was buzzing. Several people greeted us as we found a table. We picked up a paper, and the headline read, "**It looks like the winners of the Preakness and Derby will be the horses to beat in the Belmont.**" It talked about a couple of new arrivals and the second-place finisher in the Preakness but said "For all intents and purposes, it looks like the winners of the first two legs of the Triple Crown should slug it out for the third."

I said to Norm, "I also think Cornish Memories will be really tough. What scares me most is the way he rated in the Preakness."

Norm simplified things when he said "They all scare me, but if Charlie runs his race, he'll win."

I asked, "Did I mention that I find Vickie very attractive?"

"Hundreds of times. Why don't you tell her?"

I said, "She's just a friend, Norm, and friends can be pretty." He got a big smile on his face, but it went away when I explained **"Not all friends are pretty, Norm!"**

Several of the people wished us good luck as we walked out of the café. We went up to the track to watch the horses work, and I was still excited about the play. I said, "Norm, I never dreamed that I would enjoy a Broadway play. That thing was a hoot, as Liz would say."

"I felt the same as you the first time I went to one, and I almost burst my bladder too."

I said, "It's hard to get up when the play is going on, and I'm sure a couple people were upset when I walked in front of them, but the decision to go before intermission was a good one. I appreciate you telling me."

After watching several horses work, I decided to go back to the trailer to take a nap. I slept a couple of hours, and when I walked outside, Norm was sitting in a lawn chair. "Why are you out here?" I asked. He told me he was enjoying the day and thinking about Charlie. I said, "It's hard to believe I could miss a horse as much as I miss him." He nodded and went back to enjoying the weather.

The next morning, Tom called at seven and said, "Time to get up, boys."

I replied, "I've been up for a couple hours."

He said, "I wanted you to know, the horses are coming in today."

I replied, "We've been excited to see them and even Steve."

"How do you like New York and Atlantic City?"

"We've had a wonderful time and met some unbelievable people. Let me tell you about a trainer we met. He gave Steve his first job at the racetrack."

"That's amazing," he said before asking "What are the chances?"

I replied, "You're the casino man, so you'd know better than me, but I'd love to get those odds on any wager. We went to a Broadway show, if you can believe it."

"Liz and I go every time we're in New York, and we love them. You saw *The Lion King*, I presume?"

"We did, and I was blown away by the entire production."

He said, "We're coming in a couple months, and we have tickets." I was surprised when he asked, "Jim, What's the number-one rule when going to a Broadway play?"

Without delay I said, "Pee before you go in."

He laughed for at least a minute before saying "Obviously, you didn't."

I said, "Norm warned me before the play, but I wasn't happy about going, so I didn't listen."

"Did you get caught in the lines?"

"No, I told Norm it would be tough to wait until intermission, and he told me, if I never listened to him again, go before intermission."

"If you've thanked him a hundred times, a thousand would be better. I was stuck in the lines, and I actually thought about using the coat pocket of the guy in front of me," he said while laughing.

That got me laughing, and I said, "I wish you were coming to the race." As we were saying goodbye, I said, "One thing I have to know, Tommy, you wouldn't have used his pocket, would you?"

He answered, "You know about desperate times and desperate measures, I presume." We were both laughing when we hung up.

When I saw Norm, I told him about our conversation, and it got me laughing again. "Why is that so funny to you?" he asked.

I answered, "I can visualize the look on the man's face when he realized his pocket was being used as a urinal. He would more than likely have been a little angry, but he would have had to admire Tom's ingenuity."

He shook his head and said, "You're giving that way too much thought."

Steve's plane arrived at 11:00 a.m., and we picked him up. That airport is a crazy place, and if you're not alert, you'll get run over. I was glad our truck was bigger than the cabs because those guys are fearless. More probably, they're nuts. We did make it to the pickup area in one piece, but in no way were our nerves intact. I shook Steve's hand and said, "Hang on." Norm was out among them again and was dodging left then right. I closed my eyes and said, "Tell me when we're safe."

Steve said, "I forgot how bad this can be."

I replied, "**You have to forget, or you'll have nightmares the rest of your life!**" It was good to get out where people acted like life had meaning, and I was very happy when we were in the safe confines of the track. The horses were not due in for a couple of hours, so I told Steve about meeting Clints Junior and Senior. He got a different look on his face, so I said, "We didn't obligate you to anything, but it would mean the world to him to see you."

"Do you really think he wants to see me?"

"It would mean more than anything I can imagine because he thinks of you as a son."

"When I went out on my own, one of his clients asked me to take his horses. It was just a couple bottom claimers, but Clint didn't have that many horses at the time. It made me feel terrible, so as my stable grew, I sent some clients his way without him knowing. For years, I've wished I would have sat down and talked to him, but I felt really guilty."

I said, "He has cancer, so you may not get another chance."

"By all means, let's get over there." He looked at his watch before saying "We have just over an hour." Clint had given me his phone number, so I called him, and he was excited when I told him we'd come right over.

It brought tears to my eyes when they hugged. They had both made errors by not talking to each other, but they both thought the other was upset. It's hard to make up for thirty years in an hour, but they came close. Clint said, "That horse is one of the best I've seen. His heart is the size of a washing machine."

Steve replied, "Well, maybe a washtub. We couldn't be more pleased with the way he's going right now." He turned to me and said, "This is the guy that taught me not to overtrain. I can still hear him saying 'You don't have to get fit what's already fit. The key is to keep them there without hurting them and not letting them peak too soon.' That's the best advice I've ever gotten."

"No works between the derby and now?" Clint asked.

Steve said, "Just one and then good, long gallops, as you taught me."

Clint asked, "Can he beat this bunch?"

Steve surprised me when he said "With racing luck, I don't think there's a three-year-old in the world that can touch him." He told Clint that Charlie and one of his other horses did require more works than any he'd ever trained.

Clint replied, "The great horses love going to the track."

Steve looked at his watch and told him he should get back to the barn. Clint said, "Really quick, I wanna show you what the boys did for me." He had the picture in the center of his pictures and trophies.

Steve said, "Whoever put this together did a great job."

Clint pointed at Charlie's ears and said, "That's why I said a heart as big as a washing machine."

Steve started for the door and said, "Have Junior bring you by the track if possible. You know I'll be at his stall, as you taught me."

"I'll do that, not only to see you but I have to see that monster up close."

"I've really missed you," Steve said before almost running outside. *He's emotional.*

I put my hand on Clint's shoulder and said, "I think he's missed you."

On the way back to the track, Steve started to cry before saying "So many years lost to a man that I thought of as a father. Pride is such an ugly thing."

I replied, "There are at least a million divorce lawyers that'll disagree with that, but I certainly agree. Thank God, you have some time and a common love to share now. That man loves Charlie."

Steve said, "Him and about a hundred million people around the world. It's unbelievable how people are being drawn to him, and also you two. It's all over how a couple old buddies stumbled into the greatest horse in the world."

Norm said, "It's been a fun ride, and we're glad you and Vickie are our drivers." I reminded Steve that Vickie was the better-looking driver.

He asked if I was starting to have feelings for her, so I replied, "I just enjoy looking at her. Did I tell you my girlfriend grew up across the street from Clint?"

He had a puzzled look on his face before saying "That's where I met her."

Norm said, "It really is a small world."

We were at the track to meet the van bringing the horses from the airport, and when Charlie walked off the van, I felt like I was seeing a long-lost love. That's corny, I know, but that's how attached you become to some horses. I asked Steve if he needed help getting him to the walker. "Ordinarily, you know I'd say yes, but I'm not sure how he'll react to that long flight." He took hold of his shank and walked him to the walker like a stroll in the park. He turned to me and said, "I'm sorry, I should have known he'd be a real professional, like he is with everything that's thrown at him."

Slim was another story; he was washed out and a real handful. Steve was completely winded when he got him settled, and said, "That's what I thought Charlie might do, but his class shows through in every situation." He told us he was expecting a monster race out of him. I asked what he thought of Slim's chances. He answered, "If he settles in, I think he can win, but what you just saw takes a lot out of horses. I'm not talking physically tired, but the stress can throw their blood levels off, as you well know." He told me he'd check the blood before the race. He went on to say "You don't know how much a level head means with these horses. That's what is meant when trainers talk about good and bad shippers."

He told us how happy he was that we helped him get back with Clint, so I said, "You're two really good men that have meant so much to each other."

"A million times he told me about the horse he was looking for, and as far as he's concerned, Charlie's that horse. He was very specific about the speed, stamina, horse's build, but always at the top of the list were heart and mental attitude. Believe me, if Clint says it, Charlie's the real thing." He asked if we would mind making Clint assistant trainer.

I said, "If there are no legal problems, it would be great."

He replied, "I'd stipulate for this race only and give him half of my commission."

Norm was elated about Clint being involved, so he said to me, "If he wins, I suggest we also give him 10 percent."

I replied, "You know I'm for it. It would be fantastic to give him a boost." *No doubt, God would like us helping a good man like Clint.*

Norm said, "The money would be nice, but to finally have his name linked with the horse he's always searched for would be worth far more to him." We agreed it was great to have other people love Charlie as much as we did. I couldn't help wishing Linda could be there to enjoy him. I smiled as I thought about how much Vickie would like Clint. I wondered why I was thinking about both of them at the same time. *I'm more confused than I was in junior high.*

Slim cleaned up his feed, and Steve told us it was a good sign, but he'd still draw the blood. I said, "This is why I've been making money betting just the horses you and Vickie give us. There's no way I can get some of these facts out of the form."

"We do the best we can, but we can't list everything. That's one reason I'll scratch Slim if his levels are off. Not only would it be unfair to Tom and Liz but also to the betting public." I really liked his integrity and wondered if all trainers were as thorough as he was.

I was getting hungry, so I told Norm it was time to eat. I then told Steve it would do no good to ask him to dinner, but I'd be happy to bring him something. I expected to hear about food Sandy sent, but he said, "A hot beef sandwich sounds good."

He started to reach for his wallet, but I said, "It's on me." I handed him the three hundred I put away for him, and he didn't argue because he knew it was part of my master plan. We ate our dinner before taking the sandwich back to Steve. I said, "If you want us to, we'll hire an armed guard to be here through the race."

"No, I need to be with them myself, but you guys are a huge help bringing me food and staying while I shower." He told us he didn't want us paying for his meals, so we told him we'd increase his win tickets. He said, "Notice, I'm not arguing anymore. I'm convinced that your plan is working. Don't think I'm super-stitious, but I don't change something when it's working. Don't tell anyone, but I haven't washed the undershorts I wear on the day Charlie runs since his first win."

I replied, "I have a feeling I won't have to tell anyone. As a matter of fact, I noticed the interviewer stayed away after the derby. He got a sick look on his face... **Gotcha,** I promise I'll tell you if I notice."

He said, "You really do have a mean streak."

I replied, "Only with people I like."

I called Vickie and told her the horses arrived in good shape. I didn't mention what Steve said about Slim because I didn't want her to worry. I told her about our travels and adventures. She loved hearing about the play and couldn't stop laughing when I told her Tom almost urinated in a guy's pocket.

She said, "You two are so much alike." She usually told me I was a big talker when I told her I'd see her in my dreams, but that time, she told me she was going to sleep and looked forward to seeing me. After we said "good night," I thanked God one more time for sending her to help me with my healing process. I couldn't help wishing she were closer to my age. *She couldn't be as attracted to me as I am to her, and it would crush me if she used me and tossed me away.*

The next morning, Charlie galloped, and Steve told the gallop boy to keep him on the outside of the track because he could be hard to hold when working horses went by. He galloped two really strong miles, trying to go every time a working horse passed them. I said to the guys, "He's full of vim and vinegar, so let's hope he doesn't get rank."

"Vickie knows him so well that she can handle anything he might throw at her. She says his intelligence keeps him from running off. According to her, he's the most push-button horse she's ever been on. Having said all that, I worry about it too," Steve said while trying not to laugh.

I replied, "You say I'm crazy." He told me he was just cautious. Charlie was wild-eyed when he came off the track. It could have been my imagination, but I was sure that, at one point, flames shot out of both eyes, and it took the entire gap to get him off the track safely. He was mad because he wanted to run and wasn't able to.

Steve said, "He's not happy with my plan, but he's in perfect shape, so watch out when Vickie gives him his head."

I said, "I've learned to have faith in your plans, as you have in mine. Don't worry about Norm or me doubting you since the time you worked him that mile."

"So you doubted me then, did you?"

"I didn't doubt your training ability, just your sanity," I explained.

"Oh, that makes me feel better. We really do have to work on that mean streak, so would you like to put Charlie on the walker?"

I took one look at Charlie and said, "No, thank you, we'll work on that mean streak later."

Slim worked a half in forty-six flat and was dancing when he came off the track. I said, "He looks fantastic, so would you mind if I call Tom?"

"Please don't until after I run the blood panel. Never build a client up to make it further to fall. I told Tom I was concerned about his travel, and he knows we may scratch him."

I replied, "I'm glad I asked before calling." They were on the walker across from each other and seemed to enjoy each other's company. The sun was shining, and both of their coats shined like brand-new pennies. *I should take this picture and put it in the dictionary under the word* content.

I told Steve he had a special gift of caring for and understanding the horses. He said with a big smile, "They're my life."

I said, "You've been giving us a special rate on day money, but I think it's time you get us into line."

"We're back to not changing things that are working, and you guys pay me more than the difference in tips every month." With a big smile, he said, "I really shouldn't tell you this, but if he wins this race, my commission will finish paying off my house."

I replied, "You really shouldn't have told me because I may need a place to stay someday."

"Oh, Lord, give me strength," he said before going back to work.

I told Norm we were running out of time to go to Foxwood, and he replied, "If it's all the same to you, I've seen enough casinos for a while."

I said, "I hoped you'd say that. It'll give us a reason to come back."

Steve said, "If Charlie stays sound, he'll bring you back because the way he travels, no race is off-limits."

There weren't many chores to be done, so we finished early. "Do you wanna shower and have breakfast?" I asked Steve after the horses were in their stalls.

"That sounds great," he said before grabbing a new set of clothes. Norm and I agreed that it had been nice getting to know him better.

We were enjoying the sunshine when I caught a man out of the corner of my eye, walking toward the horses with his hand out. My reflexes from back in my wrestling days were still intact. I jumped up and hammered down on his hand, causing some pills to fall to the ground. He was more interested in getting the pills than coming at me, so he knelt down to get them. That was a mistake. I'd watched way too many MMA matches to miss out there. I planted my knee on his right temple as hard as a 250-pound man could, and he was out like a light. I searched his waistline and found a .45 automatic. I tossed it to Norm and said, "Try to get as few fingerprints on it as possible."

Then my fun started. I remembered a wrestling move I used quite a bit when I was in school. I put him on his stomach and lifted his butt. In wrestling, I would reach through his legs to apply a half nelson. Then I would bring his head back to put him in a hold called a reverse cradle. I would then tip him up on his shoulders for the pin, but that time, the rules were out the window, so I grabbed a handful of his hair and pulled his head through. I tipped him just enough that, if he tried to move, this overweight body would snap his neck. I had all my weight pushing against his butt, but didn't apply quite enough pressure to snap his neck. Any struggling might do the job, however. I made myself as comfortable as possible before telling Norm to grab the pills and call 911.

"What if he tries to get away?" he asked.

"If he wakes up and starts to struggle, the last thing he'll hear is the snapping of his neck. Hurry and call them because every fiber in my body is crying out for me to push." After he called 911, I said, "Get the security guards here as quickly as possible because I'm not in the shape I was in high school. I'd hate the slumping of my tired body to do what I'm fighting with every fiber of my body not to do." He started to rouse around, and I said much calmer than I thought possible, "If you wanna live, don't move."

He gasped, "I can't breathe."

I said, "The fact that you are breathing means I still have my composure, but that could change at any time. You really don't wanna push it."

He started to struggle a little, so I applied just a tiny bit more pressure. "**My neck, my neck!**" he screamed.

"Your next movement will be your last," I said. He relaxed with a gasp as the security guards came running back. I asked them if they had cuffs, and they did, so I lifted his head to where his neck was out of danger before using all my weight to drive him down on his face. "Put them on him," I said, and believe me, it took all my willpower to not punch him in the side of his head.

Steve was back by then and asked, **"What happened?"**

I answered, "Norm has his gun and the pills he tried to give Charlie. They're evidence, so let's touch them as little as possible."

One of the security guys said, "He knows what he's doing."

"I watch too many police shows," I explained. Both the guards asked if I'd show them the move that gave me my advantage. "When this is over, I'd love to, but it's just a modified wrestling hold."

Steve asked, "What's that in your hand?" I hadn't noticed, but my hand was full of his hair.

I said, "His barber won't have to take much off the top." The guy complained about his neck and said he wasn't doing anything wrong.

The bigger of the guards said, "If you open your mouth again, I'll hit you so hard, you'll be complaining through a jaw held together with wire." As he walked past me, he whispered, "I'm betting your horse."

I said, "If he didn't get any of the pills delivered, I am too."

When the policeman arrived, one of the security guards came back to help. The policeman was very young and acted like he was wet behind the ears. He heard about the beating the guy took and seemed to be siding with him. He stuck his chest out and said, "Give me your side of the story." I took him through the entire sequence of events before he said "You may have a problem because it's his word against yours."

I'd never seen Steve angry, but he got up close to the officer and wrote down his badge number while asking "Young man, what is your captain's phone number?"

"And just why do you need that?" the kid asked through a smug smile.

Steve answered, "So I can get somebody down here that knows what the hell he's doing." The officer started to say something, but Steve spoke first. "We're protecting a multimillion-dollar horse from being drugged, and you're saying it's his word against ours. If you'll not give me his number, I'll get it and tell him you're totally disrespectful."

Again, the policeman started to speak, but the big security guard stepped in and said, "I'll show you why he said you don't know what you're doing." He dwarfed the cop, and I could see the kid was intimidated. The guard pointed to just above the stall door and showed him a security camera. "Whatever took place will be right there." He paused to speak into his radio and asked for the kid's supervisor. "I came here to explain the security system, but you're so full of yourself, you didn't allow me to explain anything. I think it's best if your boss is here before we talk." He called up to the security room again and told them to copy off the last half hour of activity at Wrong Way North's stall.

I said, "Excuse me, can they see where the pills landed? We need to know if any bounced into his stall."

"Get a super-slow-motion of the pills leaving the perpetrator's hand to show where they bounced when they hit the ground. Please have it at the stall ready to play in ten minutes. Put a rush on analyzing the pills, and bring the .45 back down, ASAP."

The policeman asked, "Why didn't you tell me there was a gun involved?"

That wasn't his finest moment. The guard turned to him with a really angry look on his face and said, "You wouldn't shut up long enough for me to say any-thing. **Now one more time**, I think it best we wait until your boss gets here to discuss this further."

I got down on my hands and knees and went through the straw at the door-way of Charlie's stall. I didn't know if it was good news or bad, but I didn't find any pills. When the player and film arrived, the security guard fast-forwarded to the part where the pills hit the ground. The slow-mo showed they didn't bounce toward the stall. The force of my hand going down caused them to bounce behind him, away from the stall. *That's a relief.*

When the police supervisor arrived, I could see he was irritated. He asked, "What's going on?"

The guard said, "I think your young officer has much to learn."

The supervisor asked him if he was to take his word against his officer's. I flashed a look at the young officer just as a smile crossed his lips. The guard said, "**Sir, you do not!**" He started the tape, and it had everything about the confrontation.

The supervisor looked at me and said, "You were well within your rights."

The guard fast-forwarded to the part where the officer arrived and said, "Here's the part you need to see." It showed that the kid's mind was made up before he arrived. Instead of asking questions, he was more interested in what he could say. He had a typical arrogant attitude.

The supervisor turned to me and said, "Sir, I'm sorry for his actions." He turned to the officer and asked him why he hadn't asked to see the tape.

He answered, "I didn't think about it." The supervisor told the guard he did a great job before asking for the gun and pills.

The guard said, "I have the gun for you, but the pills are being analyzed in our lab. You're welcome to the tape, if it'll help."

The supervisor told his officer to meet him back at the office, and after the young man left, he smiled and said, "This is my horse for the race."

I said, "Mine too. I just wish I was sure he didn't get any pills."

The guard said, "He didn't, this camera could pick up a sewing needle." He shook my hand and said, "Thanks for saving my bet, and I'll get the wrestling move off the tape."

Steve said to me, "I'll have Slim's bloodwork done today, and I'll also take blood on Charlie to make sure he didn't get any of the pills. Without it, I wouldn't sleep until the results of his postrace tests came back."

I said, "I wanted to suggest that, but I didn't wanna tell you how to do your job."

The waiting made it a long day, but both tests came back with perfect results. I said to Steve, "I worry too much, but if one pill had gotten through and showed up in his test, it would put a cloud over everything Charlie has accomplished."

He replied, "That's exactly why I ordered the test. I want the racing world to know how good he is." I know it's crazy, but I heard the music again and wondered if the others could hear it.

I said, "Steve, with what has happened, I think we should have an armed guard around him all the time. We'll be very happy to pay for it after what he's done for us." He agreed, so I went to security to make the arrangements. The big guy that we had gotten to know jumped at the chance and picked two of his friends to help out. I felt a huge relief come over me, and I was glad Steve would also be out of danger. I had no idea what went along with running for million-dollar purses.

It was two days before the race, and we were enjoying the hospitality provided by the track. Charlie galloped in the mornings and enjoyed the rest of the days. I was impressed with the way Slim had settled in. He was tearing up the track, so I asked Steve if he minded me telling Tom.

He replied, "By all means, call him."

Tom answered his phone and asked, "Why did you wait so long to call me?"

I replied, "Your darn horse is looking too good."

"Jim, I've come to realize, it's sometimes hard for me to understand where you're going with some of the things you say, but this time, I'm completely lost." *I do that to people sometimes.*

I told him to bear with me before saying "Steve was concerned that he might have to scratch him, and he didn't want me to build you up, so you'd have further to fall if he did."

Tom said, "That's somewhat like going to Texas by way of Seattle, but I'm up with you now."

I replied, "I don't understand myself most of the time either, Tom, but Slim couldn't possibly be doing better."

"Do you think he'll win the stake?"

I answered, "The way he's training, he'll be awfully hard to beat."

He asked if I'd seen the form. I told him I hadn't but I'd get one. He said, "Charlie's picked on top at two to one, and Slim's the fourth pick at eight to one."

I replied, "I'll not say Slim will win, but eight to one is way too high." Tom wanted to know if I would bet him. I said, "Just to win because I think Vickie will have a two-bagger Saturday."

"Then I'll bet them both also. Are you gonna put ten K on Charlie this time?"

I answered, "No, not enough reward for the risk. I may put five on both to win." We wished each other good luck before saying goodbye. *I sure wish they could make more races. They are a truly delightful couple.*

When I got back to the barn, both Clints were there. Senior thanked me for allowing him to be assistant trainer. I replied, "That was Steve's idea, but we're both happy he did."

"What a way to end my career, assistant trainer to a man I love like a son, with the Kentucky Derby winner going for the Belmont," he said with a big smile on his face. *Glad we can do this for him.*

I replied, "It's hard for me to believe how many dreams have been fulfilled by one horse."

"He's some horse, and I'm proud to be this close to him," he said while patting my back.

I replied, "I'm proud too and very happy Norm had a brain cramp the day he bought him."

Norm, who had been sitting, enjoying his time with the guys, said, "I knew that had to be thrown in there somewhere."

Junior said, "If we had drinks, I'd make a toast to the greatest mistake ever made." We all raised our clenched fists and said **"Hear, hear!"**

A Comcast van drove toward our barn and parked forty feet away. I walked over to meet whoever was inside, and a middle-aged lady stepped out. She introduced herself as Janet, and we shook hands before I took her over to meet the guys.

She asked if Vickie was available, and Steve said, "She has a couple horses to ride at Golden Gate today, so she'll fly in tomorrow morning."

She said, "First, Jamie wanted me to tell all of you how sorry she is that she couldn't be here." After we were set up for the interview, Janet started by introducing herself to everyone. She said, "If I'm not overstepping my boundaries, I'd like to ask about the incident from yesterday."

I motioned to Craig while saying "Let's ask him."

He was in front of Charlie's stall, and when he saw me point in his direction, he walked over to us. We explained what she wanted, and he said, "You can talk about the incident, but I wouldn't be comfortable giving out the man's name. It just so happens we received the results of toxicology report, and the pills were tranquilizers." Steve wanted to know if it was a lethal amount. "They could have been if he swallowed all four pills. They coated them with peppermint oil so he'd eat them quickly, so they had it all planned out." He told Janet she could report about the pills.

"Thank you, Craig," I said before we went back to our interview.

The first question was directed to Steve. "Since Wrong Way North missed two weeks of training, do you think he'll be as fit as he was in the Derby?"

"He only had one week off. He was out at a training farm in a large paddock the second week, and he loves to run the fence line. That keeps him physically fit, plus the mental relaxation he gets at the farm is very beneficial. If he loses, it won't be because of conditioning."

"Norm, as 80 percent owner, do you make the bulk of decisions about where and when to run?"

"I make zero decisions. That's why we have Steve, and may I say, his decisions have been great so far."

"Jim, this question is about the incident at the barn yesterday."

I said, "Please give me some leeway because there's an ongoing investigation."

She asked, "Do you feel like a hero?"

I laughed while saying "Not at all, my heroes are the men and women in the armed forces. They put their lives on the line for us every day, but all I did was react to a situation. I'm glad I could get to the person in question before he did what he came to do, but in no way am I a hero."

"One more, and then I'll let you all get back to your work. This will be in all the papers tomorrow. Someone allegedly tried to give Wrong Way North some tranquilizers. Do you have any idea why that would happen?"

"You always speculate that it would have something to do with the million-dollar purse, but we absolutely don't know that." On the air, she thanked us for giving her the interview and wished us good luck in the race.

Ten minutes later, Tom called me from Lake Tahoe and asked, "What's going on this time?" He told me ESPN reported about the interview before asking, "Are you all right?"

"No problem at all. I hit his arm from the side, and he went for the pills instead of me, so he wasn't looking at me when I hit him."

"Did he have a gun?" he asked while seeming very concerned.

"He had a .45 automatic in his belt, but it was easy to get because he was sleeping."

"What's his name? I'm well connected in the New York and New Jersey area, so I'll have answers for you before the police can find out who he is."

"You'll be the only one I have or will tell. His name is Jack Omono."

"I know who he is, so stay close to your phone, and I'll be back soon." It wasn't fifteen minutes before Tom was on the line again. "He'll be booked as a disgruntled gambler who lost a bundle on the Kentucky Derby. We know and the police know it wasn't all him, but he'll be the fall guy. Trust me when I tell you there will be no more attempts on the horses, so it's best we go along with the story. Have fun racing our horses tomorrow."

"I won't ask how you know this quickly, but know this, you are appreciated and considered a wonderful friend."

"Jim, you and Norm have become very good friends to Liz and me, and you are entirely welcome. I'll watch for you tomorrow, and I believe both horses will win." I thanked him again before we hung up.

When I got back to the guys, I said, "Tom knows people in this area who were able to find out what happened with Charlie. It'll come out as Jack being a gambler that lost a great deal of money when Charlie won the derby. Tom said he's sure he'll be a fall guy for someone, but we don't wanna know any more."

Steve said in a very stern way, "**You're right, we don't want to know any more!**" *Didn't have these problems when we ran in Yakima.*

CHAPTER 10

A Race for the Ages

Belmont Stakes day finally arrived. We woke up at six thirty, and Norm said, "Dibs on the first shower."

"Go ahead, I wanna bake in the glow of what looks like a beautiful day the Lord has given us."

"Bake all you want to, I'm hungry," he said on his way into the bathroom. I washed my face and put on a pot of coffee. While the coffee was brewing, I brushed back my hair and flossed my teeth before grabbing my toothbrush and going outside. When I went back inside, I could hear the final stages of my drip coffee brewer. I loved that sound because it told me the first cup was only seconds away.

Norm said, "Nothing like the smell of freshly brewed coffee in the morning. Have you thanked your company for the fine job they do?"

"Many times," I answered. I was fortunate to have worked thirty-seven years for a family-owned coffee company based in Portland, Oregon, and they had furnished all my coffee since I retired. Their quality is second to none, and through all the economic hard times of those thirty-seven years, one thing always held true. They wouldn't abandon quality coffees for the lure of less-expensive beans. I thanked them for that with every sip. I laughed as I thought, *That could have been a commercial.*

We both had three large cups with some lightly frosted lemon pound cake. I said, "That's a great way to start the morning."

"I love that dark roast because the flavor just jumps out and takes hold of you," Norm said while smacking his lips. I agreed with him before taking another gulp. *I wonder if Vickie drinks coffee. I'd love to lay her softly on a bed and moisten her lips with some freshly brewed coffee. Where on earth did that come from?*

When we arrived at the barn, Slim and Charlie were across from each other on the walker, and Steve was paying close attention to everything around him. Craig, the armed guard, had his hands folded in front of him while paying close attention. I thought, *This is really intense.* Craig said in his deep voice, "Top of the morning to ya, gentlemen."

I took six one-hundred-dollar bills out of my pocket and handed them to him while saying "This is two for each of you. Please give the other two guys theirs with my deepest gratitude. You can either put them in your pocket or on the horses."

"This isn't necessary, we're just doing our jobs," he replied.

I told him it was a tip for a job well done. He said, "Thank you, sir, and after watching these two horses the last few mornings, my pocket is not the place for the money."

I asked, "Steve, was your life easier before you hooked up with us?"

He thought for a few seconds before answering, "It was, but even if I hadn't made a penny more through this, it would be worth the whole world to me." He opened the form to Charlie's page and put his thumb on the spot that said "Asst. trainer, Clint Collins."

"You have no idea how I've missed him," he said in that same tearful tone.

I replied, "Pride can be a really bad thing. It only takes a second to say 'I'm sorry,' but I'd love to have a penny for every tear that's been shed in this world because people are too proud to say it. Let's get fired up and win this race so we can put sixty thousand dollars in Clint's pocket."

Steve looked at me for a second before saying "Half of my commission would only be thirty thousand."

"You were quite emotional when Norm said you both get 10 percent." He told me he had never had owners like us. I became a little emotional while saying "Most owners put a lot of money into buying these horses, and they spend most of their time trying to get their investment back. Charlie was a very special gift to us, and we're happy to share him." *I really believe that is why the blessings keep rolling in.*

When the horses were in their stalls, I asked Steve if he wanted to go to breakfast and take a shower. He jumped at it, so Norm and I settled in and helped

Craig keep watch. There was a lot going on with it being Belmont day because the workouts needed to be completed an hour earlier. I couldn't help noticing how beautiful all the horses were. When I was on the backside in Yakima, the good horses really stood out to me. All the horses at Belmont looked like the horses that were talked about in Yakima. There were more standout horses in Seattle but not as many as Belmont.

I jumped out of my chair when I saw a horse break away from a groom and head our way. I stood out in front of him, waving my arms but was just about to jump out of the way when he pulled up and turned to his left. Clint Jr. was there and grabbed his shank. After he took the horse to the groom, he came to me and said, "Be careful, there have been some horrific injuries from people standing in front of runaway horses." I told him I was looking for a place to bail when he pulled up. He laughed and said, "It seems that excitement comes looking for you. I can't tell you how much I appreciate you making Dad assistant trainer."

I replied, "We've come to like your dad very much, but the one that came up with the idea was Steve. He offered to give him half of his commission, but Norm said he'd give both of them 10 percent."

"Why would you do that for my dad, Norm?" he asked rather emotionally.

Norm answered, "Let's call it a bonus for what he's done for the sport, as well as what he means to Steve."

I said, "You do understand that 10 percent of nothing is nothing, so we have to win this race for your dad."

"I'm amazed, why would anyone give away that kind of money?" he asked.

Norm became somewhat emotional and spoke in a low voice, "We're so lucky to be here, and it's fun to share some of the rewards." *It's nice that we feel the same about sharing our very special gift.*

Junior said, "Thank you for my dad and me."

I replied, "I'm just glad you stood up for Charlie, or we may not have met you." He chatted with us for another couple of minutes before going back to his barn. He was shaking his head as he walked away, and I was sure some emotions were welling up inside him. I think the whole incident with Churchill, Steve, and us may have helped him realize how special his dad really was.

When Steve came back, he was carrying a newspaper and asked, "What did you say would be the reason he wanted to drug Charlie?"

"A disgruntled gambler," I answered.

He showed me the front page, and in bold letters, it was written, **"Gambler Loses Bundle on Kentucky Derby and Tries to Take It Out on Wrong Way North."** It went on to say "Quick action by the owners and security guards saved his chance to run in today's Belmont Stakes." It explained that the perpetrator tried to give the horse tranquilizers.

Steve said, "No doubt, Tom knows somebody." Slim was in the third race, and the race was a couple of hours away. I didn't wanna go to the other side and leave Charlie for Slim's race, so I bet him at the backside café. I bet two separate hundred-dollar wins for Steve and Vickie before betting five thousand to win for myself. I was becoming more comfortable betting larger amounts as my horse account continued to grow. I thanked God one more time for Charlie and gave special thanks for sending Vickie to help me heal. *I wish she was closer to my age, darn it.*

I told the guys I was going to the trailer to take a nap. On my way, my cell phone rang, and the caller ID told me it was Jamie. She called to pass on thanks from Janet for the last interview and asked if she could interview us again after the race. I replied, "She's welcome to interview us anytime."

She asked, "What on earth is going on out there?"

I told her what was written in the paper before saying "Nothing has gone along normally with Charlie since we bought him."

"The good thing is, he keeps winning through it all," she said before saying goodbye.

It felt good to lie down, and I was asleep in no time. I slept for about a half hour before I woke with a start. I wondered if I'd missed the race, but looking at my watch brought me some relief. I brushed my teeth and combed my hair before going back to the barn. I think Norm and Steve were getting more rest than I did. I mentioned all the activity around the track, but that didn't include our barn. I said, "You guys look entirely too comfortable."

Steve replied, "In another half hour, things will pick up." I had eaten breakfast early, so I was starting to get hungry. Norm, Clint, and I went to the café for lunch, and Steve stayed at the barn.

When Steve took Slim over, I stayed at the barn to help watch Charlie. I said, "Norm, you have to give me a blow-by-blow recap of the race."

I could hear the announcer say, "Slimsfinefood goes right to the front, and after the first quarter, he's leading by two lengths. **Oh my**, the first quarter went in a blistering twenty-two seconds flat."

I whispered, "Slow him down a little, Vickie." Turning for home, he maintained the two-length lead, and the half was forty-four and three. *Awfully fast on this sandy track. Sounds more like California time.* He drew off to win by four in one minute and eight seconds flat. "Wow, that does sound like California time!" I shouted.

I couldn't believe how quickly Tom called me. He was jumping all over the place. I couldn't see him, but I could hear all the commotion. "Eleven to one," he said. I was glad he told me because I didn't want him to know I didn't watch the race. "It's official, $25.30 to win. Man, that's great, did you bet your five K?"

I answered, "I bet that plus a hundred for Steve and Vickie."

He told me he got them a little more than that, and I was sure he meant a bunch. He said, "Since you were so confidEnt, I also bet five on him."

"The question is, did Liz do the same?" I asked.

"Wow, in all the excitement I forgot. **She did!**"

I said, "Tom, I'm happy for you, and there's no doubt Steve knew what he was doing when he claimed him."

"Steve has done a wonderful job with him all along, and he seems to be getting better. Meeting you two yahoos has made my life a lot more fun," he said while trying to contain his excitement.

"Believe me, we feel the same," I replied. I was thinking about how he just helped us.

"Good luck in the Belmont," he said while barely being able to contain his excitement. I told him I'd call him after the race. I didn't thank him again for the incident because I felt it might be best to leave it alone. *He was excited!*

Norm was excited when he came back, and said, "Steve's at the test barn. Slim just toyed with that bunch, and Vickie plans to put Charlie on the front end after that race because speed is really holding." I was excited because I knew Charlie had plenty of speed that he didn't show in the derby. Norm continued, "I was surprised at how easily Slim took the lead."

I replied, "I could hear the fractions and was worried he might stop on this deep track."

"He was pulling away at the end, and Vickie had her arm raised before the wire," he said with his voice still full of excitement. I had just heard my two closest friends beside themselves with excitement and thought, *I missed a great race.* I knew Vickie was excited at that moment, and I was eager to see her. *We couldn't find this kind of excitement anywhere else.*

After Steve brought the horse back, he said, "I was worried Vickie was taking him out too fast."

I replied, "I could hear the fractions and was saying 'Slow him down.'"

"She knew what she was doing. Slim's g'tting' really good, so he'll be in a graded stake next time, if he comes out of this race in good shape."

Slim was bouncing when he came back, so I said, "If anything shows up tomorrow, I wouldn't think it could be too much."

"Adrenaline can hide a lot," he replied. I told him about Tom's call, and while laughing, he said, "He called me in the winner's circle and told me to wave." *Darn, he knows I missed the race.*

I replied, "He could turn out to be one of your best clients because he's having so much fun."

Steve was laughing while saying "It sounded like the entire casino was in the party. I could hear somebody jumping around, and I assumed it was Tom, but it could have been anyone in the room."

We sat around the barn until the race before the Belmont, and I watched Steve rinse Charlie's mouth and flex each leg. He took him to the holding barn when the announcer called them over, but Norm and I waited until that race was over before joining them. *This is tense.*

I said, "Norm, Craig has worked a long day."

He replied, "They all worked double shifts."

I said, "I hope they were able to get their bets down." Norm told me he made their bets for them, and he matched what I gave them. I said, "That'll give them a little spending money."

He replied, "Just over 2,500 each before Charlie's race, so they're all happy."

Clint Sr. was at the holding barn to walk over with us. He said, "It's been a long time since I've gotten this excited about a race."

Charlie was eight to five, and the Preakness winner was two to one. Vickie came over and gave us each hugs. That was the first time I'd seen her since we left California because her plane was delayed. She thought she might miss Slim's race, but thank goodness, they had some tailwinds. She gave us her wink when they walked by, and when they walked onto the track, I went up to make my wagers. I bet two hundred to win for both Steve and Vickie before betting five thousand to win for myself. When I collected the ticket from Slim, I had them give me a check. That took a little longer to do than I thought it would, so they were entering the gate when I walked over to a TV.

I said, "Get him out on top, Vickie."

The announcer said, "**They're off, in the Belmont Stakes.** My heart skipped a couple of beats because Charlie hopped into the air just as they opened the gate and broke dead last, four lengths behind the field. Cornish Memories didn't try to go out, thank goodness, so he didn't open up a huge lead. I whispered, "Time for plan B, Vickie." He was right in behind the field by the first turn and was able to pass three horses on the inside. Going up the backstretch, she took him to the outside and began to make good progress. Going into the turn for home, he was sitting fourth and on the move. Coming out of the turn, he was outside the second-place horse, only two lengths behind Cornish Memories. The inside horse bolted, taking him to the outside fence, so Cornish opened a four-length lead before Vickie could get Charlie straightened out. She kept him way outside and began to whip. The move he made was unlike any I had ever seen. He went from four back to two in front so quickly that I was in total disbelief. Cornish Memories didn't see him coming until it was too late because he was so wide. Charlie won by two lengths, and the announcer said, "The last quarter was run in twenty-one seconds flat." He sounded like he couldn't believe what he was saying.

Clint looked at me and said, "In sixty-seven years, I've never seen that fast a last quarter on this track."

Charlie was breathing really hard when they came into the winner's circle, and Vickie said, "You know how I always say I haven't found the bottom of him? I just found it. He actually threw me back when he rebroke. There may have been a better horse somewhere in history, but I'd love to run against any of them."

Clint Jr. took him to the barn so Steve could stay for the interview. ESPN sent a young man to interview us, and he told Vickie he'd talk to her first. "Could you have gotten into any more trouble?"

"Not without trying to. My plan was to go to the front and let Cornish Memories play catch up, but so much for plans." After working to catch her breath, she said, "A big part of the win was being able to go by three horses on the inside, in the first turn. Steve told me he galloped him on the outside of the track all week to avoid working horses, so when we were forced so wide, I thought, he knows the territory, so I'll just leave him there. I really believe that helped us because Cornish Memories, who is a very nice horse, didn't see us coming." *This is one gorgeous lady. Forget it, Jim. She could be your daughter.*

The interviewer said, "And now to a legend of the sport, Clint Collins. Did you ever train a horse that was this good?"

"I've never seen a horse this good."

Stan replied, "That covers a lot of years."

"I'm excited right now, but that last quarter was better than anything I've seen, without a doubt."

Steve was next, "Anything to add to what's been said?"

"This race is dedicated to the first man I worked for when I came into this business, my mentor, Clint Collins." His voice began to break, so he excused himself to go look after the horse. Clint wiped a tear from his eye after Steve left.

"Norm, when did you know you would win?"

"When he crossed the finish line. I would normally say when he took the lead, but the way things were unfolding, I half expected him to fall down."

"Jim, do you wanna talk to us about the attempted drugging incident?"

I replied, "I only know what you've read in the papers, but I'm glad he didn't get the drugs delivered so we could run. Since we're in New York, where 9/11 occurred, I'd like to thank the men and women of our armed forces, firefighters, and police force. We hope they enjoyed the race as much as we did."

The trophy was given to Norm, and he showed a huge amount of class by giving it to Clint while saying "This one's for you, my friend."

When we were back at the barn, Charlie's head wasn't hanging, but he wasn't dancing on the walker. Steve said, "When you hear a horse gave his all, you just saw an example." He shook his head while saying "You very seldom see a first quarter of twenty-one flat on this track in a sprint, but to do it at the end of a mile and a half is unheard of." We all cheered and expected Charlie to look up, but he continued to walk slowly.

I asked, "Steve, will he be okay?"

"He will, for sure. This is the first time he's had to empty the tank to win, and it took a lot out of him. He's earned a couple weeks at the farm with that performance."

I stepped away to call Tom, and his words were "He silenced the crowd. We all hoped he'd get second when he was forced wide in the final turn. When he started to move, the cheers came, but when he caught the leader as quickly as he did, a dead silence came over the house." I could hear him sigh before saying "After a minute or so, a man said, 'Remember this moment because we just witnessed greatness.'"

I replied, "Like you, I was hoping for second, but when he went so wide, I thought, maybe third. We had a very good day, my friend."

"In the theme of Charlie, let's call it a great day," he replied.

I said, "Slim's getting better all the time, and Steve is talking graded stakes for him. Would you like to put Charlie's win pictures from the Derby and Belmont up in your sports book?"

"I'll put them front and center," he answered. *He's still excited.*

I said, "Put Slim with him because they're brothers. We'll win many more pictures of both of them before they're through."

Vickie was at the barn when I arrived, so I gave her and Steve their tickets. "What a day," she said.

I replied, "What a training job and fantastic ride. Did you think you could win when you got him straightened out?"

"No, I hoped for second or third. Charlie was probably the only one in the place that knew losing wasn't an option." She told me she loved him before but never dreamed he could do that. I hugged her and told her I was glad she was his pilot. She kissed my cheek before saying "Thank you for saving him so we can celebrate this win."

While looking into her gorgeous blue eyes, I said, "It really was nothing, but after all he's done for me, I'd gladly put my life on the line for him."

She told me we were all like family to her, and I thought *Wow, she shouldn't look at me that way.* I kissed her a little more sensually than I should have before saying "You're all I've thought about for the last few weeks." Janet from Comcast drove up and asked if she could do an interview. *I'm glad she arrived when she did.*

Vickie replied, "As long as I can sit, I'll stay." She whispered to me, "You keep getting saved by the bell, sweet boy." I smiled and asked her if the three-knock-down rule was in effect.

We all agreed that we were tired but I kept shooting glances Vickie's way, with all kinds of emotions running through me.

Janet said, "Not a very lively bunch."

I replied, "The only one more exhausted than us is Charlie."

When the cameras were set up, Janet went to Vickie first. "What an amazing ride, would you say it was your best ever?"

She answered, "No, I can't take any of the credit because it was all Charlie."

"Still, you made the women of America really proud."

Vickie looked into the camera while saying "Sorry, ladies, but the hero here is all man."

"Very honest answer," Janet said while shaking her hand.

She asked, "Steve, have you ever had a horse run this well?"

"I'll say what Clint said earlier, I've never seen one. That last quarter will be talked about as long as horsemen sit in bars and cafés and talk about the great races of history. I'm so proud we were here to witness it."

"Jim, do you have anything to add?"

"I have a question, are the Blue Angels in town?"

"I don't know, why do you ask?"

"I'm sure I heard a sonic boom when Charlie was running down the lane, so either the Blue Angels are in town or he broke the sound barrier."

She laughed and said, "Jamie warned me that you might kid a little."

"Norm, anything to add?"

"How can I follow the sound-barrier remark? I wanna thank Steve, Vickie, and Clint for all they've done and say how proud I am of our entire team."

"That leads us to the mentor, Clint Collins." She shook his hand and asked, "Can you put into words what today has meant to you?"

He didn't know where to start. "The week has been so great. I learned that my pride can get in my way, as many have before me. I saw the best race, as far as overcoming adversity, that I've ever seen. I met two guys that America should be proud of." With tears in his eyes, he said, "Their love of fellow man surpasses anything I've ever seen." He shook both our hands and said, "Godspeed the rest of the way, boys." We both told him we felt lucky to get to spend some time with a man of his stature.

No one wanted to go to dinner. We were all drained from the day or, I should say, the week, so I left and bought a bucket of chicken. All but the two Clints stayed until after midnight, and I believe it was hard for any of us to stand up. I told Steve his friend Clint was a special man before Norm told him he hoped the money would help with his retirement. Steve said, "I'm so glad we reconciled while he's still alive."

I replied, "Believe me, Steve, he is too." We got to the trailer at one thirty, and I don't remember my head hitting the pillow. We didn't wake up until after 10:00 a.m., and neither of us wanted to get up, so we didn't move or speak for at least a half hour. *I almost said too much to Vickie, so I better be careful.* **That kiss was amazing!** *I can't do this.*

Finally, Norm said, "You take the first shower."

"You must be tired because you usually want the first shower."

"That took a lot out of me yesterday," he said while sucking in sharply.

I told him I felt the same before saying, "I'm proud of our horse's place in history." Before going into the bathroom, I said, "If only he had run in the Preakness."

Norm replied, "Be happy about the races we've won."

"I keep thinking Vickie could have won the Triple Crown," I said through the door.

After getting cleaned up, we went to the café for breakfast and lunch combined. It was 11:30 and the place was buzzing about the race. Pretty much everyone agreed that last quarter would be talked about for a long time. One guy said, "Cornish Memories also ran a great race." *He's really improving and I'm sure we'll meet again.*

When we arrived at the barn, Steve told us Charlie was coming back around so he would take him home the next day. Norm asked. "What'll you do with him when he gets back to California?"

"It's three months until the Longacre Mile so I wanna give him a couple weeks at the farm. He'll have one or two races leading up to the Mile, but I find it strange that a grade 3 is what we're aiming for. I understand it's your home, though."

I replied, "I've always dreamed about that race, but I wasn't bold enough to dream about the Triple Crown races. It'll be fun taking the winner of two of those races back home. A few years ago, the winner of the Mile went on to win the Breeder's Cup Classic, so it's not an easy race."

We went to the office to thank them for their hospitality, and everyone there was full of excitement. The racing secretary told us to have Steve call if he wanted to run either of the horses at Belmont again. I said, "I wouldn't be surprised, if they stay sound." I gave them an address to send us our money as soon as the tests came back, and said, "Clint Collins should get 10 percent, so please give it to Junior." We signed some papers releasing the money, and they all told us we were more than generous. On the way out, Norm and I agreed that it made us feel good to help Clint. I said, "Don't think God isn't taking notice. *Good things happen to good people.*

He said, "You and Vickie are getting closer."

I replied, "I love calling her my friend, and it makes me feel good just looking at her." He told me she looked quite a bit like Linda, so I said, "It's scary how much she feels like her when she's in my arms." I was surprised when he asked me if I had made love to her. I replied, "Heavens, no, she's younger than Tammy, but don't think I haven't thought about it." *How could any guy not think about it?*

We were up early the next morning and stopped to tell Steve what we did with Clint's commission. After setting our GPS for locations along the way, we took turns driving and were able to stay on the road for eleven hours a day. The roads were very good all the way back, so we made good time. When we were coming to northern Nevada, I said, "Let's go see Tom."

Norm replied, "We owe him."

I said, "It's good to know people. I wonder if we should talk to him about the incident, but I guess, if he wants to talk about it, he can bring it up. If he doesn't, I think we should leave it alone." We decided to go with that because Steve certainly got away from it when we talked about it. I told him, sometimes, ignorance really is bliss.

Norm reminded me, "Like you and the saddle incident, so long ago."

We hadn't taken the trailer to the casino, so they showed us where to park and plug in. We were feeling a little cramped, so we decided to stay in the hotel. Like always, they gave us a suite for as long as we wanted to stay. Tom and Liz were off the day we arrived, but the lady checking us in offered to call them. I told her to let them enjoy their day off and tipped her a hundred dollars for always being so nice.

We played for a while but were hitting nothing, so we went to the buffet and spent a full hour browsing and eating small amounts of several foods. We were tired from the drive, so we decided to go to the room early. I looked out the window to admire the lake, and Norm said, "This is why we came up here every year, but we came during the winter so we could ski."

I turned to ESPN, but there was nothing on that interested me. Norm was in his room, watching a baseball game, and asked me why I didn't watch them. I said, "I enjoy going to a game with a group of friends and making a dollar wager on the final score, but I'd rather watch grass grow than watch a game on television. I do sometimes watch a couple innings, when the Mariners are playing."

I fell asleep on the bed with my clothes on but woke up a few hours later. The TV in Norm's room was on, so I went to the bathroom before creeping into his room to turn it off. He was snoring, so I knew he was alive. I took my clothes off before going back to bed and was asleep as soon as my head hit my pillow. I dreamt about how excited Vickie was after the Belmont. I had been trying to convince myself that we were just friends, but I was losing the battle. Not only was she beautiful but she was also fun to be around. *I know it's stupid, but she appeals to me way too much.*

The sun coming through the window woke me at six thirty, but I decided to stay in bed until Norm woke up. I was almost asleep when he yelled "Top of the morning to ya!"

"Good morning," I said while rolling out of bed. I made the in-room coffee while whistling a happy tune.

"That whistling is a pain," Norm said, so I asked if he'd rather I'd sing. "**Whistle all you want to!**" he shouted.

After getting cleaned up, we went down to breakfast and decided on the buffet. We had two cups of coffee before looking at the food line. We were about to go through the line when a familiar voice asked if we minded having some company. "How was your day off, Tom?" I asked as I stood up. He told us it was great but wanted us to know we could have called him. I replied, "I've come to believe we can count on you for almost anything."

Norm and I were eating breakfast, and Tom was drinking coffee. I almost choked on my food when Tom told us he wasn't involved in any criminal activity. I said, "Nothing like coming to the point."

We told him we didn't think he was, and he said, "You didn't ask how I could fix the problem so quickly."

I replied, "We talked about it and decided you'd tell us if you wanted us to know."

He explained, "I know some people who may or may not have ties to the underworld. They've helped me in that area a few times, when people run up gambling debts and try to skip out. I was familiar with Jack because we've had to collect from him a couple times. He'll do anything to get gambling money, but he's really low profile. He would have shot you if you had given him the chance, though."

I replied, "I figured there was a reason he was carrying the gun. Your integrity has never been in question with us, Tom, and Steve has thanked us numerous times for bringing you to the barn."

After I finished eating, I told them I was going out to play. I bought my Keno numbers for ten games and walked around until I found a machine that appealed to me. I put twenty dollars in, and the first spin produced thirty-five dollars. The next several didn't hit, so I thought, *Double up and catch up.* I started playing two hundred credits and hit five bonus symbols. That gave me twenty-five free games, and I played in the bonus games for a long time. Every time I was almost out of games, I'd hit more, so when the bonus round was over, 540 dollars rang up. *That more than makes up for yesterday.* I played five more times at two hundred credits but hit nothing, so I printed out my ticket. Norm was playing blackjack, and as always, he was playing with the prettiest dealer in the house. "You doing any good?" I asked.

"No, the table has been against me the whole time."

I gave him a hundred and said, "Play on house money for a while." He wasn't the only one at the table, indicating that the table had been leaning toward the house, so I bought a hundred dollars in five-dollar chips and said, "This table is about to turn." My first hand, I was dealt thirteen and the dealer had a six showing. Both Norm and I stayed, and the dealer broke. I won seven hands in a row, and after the third, I was playing twenty-five dollars. After playing for a short time, I collected three hundred dollars and tossed a twenty-five-dollar chip to the dealer before telling Norm he was on his own. I made 175 dollars there, and when I checked my Keno tickets, I had eighty-six dollars coming, so I doubled my money there. It's funny how, many times, when Lady Luck smiles your way, it seems to cover all the games. *Foxy little lady, that Lady Luck.*

I went out by the lake to watch people for a while, and the water was beautiful. There weren't as many types of exercise as there were in Atlantic City, but there were a lot of people out. There was a young couple with two little girls, so I watched them, and my mind drifted back to when our girls were that age. *Way too quickly, time goes by much too quickly.* My dad once told me, "If you wanna get old, just hang around because time stands still for no man." I thought about how the last twenty years seemed like a couple of weeks and promised myself that I'd enjoy every day I had left. For some reason, Vickie crossed my mind right then. She was visiting my thoughts more every day. *I wish she wasn't so young because I don't like seeing old guys hit on young women.*

After about an hour, I walked back inside. Norm was at the same table and had a nice stack of chips in front of him. The dealer had gone all the way around and just returned to his table. She asked me if I wanted some chips, so I asked, "Norm, will you play for a while?"

He answered, "Until she moves again." I bought a hundred in five-dollar chips and lost the first three hands at five dollars. The table was starting to turn in our favor, so I kicked my bets up to ten dollars and then twenty-five. We played until they changed dealers, and I threw her two twenty-five-dollar chips on her way out. I guess, if the truth were known, Norm wasn't the only one who liked pretty dealers. We played a couple of losing hands with the new dealer before cashing in.

After dinner, I told Norm I'd stay down for a while, so he threw me a black chip and said, "Play on house money for a while." I found a unicorn machine that wasn't being played and inserted a twenty. I played on it for over an hour, but in the end, my twenty belonged to the house. I told Norm I was going up to the room, and from the looks of his stack of chips, his luck was still good.

I looked out the window for some time because the lights glistening off the water were beautiful. The ringing of my phone startled me, and Vickie asked, "Where are you guys?" I told her we stopped to see Tom and Liz on our way back. "I thought you might be there. When is it my turn?"

I answered, "Sweetie, you're here with me now."

I thought I was being cute, but she asked, "What exactly are you doing about that, lover boy?" *Wow, that stopped me in my tracks.*

I said, "Believe me, Vickie, Tom would love to have you come up here with us." I realized that my face was hot and flushed.

She was kind enough to let me off the hook. While laughing, she said, "I called about a first-time starter in the first race tomorrow. We're starting her low because her best works are hidden and the breeding is pretty common."

I said, "Just a minute, **you're gorgeous**! Sorry to interrupt you, but I was thinking it and had to say it." *Can't let her know she embarrassed me.*

She replied, "You're silly, the filly should go right to the front and go on with it."

I asked, "Do you mind me telling Tom about the horse?"

"That would be fine," she replied. We chatted for a few minutes before I thanked her for the tout.

"Just a minute, **you're not so bad yourself, sweetie**. Sorry to interrupt you, but I was thinking it. so I had to say it. I'd love to go the lake with you sometime." *She's good.*

After we said goodbye, I shook my head and thought, ***She's younger than my daughter!*** She really had me twisted in knots. I'd tell myself that our relationship was all business and think how much I cared for her at the same time. I could tell she was enjoying herself, and she was very good because, during that entire conversation, she never changed the tone of her voice. I had all kinds of feelings running through me. *If only she wasn't so young.*

I watched television for a while before drifting off to sleep. Having separate bedrooms was nice because I didn't hear Norm come in. I left the curtains open, so I woke up early, but I lay there for a while before going into the bathroom. I was so comfortable and so happy. I didn't know if I should flirt with Vickie so much, but she had me feeling better than I had in a long time. On my way out, I peeked in Norm's room, and he was sleeping like a baby.

On the elevator ride down to the casino, I thought about my conversation with Vickie. I was trying to be really cool flirting with her, but she totally turned the tables on me. She was not only lovely but also very sharp. Without a doubt, she had me eating out of her hand. I thought back to the times I enjoyed teasing girls and marveled at the way she turned things around on me. *I can't let her know how confused I am. Cute lady.*

I love new days in a casino. I bought my Keno tickets for ten games before going to the sports book to see if the entry sheets were out. The eastern tracks were out, but Golden Gate wasn't. I thought about playing a slot machine, but a leisurely breakfast sounded better. I went to the buffet and had them cook me an omelet. I also had a small piece of french toast and loved how the syrup and eggs tasted together. I was just about ready to go into the casino when Tom walked up and asked, "Do you have time for coffee?"

"I sure do, as a matter of fact, I was gonna look you up because Vickie gave us a horse for today."

He said, "We should do something nice for her."

I replied, "I always get her a win ticket." He told me he did that also but thought something really nice was in order. He laughed when I said "I won't tell you what I think is in order."

"I think Vickie says it best, **talk, talk, talk**. Do you ever think of her romantically?"

"I think she's beautiful, but she's younger than my oldest daughter. Why would you ask me that?" He told me Liz thought we'd make a cute couple, so I said, "Tell Liz I love her for thinking of me, but there's no room in my life for a woman right now. Vickie does have me thinking about women again, but the age difference will always be there. No doubt, I've thought many times about being with her, but I respect her too much to take advantage of her."

"You do think of her romantically then?"

"I'm old, but I'm not dead. Believe me, I've thought about it many times, but I'd never do anything until I knew I could devote myself to her." He told me he respected me but didn't think he could show that much restraint. "You're twenty years younger than me, and I wouldn't have been able to at your age." *Linda and I had an amazing love life for forty years.*

He asked, "Where is Norm?"

"He plays into the early morning hours, so he was asleep when I left the room. With him snoring in his own room, I'm able to sleep without my earplugs, so thank you for the suite."

"Please believe me, that room is yours anytime you want it. **Vickie really is attractive**, you know." After a couple of cups of coffee and me asking if he was the one who thought about her romantically, we stood up to walk out. "Like you said, it wouldn't be possible to not think about it, but believe me, Jim, I have my hands full with Liz."

I replied, "Don't be offended, my friend, but I have no problem at all believing that."

I went into the casino as he walked back toward his office. I checked my Keno tickets and had six dollars coming, so I gave the girl the dollar bill and added fifteen dollars to play the games five more times. I thought about the conversation with Tom. *If I was younger and able to think about another woman, Vickie would be number one on the list.* I was thankful that she had me taking notice again. I just wished I could get her off my mind. ***I'm too old to be this stupid.***

I went by the sports book to pick up a Golden Gate entry sheet, and there were ten horses in the first race. Vickie was on the seven, and I decided to wager early so I wouldn't forget. I put fifty to win and place on her horse. There were nine horses in the second, so I wheeled her horse to all in the second with ten-dollar doubles. I walked by the blackjack tables but didn't find Norm. The dealer was there from the day before, so I asked if she'd seen him. She hadn't, so I was a little concerned. I went up to the room to see if he was still sleeping.

The maid was making up the room and told me he was gone when she arrived. I gave her a twenty and said, "My wife always left a gratuity for housekeepers, but I never think about it." I walked outside, looking for him, but he wasn't by the lake. I went back inside and looked in the buffet. I could see him through the window, so I told the lady at the counter I had eaten but I'd like to go in and let my friend know where I was.

She said, "I saw you with Tom, so go right in." He was just finishing his breakfast, so I didn't sit down. I thanked the lady at the counter as we were walking out before Norm asked what I wanted to do. I told him about the horse in the first race and told him I bet it early so I wouldn't forget.

He thought that was a good idea, so he went to the sports book to make his wager. He said, "The filly is ten to one."

I explained, "Vickie said they were able to hide the works, but she did say the clocker will bet him."

Norm told me he had been playing a game that was new to him. The game was pai gow, and he explained how to play. "The dealer will actually set your hands for you until you're comfortable setting them on your own. There are two hands, with five cards on bottom and two on top. Your bottom hand must beat the top, and either the dealer or the player must win both, or it's a push. The player can play up to as much on his bonus wager as the wager itself." I thought it sounded complicated but told him I'd give it a try. We played for several hours, and I never did win much, but I didn't lose much either. We both finished down about a hundred, but we had a great time.

It was 3:00 p.m. when we walked away from the table, and we were both surprised to notice how much time had passed. I said, "I wanna check my Keno tickets." I stopped in my tracks and shouted, "**We forgot the race!**" Norm told me he couldn't believe we both forgot it. I said, "With two of us, you'd think there would be a brain in there somewhere."

We stopped by the Keno area on our way to the sports book. I had thirty-three dollars coming, so I gave three to the girl and put the remainder in my pocket. When we arrived at the sports book, I said, "You check your tickets first." He had fifty to win and place and was very pleased when the machine told him he had 680 dollars coming back. I said, "Good, that means she won." I got that plus I had the double five times, so my total was 1,320 dollars.

Tom walked up as we were leaving the sports book and asked if we bet the race. Norm said, "Luckily, Jim had me bet it early, or I wouldn't have."

Tom said, "I looked through Keno, blackjack, and slots but I couldn't find you."

I replied, "Norm showed me a new game called pai gow."

He said, "I didn't think to look there."

He asked if we enjoyed the game, and I laughed while saying "Enough that we forgot about the race."

"Liz will get a big kick out of this. She was here for the race and said, 'Those guys are hoots, so they could be anywhere.'"

I said, "Tom, I got the money, and that's great, but please give me a replay of the race."

"It was pretty simple, the filly went out on top and never looked back."

I said, "That's what Vickie said should happen." Tom gave me two hundred dollars and asked me to give it to her, so I took two hundred from what I collected and told him I'd give her four and make sure she knew half was from him. We talked for a while about how much fun the horses had been before Tom gave us a voucher for the restaurant on the top floor. I said, "You've done too much for us already. We've known you for less than a year, and you feel like a lifelong friend."

"You guys earn the comps, and Liz and I feel the same about our friendship." He wanted to know how long we were staying, so we told him it would be no more than another day.

After a very nice meal, I decided to play a little longer since we were going home the next morning. We found two empty seats at a pai gow table and played for a couple of hours. I could tell when the smoke was getting to me, so I told Norm I was going to the room.

I decided to go out by the lake before going up. There was a very soft breeze, and the lights on the water were magical. Once again, my mind drifted back to when Linda and I went there on vacations. We didn't spend very much money gambling at first, so we spent a good amount of time by the lake. She loved to play the slots, but we couldn't budget too much. *I sure wish she was here now.* It would be very different for her, not having to watch so closely what she spent, but maybe it wouldn't be as much fun. At least once a day my eyes teared up, but that was part of my healing process, and the memories were too precious to let slip away.

When I was in the room, I turned the television on and watched a movie for a while. I became bored with the movie, so I started flipping through the channels and came across an old *Bonanza* rerun. It reminded me that Linda and I stopped at the Ponderosa the first time we went to the lake. I was glad we did because a couple of years after that, they closed the place. When we arrived, I asked her to remind me to go upstairs because, in all the shows I watched, I never did see the upstairs. The actors were always at the top of the stairs, coming down, or at the bottom, going up. I was surprised to find there was no upstairs. The staircase stopped at a door, and that was it. It looked like a big house on television but was a really small model house. I guess that's what they refer to as the magic of cinema. After *Bonanza* was over, I turned off the television and went to sleep. Norm made a noise when he came in at 1:00 a.m., so I said, "This is early for you." He told me he started getting tired and his luck turned at the same time. I said, "Vickie bailed us out again."

I made sure to close the curtains so I wouldn't wake up as soon as the sun came up. It was a good decision because I was able to sleep until eight thirty. We took our time getting cleaned up and had a long, leisurely breakfast. As he had begun to do, Tom had coffee with us before we left.

A slight drizzle welcomed us back to Northern California. It was more of a rolling fog than rain, but after the glorious mornings we'd been waking up to, it was a bit of a downer. Norm took the first shower, so I started the coffee. I was hungry from skipping dinner the night before, so I rummaged through the freezer and found about a third of a lemon pound cake. I thawed it in the microwave and found some of the bounce was out of it. After taking the wrapper off, I gave it a good visual once-over, looking for mold. By that time, my hunger was more noticeable, but I almost dropped the cake when Norm bellowed how good the coffee smelled. There was no mold, so I popped it into the microwave again. When I opened the door, the aroma mixed with the freshly brewed, dark-roast coffee, was overpowering. *Sixty-four years old, and my sense of smell is alive and kickin'.* For a moment, I wondered how well the rest of me would work but laughed, knowing Vickie had certainly put some lovely visions in my head. I poured us a cup of coffee and divided the cake into two pieces.

Norm asked, "Aren't you gonna shower?"

"Not until after I eat, so if I'm offending you, it's not too bad outside."

"I'll put up with you. To good food, good coffee, and best of all, good friends," he said while tapping his cup to mine.

"I agree with all of that, especially the coffee," I said in return. He rolled his eyes and shook his head before taking another bite.

The dirt at the barn was a little wet but just enough to irritate us by sticking to the bottoms of our feet. We could tell Steve was happy to see us when he said, "The prodigal sons return."

I started looking around frantically, so he asked me what I was doing. I said, "I'm looking for the fatted calf for our feast."

He laughed while saying, "If you're lucky, I'll buy you a burger." He walked over and gave us both hugs.

This is not Steve, I thought, so a chill went up my back. **"What happened to Charlie?"** I asked with noticeable fear in my voice.

236

I must have had a really frightened look on my face because it scared him and he asked, "**What did you hear?**"

"Nothing, but you're never this affectionate, so I thought something must have happened."

"Don't do that, you scared the daylights out of me."

"Right back atcha," I replied. *That really scared me, so I need to relax and enjoy this journey.*

He said, "I hugged both of you as a thank-you for the entire trip. What are the chances you'd run into Clint while you were there? I want you to know how much I appreciate everything you did for me and for Clint. He sent a thank-you letter to all of us, and I'll have it for you to read in the morning." *I hope Vickie's happy to see me.*

CHAPTER 11

A New Addition

Vickie was riding up on a filly, and Steve wanted us to go up to the track to watch her. He told Vickie to let her stretch her legs the last quarter before asking us, "Do you remember the colt that ended his career in his first start? This is his full sister, and she might be better than he was." We watched as Vickie took her from a jog to a really nice gallop. *Very nice action,* I thought. When she hit the quarter pole, her back lowered a little, and she was in full stride. Coming out of the turn into the stretch, I paid special attention to see how she changed leads. I didn't see her change, but a couple strides down the lane, she was on her right lead. I wondered when she changed or if she was on her right the whole time. She hugged the rail, so I didn't think that was possible. No sense in wondering about it, so I blurted out, "I didn't see her change leads."

Steve had a big smile on his face when he said, "She's an athlete. Vickie says she changes more gracefully than anything she's been on."

As she was galloping on around, the clocker asked, "Did you want a time on that, Steve?"

"I just told Vickie to stretch her legs a little, but if you have a time, I'll take it."

"I caught the quarter in twenty-three flat." Steve apologized and told him he'd call it up in the future. His response was "As much as I've made on Wrong Way North, you can't ruffle my feathers. If that's Jim and Norm with you, I wanna say unbelievable Belmont win." Norm told him we were still in awe of what he did.

"Good luck with this one," he said before closing his microphone. When Vickie brought her off the track, she wanted to know if he timed the quarter.

Steve said, "He called it down as twenty-three flat."

"I swear, she could go in twenty-one and change anytime she wants to, and for a big filly, she hits the ground very softly."

I said, "Here's the real question, how about the third quarter?"

She smiled and said, "Smarty-pants, but a very educated question."

I said to Steve, "Maybe I was a salesman for too long because this sounds like a sales pitch."

Norm added, "If it is, I'm interested."

I said, "Just a minute." I ran over to Vickie to give her the four hundred dollars and made sure to let her know two of them were from Tom. "One question about the filly, does she relax well?"

"She's really doing well, and you know I've always told you the truth." After hugging her and telling her how much I missed her, I turned to walk away.

I turned around and said, "I **will** make you mine one day."

She laughed really loud before saying "You already have, lover boy, but you're not smart enough to know it."

I laughed before saying "I love flirting with you, and I really did miss you." *She's so much fun.*

I said, "Steve, sorry to run off, but Tom wanted me to give her some money."

"Vickie told me she gave you a good tout," Steve replied. I told him I asked Vickie if it was all right to share the tout with Tom. "He's part of the family now, so you can include him in all of our information, but let him know, shared information is all it is. No money-back guarantees."

I said, "I left before I found out if the filly's for sale."

He replied, "I'll let Norm run it by you."

Norm explained, "The wife was distraught after the colt broke down in his first start and couldn't risk going through it with a full sister. Apparently, when she said she couldn't go through it, she was convincing enough that her husband took the filly out of training. Steve told him he'd work with her and try to sell her. He told me he wouldn't sell her to us without seeing a couple works, and today was her second work. He really likes her."

"What would you think about asking Liz and Tom to be partners?"

He said, "You didn't ask the price." I told him I knew he'd tell me, so he said, "We could pick her up for thirty thousand, and she can run in forty-five days, if all goes well."

I replied, "A year ago, I would have choked, but now, I say that might be a real bargain. If Tom gets in, I'd like for each of us to have a third."

He answered, "I was gonna suggest that."

We asked Steve if he would mind us offering Tom a third. He said, "They're fantastic, and I'd love to train another horse for them." I asked to be excused so I could call Tom.

I explained the offer to Tom, and his only question was "Did Steve tell you he likes her?"

"He said he likes her very much," I answered.

"Count us in."

"If you're gonna play hard to get, heck with you," I said while laughing.

He laughed out loud before saying "Jim, you can verify this with Liz, one thing I'm not is hard to get." *They're a fun couple.*

I said, "You're a hoot, Tommy, and it's good to call you partner. I'll call you when things are ready to be finalized."

Steve told me he heard a lot of laughter and wondered if Tom laughed at us. "Heavens, no, his only question was if you liked the filly, and as soon as I said you did, he was in."

Steve replied, "That's the kind of statement that makes seven days a week worthwhile. If the filly's doing well in the morning, we'll sign some papers and give them a check."

"Does she look good now?" I asked.

"She sure does, but it's a formality. You don't get this opportunity when you claim them."

He asked us if we wanted to go see Charlie. We drove about ten miles out in the country, and it was good to see that, with all the growth to Northern California, there was still some farmland. I was excited when we pulled in because Charlie was out in a good-size paddock and seemed to be enjoying himself. It was obvious that he recognized Steve's pickup, and he acted like he was happy when Norm and I stepped out. He streaked across the paddock, kicking his hind legs out behind him. We walked over to the fence, and he came over to me so I could scratch his neck. After laying his head on my shoulder, he purred like a little kitty. That part about purring might be stretching the truth a little, but he was happy to see us. We hung around the farm for a while, and the manager came out to meet us. He told us they had come to love Charlie and hoped that, when his racing days were over, they might adopt him.

Norm said without hesitation, "I'd love that."

They shook hands to seal the deal, and Steve said, "That shake is as good as a written agreement." Norm told him we wanted Charlie to enjoy his retirement.

Before heading to the truck, I kissed Charlie's jaw, and when we were in the pickup, Norm told me it creeped him out. I said, "You have your fetishes, let me have mine."

Steve shook his head and said, "You two belong in an institution."

I replied, "Linda was much nicer, she said we acted like we were married."

We hung around the barn until Steve went home, and when we stopped by the café for dinner, we smelled the ribs as we walked through the door. The man taking the orders said, "Let me guess, the rib dinner." We both smiled and nodded. He said, "That Belmont was a race for the ages."

I replied, "We'd like to take some credit, but we were as shocked by the stretch run as anyone that saw the race." We took our number and found a table. The same guy brought our meals to us and asked if we knew when Charlie's next race would be. I said, "We'd normally have an answer, but right now, we don't know. Our goal is to run him in the Longacre Mile, but he should have at least one race before then."

With a big smile on his face, he told us he started out at the backside café at Longacres before saying "You have no idea what having the Kentucky Derby winner run in Seattle will do for those race fans."

I said, "Believe me, I know about the Seattle sports fans. If any team in Seattle is winning, the stadiums sell out, and if they ever win a World Series, I hope the city survives." He was laughing as he walked away, but I wasn't kidding.

After dinner, we went back to the trailer and watched television for a couple of hours. We talked about Charlie and the new filly. We also talked about Liz and Tom being our partners. I said, "I can't remember a couple that I felt so deeply for so quickly." Norm wanted to know if Liz's beauty had something to do with it. "Maybe a little at first, but as soon as I got to know Tom, I stopped thinking about her looks."

He nodded and said, "**Ya**, me too."

"She is nice to look at," I said while sighing.

Again, he said, "**Ya**, me too."

I said, "Our little jockey isn't far behind."

One more time, he said, "**Ya**, me too." *That boy needs to work on expanding his vocabulary.*

We arrived at the track bright and early the next morning and asked Steve if we were the proud owners of a two-year-old baby girl. "As soon as you give me a check, you are." Norm wanted to know if Tom would have to sign some papers. "He faxed me a notarized statement, giving me power of attorney in this purchase," Steve replied.

I said, "I'm impressed. Those are big words for a poop scooper."

He explained, "I finished two years of college along the way, but I did go to some classes smelling like horse poop."

"If you'd had Charlie back then, the students would have thought you were wearing expensive cologne," I said while laughing.

"Wait a minute, you told me his poop smelled bad."

I replied, "That was before he won the Derby." We signed the papers, gave him the check, and asked the filly's name.

"I didn't mention, the wife was so against running her that they didn't file for a name."

I said, "I have one request, Run Linda Run."

Right away, Norm said, "That's my name also. I'll call Tom, and he'll agree."

Steve told us he'd send it in at lunch, before saying "If it's okay, I'll send a couple more with the name Linda in them because that name might be declined." Both Tom and Liz were happy with the name selection when Norm told them.

We each cleaned a couple of stalls, and I was breathing hard when we finished. "Hard to believe you can get out of shape for this," I said. We went down to the filly's stall to take a good look at her. She was a bay with a white blaze down the length of her face. I said, "She could be sixteen hands right now, and she'll surely grow some more." Norm reminded me that fillies mature younger than their male counterparts did. I said, "She'll be considered a big filly, even if she's done growing. We know she has speed but not how far she can carry it. Vickie told me she relaxes very well, and that's important for distance horses."

Steve said, "Her dam is by Seattle Slew, so she should have speed and be able to carry it a route of ground."

"Who's the sire?" I asked.

He answered, "A son of Desert Wine."

I said, "That's speed and distance."

Norm reminded me of a filly we owned, named Class a Wine. She could sprint and route. I smiled as I remembered, we called her Classy, and she most certainly was.

I asked Norm if he wanted to drive to Seattle to nominate Charlie to the Mile. He said, "You just wanna be back on the road."

I replied, "I think you're right, I'm feeling a little restless." He agreed to go but wanted to play golf and leave the next day.

I shot par on the first hole, and Norm made bogey. We both played good for our talent level, and Norm ended up four over par. I was five over and said, "That's the first time you've beaten me." He told me it would be the first of many, and I believed him because he kept his game under control better than I did. I was just happy we were getting out in the fresh air. *Life sure seems brighter than it did a year ago. Has all that has happened been a special gift from God, and could Vickie be included in the blessing?* I remembered back to the lady in the wheelchair and wondered if she was an angel.

"Let's pick up a couple nice steaks and eat at home tonight," I suggested. We picked up two T-bones that were over a pound each, plus two really nice baker potatoes. We also bought a package of sliced mushrooms for the steaks. Thirty minutes after we were home, dinner was on the table, and the steaks were better than we hoped they'd be. Our drink of choice was root beer, and it went really well with the steaks.

Norm said, "Back in my drinking days, I would have had a nice red wine with this steak."

I replied, "Back in my drinking days, I wouldn't have tasted dinner."

The next morning, we arrived at the track early. Slim was working five eighths in preparation for his upcoming seven-furlong grade 3 race. He looked magnificent going onto the track, and it reminded me of the first time I saw Vickie in Seattle. Steve said, "Save him the first quarter, and let him finish strong." She nodded, and after looking both ways, they jogged away. At the top of the backstretch, she put him into a slow gallop as Steve called up, "Slimsfinefood going five eighths." The five-furlong pole was just to our left, so I was looking right into Slim's eyes when she shook the reins. His body lowered, and in two strides, he was up to full speed.

When they flew past us, I spoke louder than I meant to. "She really looks good goin' away."

Steve said, "You mean he looks good."

"Oh yes, that's what I meant to say."

Steve said, "So much for saving him at the start." Slim hugged the rail all the way around the turn, and entering the stretch, he popped back onto his right lead and was gone. Vickie shook the reins twice, and that was the only time she prompted him. The clocker asked Steve if he could speak candidly.

Steve laughed and said, "You're making this sound like a spy movie."

"Off the record, he worked in fifty-eight and one, but the form will show fifty-nine and three. Here's what you'll like. He galloped out six and a half in one-fifteen flat, and the mile was one thirty-six flat. Best of luck, my friend."

Coming off the track, Vickie said, "He's light-years ahead of where he was when he came to the barn. He's relaxing so much better than before, so believe me, he'll be hard to beat Saturday." When he was on the walker, we stood and admired him. The work took very little out of him, so I told Vickie he might be catching up to Charlie. She smiled and said, "Their talent level is not that far apart, but Charlie will find a way to beat him every time. The Belmont closing quarter wasn't possible for any normal horse, but Charlie did it. I love that about the great horses. Nobody can explain just what they do but know they dig down and find a way to win."

I had shivers going up my spine and said, "You just mentioned Charlie with the great horses."

With no hesitation, she said, "Not only with them, right at the head of the class." A look of pure love swept across her face as she said, "I've never been on anything even close to Charlie. Again, I can't explain it, I just know it. **We're not planning to run them in the same race, I hope? Please say no!**"

I answered, "As long as the ownerships stay as they are, that'll never happen." I asked her if she heard Tom and Liz were partners in the filly.

"That's fantastic," she said before asking if the filly had a name.

I answered, "She hasn't been named, but we turned in Run Linda Run."

"Isn't that your wife's name?" she asked. Before I could answer, she lunged at me and threw her arms around my neck. I knew she did it to hide the tears that were filling her eyes, and I was glad because it hid those in mine. It was the warmest hug she had ever given me.

I whispered, "Please don't read too much into this, but I love holding you in my arms."

She started to speak, but Norm asked, "Are you two falling in love over there?" *Saved by the bell again.*

I replied, "She's in love all right, but you and I are outta luck, because Charlie has her wrapped around his little hoof."

She laughed while saying "I've never heard it put that way, but you're absolutely right, he has my heart." She shook our hands before going back to work. I thought, *That felt a lot like hugging Linda.* No doubt, my feelings for her were getting more intense. *I better never be alone with her.*

Steve brought us the letter from Clint and said, "Sit down before you read it."

Norm took the letter, and I asked him to read it out loud. He started by telling Steve how happy he was that they were able to reconcile before he died. He told him how much he enjoyed our company and just how much he loved working with Charlie. It read, "When you look forward to working with a horse as much as I did with Charlie, it would be normal to expect a letdown, but in this case, I couldn't have dreamed that final quarter. He took me to the top of the world, and words can't express my gratitude about the money."

Norm said, "I'm very happy we could help him." I looked for Steve, but he had walked away. I presumed it was for the same reason Vickie hugged me. *She felt amazing, but what if I get serious and she's just having fun? Can't do it, Jim.*

We worked around the barn for a couple of hours before Norm asked Steve if it was too early to nominate Charlie to the Longacre's mile. "It would be fine to nominate him anytime, and the fee is five thousand dollars."

Norm said, "I think we'll go up to pay it and spend some time around Jim's kids."

"That sounds great, but don't forget about the race Saturday because Slim will be double tough." His wife was busy at lunchtime, so we took him to lunch at the backside café. Steve kept to himself for the most part but was a very respected trainer by his peers.

One trainer said, "Nice work by Slimsfinefood this morning, Steve."

Steve replied, "Fifty-nine and change surprised us, but he's feeling really good right now." After we were seated, he said, "Always give enough information to keep them from digging deeper." I had learned what I knew by watching trainers, but Steve was really trying to pass his knowledge along to us. I knew I'd never work seven days a week no matter what, but I did enjoy learning about the horses. We ordered burgers, and Norm paid the bill. When we sat down, Steve asked Norm what he got out of Slim's work. Norm laughed before telling him he was superfast.

Steve turned to me and nodded. "Well, like Norm said, he's definitely fast. Also, the way he changed leads, tells me he's a fantastic athlete, plus he's sound in the front end."

Norm wanted to know how I got that out of him changing leads on time. I said, "He's transferring his weight from one side to the other, so if either side was sore, he would be reluctant to have his weight on that side."

"You've been learning as you go," Steve said.

I chuckled before saying "I've always listened to what trainers have said, but this is my first quiz. Thank you for that, Steve. I feel the trainer that most readily shares his knowledge is the one with the most knowledge to share." After lunch, we told him we had some calls to make before heading north.

He said, "You guys be careful and make it back for the race, if you can."

I replied, "We should make it, but if not, we'll watch it somewhere."

My first call was to Tom to tell him about Slim's work. I said, "The best parts were hidden, so he should have some odds. Vickie's really impressed with the way he's improving, and she expects him to win Saturday. We may not make the race because we're going up to Washington to see the kids, but we'll try to make it back. If we can't get back in time, we'll certainly watch it somewhere."

I called my daughter in Portland to tell her we were going that way, and she said, "If you wanna stay in the yard, go ahead and park." I told her we weren't taking the trailer and would probably get a room around Eugene.

With the heavy traffic, we didn't get to Eugene until ten thirty. We found a room in a nice motel along the freeway that offered a senior discount. I told the girl at the desk that something good had to come from getting old. The next morning, we enjoyed the breakfast provided by the motel before getting back on the road.

Oregon is really a beautiful state except for all the rain. You drive for miles up I-5 and see majestic evergreens all along the way. The ocean beaches are favorite vacation spots for people from all over the northwest. *I love relaxing at the beach.*

It was midafternoon when we arrived at Tammy's house. They were all home, and we had a nice visit before going out back to barbecue some hamburgers. While enjoying a beautiful evening, I asked Tammy if she and Kayti could make it over to Portland Meadows on Saturday. They both said they weren't busy, so I wrote down instructions on how to wager and told her the person selling the tickets would help her. I said, "The track is Golden Gate, the race is the seven-furlong stake, and the horse's name is Slimsfinefood." I gave her ten hundred-dollar-bills and said, "Put it all to win."

She said, "Dad, that's a lot of money to me. I can't bet that much."

I gave her another thousand and said, "This is for you and the kids, but the other thousand must be bet. If he wins like we think he will, this will pay some bills for you." I gave Kayti two hundred and said, "Put it on his nose, and that'll pay for your gas to and from school for a while." They both thanked me, but I could tell they were apprehensive. I said, "If he wins, you're in hog heaven. If he loses, turn around and walk away, knowing you've lost nothing of your own." They said they would, but I could see they were still very concerned. *I would have been too before Charlie.*

Tammy told us she could find places for us to sleep if we wanted to stay, but we both wanted to drive a while. I said, "If the horse wins, have them pay you with a check because I don't want you two walking out with that much cash." I gave her a twenty and said, "This will get you both into the track and buy you a sandwich." We all hugged before Norm and I started to walk out. As an afterthought, I said, "Kayti if you talk to Jamie, tell her we plan to run in the Longacre Mile, and we hope she can do an interview." She promised to call her before giving me another hug. I whispered, "Make sure your mom makes that bet."

It was nice driving to Seattle instead of Yakima because Seattle is a straight shot up I-5. We drove as far as Tumwater before deciding to get a room. We pulled into a beautiful motel, and Norm told me he'd register. As he was walking in, I said, "Don't forget the senior discount." As we were taking our luggage in, I said, "This is really nice, it must have cost a bundle."

"Quit crying, I got the senior discount," he said while shaking his head.

A couple of minutes after we were in the room, my phone rang. Tammy said, "Sorry to bother you, Dad, but this is too much money for me to bet."

I said, "Let me explain something. Before Charlie, I didn't even like betting five dollars on a race, but believe me, back then, losing five dollars hurt me more than a thousand now."

"How can you say that?"

I answered, "My horse account is separate and is over half a million dollars." There was dead silence until I asked if she would be all right betting the thousand.

She said, "I guess it'll be okay."

I said, "Now, we expect this horse to win, and it'll be quite a thrill, but don't get hooked on gambling. All those years your mom and I went to the races, we usually lost money. We bet really small and considered it our entertainment. The only reason I'm winning now is I only bet Charlie and a few other horses in the barn. Have fun, and don't get hooked."

After we hung up, I went to bed feeling really good. I could have given her twenty thousand dollars, but I wanted her to experience the thrill of winning. *I hope he goes off at twenty to one.*

The next morning, while enjoying the breakfast provide by the motel, Norm asked about my phone conversation with Tammy. I said, "She's not a gambler, so she was hesitant about the amount, but she'll be okay."

He said, "I heard you tell her not to get hooked on gambling, and that was good." He told me about working for a track in the Midwest while he was in college and spending too much of his wages on gambling. He said, "It **can** get in your blood."

I told him I was glad he got it under control because I knew it could be a problem. I laughed while saying "If it wasn't under control, you'd bet more than forty cents when playing slots."

When we walked into the racing office in Seattle, they were delighted to hear that we were running in their race. The racing secretary said, "The city will have a party."

"We're coming home, and so is Charlie." I reminded him that he won his first two races there. He showed us how proudly they displayed his two win pictures, so I asked if he'd like the Derby and Belmont pictures to hang by them. He was very happy that I offered. We had a few extra in the truck, so I went out and grabbed one of each. After I gave them to him, he showed them to everyone in the office while telling them we were coming to the Mile. You'd have to know racing to understand the applause that rang out all over the office. People were jumping up and down, and I was overwhelmed by the reaction. I couldn't believe the number of lives Charlie had touched. They all came over to thank us for not forgetting their track, so I said, "This is our home."

"Norm, let's have lunch at the Space Needle. I went to the top in 1962 when it was built for the Seattle World's Fair, but we couldn't afford to eat there. I don't know how tall it is, but I know it's much taller when you're on top looking down than it is when you're standing on the ground, looking up." He mumbled something about the same height, but I wasn't listening.

We enjoyed the meal, and the view was great, so I told him we should bring Vickie when she was in town to ride in the Mile.

"You should bring her here," he said.

I replied, "We're all good friends."

He asked, "Are you totally oblivious?" I told him I had no room in my life for more than friendship, even if she was interested. He said, "She's a very lovely girl, and a blind man could see she cares for you."

"I think about that every day, but I have too many issues to pursue her. You don't know how much I enjoy the feelings she's brought back to me, though." *Too much difference in our ages.*

"Believe me, I've seen the change in you," he replied as we were walking to the cash register.

We went down to Pike's Place Market and spent a full hour walking around. We explored part of the underground city, and Norm said, "Lotta history."

We walked on Second, Third, and Fourth Streets, and I showed Norm where we stayed when we went to the World's Fair. He said, "Doesn't look very safe."

I replied, "My dad had a friend he called Tiny. He was about six feet tall and weighed over four hundred pounds. He managed the hotel and told us not to leave our room for that reason." I laughed and continued, "He carried a leather flapjack and used it on more than one occasion. He came to Yakima to pick us up and gave us a room for a couple nights because he thought of us as family."

After spending the night in a nice motel, we went to the food court at South Center Mall for brunch. After finishing our meal, we decided to head back so we could make the race. It took us the rest of the day and into the night to reach Northern California, so I asked him if he wanted to get a room or drive on in. We decided to drive until we were both too tired and made it home as the sun was coming up.

We slept until late afternoon, and after having dinner at the backside café, we went to the barn. We didn't go inside the shed row but walked outside to where the filly was standing in her stall. We were enjoying the cool night air when Norm asked if I remembered being there with Charlie. I answered, "Maybe a little, but we've lived a couple lifetimes since then. I can't say this is my favorite time since Charlie because he's never let me down. If he never wins another race, he'll never disappoint me." Norm told me he had many more wins in him.

Saturday morning arrived with a cool breeze. It would be Slim's first graded stakes race, so I could only imagine how excited Tom and Liz were. *Why wonder?* I called Tom, and he answered by asking "How do you do it? My stomach's in knots."

I laughed and said, "Take two aspirins, and call me in the mornin'."

He yelled, "**I'm dying here, and you're makin' jokes.**"

"I'm sorry, Tom, but I don't know what to say. The first time we ran in a stake, I kind of went into shock. That was the Spokane Derby, and it was several years ago. The bigger the stake, the more exciting it is."

"Jim, how did you get through the Kentucky Derby?" he asked with a sigh that lasted longer than I thought possible.

I thought for a bit before answering, "I believe I was in shock the entire day. Aren't you happy you can experience this much excitement? If Slim wins, and I think he will, I'll take care of you."

He said, "Have Norm make sure Liz is all right because she's in worse shape than me."

I replied, "Don't be offended, old buddy, but he has much the best guard duty."

"I'll tell her you said that," he said while trying not to laugh. I asked what time they'd be down, and he answered, "About two or so."

I said, "We'll see you then, and drive safely." I thought back to the times I was where he was, and laughed. *No doubt, his anxiety level will increase as post time draws nearer.*

We picked up a program when we went to breakfast, and while we were waiting for our meals, I flipped to Slim's race. His morning line was fifteen to one, so I told Norm I'd be happy if he went off at that. He replied, "I think his odds will go up from there because a sprinter from Southern California is the morning-line favorite, and he'll get a lotta play."

I replied, "It does look like he'll take most of the action. Let's just hope Slim is good enough to beat him." One of the gallop boys we knew from eating at the café walked up to ask if we thought Slim could win. Steve's words echoed inside my head. *Give them enough information that they don't dig deeper.* I said, "I'll play him with the favorite in the exacta because we think he should run very well." He thanked me before going back to work.

The hours passed quickly, and Liz and Tom arrived at two thirty. I looked at them and started to laugh while saying "You two look like a couple deer caught in a car's headlights."

Tom could hardly speak, and in a shaky voice, he said, "I don't know if it's worth it, Jim."

I asked, "If you weren't here, where would you be?"

"At the casino, I suppose."

"On a scale of 1 to 10, how excited are you right now?"

He answered, "**Twenty-five!**"

"When was the last time you saw anyone this excited in your casino?"

"Maybe never," he said as he started to relax a little.

"This is one of the most exciting times you'll ever experience, so grab it and hang on tight. These times come along way too seldom." Both their breathing patterns were starting to level out, but they still had a long day ahead of them. I said, "We'll be with you the rest of the day, and you'll be fine."

He said, "I have to go to the bathroom."

I pointed to the bathroom and said, "You're on your own, my boy."

That broke the ice for Liz, and she said, "You're a hoot. I guess your loyalty has its limits."

I replied, "I have lines I refuse to cross."

When Tom came back, he was laughing and shaking his head. "You'll be with me all day, huh?" Liz looked puzzled, and Tom laughed when I told him I was afraid he might pee in my pocket.

We had fun the rest of the day, but I was happy when they called the horses to the holding barn. Steve took Slim over, and we waited until the end of the next race to join them on the walk over. Liz was gorgeous in her tight-fitting jeans. She told me how happy she was that the filly was named after my wife, so I thanked both of them for their support.

Tom said, "She'll be fun." Vickie had called Liz and told her how well she was doing. *It sounds like she and Liz are becoming friends. They're both tens, as far as I'm concerned.*

Norm said, "If she turns out to be as good as Charlie and Slim, we're definitely dreaming." Tom and Liz looked a little more relaxed when we walked into the paddock.

When Vickie walked in, she hugged Tom and kissed Liz's cheek before saying "Expect a good race."

Slim was twenty-five to one because the favorite was taking most of the money at two to five. I said, "Tom, Slim better be as good as they think he is because the favorite is really good."

"What will you bet?" he asked.

I answered, "Three thousand to win and a hundred-dollar exacta with Slim on top of the favorite." *I'll stick with what Vickie tells me.*

251

He said, "I'll do the same." Liz asked him to bet the same for her, and when we walked away from the window, Slim was twenty to one. *If he runs the way Vickie thinks he will, we're in for a nice payday.*

When the gate opened, the announcer said, "They're off, and Slimsfinefood goes right to the front."

I was standing by Tom and said so he could hear, "Vickie, this is seven furlongs, so save him."

I could tell he was getting more manageable because, with very little effort, he came back to a length in front. Tom asked, "Are we in trouble?"

I answered, "You're watching a master artist at the top of her game. Watch how he leans into the turn and how he stays glued to the rail." I was having fun calling the race for him. Coming into the lane, the favorite had moved into second and was in perfect position to pounce, but then he wasn't. Three right-handed smacks with her whip, and Slim was gone. He drew out by five, and Vickie put away her stick. The winning margin was four lengths, and the time was two ticks off the track record. I held Tom's arm, and Norm held Liz. *What's fair about this?*

Vickie brought Slim into the winner's circle with her right fist pumping. She looked at Tom and said, "You haven't seen the bottom of him, so I'm sure he has a grade 1 in him." Tom just smiled because he was totally out of it. *I remember being where he is.*

Vickie asked me if he would be all right, and I replied, "Tomorrow he'll wake up and try to figure out where he's been, but believe me, he's in great shape. Sweetie, with the sun shining behind you like that, you look like a beautiful angel." She laughed and told me I was crazy.

We were taken to a stand where a man from ESPN interviewed us. When he asked Tom a question, he pointed to me and said, "He's speaking for me."

The question was "How do you feel about your first graded win?"

I answered, "He'll be somewhat embarrassed when he sees this on television, but what a boost it is to horse racing." I put my arm around him and said, "How many of you out there have been this excited? You ask how he feels about the win, you can't find this kind of excitement any other place. After winning the Kentucky Derby, I was like this for at least twenty-four hours, and I wouldn't trade that experience for anything in the world."

"Since you brought it up, how is Wrong Way North?"

I said, "He's doing great. Please don't think me rude, but this day belongs to Tom and Liz."

As we were walking off the podium, my cell phone rang, and I saw it was Tammy. I asked Steve to keep an eye on Tom, and he told me to hurry because he should get back to the barn. Tammy was so excited that she couldn't hold still. I said, "I have to go, but I'll call you back in a little while." I asked if she got the money in a check, and she told me she remembered. I told her again that I'd call her soon.

When we walked to the barn, I was holding Tom's arm, and Norm was holding Liz. We sat them down in lawn chairs, and I got up close to look in Tom's eyes, and they were totally dilated. Liz asked what happened to him, so I got up close and looked into her eyes. I said, "Fully dilated, so you'll have many questions tomorrow also." She told me she was fine, and I said, "You most certainly are, but you'll have questions in the morning." I asked if they were staying the night, and thank goodness, the answer was yes. I told them to take care of their winning tickets and we could cash them the next morning.

Liz asked, "**What tickets**?" We found where Tom put them, and she tucked both sets safely into his wallet. After a couple of hours, I asked them if they wanted to eat dinner. They both said they weren't hungry, so I locked their pickup and took them to their room. Tom thanked me on my way out, and I told him to call us the next morning.

When I got back to the track, Steve and Vickie were standing by the stall. I gave them their win tickets, and we all started to laugh. Vickie asked if they were all right, and I answered, "In the morning, the sky will be beautiful even if it rains, and life will be unbelievably bright."

She batted her beautiful blue eyes and said, "You seem to know a lot about this." *Why does she excite me so much?*

"I've been there but not often enough, and it seems you were a big part of the excitement." I hugged her and told her the ride she put on Slim was exciting to the point of being X rated. She laughed for several seconds before telling me how happy it made her that I pleased her. *She says some of the sweetest things, and she has no idea how much she pleases me.* **Maybe she does!**

Tom called at six the next morning and asked, "**What happened**?"

I answered, "Your horse won his first graded stake by four lengths."

"I remember that but not much after."

I said, "Welcome to a really common club. Football players and boxers are very familiar with the feeling, but they're in danger. What they experience is caused by a blow to the head, and brain swelling may occur. In our case, and this is only my opinion because I've never gotten a medical opinion, I think our brains have a safety switch to keep us from harm when we get too excited. I suppose our blood pressure could go up enough to cause a stroke, if not for the safety switch. Again, my medical knowledge is very limited at best, but I do know that things slow down to a crawl."

He replied, "I'm glad you said that because I could see your mouth moving, but the words were coming out really slow."

"How does the world look right now?" I asked.

His answer was "Brand-new, and **we own a graded stakes winner!**"

"We left your pickup at the track, so relax for an hour or so, and I'll pick you up. Congratulations, and onward and upward from here, my friend."

I called Tammy at seven thirty and woke her up. I said, "Sorry, I forgot you're a late sleeper."

She was excited in a sleepy way and said, "My check is over twenty-four thousand dollars, and Kayti collected over 4,800. Thank you so much."

I said, "If you'll put away a thousand in a separate account, I'll let you know about a few horses when the reward exceeds risk."

"Dad, Kayti was so excited that I almost had to tackle her. This was her first-ever horse race, and what a thrill she had."

I said, "I'll talk to you soon, and don't you or Kayti bet anything until I say." She asked what my account was up to, and I said, "We were so busy that I didn't cash my tickets, but from what you told me, I have close to a hundred thousand coming from this race."

"Keep it going, and don't forget us when a bet comes along," she said before we hung up. I said a silent prayer asking God to please not let them get hooked on gambling. I was happy they found winning the race so exciting because to me there aren't many things in life that compare to having your horse win a big race.

After getting cleaned up and eating breakfast, we went to pick up Tom and Liz. When she opened the door, she asked, "**What did I do?**"

Norm replied, "You were a perfect lady, and at no time did you seem any different."

She said, "After the race, everything was in slow motion. I kind of remember most things, but all things are blurry." I had to tease her a little, so I told her I enjoyed her table dance. She smacked my shoulder and said, "**Stop that!**"

Tom said, "Times ten for me about things being a blur."

I told them a story about when I was a sophomore in high school. "I wrestled, and one time in practice, my head was slammed against the mat. I couldn't remember my locker combination, so I walked out to the gym and ask for help from the basketball coach, who was also my PE teacher. He pointed his finger to the door and said, '**Get your butt in there!**' Come to find out, I was just wearing my jock strap." *Glad I was wearing that.*

Liz burst out laughing while saying "You're humoring us."

"No, I assure you, I'm telling the truth. I was literally seeing everything from a different plane, and to this day, I don't know how I unlocked my locker or how I got home. The next morning, I woke up with crusted blood from my nose and my right ear. I assume I could have died and nobody knew. I told the coaches off, but they reminded me that I had a tendency to play practical jokes."

Liz said, "We never would have known, sugar."

"What I had was a concussion, but your mind works pretty much the same way. Again, this is purely speculation, but I think God gave us a safety switch in our brains, to protect us from pain and anguish during serious trauma. I'm sure many studies have been done on it, but I've never taken the time to read about it."

Before we left the room, Liz said, "There's one thing that bothers me about your concussion, Jim. Why didn't your parents see the blood?"

"That's bothered me for years. It wasn't just my parents, but the coaches, other wrestlers, and my brothers. I've come to believe the bleeding occurred during the night because, in the morning, I had blood all over my mouth from my nose and from my ear, all the way down to my shoulder. I didn't have it checked out because I felt fine. Maybe there was swelling and, during the night, the swelling went down, allowing the blood to escape. That's purely speculation, so maybe I should ask a doctor."

"You're lucky to be here," she said.

I replied, "I've thought about that many times." Tom laughed when I told her I was surprised a jealous husband hadn't killed me.

She said, "Honey, Vickie has you pegged, you do a whole lotta talkin'."

We went to the backside café so Liz and Tom could enjoy the buzz about their horse. When we were sitting at our table, many trainers and backside workers came by and told them how happy they were that Slim beat the horse from down south. Tom and Liz soaked in the praise with their usual modesty.

The guy I told to put Slim with the favorite in the exacta came by and told me he just put him on bottom. He wanted to know if I boxed them, so I told him

I always did. He thanked me before walking away, and I told Tom about our conversation. Being the nice guy he was, he wished the kid would have hit the exacta, but the kid was like most and thought the favorite couldn't lose. The favorite lived up to his hype but was beaten by a rising star. *That claim looks awfully good now.*

When we reached the barn, Vickie was there and had brought a dozen sweet rolls for the workers. She gave both Liz and Tom nice hugs, so I said with a pouty face, "I didn't get my hug in New York."

She said, "Jim, you have to stop begging." She then walked over and gave me the warmest hug ever while saying "Thank you so much for everything you've done for me." I turned to Liz and told her I didn't mean to steal her thunder, but I took my hugs where I could get them.

She said, "Get over here, you big galoot." She gave me a really tight hug while thanking me for taking care of Tommy. She then kissed my cheek and said, "That's for telling Tom, Norm had the best guard duty."

Vickie kissed my other cheek before saying "It was a nice thing to say, sweetie pie."

A big smile swept across my face as I said, "**Take that, Norman!**"

We were looking at the filly when Steve came up and told us he had bad news and, hopefully, good news. "The name Run Linda Run was declined, but Sandy also sent in Lindalovestorun, and that name was accepted."

I said, "Thank Sandy for me because I like it even better." Everyone seemed to be happy with the name.

Tom asked if he could go into the tack room. He brought back a bottle of champagne with some plastic glasses and said, "This was for the race last night, but as you know, I was in no condition to drink." He poured each of us a glass and said, "Let's drink to Slim and Linda."

I took a glass and said, "Now that I'll drink to."

I told Tom it was good champagne, and he replied, "It's from our top-floor steak house. Only the best for my partners." He thanked us again for keeping them safe. *This really tastes good after so many years without a sip.*

I said, "We have to cash our tickets." Tom had a look of horror on his face, but before he could say anything, I said, "Liz put them in your wallet."

He pulled out both sets of tickets, and combined, they had six thousand to win and a two-hundred-dollar exacta. He said, "I wonder what this pays."

I answered, "Around two hundred thousand." Tom couldn't believe it, and Liz told us she was goin' shopping. When I collected my tickets, I found the exacta paid only ninety-eight dollars. The favorite running second knocked it down, so in all, I collected just over eighty thousand. I had them pay me with a check and told Tom I misjudged what the exacta would pay. He was still totally delighted, and Liz was still goin' shopping. *What a fun couple.* I loved both of them, but I made a mental note that, next time, Norm would take care of Tom.

They thanked us for a wonderful time, and I told them I'd let them know how the filly was progressing before they headed up the mountain.

Steve went to lunch with us. Charlie had been out for two weeks, and the Mile was three months away. He told us he was torn between running him and giving him some more time off. He told us the race after the mile would be the Breeder's Cup and I still wasn't to the point where I could think about him running in a Breeder's Cup race. Steve told me his last race would have won any race, so I said, "It's a decision I never thought I'd be involved in making." Steve really didn't need to include us in the decision, but he chose to. We decided to give Charlie more time off and work him up to the Mile. Before Steve left, he told us he'd work the filly three-eighths the next morning.

We were at the gap when Vickie brought her up, and I said to Norm, "I still love this stage in a horse's career. She gives us so much hope, but the true test will be when she runs." They started to jog in the opposite direction, and when they reached the top of the backstretch, Vickie turned her around and put her into a slow gallop. Steve called the three-eighths work up to the tower. When they came by us, she was in a fast gallop, and when they reached the pole, Vickie shook the reins. It was beautiful, watching the filly respond. She switched to her left lead at the same time she leaned into the turn and hugged the rail all the way around. She switched to her right lead like a horse that had been running for years, and Vickie tapped her lightly once to get her used to the whip. She was in full stride right away, and they worked a good hundred yards past the wire before galloping out another quarter of a mile.

The clocker called down, "Lindalovestorun, three-eighths in thirty-five flat. She's lookin good, Steve."

When Vickie brought her off, she told us she was ahead of schedule. Steve put her on the walker after her bath, and we had to make sure she didn't get her front feet too high, but other than that, it was fun to watch her having fun. She was starting to get muscle definition in the back end, and her coat was shining in the morning sun. *The only thing brighter than her coat is her future.* I felt that for whatever reason, God had really smiled on me, and again I wondered if Vickie was part of the blessing. Just maybe, he was filling the hole in my heart that was created when Linda died.

Norm brought me back to the present when he said "If she stays sound, she might be a really nice filly."

Steve replied, "She's coming along like a real runner. She has a lot of speed, so she may shin-buck, but if she doesn't, she could be in a race in four or five weeks." We watched Slim jog, and he was looking better all the time. I told Steve how proud I was of him for the way he had brought him along.

He explained, "The big thing was gelding him and then listening to what he tells me." I laughed and asked him what he said about being gelded. He replied, "I know what I would have said, but he was happy. He loves to run but was getting really sore in the back end. Look how content he is now."

I asked, "Why didn't they geld him?"

"He's well-enough bred that, if he had run as a colt, he might have been a good stallion prospect. I'm sure most of the damage was done in the race we claimed because they couldn't have run him much longer, as sore as he was getting."

I said, "I hope you don't mind me asking, has the filly been sutured?"

He told me she had before saying "You really got involved in the backside work to know about that."

I told him about helping a vet suture a filly in Yakima, before saying "I was scared half to death."

He said, "I don't think I'd get in the stall when that was going on."

"I had a lip chain on her and pulled really hard every time she started to move. Her mouth was quite bloody, but I figured it was better her than me." *That filly was mean. I don't remember ever hating a horse other than her.*

We grabbed a couple of steaks and a frozen pasta dish at the store on our way home. During dinner, we reran our conversation with Steve, and I said, "Even though Charlie has won two legs of the Triple Crown, it's hard for me to believe he'll run in the Breeder's Cup."

Norm asked, "I wonder which race he has in mind."

I replied, "Being able to run on grass and dirt gives him a few options. I'm happy he'll not run before the Longacre Mile."

We talked until almost midnight before turning in, and I whispered "good night" to both Linda and Vickie before falling asleep with my arms wrapped around my pillow. *What's going on with these feelings I have for Vickie? Totally stupid.*

We were up at five thirty the next morning and at the track by seven. When we stopped by the café for breakfast, Vickie was having some fruit. She moved over to join us and said, "Slim's gettin good." She told us she thought Steve would put him in a grade 1 going a mile at Hollywood Park in three weeks.

I asked, "Will he get the mile?"

"The way he's relaxing, I believe he'll go at least that far, but the competition's the question. He has risen fast, but that's a big leap." I told her how happy I was for Liz and Tom before she said, "Steve told me Charlie's next race will be the Mile." Norm told her we were happy about that, and she said, "He's also considering the Breeder's Cup Classic."

A shiver went up my back, and I asked, "**Did you say the classic?**"

"I hope I'm not speaking out of turn, but I'm sure that's what he's thinking." She asked Norm if she would have the mount.

Norm replied, "Thanks for not taking things for granted, but you have the mount as long as you want it."

Before she could thank him, I said, "Until Superman starts riding, you have the mount."

"I won't worry until I see the caped crusader in the jockeys' room," she said through a very pretty smile. She winked at me when I asked her if I could go into the jockeys' room with her if I wore a cape. She whispered, "You say some of the cutest things. If you let me pick out the cape, I could be persuaded." I kissed her cheek and told her she was sweet.

As she was walking out, I said to Norm so she could hear, "It sure seems like I should have gotten a hug there."

She turned and threw me a kiss. She then walked back and told us she had forgotten, she was on a horse in the third but thought it still had some learning to do. "I only tell you because he could jump up, but I wouldn't put much on him."

We both told her we'd sit that one out before wishing her good luck. Before she turned to leave, I said, "I got excited because I thought you were coming back to hug me."

She laughed and said, "You're so cute."

I said, "Norm, I told you I'm cute."

He hurt where my feelings should have been when he said, "She was calling you a cute old man." It hurt because that's what I was thinking.

I said, "Things sure move fast in this business. Can you believe the five-million-dollar classic?"

"I don't believe or disbelieve anything anymore. I just pinch myself every morning to be sure I'm awake."

After walking to the barn, I asked Steve which Breeder's Cup race he had in mind for Charlie because I didn't want him to know Vickie told us. He told me he was thinking the classic before saying "His last race would win it." That was as confident as I'd ever heard him be.

I said, "It's hard for me to wrap my mind around running in the race that I've been watching on television for so many years."

"You probably thought the same about the Kentucky Derby and Belmont."

I replied, "They still don't seem real."

His eyes narrowed a little as he said "Before Charlie, I'd almost given up on being here."

I asked, "Would you rather go back to a less-stressful life?" His reply was a resounding **no**. I told him Norm and I were having a ball but found ourselves thinking it was all a dream.

He continued, "I already had some very nice horses in my barn, but one day out of the blue, my rider told me a horse she thought was special was coming down from Seattle. She told me, if I wanted him, he was mine, and explained that Norm asked her to find a trainer. I'm sure glad she chose me." He shrugged his shoulders before saying "I was really taken aback because I've never had a jockey find a horse for me. I'm glad I had so much confidence in her horsemanship, and the rest is history."

Norm said, "We're happy she chose you."

I added, "It was kind of like the perfect storm. Three separate entities came together to make a perfect team."

Steve told me he loved the movie, before saying "I never thought about it, but everything did fall into place very nicely. Let's hope he stays sound for a few years because he has many more wins in him, if he does."

I replied, "I'm sure we've said all of this before, but I never get tired of saying and hearing it. Talking about things falling into place, if Norm hadn't told me to be really still a few horses before Charlie, I would have told him he was bidding on the wrong horse." Steve and I couldn't hold back our laughter when Norm told us he had his eye on Charlie the whole time. I said, "Because of his breeding, I'd believe you if I hadn't seen the look on your face." *God knew what I needed, and I'm starting to believe Vickie was part of his plan from the start. I was awfully close to giving up.*

We cleaned some stalls before saying goodbye to Steve on our way to the golf course. We were playing very competitively again, and with two holes to go, I was even par. Norm was a shot behind me, but I double-bogeyed the next hole while he shot par. He was one shot up going into the last hole and put his tee shot five feet from the pin. My tee shot landed six inches from the cup and stuck right there. When we reached the green, I told him I'd mark my ball, but he grunted, **"Just pick it up!"**

When he was over his ball, I said, "There's no pressure, so take a deep breath and put it in."

"Is this a little gamesmanship?" he asked.

I answered "Nope, I'm rooting for you."

He took two deep breaths and dropped the putt in the center of the cup. I shook his hand and said, "You're improving like Slim." We ate at the pizza restaurant on our way home, and after watching television for a couple of hours, we said "good night." Again, I whispered "good night" to both Linda and Vickie. *Mmmm, life seems so much brighter now.*

The next two weeks went by quickly as we played golf almost every afternoon. We also made several trips out to the farm to see Charlie, and every time we walked up to his paddock, he came over to lay his head on my shoulder. After a few minutes of letting me scratch his neck, he'd take off bucking and throwing his hind legs from side to side. Norm told me he was starting to worry about us. I said, "It's so good to see him this content, and he looks like he's put on fifty pounds or more. I hope that's a good thing."

He shrugged his shoulders before saying "Let's just hope it's all muscle."

"He'll have two months to get ready for the Mile so Steve will make sure he's razor-sharp. There shouldn't be that much in the race for him to worry about unless one of the local horses is a real monster."

Five days before Slim's race, I asked Norm if he wanted to go up and see Tom. We told Steve and Vickie we were going up to the lake, and Vickie told us the horse she told us not to bet before was in the next day. The horse finished fourth, only beaten two lengths, and she said, "He's improving. They're taking him up from maiden thirty-two thousand to maiden forty thousand, but the horses will be pretty much the same. Be sure to share that with Tom, and tell him I said Slim will be really tough. Do you know if they'll make his race?"

I answered, "We'll find out when we get there, and I promise, I'll call to let you know tonight." It was 10:00 a.m. on Tuesday, so the traffic wasn't too bad. I called to make a reservation as we were driving. My heart was racing a little, and I wondered if I was excited about calling Vickie. *She has added so much to my life.*

The lady making the reservation said, "Say no more, your room will be ready when you get here, and I'll tell Tom you're on your way."

When we walked into our room, we saw a bottle of the same champagne we had at the track. Beside it was a bowl of perfectly shaped and perfectly colored strawberries. I said, "All of this for someone who plays penny slots." He told me not to forget he played cards once in a while, but I knew most of our comps came from his play. *What a wonderful adventure this has been. Please, Lord, keep Vickie safe, and thank you for helping me heal.*

CHAPTER 12

Nice to Be Spoiled

I answered the room phone, and Tom said, "Save your appetite because Liz and I are taking you to dinner. I hope you're hungry because my chef has a special meal planned."

I thanked him before saying "So I don't forget, Vickie likes her horse in the third tomorrow."

After thanking me, he said, "Meet us at the main entrance at seven."

It was three thirty, so we had time to play before getting dressed for dinner. Norm went to a blackjack table, and I bought my Keno numbers for ten games. I walked to the sports book and asked if they had racing forms for the next day. They apologized and told me, because of transportation problems, they wouldn't be in until the next morning.

I sat down at a unicorn machine and inserted a twenty. I started playing two dollars a spin, and on the fourth spin, the screen was almost filled with unicorns. *This could be a good week for the horses*, I thought as the credits mounted up. The credits stopped at 280 dollars, and I had so much fun that I didn't notice the time slipping away. I looked at my watch, and it was five fifteen, so I printed my ticket. I thought about checking my Keno tickets, but I had seventy two hours to collect, so I decided to wait. Norm was at the table where I last saw him, so I walked over and tapped his shoulder while saying "Time to go, buddy."

He looked at his watch and asked the dealer to color him up. He had over four hundred dollars, so he gave the dealer two twenty-five-dollar chips before putting the rest in his pocket. After hurrying to get cleaned up, we met our hosts, a little winded but two minutes early.

I thought we were dressed well, but Liz and Tom put us to shame. Tom had a dark blue suit that had to have cost two thousand dollars, and Liz was wearing a sapphire dress that molded perfectly to her gorgeous figure. I said, "You'll have to forgive me, Tom." I turned to Liz and said, "**You're breathtaking**!"

He smiled and said, "You're forgiven this one time." She gave both Norm and me nice hugs before Tom said, "This night belongs to the three of you."

"Three of us?" I asked. They took us to a table in the corner overlooking the lake. There were windows from the floor to the ceiling, and the lights reflecting off the water were intoxicating. In the center of the rather large table was a vase that contained a dozen of the deepest-red roses I'd ever seen. On two sides of the vase were tripods, holding win pictures of Charlie from the Kentucky Derby and the Belmont Stakes. I turned to Tom and asked, "The third you were speaking of?" He nodded, so I gave him a warm but masculine hug. To top it off, when we sat down, three violinists came over and played "New York, New York." Norm and I were overwhelmed, so I asked, "How did you put this together in such a short time?"

He answered, "I have a pretty good staff."

The dinner consisted of seven different lobster dishes, and each one was better than the one before. The entrée was a lobster tail that had to weigh a pound and a half, removed from the shell, and swimming in a butter and tarragon sauce. I must say, it was one of the best meals I'd ever eaten. At the end of the meal was a small bowl of very lightly flavored lobster ice cream. The thought wasn't at all appealing to me, but it was delicious. We topped it off with a cup of medium-roast arabica coffee. I believed it was Costa Rican, but I had been out of the business a while, and my taste buds weren't as keen as they once were. As I pulled out my wallet, Tom said, "This is on Harrah's."

I put two one-hundred-dollar bills on the table and said, "This is for the staff."

Norm matched it and said, "Tell them they deserve much more."

Tom asked us, "What are your plans for Slim's race?"

I replied, "We thought we might watch it here with you, unless you're going to the track."

He asked, "Do you two mind if we spoil you?"

Norm answered, "Jim certainly doesn't, so that sounds great to me."

Liz laughed and, in her cowgirl way, said, "You two are hoots."

"What did you have in mind?" I asked.

He replied, "I thought we might stay at Caesars Palace in Vegas until Saturday and fly to the race from there. It'll all be on Harrah's, of course."

"That sounds fantastic, but will they let you do that?" I asked.

He answered, "Please don't think I'm being presumptuous, but they pretty much give me a free hand as long as my numbers are in line. On top of your other play, your horse wagers really help my bottom line." I told him I hadn't thought about the horse betting even though I always gave my card out of habit. He said, "If you didn't wager what you do, we'd still find a way to make this happen."

At the end of a wonderful evening, we thanked them and told them we were totally overwhelmed. Tom told us to be rested because our week was just beginning, and we agreed to meet at eight the next morning. *They're amazing.*

I was pleasantly surprised when I checked my Keno tickets and 356 dollars flashed onto the screen. I gave the girl twenty-six dollars, and the remainder went in my pocket. Norm was already playing blackjack, so I told him I was going up to the room. He promised to be quiet when he went in.

As soon as I was in the room, I called Vickie. I was surprised at how fast my heart was beating as she had me take her through the dinner step by step. She said, "The roses I can see, but three violinists playing 'New York, New York' is amazing."

She wanted to know how the other patrons in the restaurant reacted, so after a few seconds, I said, "I really couldn't tell ya."

She whispered, "It sounds like you were overwhelmed."

I replied, "We were both completely speechless." She asked me to describe Liz's dress, so I said, "She's about five nine, and her dress rose from the bottom of her ankles to the top of her shoulders." I took a deep breath before saying "It was cut just low enough to show she's a lovely woman but high enough to show her class. It was a beautiful sapphire color, and her earrings matched perfectly." I took another breath before saying "She carries herself like a runway model."

"Did you know she was, for a few years?"

I replied, "This is the first I've heard of it, but it would be a shame if she hadn't been. What I really enjoy is her Southern accent."

Vickie laughed while saying "She told me she lays it on a little thick around you because she can tell you like it. She really enjoys kidding with you."

I whispered, "We all agreed to have dinner together the night of the race, no matter what the outcome. We'll take them to Slim's, so please make plans to go with us. You've become very special to me, but please let me know if I become a bore. I wish I didn't find you so attractive because I've already lived my life."

"You're certainly not boring, Jim. I felt like I was at dinner with you, the way you described the evening, and it makes me happy that you find me attractive. I like the way you look too, and I promise, I don't care at all about our age difference. Thank you so much for calling me." *I'm being foolish, but I'm having more fun than I've had in a long time. She's from a different time.*

I was asleep by ten o'clock and didn't wake up when Norm came in. I had called for a six-thirty wake-up call and was glad I did, because I was sound asleep when the phone rang. I stopped by Norm's room after brewing some coffee and said, "Get up, buddy." He didn't move, so I went over and shook him.

It startled him so he sat up with an angry look on his face and snarled, **"What are you doin'?"**

I said, "We have to meet Tom at eight." He shook his head for a few seconds before telling me he didn't get in until four. I told him he could sleep on the plane.

"Are we flying?" he asked.

"Tom said it's on Harrah's, so I presume they bought us plane tickets."

We had coffee in the room before going downstairs. They were dressed as casually as we were, and Tom wanted to know if we were ready to go. We apologized before telling him we'd have to grab our bags. He said, "No hurry, get what you need for a great time." We were back down in fifteen minutes, and they whisked us to the Reno airport in the corporate helicopter. We boarded the corporate jet right away, and I thought, *Let me catch my breath.*

Tom asked if we wanted some breakfast, so I said, "Just a cup of coffee and a roll for me, please." Norm had the same, and there was a bowl of assorted fruits sitting out, so I nibbled on a few strawberries. I was surprised at how quickly we landed in Vegas, and a limo picked us up to drive us to the hotel. I told Tom he was sweeping me off my feet.

Liz laughed while saying "We have to watch them, Norm."

"Jim's a weird duck, all right," he said, and Liz laughed out loud.

Tom said, "Jim, I think they're having fun at your expense."

I replied, "I'm having way too much fun to pay attention to them. We have to remember the third race." It was eleven, so we had plenty of time. Tom told us he had some business to take care of and asked Liz to bet a hundred to win and place on the horse for him. He told us to have fun and he'd call us when he was free. I said to Norm, "I'll bet now so I don't forget." Liz wanted to know if she could tag along with us, so I showed her how to find the horse in the entry sheet, and she knew what to do from there. I bet three hundred to win and place on him and bet a fifty-dollar win for Vickie while making sure to use my player's card. Liz told us she wanted to freshen up and rest until the race. I said, "Before you leave, I wanna tell you about my conversation with Vickie last night."

Her face lit up as she said, "I'd love to hear about it."

I said, "She had me walk her through the dinner and surprised me when she asked me to describe your dress."

Liz smiled and said, "That's a girl thing."

I continued, "I must say, I described it rather well. Vickie has become a very special friend, and I love our phone conversations."

She looked a little disappointed while saying "Yes, she's a very special lady, and she's become a dear friend to me too. Please forgive me for thinking she means more than that to you."

I said, "I don't know how you can tell, but I do find her very attractive, and I think about her way more than I should. I wish she wasn't so young."

She said, "Women have a sixth sense about matters of the heart. Your face lights up when she's around, and she certainly doesn't seem to worry about your age difference. Don't be late for the race, sugarplum." *Would it be possible for us to be together?*

Norm went over to play pai gow, and I walked over to the Keno area. I bought my tickets for ten games and sat down because my brain was overloaded from all the frantic activity. It was nice to relax, and my mind drifted back to the times Linda and I went to Vegas. We stayed at the Flamingo, just across the street, but spent many hours in Caesars. She loved to walk through the Forum shops and dream about buying some of their items. We both had good jobs, but most of their products were out of our price range. She loved to dream but was very happy playing the penny and nickel slots. We always played close to the vest and almost always went home having spent far less than we budgeted. I told my friends that they don't have to gamble to have fun in Las Vegas. I also told them to get player's cards if they planned to gamble, and they would get their rooms comped.

"**Sir, sir**" brought me back to the present, and the girl at the counter pointed to the board. My 1, 3, 5, 7, 9 had hit along with two even numbers, so I made 1,100 dollars. She had a very nice smile on her face while giving me two thumbs up. I had eight games left, so I asked her how long she'd be working. She was going off shift in an hour, and I wasn't sure my games would be completed by that time, so I walked up and gave her a hundred-dollar bill.

She wanted to know what it was for, so I explained, "If you leave before I collect, I wanna make sure you get your tip, but if you're still here, you know you've received it."

"Thank you so much, and good luck the rest of your games."

It was twelve fifteen, and post time was one o'clock. I still had seven games to go, so I walked over to where Norm was playing cards and invited him to lunch. He had the dealer color him up, and he lost a couple of hundred but told me he'd win it back on the horse. I wondered if we were getting too accustomed to Vickie's and Steve's touts coming in. *I've never been this lucky for so long.*

We went to the food court to ordered fish and chips and sat there for about thirty minutes before I said, "Let's go watch the race."

Liz was standing in the sports book, but Tom hadn't arrived. She said, "Tom called and said he might be a couple minutes late. Would you mind if I sit with you two country boys?"

The horses were entering the gate when Tom walked in and he asked, "Did I make it?"

Liz said, "He's number 4, and they're going in the gate right now."

I smiled as I noticed how she had gotten into the swing of things. "They're running" rang out, and the four broke close to the front. Vickie took him back to midpack and let him settle on the rail. The race was going a mile and a sixteenth, so she wasn't rushing him. Two horses were fighting for the lead, a good five lengths in front of the pack. I said to Liz, "They're frying each other, so our danger will be coming from off the pace." Vickie maintained her position, saving ground through the first turn, and about a quarter of the way up the backstretch, she shook his reins. One of the horses on the front end was going backward fast, so Vickie swung her horse to the outside to avoid him. By the time they entered the final turn, she had him in third, two wide. The leader had come back to a length in front, and the horse coming back bothered the horse inside of her horse just enough to give her the lead. They still had a quarter of mile to go, so she started whipping really fast. A horse was gaining, but they reached the wire a half length in front. *Glad I'm not feeding that horse.*

I said, "I sure hope our filly is better than him." Tom told me he thought he looked good, so I replied, "It took too many races to break his maiden, and she asked him for his life to win this time. I wish the owners luck, but I expect him to run right on the bottom.

The horse paid $17.80 to win, and because the second-place horse was eight to one, he paid $10.20 to place. Vickie received over 450 dollars on the ticket I bought for her. I received 4,200 and tipped the ticket seller a hundred dollars. Tom collected his tickets right behind me, and when we walked a few steps away, he said, "You're certainly generous with our employees."

I told him I felt blessed with all that had happened to me, and I enjoyed sharing the blessings, before saying "I need to collect my Keno tickets." Tom asked if I was still tearing them up at Keno, so I said, "I've been on a good run." The machine showed that I had 1,172 dollars, and there was a different girl at the counter, so I gave her the seventy-two dollars.

We all went to dinner together and talked about the nice ride Vickie put on the horse. Liz asked why she whipped him more than she whipped Charlie and Slim. I said, "He doesn't run as willingly as they do. Some horses require more prompting than others, and there are some horses that will stop if they're whipped at all." I smiled while saying "They're as confusing as women."

She raised her eyebrows while tilting her head to the left before saying "**I believe** that would be men." We both laughed when I told her I thought we might have a difference of opinion.

The dinner was succulent prime rib with a delicious horseradish and wine sauce. The side dishes were slightly undercooked asparagus and baby-red potatoes, served in a butter sauce with a hint of saffron. The crispness of the vegetables was a wonderful touch. The dessert was a delicious pineapple upside-down cake, swimming in a buttered brandy sauce. It was served with a triple espresso, flavored with brandy and cinnamon. Our server was a beautiful young lady who had to have attended culinary school because she had a wonderful knowledge of every dish and just how they should be presented. Tom said, "Your money's no good here because this meal is on Harrah's." I asked if anyone would be offended if I left a gratuity for the chef and our server. Tom said, "We're never offended when our employees are rewarded for doing outstanding work." I left two one-hundred-dollar bills. One was designated to the chef and the other to our server. They gave me a notepad and a fancy Caesars pen, so I wrote, "Thank you for a very memorable dining experience." I then lifted the pen to Tom, but before I could ask, he nodded for me to keep it. I didn't notice how much Norm left, but I was sure it was as much as I did.

While enjoying a hot cup of coffee, I asked if they would mind me sharing a story. I began, "Linda and I loved taking advantage of the buffet deal when we were in town. We could eat at any of the seven outstanding Harrah's buffets for twenty-four hours, for only forty-five dollars, with our player's card. Three buffets that stood out to us were the Flamingo, Paris, and then we came to Caesars. When we started to eat, Linda told me her food was fantastic. It was like fine dining. We belonged to a chef's society with my job, so we were accustomed to really well-prepared meals, but the buffet at Caesars topped them all."

Tom said, "That buffet deal has been a real success for us."

I continued, "We decided we could eat four meals each twenty-four-hour period, and that's eleven dollars a meal. We've paid more than that for burgers and fries on the strip. We made it our goal to not overeat at each setting, but we didn't achieve our goal at Caesars."

After dinner, Tom said, "We'll leave you alone after tonight, but if the ride in the chopper didn't bother you, we'd like to show you the city." Actually, my stomach did a few different things as the very skilled pilot took us in for some dynamic views of the strip. I was happy I didn't lose that delicious dinner, but it was a little iffy a few times. I could tell that Tom was very proud to be employed by Harrah's, as he pointed out each of their locations.

I said, "Linda loved this city, so I wish she had seen this with us." Liz told me she would love to have met her, and I told her they would have liked each other. I was a little surprised when Norm told her she looked a lot like Vickie.

After we landed, we sat in the helicopter for a few minutes while Tom told us about a meeting he attended. He said, "Because of the relationship we've developed, Harrah's would like to display very prominently the win pictures of the Kentucky Derby and Belmont Stakes in all of our sports books."

Almost before he finished speaking, Norm told him he loved the idea. Tom had us follow him to a banquet room where two pictures were set up on tripods and were surrounded by deep-red velvet. The pictures were three by five feet, and I couldn't believe how clear they were, being blown up as much as they were. Tom told us his graphics department did a great job.

I looked around the room before zooming in on the tripods and asked, "Who put this together?" Tom told us Liz set it up. I stepped closer to the pictures and startled everyone when I looked at the Belmont picture and said, "I don't think we can use this one." Tom wanted to know why, so I said, "It makes me look fat."

Norm said, "It's not the picture."

I replied, "Okay, we'll blame it on Caesars' buffet." We all agreed the idea was fantastic before I said, "If he wins the Breeder's Cup Classic, I think that picture will fit in nicely, and I'll diet for that one." We thanked them for a very memorable evening before parting ways.

The next three days, we were on our own. We spent most of our time in Caesars, and we did take advantage of the buffet deal. Norm agreed about the quality of the food at all the buffets we visited but loved Caesars most of all. We didn't win any more sizable pots, but we both ended the week ahead because of the horse. Norm asked if I bet a win ticket for Vickie, and I told him I bet fifty to win. "How much was that?" he asked.

"Four hundred and fifty dollars." He forgot to bet for her but didn't want to give her that much, so I took a fifty out of her stash and put it in my pocket before saying "Give me a hundred." I folded it in with the other four and told him I'd tell her it was from both of us, but on one condition.

He looked at me suspiciously and wanted to know what it would be. I told him he had to admit it was the picture that made me look fat. He said, "I'll lie for 350 dollars." *It's hard to believe I call him my friend.*

We took the corporate jet to Los Angeles at ten on Saturday morning. Slim was in the seventh race, so we had plenty of time to take a scenic flight over the Grand Canyon. I said, "Just like women."

Tom asked, "What's that?"

I said, "God outdid himself when he created this, just as he did when he created women."

Liz, with that gorgeous Southern accent, asked, "Well, aren't you sweet, sugarplum? Did you say those nice things to Linda?"

I answered, "Regrettably, not nearly as often as I should have." *Wish I could have some do overs.*

Tom said, "I'll bet you were a romantic rascal."

I replied, "According to Linda, not so much."

Norm was quiet, but he picked his spots. He said, "She was very sharp and knew what she was talking about."

Liz was serious when she said, "It seems you were very close to her too, Norm."

He replied, "After my divorce, she welcomed me into their family, so I miss her almost as much as Jim does."

She said, "She sounds like quite a lady." I kept looking out the window at the canyon to hide the tears that were filling my eyes. I knew I should let go, but it wouldn't be for a long while. That was why I didn't have room in my life for any woman, including Vickie. *Well, one of the reasons.*

We landed in LA at eleven, and it was noon by the time we reached the track. We went through the back gate and were directed to the stakes barn. Steve was sitting in front of the stall, enjoying the morning. Vickie had arrived and, not having other mounts, was sitting with him. I gave her five one-hundred-dollar bills and told her they were from Norm and me. Tom also gave her some bills while thanking her for the tout. I said, "Sorry to leave you out this time, Steve."

He replied, "It wasn't my horse."

Tom said, "You'll get yours today." Steve told him he should run really big, but it was a tough bunch.

Liz replied, "Not as tough as Slim." I loved that she was having so much fun.

Slim was the number 2 horse in a field of eight, and his morning line was six to one. Two horses would take most of the action. The one was two to one, and the three was eight to five, so I said, "I'll make a trifecta bet before I forget."

Tom walked with me and asked what I was betting. I answered, "It's as easy as one, two, three." I bet a ten-dollar tri box, 1, 2, and 3, so Tom did the same. We wagered at the backside café, so we sat down at a table that Norm and Liz had grabbed for us. I said, "They have a nice spread for the owners of stakes horses in the turf club, if you wanna go over."

Liz told me they spent their lives putting on those functions before saying, "Right here is what interests me most." Both Norm and I told her we couldn't agree more, but Tom told her he liked being spoiled sometimes. Liz replied, "Honey, if I spoiled you any more, you couldn't handle it." *That Texas girl might be quite a handful.*

We were sitting at the barn with Steve after Vickie went to the jockeys' room, and right after the sixth race, word came back that a nice filly broke down. A few minutes later, the horse ambulance came back and parked about thirty yards from us. The filly was taken off, walking on three legs. The vet took a close look at the injured leg. He then looked at the trainer and shook his head. They took her as far as they could from prying eyes and put a needle in her neck. She went down slowly and was gone when she hit the ground. Liz was visibly shaken, so I said, "This is the ugly side of the sport."

She whispered, "That could have been Slim or Charlie."

I said, "It certainly could have. They put their lives on the line every time they go out, but they're doing what they love."

She said with tear-filled eyes, "Let's enjoy every minute we have with them."

Norm chimed in, "Jim and I decided that a long time ago, when one of Steve's horses broke down." *Glad he didn't mention he was our filly's brother.*

She took a long and loving look at Slim before saying "You be careful sweetie." I could see that Tom was badly shaken too. Unless you've owned horses, you can't know how attached you get to them, and that's why I pray every time one of our horses goes to the track. I thought back to a time at Longacres when a big man was reduced to tears out in front of the grandstands. His horse broke down in a race, and his wife was trying to console him, in front of all the racing fans. It had been over twenty years, and the sight was still fresh in my mind. The horses really do become like members of your family. *I hope Charlie never breaks down.*

Liz had relaxed by the time Slim was called to the holding barn, so I said, "You're both calmer today than you were last time."

Tom told me they had both taken a tranquilizer, and Liz said, "Those things really work." We walked into the paddock together, and Slim was nine to one. The one had taken over as favorite at four to five and the three was five to two.

When Vickie came in, she walked over and hugged Liz before shaking Tom's hand. "He'll run good," she promised. *She's so pretty.*

Steve legged her up, and she winked at us as they walked around. Liz smiled when I said, "That's what I was waiting for." When they walked onto the track, I went inside to make my bets. I was a little over four thousand up from our week at Caesars, so I decided to bet a thousand to win and place. I'd have a nice profit for the week, no matter what the outcome. I also bet hundred-dollar win tickets for Vickie and Steve. We found a spot where we could watch the race on a television monitor.

Slim was eight to one when the gate opened. The one and Slim went right to the front, but Vickie pulled gently on Slim's reins, and he came back with no effort at all. She settled him two lengths off the lead, and the three was in fourth, three lengths behind them. Slim was in a beautiful rhythm, two lengths off the leader, and three quarters of the way up the backside, she shook his reins. He moved into striking distance, so she looked under her right arm to make sure she wouldn't get boxed in. Since nothing was closing, she kept him on the rail going into the turn. She was so close to the leader that I was afraid they might clip heels, and coming into the stretch, the one went just wide enough to let her through. She popped

Slim twice, and he opened up a three-length lead, but the three was rolling. With a hundred yards to go, he pulled to within a length, but Vickie heard him and went back to the whip. Slim pinned his ears and was pulling away at the wire. The three was second, and the one held on for third. Liz was jumping up and down but well within herself. I grabbed Tom's shoulder and said, "You're now the owner of a grade 1 winner."

He replied, "Yes, and he looks like he can go a mile or more."

I replied, "He was pulling away at the end."

Norm said, "The way he's relaxing, we have no idea what his limitations are." I thought back to a little horse named Northern Dancer. He was not only a great runner but also maybe the best sire of his generation and the reason I wanted Charlie.

When Vickie came into the winner's circle, Liz gave her a high five. Tom took hold of her and said, "Be careful, sweetie." Slim was pure class, standing for the picture.

A man from ESPN took us to a platform for the postrace interview, and the first question was directed to Steve. "Can you believe how this horse is improving?"

He answered, "He has surprised me all along, and the way he's learning to rate, I really don't know how far he'll go."

The interviewer asked, "Do you know what's next for him?"

"We'll see how he comes out of this race, and if he's doing well, we'll explore some options."

Vickie was next, and the question was "Does he feel like a different horse now?"

She answered, "He's gotten better with every start. The biggest difference is how manageable he's becoming, and I'm excited to see where we go from here."

The next question was "Would you like to compare him to Wrong Way North?"

Vickie smiled and thought for a few seconds before saying "No, thank you." She headed to the jocks' room for her shower, and I thought, *That was a thoughtful answer from a very beautiful and articulate lady.* I found myself admiring her more every day and hoped I wasn't setting myself up for a fall. **She's way too young, Jim! Don't be stupid.**

Liz was next. "What's your biggest thrill so far?"

She had the sweetest look on her face when she said "The relationship we've developed with Jim and Norm and the joy it's brought to my wonderful husband." It made me wish Linda was there to enjoy the journey with us.

He said, "Tom, you're much more relaxed this time."

Tom laughed and said, "That last race really got to me." He put his hand on my shoulder and thanked me for helping him get through it.

"Where do you go from here?" he asked.

Tom answered, "Steve's in complete control, and we know he'll make the right decisions."

He turned to me, and I said, "This is their day, and I'm very happy I could enjoy it with them."

Norm said, "I have nothing to add, except to say another beautiful ride by Vickie." Liz took the trophy and hugged it to her bosom.

Later, when we were alone, Norm told me he was envious of the trophy. I told him he was sick, but as much as I hated to admit it, it had crossed my mind. I didn't know how a guy could look at her and not have those thoughts. *Sorry, Tom, but looking's not that bad.*

The win paid $18.60, and the place was $7.20. I was happy to see the trifecta paid 114 dollars, and we all had it ten times. I collected the tickets for Vickie and Steve along with mine, and they were pleased when I gave them each nine hundred dollars. "Why so much?" Steve asked. I told him I bet a hundred for each of them.

Norm wanted to know if I could believe the wagers we were cashing since Charlie. I said, "The breakage alone is more than the tickets I collected before. Sixty cents on each two dollars is a lot more when you bet a thousand than when you bet five."

"I hear ya there," he said while shaking his head. *I hope we don't wake up.*

I asked Tom if he'd like to go to the restaurant his horse was named after. He said, "Let me call the pilot and see if we can."

The pilot said, "No problem, I'll just cancel the flight plan. Call an hour before you get here, and I'll file a new one."

As usual, Steve had to stay with the horse, but Vickie was very happy to join us. I heard her tell Liz how much she loved the restaurant, and when we walked through the door, Slim was there to greet us. He said, "My favorite people, I hoped you'd be in tonight." He shook my hand and then Norm's before shaking Tom's. He hugged Vickie and asked Tom if he minded him hugging Liz.

"By all means," Tom said.

He hugged her and told them how nice it was to meet them. He asked, "Tom, what would you charge me for a win picture?" Tom told him he ordered extra and would be glad to give him one. We sat down at one of the rustic tables, and everyone ordered steaks, even Vickie.

Liz said, "This reminds me of home because we always butchered our own beef." Vickie ordered her steak medium rare, and Liz ordered hers rare or, as she told the waitress, "Cut its throat, wipe its butt, and put it on a plate." The rest of us ordered them medium while trying not to visualize what Liz said. I was happy to see Vickie finish her steak, but she just nibbled on the side dishes.

In a very casual voice, I said, "If you hadn't gone to the jockeys' room so quickly, I was gonna offer to wash your back."

She was taken so much by surprise that she took about three double takes, and as she processed what I said, a smile crossed her lips. She made everyone laugh when she said, "**You're so full of crap!**" I smiled and winked at her but didn't let her know it had crossed my mind.

A few people congratulated Tom as they walked by before he ordered a bottle of champagne and poured us all a glass. Everyone said no to dessert, and when Tom asked for the bill, the waitress said very softly, "Slim will catch it." *I wonder how much he made this time.*

I took out a hundred-dollar bill and said, "This is for a job really well done." Norm and Tom did the same, and the waitress showed her appreciation with a warm smile.

Tom called the pilot to tell him we'd be ready in an hour. Vickie hugged Tom before kissing Liz's cheek. I didn't even have to beg; she came over and hugged Norm first. She laughed and shook her head before hugging me and said, "Some of the things you say tickle me so much." She had driven to the restaurant, so we said "good night" at her car before taking a cab to the airport.

I told everyone how much I loved seeing Vickie eat real food, and Liz said, "It must be hard to diet all the time." She tapped my shoulder and whispered, "You better be careful teasing her."

I replied, "I love making her laugh."

She told me one more time, "She's a very lovely lady, and a blind man could see she cares for you." I agreed that she was lovely while thinking, *There wouldn't have been any harm in me washing her back.*

As we were flying back to Vegas, we talked about how great a job Steve had done with Slim and how hard he worked. I said, "I think the whole team meshes together really well, and Vickie's a perfect fit for the horses." I exhaled for several seconds while thinking, *Wow, does she fit that saddle!*

Liz asked how the filly was doing, and Norm answered, "She's probably five weeks from a race and working really well."

I added, "If she doesn't shin-buck." Liz knew about that from the horses they had on the ranch. I looked out the window while wishing Linda had been with us. *What are these feelings I have for our jockey?* I wondered as we started our decent into Las Vegas. I had told myself many times that she was too young for me, but I couldn't shake the feelings I had for her. *It's not like she's underage.*

Tom told us we'd leave for Tahoe at eleven the next morning. The entire week had been fantastic, and we promised to get together again soon. Liz suggested that we take Vickie to the lake with us sometime, and I told her we would.

Tom asked if we minded him putting Slim's pictures with Charlie's, and I said, "I was gonna mention that. Make room, because I expect big things from the filly."

We said "good night" before Norm went to play cards, and I went up to the room, out of the smoke. I thought about the beautiful ride Vickie gave Slim and how pretty she was before whispering "good night" to her and Linda. *So confused.*

Norm didn't wake me when he came in, so I slept until seven thirty the next morning. When I got up, I peeked in his room, and he was sleeping, so I decided not to wake him until after my shower. Before walking out, I yelled for him to get up, and he told me he would.

I bought my Keno tickets for five games before going to the food court for breakfast. I found a café that featured Belgium waffles and three different coffees, so I had a waffle with blackberries and whipped cream. The coffee I chose was a French roast because dark-roast coffees go well with sweet foods. After eating, I checked my Keno tickets and had nothing coming back. I played some slot machines for twenty minutes but hit nothing. *Time to get outta Dodge.* It was ten fifteen, so I decided to get my bags from the room. When I stepped inside, the room was dark, so I looked in Norm's room. He was still sleeping, so I yelled, "WE HAVE TO MEET TOM IN A HALF HOUR!" He jumped out of bed and told me he'd make it. While he was in the bathroom, I put my things together. He went running out while still dripping and threw his clothes on. We arrived at our destination at eleven sharp, and I told him it was a good thing he didn't have much hair to comb.

The flight back to Reno was beautiful, and during the flight, Tom asked if we wanted to stay a few days. We both thought it best to go home. When we arrived at the hotel, we thanked them for a wonderful time while knowing we had made some fantastic friends. We promised to watch Slim's next race together and agreed that we were excited to see the filly run.

We made it back to our trailer at seven thirty. We had eaten too much the entire week, so we had peanut butter sandwiches for dinner. We sat outside until midnight, and Norm had to wake me to go to bed.

The next morning, we were at the barn at seven. The filly would work a half, so we both cleaned a stall while waiting for her. Steve said, "Slim came back really good, so he'll jog after the filly works." When it was time for the filly to go out, Steve called us to watch her. He told Vickie not to ask for too much but let her have her head down the lane. She jogged her around to the finish line and settled her into a nice gallop. She looked fantastic coming into the backstretch and reached the half-mile pole full of run. Steve called up, "Lindalovestorun working a half." Vickie shook the reins, and they were in full stride by the time they passed the pole. She was on her right lead, going smoothly, and a stride before the turn, she flashed onto her left lead while leaning into the turn. They never were more than a foot off the rail, and almost undetected to me, she switched back to her right lead entering the stretch. *Smooth* is the word for the way she flew down the lane. Vickie was asking for nothing, but the filly was more than willing. They worked a good twenty yards past the line and galloped really strong around the turn. When they went by us, Steve listened closely to see if there were any breathing problems, but everything was perfect. *She just might be special.*

The clocker called down, "Forty-six and one, and she galloped out five in one minute flat under wraps. Looks like you have a nice one, guys."

When Vickie came back, she told us the filly was a little speed crazy but was feeling like a really good filly. We watched her for a couple of minutes on the walker. Her muscles were starting to be defined, and I asked Steve if he had measured her. He told me she was fifteen and three-quarter hands.

"Do you think she'll grow more?" I asked.

"Probably not much, but she's plenty big right now." We went to the track with Slim, and Vickie jogged him a mile and a half. His coat was glistening in the morning sun, and while they were going around, I asked Steve how Charlie was doing. He told us he'd come back to the track in seven days before saying "He has really enjoyed his time off, but it's time to get him ready for the Mile." I swear I could hear the inspirational music being played somewhere.

When Vickie brought Slim off, she said, "He felt like he could run this week."

Steve laughed before saying "There's a mile, grade 2 on the grass, in three weeks. Let's gallop him on the surface tomorrow to see if he can keep his feet under him."

Norm and I both cleaned another stall before going out to play golf. After a competitive round, we went to the pizza restaurant for lunch because we were both hooked on their Italian sub and salad bar. It was a nice meal and wasn't too high in calories. We had been enjoying too many buffets.

We arrived at the track at seven the next morning, and Slim would gallop on the grass to see how he handled it. While we waited for him to go out, I cleaned the filly's stall. I noticed some blood along one wall, so I called Steve over to show him. He showed me where she scratched her right hind leg and told me it was nothing to worry about, but he'd keep an eye on it. He was happy I noticed.

We went over to watch Slim, and he walked onto the track like he owned it. He was showing an attitude much like Charlie's, and it was obvious he was proud of himself. I was starting to believe that Charlie might just have his hands full with him. Steve said, "Gallop him a slow mile to see how he handles the lawn." They jogged around to the finish line where she asked him to pick it up a little. He settled into a really nice rhythm, and when they went past us, they both looked fantastic. He was getting a good hold of the surface, and turning for home, a horse worked past them. He grabbed the bit and started after him, but Vickie got control of him right away. Steve said, "He's really learning to follow instructions." *I wish she'd follow mine.*

I asked, "Not that they'll ever meet, but how do you think he and Charlie would stack up now?"

"Slim's improving all the time, but Charlie would still get my money. It's a nice thing to think about."

When Vickie brought him off, she said, "He may be better on the grass."

Steve replied, "We'll work him on it in a couple days, and that'll give us a better idea." Slim was full of himself on the walker, so I asked Steve if I could call Tom to give him an update.

He replied, "Let's wait until after he works because I wanna be sure he can handle the surface before we tell him."

Norm and I each cleaned another stall and finished just in time to walk to the track with the filly. She was feeling and looking great. She tried to go, but

Vickie was able to keep her in hand. It wasn't easy because she was really full of herself.

When Vickie brought her in, she said, "If we do that very many times, I won't have to worry about dieting." On the walker, the filly was bucking and playing, so I thought, *She's improving every day.* I smiled, knowing she was named after Linda.

After the stalls were cleaned and the horses were put away, we invited Steve to lunch, but he told us he promised Sandy he'd go home. Norm and I ate in the café, and one of the gallop boys asked how Charlie was doing. Norm said, "He'll be back in training next week. We gave him some time off so he could enjoy being a horse for a while."

The young man said, "He certainly earned it with that Belmont win."

After lunch, we decided to go out to the ranch to see Charlie. The ranch manager met us and told us he was doing really well. We walked over to his paddock, and I said, "He looks bigger."

The manager replied, "He's put on some weight, and that's good because he was a little drawn up after that last race. Steve told me he'll take him back to the track next week. Do you know where he'll run next?" We told him it was the Longacre Mile, and he was a little surprised. He said, "He'll blow those horses away."

I stood by the fence and let Charlie lay his head on my shoulder. After I scratched his neck for a couple of minutes, true to form, he ran across the paddock, bucking and throwing his back legs from side to side. Again, the music was playing, and I thought, **Here we come, Seattle!**

Norm said, "His earnings are over two million dollars, and he's just getting started, so I'd say that wasn't a bad mistake at all." *Definitely a blessing.*

The next day, Slim galloped on the turf even better than the first time, and the filly galloped a really strong mile. When Vickie brought her off, she said, "Maybe we should work both of them tomorrow." We cleaned some stalls before going out to play golf, and while we were on the course, Norm asked me if I could believe how things had gone the past year.

I answered, "I think about it all the time. We started with a two-thousand-dollar mistake, and somehow, we met Tom and Liz. I have as much fun watching their horse run as I do Charlie. I still don't know how we ended up with the filly. I know we bought her, but it was like she was just handed to us. The money's not a concern because I've never had money like I do now. It seems that every time we turn around, something good happens to us, and I keep wondering, why us?"

"That's saying a whole bunch at one time, but I feel the same. It's like being on a merry-go-round and we can't get off. Don't get me wrong, I don't wanna get off, but I keep wondering how we got here in the first place." *Too amazing for words.*

The next morning, we were at the track at six. There was a fine mist in the air, so I asked Steve if it would be a problem, working Slim on the grass. He said, "No, you don't usually get here this early, but it'll burn off in the next hour."

I looked forward to seeing how he could handle the grass so I could call Tom. Steve told us he'd work the filly a half and let her gallop out a strong mile. He would work her first to let the grass dry a little more. We both cleaned two stalls while waiting for Vickie to arrive. I told Norm and Steve I was going to the café for coffee and asked what they wanted. Steve said, "Coffee black and a cinnamon roll, please."

Norm said, "Same here, except cream in the coffee." I went in and bought a cup carrier with three cups of coffee and three fresh cinnamon rolls. Vickie was there when I walked back doing my balancing act and laughed at the way I was trying to watch the carrier and the ground at the same time.

I said, "Gentlemen, a little help, please." Steve came over and grabbed the carrier. Norm told him he ruined everything because he was having fun watching me struggle.

I asked Vickie if she wanted coffee and a roll. "No, thank you, I need to get to work," she said while flashing her lovely smile my way.

I said, "That's too bad, I was gonna give you Norm's."

She laughed and shook her head while saying "All this time I thought you two were friends." As they were jogging around to the finish line, I passed out the coffee and rolls.

Steve called up, "Lindalovestorun, going a half."

"Nothing like coffee in the morning, and these rolls just came out of the oven," I said. They both agreed with their mouths full. The pole was right in front of us, and Vickie sat her down right there. The filly lowered her body and was in full stride right before our eyes.

Steve said, "She responds so willingly." Going into the turn, she changed to her left lead and leaned in so far that she was leaving hair on the rail. Watching her take the turn so easily, he said, "She's some athlete." She came out the other side and was on her right lead before any of us could see it. With no coaxing at all, she flew down the lane, and Vickie let her keep the bit almost to the turn. She started to bring her back a little, but she was in a full gallop when they went past us.

The clocker asked Steve if he wanted the off the record first, and he said, "That works for me."

"Forty-five and two, but the recorded work will be forty-seven flat."

"Did you catch her five-eighths gallop out?" Steve asked.

"I don't think we can call this a gallop out. I got her in fifty-nine and four."

Steve said, "Vickie was a little slow pulling her up." He thanked him for helping to preserve her odds.

"I've made way too much money on you to stop now," he replied.

I asked Steve if other people on the track could hear the conversation. "There are separate controls for everyone calling in," he answered.

I said, "That certainly helps us."

Steve replied, "Believe me, it helps him too. He's quite an athlete when he goes to the betting window."

When Vickie came in, she said, "Much better, she saved some for the finish."

Steve said, "I guess she did."

She asked, "Did I do bad, boss?"

"No, she was just full of herself."

"Exactly, what are we talking about?"

Steve said, "The half was forty-five and two. Hang on, five furlongs in fifty-nine and four. Don't beat yourself up because she's just plain fast. We may need to run her sooner than we thought, so we'll work her five in five days, and if everything goes well, we'll start looking for a race."

When Vickie brought Slim to the gap, I said to Norm, "I just had a flashback." He wondered what I was talking about, so I said, "That reminded me of when she brought Charlie up that first time in Seattle."

He replied, "You're right, he was dancing just like that." As she was riding away, I thought, *That's when I realized our jockey is a lovely woman.*

Steve called up, "Slimsfinefood going six." The six-furlong pole was at the start of the backstretch, so she galloped him from the finish line and gave him his head right at the pole. He lowered his body and was off. It was easy to see that he wasn't going full speed, but he was gaining momentum as he went past us. When he entered the turn, he switched to his left lead and leaned in. Coming out of the turn, he was back on his right lead and flying. She didn't go to the whip, but he was all-out. She started pulling him up just past the wire, and by the time he was through the turn, he was in a nice, easy gallop.

The clocker called down, "One minute and eleven seconds flat. That was the six-furlong time, but the really impressive thing is the last quarter was twenty-two and one."

Steve said, "That I like."

"If you don't mind me asking, are you aiming for the grade 2 mile on the turf?" the timer asked.

Steve replied, "After that work, I'm through aiming. He'll be nominated today."

The clocker laughed while saying "That work was one thirteen and two."

I asked Steve if he minded me calling Tom, and he answered, "You've been great to wait this long, so by all means, go ahead. Tell him I'll be calling him about the nomination fees."

I said, "I'll listen to Vickie first."

She was beaming when they came off. "He's totally push button now, and I think the grass is his best surface. He's a real monster out there."

I had heard enough, so I called Tom. "Where the heck have you been?" he asked.

"Like last time, I wanted to be sure before I called."

"What is it this time?"

I said, "He'll be in a grade 2, going a mile on the grass in two weeks,"

"Did you say 'on the grass'?"

"That's why I waited. Steve wanted to make sure he could handle the surface before I called you, and Vickie thinks he could be even better on the lawn."

"I sure wish you guys were up here because I'm totally beside myself. Things really move fast in this business."

I asked him if he had plans for dinner, and he didn't, so I said, "If you don't mind eating where you work, I'll buy both of you dinner tonight,"

"Sounds great, and I have something I want you to see. Bring a bag so you can stay the night." I told him I'd call if we couldn't make it. When I talked to Norm, he was ready to go. I asked Steve if he was thinking Breeder's Cup for Slim.

"Without a doubt, if he runs like I think he will."

"Would I be out of line telling Tom?"

"Go ahead, as long as you say depending on the results of his next race."

It was nine thirty, so we ran by the trailer to grab a bag, and we were on the freeway by ten o'clock. I said, "Let's miss as much of the lunch traffic as possible." We headed due east as fast as the law allowed or maybe just a touch faster. We made good time and pulled into the hotel at four thirty. Our room was ready, so we were unpacked by four forty-five. The bottle of champagne was on ice, and that, along with some chocolate-covered strawberries, was just too much temptation for us to resist. We had a glass and three strawberries each. I don't know why, but champagne goes perfectly with strawberries, and chocolate makes it even better. We showered, got dressed, and were downstairs by five thirty. I called Tom, and he told me Liz couldn't make it until seven, so we made plans to meet at the front door.

I bought my Keno tickets for five games before going in search of a unicorn machine. *What we've seen with our horses today, it'll have to be good.* There was a convention in town, and all the unicorn machines were taken. I walked around a while, but nothing jumped out at me, so I decided to watch the Keno numbers being called. I looked at the number on my ticket, and only one game had been played. It was 6:10 p.m., so I thought I'd be able to watch the rest of the games before meeting Tom. The next game started with number 5 and then 35. I thought, *It couldn't happen again.* Two other numbers were called and then 45 and 15. After three more numbers, 25 and 55, but no more 5s were drawn the rest of the game. Eighty bucks was nothing to sneeze at, though. The next three games brought me fourteen more dollars, and I had twelve minutes to get to the front door. I collected and gave the girl four dollars before going by the card tables. Norm wasn't in sight, so I walked to the door with four minutes to spare. Norm was standing there, and as soon as I walked up, Tom and Liz walked through the door. An old guy should look at Liz gradually because, again, she literally took my breath away. *She's as beautiful in jeans and a plaid top as she is in a glamorous gown.* Actually, the jeans did more for her than a dress ever could.

Tom told us right away that he wanted to swing by the sports book. They had decided to dedicate a wall to horse pictures, and Charlie's Kentucky Derby was followed by his Belmont. Next to them, Slim's grade 2 was followed by his grade 1. Over the top, in purple and gold lettering, it was written, "Where Dreams and Friendships Are Forged." Since the pictures were on the wall, they decided not to make them as big. Again, the graphics department did a beautiful job, so other than me looking overweight, they were perfect.

I asked Tom if his graphics department could make me look thinner, and Norm said, "They're good, but they're not miracle workers."

I said, "Remind me why I started running around with you."

"Now, I'll show you something we've been working on," Tom said after he stopped laughing. "We had to get written permission from Slim to make it happen, but he was more than cooperative. We had a restaurant that wasn't pulling its weight, and we got the idea when we ate at Slim's place in LA." He took us to a storefront done in the same colors as those of Slim's place. Over the door was a flashing red sign saying "Welcome to Slim's North." A small sign said, "Seating capacity: 110." We looked inside, and everything was Western. Just inside the door was a life-size cardboard cutout of Slim with his right hand forward. His arm was moving up and down like he was shaking hands. Tom said, "We negotiated a little about this."

"Did he hit you pretty hard on it?" I asked.

He laughed while saying "One of every win picture Slim gets. He's dedicating a nice spot in his restaurant to him because of his name."

I said, "It better be a large spot."

Liz replied, "I like the sound of that. Come on in, we have a table in the corner."

I said, "Dinner's on me tonight." After we were seated, I noticed some pictures on the wall. Norm and I walked over and saw Charlie's derby and Belmont pictures, followed by Slim's two graded stakes pictures. Already, there were several others donated by their customers.

Tom came over and said, "We're surprised by the interest this wall is creating. The place opened yesterday, and all of the tables were full. Many of the people coming in brought pictures of their own. We hope to project a down-home attitude that'll keep them coming back, so we set our prices where locals can afford to come here when they take Mama out to dinner. The food will be the best, so our food cost is over 40 percent, but rent is built in and labor is good, so we'll do well if we keep the tables turning."

We all ordered their best steaks and a bottle of red wine. While we were waiting to be served, I filled them in on the filly and Slim. Tom told me he had been wondering all day about running Slim on grass, so I said, "I'm not skilled enough to know how Steve came to this point, but Vickie says he should be better on grass. Hold on to your hats, his ultimate goal is the Breeder's Cup Mile, if he wins in two weeks."

Tom looked a little dazed while asking, "How did we get here so quickly?"

Norm said, "We've been questioning that the last couple days but one thing we've realized, we enjoy watching Slim as much as we do Charlie."

Liz replied, "Tom and I have been saying the same thing." She raised her wine glass and said, "To Slim and Charlie."

After tapping our glasses together, I said, "And to a very promising filly."

The steaks were outstanding. The beef was top-quality, and they were prepared just the way we ordered them. I was startled when I recognized a booming voice behind me, so I turned to see Slim standing close to the table. He told us he would have been earlier, but the guy up front kept wanting to shake his hand. "Are we talking about the cutout of you?" Tom asked.

He replied, "I reckon we are. He sure is a friendly cuss." I offered to buy his dinner, but he told me they fed him on the plane. He said, "Tom, your plane is a nice ride, but that helicopter keeps you guessin'." Tom told him the helicopter bothered him at first too. Slim sat down with us before saying, "This place looks familiar." Tom told him he was so taken in by his restaurant that he wanted to do something like it. "I really do like that cutout of me," Slim said.

Tom said, "Liz is from Texas, and she fell in love with your restaurant when we had dinner."

"That reminds me, there's one more thing I want." Tom thought it was a little late to be asking but listened. "A really nice picture of the two of you to put in Slim's display. Tom, you're not bad, but she'll really dress up my place." Tom thanked him before Liz leaned over to kiss his cheek.

"We'll have one made up for you in a nice Western frame," she promised. I admired how quickly people were drawn to the couple. I knew that I and Norm certainly had been. We sat there talking until after midnight. Slim was there to sign some takeout menus for customers the next day at lunch. He was really excited when Tom told him Steve was thinking about the Breeder's Cup, if Slim kept running like he was. He didn't go into the part about running on grass, and I wasn't sure he had fully grasped it.

I paid the bill and left a two-hundred-dollar tip before Tom said, "Jim, you're too generous." I told him it had been working for me, so I wasn't about to change. We said "good night" and went out to play pai gow for a while. We both lost a hundred dollars but played until three in the morning. We were getting some points on our player's cards, and the smoke didn't seem to bother me too much. Maybe many of the smokers had already gone to bed.

We went up to the room at the same time and went to sleep without turning the television on. I woke with a start at ten the next morning when the maid knocked on the door. Through the door, I asked her to leave a set of towels and told her everything else would be fine. *We'll stay another night now.* I slipped my jeans on and grabbed the towels. Norm was still sleeping, so I got cleaned up quietly, and as I was leaving, he asked if we were going home. I explained what happened with the maid, and he said, "That's great, I feel like playing for a while." *It's nice to be retired.*

Before I could get out of the room, Vickie called and asked if we were staying. I told her we would for one more night anyway. She didn't beat around the bush. She said, "Play me in the fifth."

Without thinking, I said, "I'd like to play you somewhere."

She replied, "All I get out of you is a whole lotta talkin', sweetie." While laughing, she said, "The horse is a maiden special weight, first-time starter. He's worked head-to-head with a stakes horse in the barn, and his morning line is five to one. There's an eight-to-five horse from Southern California in the race, but if he was great, they'd break his maiden down there. He should help with our odds."

I told her she was sweet for remembering to call us about the horse. She wanted to know if we spent some time with Tom and Liz, so I said, "We were at dinner until after midnight because Slim's up to help kick off the new restaurant."

She said, "I need to get away for a few days pretty soon, and I think it would be fun to come up there."

I replied, "I'll bring you up, if you'd like, and Tom said he'll give you a suite at no charge. Forgive me, I mean we'll bring you up."

She said, "Please stop that, Jim, I'm not afraid you'll rape me. Believe me, sweetie, I can take care of myself." *She sounds frustrated.*

"I don't like old guys hitting on young ladies, and your friendship means too much to me to offend you that way. I'd rather apologize than have you find me disgusting."

"**Listen to me**, I'm not that young, and you're not that old, so please stop worrying about making me mad. I've already told you how much I enjoy our flirting."

I whispered, "Just say the word, and we'll bring you up." I promised her that we wouldn't get in her way once she was there. She laughed and told me she would want me to show her around. I said, "I would like that very much." I thanked her again before saying goodbye. I was really trying to keep our relationship business, but it wasn't easy. I didn't know if she was interested or just flirting with an old man. *"I'm not that young, and you're not that old"?*

Norm was out of the bathroom, and I told him about the horse in the fifth. He told me he'd be ready to go in fifteen minutes, so we agreed to meet at the sports book. I went down and bought my Keno numbers for five games before calling Tom to tell him about Vickie's horse. He told me he'd try to be there for the fifth but was tied up with the opening. I told him to try to make the race, but if he couldn't, I'd make his bet for him.

Vickie's horse was the four out of nine starters. I decided to bet early and bet five hundred to win and place on him. I also put him on top of the eight, who was the favorite, for a hundred-dollar exacta. I was becoming more comfortable making bigger bets as my horse account grew. Vickie had been right almost every time, and she was very confident about that one.

Norm wanted to know if I had bet, so I told him I did before saying "The horse is the four in the fifth at Golden Gate." After he made his wager, I suggested that we go to Slim's for lunch. We walked over but stopped when we saw a long line waiting to get in. We picked up some coffee and rolls at the food court and would try Slim's later.

At a pai gow table, we started out playing ten dollars on the wager and bonus. After three hands, I was down forty dollars and thought about lowering my bet but decided to go a couple more of hands. The next hand, I was dealt a straight flush, and that paid me five hundred on the bonus. I didn't win the two-card hand, so I didn't win the ten-dollar wager. Because Norm had ten out for his bonus bet, he also won some on my straight flush, but I didn't notice how much. We played there until time for the race, and I cashed out 450 dollars ahead. I gave the dealer a twenty-five-dollar chip before we walked away.

The horses were in the post parade when we walked in. Liz and Tom had slipped away from Slim's and were sitting at a table. Tom said, "The horse is beautiful." I told him what she said about him working head-to-head with a stakes horse. They had each bet three hundred to win and place, and the horse was nine to two when they entered the gate. "They're off and running" rang out, and the eight went right to the front. The race was six furlongs, so there was only one turn. Vickie kept her horse two lengths behind the leader, going into the turn. She looked under her right arm and was in the clear, so she hugged the rail as she got closer to the leader. The eight hugged the rail, so she took another quick look before swinging her horse to the outside. She popped him three times and put her whip away. They won by six widening lengths, but the eight was in a photo for second, and I was afraid he didn't hold on for my exacta. Sure enough, when the results were posted, the eight was third, so I missed the exacta but still did really well. I had purchased a fifty-dollar win for Vickie, so I had a nice tip to take back to her. *She's so sweet to keep giving us these touts.*

I told Liz what I was thinking, and she said, "Sugar, you know why she gives you these tips. We can all see how much she cares for you. I hope you defeat your demons before she finds someone and you worry about your age way more than she does." *I hope we can be together someday.*

I gripped her hand and said, "I care for her very much, but I don't want a one-night stand with her. If we can somehow get together, I want all of her."

She smiled and said in a low whisper, "As much as you care for each other, things will work out."

I whispered, "Thank you for your support, Liz."

Norm asked Tom if Slim went home, and he answered, "Ya, and he was really worn out."

"That man's a hugger," Liz said while laughing.

I replied, "He's one of the best front men I've seen. I don't think anybody gets by him in his restaurant, and it's clear that he's the reason many of them eat there."

"Along with the best steaks in LA," Tom said.

I said, "We tried to come in for lunch today, but the line was outrageous."

Liz replied, "It's been that way all day. Please forgive me, I didn't thank you for dinner last night."

"We have a long way to go to catch up to what you two have done for us," I replied.

Tom said, "But you used your money."

I replied, "No I didn't, I used Charlie's." They liked that, and we agreed it would only get better when the filly started running.

"How long are you staying?" Tom asked.

I said, "At least tonight, if we're not a bother."

He replied, "Listen to me, that room or one just like it is yours anytime you want it for as long as you wanna stay."

I said, "When Vickie called to give me the tip, she indicated that she'd like to come up soon." Liz told me she'd love to go shopping with her, so I told her I'd try to keep my hands off her long enough to let them shop. Her laughter filled the room as she said, "Vickie has you pegged, sugar, **you're a big talker!**"

When I checked my Keno tickets, I only had three dollars coming, so I gave them to the girl and played ten more games. I found a unicorn machine that wasn't being played, so I put in a twenty and started playing one dollar a spin. On the fourth spin, I won 120 dollars and played on that until dinner time. I cashed in sixty-two dollars and thought, *I had all that fun and tripled my money. Where else could I have that much fun and come out ahead?* That made me a little sad because Linda and I said that every time we went to Vegas.

When I found Norm, he told me he was starving, so I asked if he wanted a steak. He told me he'd rather go to the buffet. When we arrived at the counter, he told me to put my money away. I was in hog heaven because they had both my crawdads and hot and sour soup. I said, "Life is good." He reached over to pinch my arm, and I said, "Ouch, that hurt."

"Just making sure we're awake." I told him to use his own arm next time. Before we left, I put a fifty on the table, and Norm frowned before asking, "A fifty-dollar tip at a buffet?"

"It's been working well so far, so I'm not about to change." He put a ten with it, and we walked back into the casino. I said, "One thing has always held true with you, Norman—**you're cheap!**"

"I told you, I have to pay 80 percent of Charlie's bills," he said while trying not to laugh.

There were a couple of open seats at a pai gow table, so we sat down. We started playing ten and ten and had played for about fifteen minutes when I saw Norm tense up. When he turned his cards over, he had a joker-aided royal flush, so they paid him fifteen one-hundred-dollar chips. I collected a hundred dollars because I had ten dollars on the bonus line, plus he slid three black chips to me and said, "Play on house money for a while." We played for several hours before I went up to the room. It was ten thirty, and I thought about calling Vickie but decided it was too late. Again, I wondered what was going on with the feelings I had for her. *I can't fall in love with her at my age.*

The next morning before going home, we thanked Tom for everything and promised to keep him posted about how the horses were doing.

We were happy to see that Charlie was back at the barn when we walked in. It was afternoon, so all the chores were done. Steve was ready to go home for a while, so we decided to go to the trailer until feeding time. After lying around for a couple of hours, we decided not to go back to the barn.

The next morning, all three horses were scheduled to gallop. Charlie went really slow and wasn't breathing hard when Vickie brought him off. She said, "He's put on some weight, so he'll be perfect for the Mile." I asked her if putting on weight was good, and she answered, "Absolutely, he was a little drawn up after the Belmont. He'll keep this weight and turn it into hard muscle. He's kept himself in good shape and will peak for the Mile."

I asked her why she smiled at me the way she did. She answered, "I missed having you around."

I said, "We missed you too." I was doing my best to not let our conversations get too personal, but her blue eyes were driving me crazy. *I can't go through that pain again.*

The filly was next. She galloped a mile and wasn't breathing hard when Vickie brought her off. "One more work, and she'll be ready to go," Steve said.

"When will she work?" I asked.

He answered, "She'll work five-eighths in the morning."

Slim was the last to go to the track, and he looked huge and menacing. He stood straight up on his back legs before walking onto the turf, and Vickie yelled, "Giddy up!" She seemed awfully happy, so I wondered if she might have met someone. *I hope not, but it might be best for both of us if she did.*

Steve said, "Two strong miles." She jogged him around to the finish line before letting him settle into a nice gallop. When they came by us, Steve said, "He's really reaching, so I wish the race was today." I asked if he'd work before the race, and he answered, "No, just long, strong gallops. He's plenty fit, so now we'll keep him that way without letting him peak too soon." He laughed and reminded me of what Clint said. (You don't have to get fit what's already fit.) Slim went around twice and looked like he wanted to go again.

When they came off, Vickie said, "He's getting better all the time. If we can keep him right here, he'll be really tough to beat." His race was a week away.

The next morning, Charlie went to the track first. He galloped a nice, easy mile and was playing when Vickie brought him off. "That's my Charlie," she said.

Steve put him on the walker, and Norm and I watched him until Steve told us the filly was going to the track. I said, "The horses are doing well, but I'm gettin' tired."

"Work her five-eighths, and keep some for the finish, if she'll let you," Steve said before calling the work up to the tower. They jogged around to the finish line before Vickie let her pick it up to a nice gallop. The five-eighths pole was a furlong to our left, and a few strides before the pole, Vickie shook the reins. Her body lowered, and she was in full stride by the time they reached the pole. She seemed a little more under control as they went by us and picked up speed through the turn. Going for home, she was really laying it down, and Vickie let her work about thirty yards past the finish line. She had her under wraps by the time she leaned into the clubhouse turn, and they galloped out pretty fast. Steve told us she was ready.

The clocker called down, "One minute and two-fifths. She really picked it up coming out of the turn and galloped out six in one twelve and two."

Steve thanked him and said to us, "She's looking good." When Vickie brought her off, she and Steve agreed that she was relaxing much better.

Slim galloped another strong two miles and looked great coming off the track. Vickie said, "He couldn't be doing any better. It would be nice if they could both run Saturday."

Steve told us he'd ask the secretary to hang an extra before saying "There's something about having a Kentucky Derby winner in the barn that seems to give us a little leverage."

I called Tom and said, "Get ready because Slim sure is." I told him what Vickie said and that Steve would try to get a race for the filly. He asked if she was ready to roll, and I told him she was breathing fire.

I told him I hoped they could make the races, and he replied, "It looks like we can right now, but I'll call if something comes up."

Entry day arrived, and a two-year-old filly maiden special weight was listed as an extra. That race received eight entrants, and one of the others didn't fill, so she was in. She drew the 3 hole, and Steve said, "With her speed, 3 will be perfect." Slim was the five horse in a field of ten, and Steve told us he didn't care where he drew in. The way he was relaxing, he could sit just off the pace, if not have the lead. He said, "I'd like for him to come from just a little way back on the grass, but it's nice having a horse with his versatility."

Friday night, Tom called and told us they wouldn't make the race before saying "The new restaurant is making so much noise that corporate is sending a team in on Saturday. They're thinking about putting Slim's in all of their hotels." I asked if they would have to negotiate with Slim. "Oh, absolutely, this could mean a lot of money to him." I told him I would root Slim home for them.

He wanted to know about the filly, so I said, "She's in the fifth and should have the lead, so let's hope she keeps it." The last thing I said was "Vickie thinks she'll win."

The next morning was beautiful. There was no morning mist, just beautiful sunshine. We had breakfast in the café and picked up a program. The filly was listed at eight to one, and Slim was the second choice at seven to two. They both had eight-to-five favorites in their races.

After breakfast, we walked to the barn and told Steve there were eight-to-five favorites in both races. He said, "They're both being brought up by the same trainer. In the fillies' race, the favorite just missed in a maiden special weight at Santa Anita. In Slim's race, the favorite is a grade 1 winner on the grass. We wanted to find out if Slim's good enough to go to the Breeder's Cup, and this will certainly let us know." He told us we arrived just in time because Charlie would work a half. We walked up with him, and he called up, "Wrong Way North working a half."

Our friend, the clocker, asked, "Is he still around?"

"Alive and kickin'," Steve replied. Vickie jogged him around to the finish line before putting him into a gallop. The half-mile pole was right in front of us, and just before the pole, Vickie shook the reins. His back lowered, and he was in that beautiful stride, right before our eyes. He leaned into the turn and hugged the rail all the way around. I could see his back end lower a little more as he picked it up down the lane. She worked him a little past the line and had him in a fast gallop through the turn.

The clocker said, "He's back, the half was forty-five and two, and he galloped out six in one eleven flat."

Steve said, "He's a little more fit than we thought he'd be."

When Vickie brought him off, she had tears streaming down her face, so I asked her if she was all right. She pointed to her face and said, "Happy tears." Steve had hold of Charlie's halter, and he was being completely calm, as if to give Vickie her time to speak. She said, "Just when I thought Slim might give him a run for his money, he brought me back to reality. This guy is in a league all by himself. Norm, Jim, and Steve, thank you for this gift of a lifetime. In my wildest dreams, I never dreamed this big." She brought tears to my eyes when she hugged his neck and told him how much she loved him. Through it all, Charlie was thinking, **All right already, where are my oats?**

After Vickie gave us nice hugs and walked away, I asked Steve if she just said we shouldn't bet Slim. He laughed and replied, "Slim will run great, but what you just heard is Charlie will be double tough in the Breeder's Cup Classic." We watched Charlie bounce around on the walker for thirty minutes. He looked at us each time around as if to say "Just another day and, hopefully, another bucket of oats." *If he wins the classic, I'll add a glass of champagne to his feed.*

I said, "Vickie couldn't have said it better, I didn't know I could love an animal this much." Both Steve and Norm agreed with me.

I was happy when the horses were called to the holding barn for the fifth race. I felt an excitement set aside for first-time starters, and she was even more highly touted than Charlie was. I was full of anticipation as we walked over, and my mind drifted back through the years. I recalled many of the best fillies of all time and hoped she might fit in there someplace, but the true story wouldn't be told until she showed she had the fire in her belly. So many talented horses don't have the heart, when the goin' gets tough.

In the paddock, she pranced like the princess she thought she was. Vickie came in and hugged us before saying "I wish Liz and Tom made it." Steve legged her up, and she winked at us as they came around. Everything said bet her big, but in the back of mind was the image of a filly we had in Spokane. Nothing could touch her for a quarter of a mile, but she wasn't a quarter horse. I bet two hundred to win and place, and that was like the five dollars to win and place I bet before Charlie.

She was ten to one when they entered the gate, and the favorite was two to five. When the gate opened, our filly went right to the front and opened up three easy lengths on the field. Just as she had done in her morning workouts, she switched to her left lead and leaned into the turn, but coming out of the turn, she went quite wide.

I said, "She didn't switch back to her right, so she's either confused by the crowd noise or hurting on the right side." She had four lengths on the field, but her stride was shortening, and the favorite was closing fast. Vickie was holding her together as best she could, but it was obvious that she wouldn't hold on. The favorite went by her and won by a length, but she finished two lengths in front of the third-place horse.

When Vickie was bringing her back, I could see she was off on her right front, so I prayed, "Lord, please let her have shin bucked." Vickie got off about thirty yards from where we were and led her back. She was visibly limping by that time, so Steve asked Vickie if she knew what happened. She told him she couldn't be sure but suspected she blew her right shin. I prayed, "Lord, please let her be right."

Steve felt up and down her leg before saying "No bone displacement or bowed tendon." The track vet came out and confirmed that she had indeed shin-bucked, so I felt like a thousand pounds had been lifted off me.

I said, "Steve, I only ask because I know Tom will be calling. Will you pin fire her and go on?"

He answered, "She's way too nice, so she'll come back as a three-year-old."

I said, "Please call and let the people we bought her from know she shin-bucked because this has to have brought back some ugly memories." Steve told me he'd call them right away.

Five minutes later, my phone rang, and Tom asked if she was done. I said, "For this year. Steve said she's way too nice to take any chances with her, so she'll come back next year. She totally blew her right shin but kept trying through the pain." Tom told me he was a runner in school and had what were called shin splints. He told me how painful they were, so I said, "That's the same thing, and with some time off, she'll be fine. We'll get the big money with Slim." He thanked me and told me he'd call back after Slim's race. *Scared me!*

Back at the barn, the filly was in some pain, but Steve told us the vet gave her some pain meds and they should kick in soon. He said, "Vickie said it happened going into the turn."

I replied, "I noticed that she didn't switch back to her right lead and thought she must have shin-bucked. Thank God it wasn't more than that."

He said, "She tried awfully hard in a lot of pain, so believe me, Jim, she has a huge heart. Sometimes, horses remember that terrible pain and never come back to what they could have been, but with some time off, she'll be fine."

She was comfortable in her stall when the horses were called over for the seventh race. When we walked into the paddock, Slim was five to one, and the favorite was four to five. Slim was the third choice because the form showed he had never run on grass, and thanks to our friend in the morning, his works looked pretty ordinary. When Vickie came in, she asked about the filly, so I explained, "She's resting comfortably in her stall, so the pain meds are doing their job."

Steve legged her up, and she winked on the walk-around. That time, there was no gnawing down deep in my stomach when I went up to bet. He had gone up to six to one, so I bet three thousand to win for me and a hundred for Steve and Vickie.

When the gate opened, Slim had gone to seven to one, and the favorite was one to five. The favorite went right to the front and maintained a two-length lead around the first turn. He really was a beautiful horse and looked strong. Slim was on the rail in third, three lengths behind him, and was as relaxed as he would have been on the walker. About halfway up the backside, Vickie shook his reins, and he easily moved into second. Coming out of the turn, Vickie reached back and popped him three times. **What a sight**. Slim took the lead with a hundred yards to go and was drawing away under a hand ride. His winning margin was two lengths but looked like it could have been more. *He has improved so much.*

Norm said, "We have two legitimate Breeder's Cup horses to wager on."

ESPN did an interview after the race, and Steve was asked the first question. "What's next for him?"

I wasn't surprised when Steve said "A month off, and then we'll work him up to the Breeder's Cup."

Vickie was next. "Were you surprised at how easily he won?"

She answered, "That favorite is really tough, but Slim is improving all the time. I'm looking forward to riding him in the Breeder's Cup."

The lady asked, "Since the owners couldn't make it, would one of you like to say something?" Norm pointed to me, and she asked, "Do you know why the owners couldn't make it today?"

"They have some important business that had to be taken care of, so please don't take it as a lack of interest. They love this business and, most of all, this horse." She asked how Charlie was doing, and I said, "He's fine and will run next in the Longacre Mile, but today belongs to Slim. It looks like he has a bright future on the turf." She thanked us for the interview before wishing us good luck.

The two-dollar win paid $16.20, and I gave Steve and Vickie their tickets before collecting mine. I collected just over twenty-four thousand dollars, including eighty dollars for the filly running second. My horse account was growing and was more than my 401(K). Charlie was the engine driving everything, so I thanked God one more time for his wonderful gift.

A couple of minutes later, Tom called and said, "Slim really does look better on grass."

I replied, "Vickie has been saying that for over a week. It looks like we'll have no horses running before the Longacres Mile, so I'll be a little lost." He wanted to know the date of the race, so I said, "I'll have to check, but I think about five weeks." He asked what we would do with ourselves for that long, and I answered, "I'm not sure, but something relaxing. I'll keep you posted about the horses."

That night, Norm said, "It's nice to be back to just Charlie for a while."

"How far off is the Mile?" I asked.

"About six weeks, but we'll find out for sure in the morning."

I said, "It'll feel strange to have the prohibitive favorite in that race after watching other people win it for so many years."

"I'm anxious for the race to get here," he replied.

Charlie worked the day before, so he was just walking. Steve said, "It's a little quiet around here without the filly and Slim."

I replied, "I don't mind having things slow down a little. How many weeks before the Mile?" He told me it was six and wanted to know if we were busy for the next few weeks.

Norm said, "We've been thinking about that but haven't come up with a plan." He told us we were always welcome at the barn.

I said, "Maybe we should stay around. We could work in the mornings and play golf in the afternoons. If something strikes our fancy, it doesn't take long to hook up the trailer." Norm agreed that relaxing for a while would be good.

Steve said, "My groom needs some time off, and it would help me if you could be around for a couple weeks." We were happy to help him because he was still giving us the special rate. *He doesn't ask us for many favors.*

The next two weeks, we worked a little each morning and watched Charlie get more aggressive. Four weeks before the Mile, Steve said, "We might have a decision to make because Charlie's getting way too full of himself. If we back off too much, he might not be fit enough for the Mile, but if we continue as we are, I fear he'll get rank. I didn't wanna run him before the Mile, but he loves to run so much that I don't think I can keep him from peaking too soon." He picked up his condition book and started browsing. "Saturday, there's an allowance, three-year-olds and up. The purse is only fifty-eight thousand, but that's not why we'll run him."

I said, "That wouldn't be an easy race because older horses can be tough."

Steve replied, "Charlie will win it, and he'll be running against older horses in the mile." We agreed to enter him and see what else would be in the race. *I don't know why he's involving us in his decisions.*

The next morning, entries were taken for the race, and seven horses were entered. The race was going a mile and a sixteenth, and Charlie was in the one post. Steve told us he recognized one of the horses that had been laid off for over a year. He placed second in a grade 1 at Hollywood Park the year before, after leading every step but the last. He bowed a tendon slightly, working up to his next race, but word had it that he was training well for his comeback.

I said, "I hope not too many horses scratch when they see that horse and Charlie are in."

Steve said, "The race is set to go, so scratches won't cancel the race at this point."

I asked, "Do you think being down inside will hurt us?"

"Not at all, he'll get a good position on the rail just off the lead, and he's much the best horse, so he'll win easily. I just hope he gets enough out of the race to set him up for the Mile."

The morning of the race was ushered in by beautiful sunshine. Two horses scratched, leaving a field of five, and the comeback horse, Harlan's Choice, was in the five post. I told Norm I would prefer being on the outside, and he told me I worried too much. We were two to five in the program, and Harlan's Choice was three to one. I told Norm I wouldn't bet because the odds were too low, and he agreed to just watch the race also.

When we walked over with Charlie, he looked like he could whip the world. Norm said, "He's the most beautiful horse I've ever seen." He certainly looked different than he did when we took him to the track in Yakima.

Just before we got to the paddock, Tom called and said, "I know you don't need it, but good luck." I thanked him and told him, "You always need luck."

When Vickie came into the paddock, she hugged Norm first and then me. I looked toward the tote board and said, "No betting today." Charlie had dropped to one to nine.

She said, "Just enjoy watching him run."

I whispered, "Today, I'll be watching his rider."

After Steve legged her up, she winked and mouthed, "**Talk, talk, talk**." She was so cute, and I was having so much fun flirting with her. There was no doubt that she was helping me want to go on living. *I really needed her when she came along.*

"They're running" rang out as the gate opened, and as Steve said would happen, Vickie settled him into a nice spot on the rail, two lengths behind the five. They maintained their positions through the first turn, and starting up the backside, the jockey on the three asked his horse for run. Vickie stayed where she was, knowing he'd run himself out and hoped he might put some pressure on the five. As he was going past them, everything changed. He hadn't cleared Charlie, but for some reason, he dove to the rail. Vickie pulled back on Charlie's reins, but she was too late. He clipped heels with the three, and his head went down. Vickie lurched forward and was up on his neck. A lesser horse would most certainly have gone down, but Charlie righted himself in a heartbeat. Vickie worked herself back into the saddle, but by the time she had her feet in the irons and was ready to go back to riding, Charlie was four lengths behind the field. The real problem was the five was six lengths in front and running much too easily.

Vickie stayed on the rail going into the turn, hoping things would open up, but the inside horse hugged the rail all the way around. Vickie took Charlie to the outside, entering the lane, and they moved into second with half the lane to go. The five still had five lengths on him and had a lot of run left. Charlie made a move not unlike the one he made in the Belmont, but it was too late. At the wire, he had cut the margin to three quarters of a length but was unable to go by.

Norm had a stunned look on his face and said, "He couldn't have gotten into any more trouble."

I replied, "I hope he didn't get hurt." When Vickie brought him to where we were waiting, Charlie looked into the winner's circle with an angry look on his face. I said, "Look, Steve, he looks like he's mad."

Steve said, "He thinks the picture is part of his race, and he doesn't like that other horse being in there. Charlie could beat him with any luck at all."

I replied, "I hope we run against him again so Charlie can crush him."

When we got back to the barn, Steve went over him very closely before saying "He doesn't have a scratch on him."

Norm said, "It's unbelievable that he didn't go down."

Steve said, "Yes, and that Vickie was able to stay on. Don't take this the wrong way, guys, but he got way more out of that race than he would have if he had won easily."

I said, "Money wasn't the reason we were in the race, but it hurts to see him lose."

Steve replied, "He impressed more people with that race than he would have by running away from the field."

Right then, Tom called and said, "I'm sorry he didn't win, but the way he responded to all the problems had the club buzzing. He should have gone down."

I said, "If Vickie hadn't come out of the saddle, I think he still would have won."

He agreed before asking, "Is he all right?"

I answered, "The way Steve put it, not a scratch on him."

The last thing he said was "I and Liz are going to Seattle for the Mile if we won't be in the way." Both Norm and Steve were happy to hear they'd be in Seattle.

The next week went by quickly as we were at the track every morning and played golf almost every afternoon. Vickie came to us one morning and told us she had a horse for the next day if we were interested. It had been a couple of weeks since I'd made a wager, so yes, I was interested. She said, "She's a nice filly that's run one time. She didn't get out of the gate, so coming for home, she was hopelessly beaten. I let her run just enough to get some conditioning, so she should have good odds. They've taken her to the gate several times to school her, so when it's time for her to break, she'll get out much better this time."

I said, "I don't know how many of these touts you can give me before I fall hopelessly in love."

She flashed her beautiful smile while saying "I have a few more comin' up, sweetie pie."

I said, "You looked incredible staying in the saddle, in Charlie's race."

She replied, "I was a long way from the saddle for a while. Like dolphins are said to keep people from drowning, Charlie kept me from being hurt. He literally lifted me back into the saddle, so I think he loves me as much as I love him." I hugged her more warmly than I ever had, and I was surprised when her body molded to mine.

I stepped back and said, "Now go back to work before you make this old man cry." *She feels so much like Linda. I need to settle down.*

Charlie was galloping two miles each day, and Steve said, "No more works, just good, long gallops up to the race."

The next morning, the track came up muddy, so I asked Vickie if the filly could handle it.

She said, "I haven't worked her on a muddy track, but she's bred to like it. I expect her to break on top, and many times when horses get the lead in the mud, they keep going." *I'm not sure what she said because I can't get my mind off her last hug. Been a long time since a woman has touched me like that. I need to back away, or I'll get hurt again.*

The race was a thirty-two-thousand-dollar Cal-bred maiden race, and she was number 8. I said to Norm, "She won't get in much easier, with the Cal-bred condition." When she walked into the paddock, she was eight to one. We stood outside to watch the horses go by, and Vickie winked at us, as she almost always did.

When they went onto the track, I ran up and bet five hundred to win and place for me and a hundred-dollar win for Vickie. I thought again about how great the hug she gave me felt. I knew she was excited about Charlie, and I would never do anything to jeopardize our friendship, but my goodness, she felt good in my arms. *I'm losing my mind.*

Norm and I decided to watch the race by the finish line since the crowd wasn't too heavy, and it was nice being outside after the rain. When the gate opened, the filly was out like a shot and had three lengths on the field, fifty yards out of the gate. Vickie didn't fight her, but neither did she ask her for more. Coming out of the turn, she had four lengths on the second-place filly. She looked under her right arm, and nothing was closing, so she hand-rode her to the wire. The winning margin was five very easy lengths, and we were in for another nice payday. *She's amazing.*

The people in the winner's circle were having a great time. There were three male partners who looked to be in their midthirties, and when Vickie came out after the picture, I shook her hand and said, "It looks like one of those guys is interested in you. You seemed so happy when we came back from the lake that I thought you might be interested in someone. Is he the one?" *I hope I didn't seem desperate.*

She smiled before saying "Ya, he thinks he's quite a ladies' man, but he doesn't interest me. You're right, sweet boy, I'm very interested in someone, but it's not him." She kissed my lips quickly and winked before heading to the jockeys' room. I was a complete idiot because I stood there like I didn't have a clue. Sometimes, windows of opportunity open with women, and if you hesitate, you may not get a second chance. They don't take rejection too well. *I shoulda kissed her back, or maybe it's good I didn't. Never been so confused.*

The win paid $19.60, and the place was $8.20, so I said to Norm, "That'll pay for my trip to Seattle."

Steve thanked us for helping him after telling us his groom was back from vacation. It made us feel good to help him after all he had done for us.

That night, we talked about going to see Tammy and my grandkids in Portland before going to Seattle. We decided to go by the track the next morning and tell Steve and Vickie about our plans.

She had just taken Charlie up for his two-mile gallop, and he was in a nice rhythm when a working horse came up inside him. Charlie grabbed the bit and was after him, so Vickie gave him his head for a good three-eighths of a mile before taking hold of him and gently bringing him back. Steve said, "She's letting him have fun."

When they came off the track Vickie said to Steve, "Sorry, boss, he was getting a little too full of himself, so I thought I'd let him get some of it out of his system." *I'm a little full of myself, so I wish she'd settle me down. I'm having fun.*

Steve said, "Right here is where we want him physically and mentally, when he leaves the gate in Seattle."

I replied, "Like Vickie realized her dream winning the Kentucky Derby, we're about to realize ours." *Hope I get another chance to kiss her.*

We told them we were going up to spend some time with our families and would see them at the track in Seattle. Vickie told us she was coming up a few days early to enjoy the week's festivities. Steve asked if we had read the paper, and none of us had so he grabbed his and showed us the sports page. In big letters, it was written, **"Harlan's Choice to Face Wrong Way North in the Longacre Mile."** His owner went on to say "It was fun outrunning the Kentucky Derby winner, and I want the world to know it wasn't a fluke."

I laughed and said, "We'll hand him his butt on a platter."

Vickie was mad and said, "Last time he had everything his way, but this time, he finds out what pressure is like. He won't light the board."

I replied, "I'm glad you're on our side, little lady." *She's cute when she's angry.* I had been trying not to think about her telling me she was interested in someone before kissing me, but it wasn't working. I tapped my index finger on the tip of her nose while saying "Temper, temper, little girl." What I wanted to do was wrap her in my arms and tell her I was crazy about her.

"It just makes me mad," she said in a way that made us all laugh.

I said, "Don't lose that fire because I wanna bury him as much as you do."

"Don't worry, he'll fold like a poor poker player," she promised while little sparks shot from her big blue eyes. She smiled after I kissed her lips very quickly and told her I was practicing for my kiss after the Mile. *I won't miss that opportunity again.*

We decided not to leave until the next morning and played golf before having dinner at the pizza restaurant. We sat outside the trailer until eleven thirty, enjoying the night air and talked about the upcoming race. We had both dreamed

302

about winning that race for over twenty years, and our chance was only a week away. Norm, all of a sudden, burst out laughing and said, "Vickie was really mad."

I replied, "She loves Charlie, and she was defending him. Her competitiveness is one more thing I love about her."

"Smitten," he said before going inside. As I followed him, I told him he had to admit, she was cute when she was angry. Again, he said, "Smitten." I wasn't sure what smitten meant, but I did think she was cute when she was angry. I couldn't get our last conversation and hug out of my mind. *Could she really be interested in a man my age? Go to sleep before you go bonkers.*

The next morning, we stopped by the backside café for breakfast and told Steve we'd see him Friday or Saturday. I called Tom to tell him we were leaving, and he said, "Liz made reservations to stay at a nice hotel downtown. We stayed in Seattle a couple years ago and walked around on the numbered streets. Liz made me promise that we could stay at a hotel, we stopped in for lunch."

"When will you arrive?" I asked.

"We're due to arrive Wednesday afternoon. Liz reserved a car with a GPS so we can do some sightseeing."

"From what you've told me, that lady spoils you a little. You're a very lucky man, Tom."

"Believe me, Jim, I know how lucky I am. **She tells me every day!**" *She's a kick.*

When we hung up, I told Norm we were lucky to have met such great people. He said, "I really believe there isn't anything in the world they wouldn't do for us."

"You just like looking at Liz," I said, and for once in his life, he couldn't argue with me.

When we crossed the state line into Oregon, I called my daughter to tell her we were on our way. She asked if we brought the trailer, and I told her we did, so she promised to have things ready for us to hook up. A little while later, we saw a sign for an Indian casino, and I asked Norm if he wanted to stop for lunch. When we pulled in, I was really impressed with the exterior. After parking the truck, Norm said, "Let's play for one hour and then meet at the buffet." We agreed to call if one of us was on a hot streak.

I bought my Keno tickets for five games before going to a unicorn machine. My first twenty only lasted about five minutes, so I wondered, *Should I play another twenty or find a different machine?* Not a good decision. I stayed, and my twenty lasted maybe ten minutes that time. ***Get me outta here!*** I moved to a machine that was named after an artist or something, and it was fun because, each time I'd hit something, it made a noise and automatically gave me another spin. My twenty lasted thirty minutes in that machine, so I had enough fun to not mind losing. I looked at my watch and thought, *Just enough time to check my Keno tickets and go to the buffet.* I certainly didn't have to call and tell Norm I was on a roll. My Keno tickets returned two dollars, so I told the girl to keep them. Norm was standing with a frown on his face and said, "I just lost a hundred bucks, so this better be good food." I told him I didn't do much better.

We pulled into my daughter's yard at four thirty and plugged into an extension cord that she had set out for us. We offered to take them to dinner, but Tammy had set out some burgers and hot dogs to barbecue. That gave us more time to talk and catch up. She told me what she was able to do with the money she made on the wager, and Kayti said, "**That was awesome!** We were so excited when the horse was winning that people all around us knew something was happening. Mom was embarrassed, but not me." Kayti always had a really fun side and didn't let things bother her. *I miss Vickie.*

They were night people, so we stayed up late talking. Before I said "good night," I gave Tammy two cashier's checks for ten thousand each. One was for her, and the other for my daughter in Yakima. She told me she'd send Marcie's check to her the next morning. I told them to bet the money they held back on Charlie, before saying "He'll have low odds, but he'll win in a gallop."

Tammy said, "Kayti's modeling some wedding dresses at Bellevue Square, Friday."

"If you can stay over for the race, I'll get you a room," I suggested. *It's nice to have extra money so I can do these things.*

She nodded toward Kayti, and she said, "That works for me." Cory and Jenna were staying with friends, so we were set. I told Kayti I wanted her to meet a lady and explained that she had done some modeling in the past. She was eager to meet her.

We didn't get to sleep until eleven thirty, but the street out front was busy, so we couldn't sleep in. We looked in a window and couldn't see any activity, so we disconnected the plug and headed north. As we were driving by the Tootle River, we could still see some of the devastation caused when Mount Saint Helens blew her top. Norm asked if I remembered the day. I said, "We were on our way to Longacres when we saw the cloud coming. We thought it was a rain storm, but we picked up one of the girls' friends to take with us, and she told us it was the volcano. We made it to the edge of town but had to drive back home very slowly because we could hardly see past the front of our car. If we had left a half hour earlier, we would have been out of it."

"Wouldn't you have been caught in it?" he asked.

"No, we would have headed west at Ellensburg, and the cloud missed that area, but the mess would have been there when we got home."

When we arrived at the track, we asked if they had a place where we could park our trailer.

They had a young guy show us the way, and he said, "We're so happy you're coming. We should have quite a confrontation with Harlan's Choice in the race." I asked him if he wanted a safe bet. "What's that?" he asked with a smile on his face.

I said, "Harlan's Choice won't hit the board."

He looked at me to see if I'd laugh, but I didn't. He said, "I guess we'll have to see." After we parked, I told Norm I'd call Tom to see if I could get a wager that Harlan's Choice wouldn't be in the top four.

He said, "They bet on everything else, so I don't know why not."

When Tom answered his phone, I explained, "Vickie will pressure Harlan's Choice, and we're sure he'll stop because the form shows, in earlier races he didn't hang on when pressured. If I can, I'd like to bet that he won't hit the board."

He told me he wouldn't touch it but he'd call Vegas. Ten minutes later, he called and said, "You're set. You'll get ten to one at Caesar's if you bet against him being in the top four."

I asked, "How can I wager ten thousand?"

"Say the word, and it's done. Your player's card is on file, so I'll use it." I told him I'd have a cashier's check for him when he arrived.

I asked Norm if he wanted a couple thousand of the wager, but he said, "I'll pass because I'm not sure Charlie can go out with Harlan."

"Charlie has the speed to bury him, and if you've forgotten, Vickie's on a mission to show that last time was a fluke."

We called Steve to ask when he'd be in town, and he said, "I leave in an hour, and Charlie will be right behind me. I wanna make sure he's acclimated to the area and he can handle the track." I asked him if galloping would show him. "You're getting to know enough to be a pain," he said while laughing. I told him he would always be the boss. "I'll have Vickie blow him out a quarter a day or two before the race," he said. I wasn't at all worried because he had won twice on the track.

With all that was going on, time slipped away from us. It was three thirty, and we hadn't eaten lunch. Norm said, "Let's just eat dinner around five."

"That sounds good, where shall we eat?"

"Let's eat here at the backside café," he said before his phone rang. Steve told us he would arrive at Sea-Tac Airport at four thirty and asked for a ride. Norm told him we'd be there before saying to me, "Dinner may be a little later than we thought, so if you want something to tide you over, we better hurry." With all that was going on, I wasn't hungry.

When we picked up Steve, he told us he was hungry. I asked him when Charlie would arrive, and he answered, "By the time the van gets in, it should be about seven."

I said, "Let's eat at the track to make sure we're at the barn when he arrives."

He replied, "Now that's a plan I like."

We were sitting at the stakes barn when the van arrived, and when Charlie stepped off, he looked like a million bucks. Steve said, "He's in perfect shape, so unless he falls down, they won't beat him." He laughed and said, "If he could get up fast enough, he'd still win." I told him he was a lot crazier than when we first met him. He rolled his eyes and said, "A guy could only stay sane so long around you two." I agreed that Norm could do that.

"What's goin' on, guys?" a sweet female voice asked. We turned around, and Vickie was standing there with a lovely smile on her face.

"Why didn't you have us pick you up at the airport?" I asked. She rented a car so she could visit some of the riders she rode with in Seattle. I said, "If you can keep Friday afternoon open, my granddaughter is modeling some wedding dresses at Bellevue Square."

"I'd love to be there, and thank you for asking." I took her a little by surprise when I told her I needed her to make sure Harlan's Choice wouldn't be on the board. She winked and said, "It's in the bag, sweetie."

I whispered, "I need to speak to you on the phone tonight."

"Is there a problem?" she asked while looking concerned.

I answered, "Other than me being crazy about you, no. I've been struggling with a few things, and I think we should talk about them." She promised to call me about nine, and I told her no when she asked if I was upset.

Fifteen minutes later, Tom called to say they were in town. I asked if they wanted to get together, and he answered, "Not on your life, Liz has plans."

I said, "Now let's be sure I understand. You could spend the evening talking to us or having Liz thank you for getting her out of town. I guess that's why you make the big bucks, Tommy." He laughed and told me he'd call us the next day. I said, "Pace yourself, my friend, it'll be a long weekend."

At eighty thirty, I told Norm I was going to bed. I was sure that, with all the noise around the track, we'd be up early. I was in the trailer when Vickie called, and she laughed while asking "Are you afraid to talk to me face-to-face?"

"Maybe a little, I've been doing some soul-searching, and I feel that I haven't been fair to you."

She whispered, "I'm listening, so please go on."

"I feel like a complete idiot even talking to you about this. It's probably just in my mind, so I think I'd sound stupid. I'll just shut up."

"Yes, shut up and listen to me. You mean the world to me, so **nothing** you say would sound stupid," she told me with emotion in her voice.

I was like a bull in a china closet when I said, "I care for you way too much. I can't get you out of my mind, but I have too many issues that I'm dealing with. It's not fair to you, but I enjoy flirting with you too much to stop. I didn't expect to care for any woman after Linda died, before I saw you in Seattle. You hit me like a lightning bolt, and I haven't stopped thinking about you since."

"I know you're struggling with the loss of your wife, but that only makes me want you more. I've tried to hide my feelings for you, but it hasn't been easy. I'm sure you knew the guy I told you I care about is you." She sounded very emotional.

I said, "Please know that I'm not sure what I feel for you, but it's been driving me crazy. I can't get your last hug out of my mind because you felt entirely too good in my arms."

"I've thought about that many times also, and you don't have to tell me you were excited," she said with a nervous laugh. I told her that was embarrassing, and she said, "If you wanna be embarrassed, go right ahead, but I loved it." *That hug was amazing.*

I said, "I won't start something with you until I know I can make a commitment, but I love the way you make me feel. You're so beautiful that just looking at you drives me crazy. I hope I'm not being out of line, Vickie."

"The fact that you're struggling with this makes me care for you so much more," she said in that same tearful tone.

"Don't you have a place you need to be?" I asked, remembering that she planned to spend time with old friends.

"Yes, I have to meet some people in thirty minutes, but I have time to talk. Thank you for bringing this up because I've been going crazy, wanting to say them to you."

"I have only one question. Am I bothering you, flirting the way I have been? You mean so much to me, and I don't want to lose your friendship over acting like an old idiot."

"I absolutely love the way we've been flirting with each other, and I hope it doesn't stop. I told you before, I'm having more fun than I've had in years. Nothing you say will make you look like an idiot to me, and stop saying you're old."

"You've made me feel like a whole man for the first time in five years, so I don't wanna stop. I'll go on as I have been, if you really don't mind."

"If you stop, I'll kick your butt," she said before laughing and telling me I was sweet.

I exhaled sharply before saying "You have me as confused as a junior-high boy, but I love the way you make me feel. If you really are interested, I hope I can slay my demons, as Liz might say."

"Just knowing you care is enough for me right now. It means a lot to me that you said you want to wait until you can make a commitment because I care very much for you. If you do slay those demons, please give me a chance to make you happy." *Am I setting myself up to be hurt again? She's so sweet.*

I said, "Some of the thoughts I've been having about you make me feel like a pervert because there's way too much difference in our ages."

She whispered, "I love knowing you're having those thoughts, so I must be a pervert too." **She didn't laugh that time.**

"You'll be in my dreams," I promised before we said "good night." I could feel that my face was flushed, and I was shaking all over.

She laughed before saying "I love that I hit you like a lightning bolt, sweet boy." *There's that sense of humor again.*

I slept until seven the next morning and when we went to the café for breakfast, the girl who galloped Charlie in Seattle came up and sat beside Norm. My cell phone rang right then, and I saw it was Jamie, so I asked to be excused. She wanted to know if we would have time for an interview, so I asked when she'd be in town. She was coming in Friday afternoon, so I told her about the bridal show at Bellevue Square. I said, "Anytime after the show would be great." She told me she'd try to make it in time to attend the show. *Kayti would love having her there.*

When I walked back inside, Norm was still talking to the girl. He introduced her to me as Phyllis before she talked about how tough Harlan's Choice should be. I couldn't sit back, so I said, "I've gone all the way back to his first maiden race, and one thing really stands out." She asked what that was, and I answered, "Every time he's headed, he crumbles like a month-old loaf of bread."

"Is there a horse in the field that can go out with him?" she asked.

I smiled and said, "I know one that can. Charlie will test his heart this time for sure."

I had to excuse myself again when Tom called. "Are you just getting up?" I asked.

He replied, "You bet, and what a night that was. Liz loves getting out of town." He told me they'd run around town a while before asking if we wanted to meet them for dinner.

"We'd love to," I answered before telling him I was born in Seattle. He told me they loved going through the stores and shops downtown, so I said, "Make sure you go to the underground city at Pike's Place Market. Tom, there's one thing that makes me feel a little weird."

"Lord, forgive me for asking, what is it?"

"I enjoy coming home to Seattle so much that I feel like a salmon swimming against the current to get here."

He replied, "That's not so weird."

"The weird part is, every time I get here, I have a tremendous urge to buy a dozen eggs and pee on them. **Salmon die when they do that**!"

He took a deep breath and said, "You never cease to amaze me."

I said, "We'll see ya tonight."

When I went back inside, Norm told me he got a call from ESPN before saying "They wanna interview us in twenty minutes, if we can make it."

"Where?" I asked.

He told me it was at the barn, so we walked back, and they were setting up. I asked Steve if they cleared it with him, and they did. We were very surprised when the owner of Harlan's Choice walked up and shook our hands.

Stan, the man doing the interview, said, "I hoped to talk to you before he arrived. If you want separate interviews, I can do that." Both Norm and I told him it would be fine. He was asked the first question. "How did you beat Wrong Way North last time, and how do you plan to do it this time?"

"To answer the first part, we got a lead, and he wasn't able to catch us. As to the second part, this is a speed-favoring track, and this race is a sixteenth of a mile shorter, so I think it'll be much easier this time."

Stan asked me to respond, so I said, "I'm sure our distinguished friend knows that, when a speed horse is left alone on the lead, his race becomes **much** easier. Our plan in the last race was to stay close and go by him in the lane, but we ran into a lot of trouble, and the plan changed."

Without being asked, the owner said, "He wasn't close because Harlan's too fast."

I said, "I'm sure you don't want this interview to deteriorate any more than I do, so I'll make you a gentleman's wager. I'll bet you a thousand dollars right now that your horse won't finish in the top three."

"Are you serious?" he asked with a smirk on his face.

"This is how horse racing was started," I said. He was surprised when I told him I could get big odds in Vegas if I wanted to wager he wouldn't be in the top four.

"Let me be clear, you're saying they're betting whether or not Harlan will be in the top four?"

I answered, "That's what I've heard."

"They wouldn't bet on something like that," he replied.

I said, "If two monkeys were climbing flagpoles side by side, Vegas would find a way to have wagering on the first to the top, and many people would be there to bet."

He asked for a break, so he could call a friend in Vegas to check into it. I said, "I have time, and if you don't mind, find out the odds. I might make a wager."

When he came back, he told me he couldn't believe it. "It's true, and the odds that he won't finish in the top four are twenty-three to one." He thanked me before saying "I bet fifty thousand that he **will** be in the top four."

I said, "My bet still stands, except in the top three because the odds will be even."

He told me he wouldn't take my bet before saying, "I'm sorry if I've offended you. I know how much Harlan means to me, and I know how much Wrong Way North means to you, so I'd like to shake hands and go on."

I replied, "I like that even better."

After the interview, Stan said, "I'd like to thank all of you and wish you good luck."

I went to shake hands with Harlan's owner off the air, and he said, "Until I felt how it hurt when you said we wouldn't finish in the top three, I didn't stop to think how some of the things I've said must have hurt you. Please forgive me."

"I knew you were excited about beating the Kentucky Derby winner, so you're most certainly forgiven, and I look forward to a great race."

Twenty minutes later, Tom called me and told me I was crazy. I said, "I didn't say anything about how the wager was started."

He replied, "You goofy rascal, I mean you're crazy **good**. I just got off the phone with the CEO of Caesars, and since that interview, the wager is the hottest bet in Las Vegas. Over a hundred million has been wagered, and there's two days to go. He loved the remark about the monkeys, and I think he might start looking for some. Let's have dinner here at our hotel, my treat." I could tell he was trying not to laugh, but it gushed out like a waterfall. "Please forgive me, buddy. We mean this in a good way, but Liz and I have come to the conclusion that **you really are** the craziest guy we've ever met."

"What time for dinner, and can we bring Vickie?" I asked while trying not to laugh.

"Absolutely, I didn't know she was in town. It'll be a party, and let's make it seven thirty," he said. I could tell he was looking forward to having some company. *Liz just might be too hot to handle, and women do love getting away.*

I called Vickie and asked if she could make the dinner. "You bet I will. Let me ride from the track with you so I don't get lost because I never spent much time downtown."

I told Steve I knew he wouldn't go, but I had to ask. He said, "I can't, but if you'll stay with Charlie, I'll get something now." Norm walked to the café with him. It was three thirty, and it seemed like we just ate breakfast.

When Norm got back, he wanted to know if I was hungry. I answered, "Too much goin' on." He brought me a candy bar to go with my coffee, so I said, "I never turn down the combination of coffee and chocolate."

We walked into the restaurant at 7:25 p.m. Tom and Liz had a nice table in the corner, and when we walked up, there were hugs all around. Tom said, "Jim, today topped everything I've seen you do."

I laughed and said, "I guess I get worked up when it comes to Charlie."

He told me he was getting hourly texts from the CEO of Caesars and said, "Before the interview, they were having a great time with the wager, but since the interview, in his words, it's gone viral. Just a minute, the last reporting just came in. It's over 112 million."

"Million what?" I asked.

"That's how much has come in on the wager," he replied.

I asked, **"You're saying that much money has come in on this one bet?"**

"That's exactly what I'm saying."

I thought for a bit before saying "I don't think the bet involving the monkeys is far-fetched at all."

Liz started laughing hard enough that tears were running down her face, and she said, "Honey, when you said that today, I almost wet my pants, so please don't bring it up again." She asked Vickie to go with her to fix her makeup.

Laughter is contagious, so Vickie replied, "Mine needs a little touching up too."

When they were gone, Tom said, "I don't think I've ever seen Liz laugh that hard. I asked her why she found it so funny, and her answer was 'I could visualize the monkeys running up the poles with their bare fannies showing.' She started laughing all over."

"Now that's funny, I can actually hear it in her Southern accent," I said while laughing out loud.

When the ladies returned, I told them they were ravishing. Vickie thanked me, and Liz told me, if she laughed any more, she would become dehydrated. Tom shook his head while saying "You haven't heard the last thing Jim told me about Salmon."

Liz stopped him and said, "If I laugh any more, my tear ducts will dry up."

I was surprised when Tom said to me, "I know you worked for a coffee company for thirty-seven years, but you've never mentioned the name. Is there a reason?"

I thought for a few seconds before saying "I guess I didn't want you to think I was making a sales call. I usually met people involved with restaurants during sales calls because my primary job during my working years was acquiring new accounts and retaining existing business. The company's name is Boyd Coffee Company. They've been in business for over a hundred years and provided a good living for me and my family for more than a third of that time. I'm sorry I didn't mention the name, Tom."

He said, "I only asked because Liz wants to look at that coffee to use in Slim's North. Hopefully, it'll go nationwide, but you do understand, it would have to be very good coffee."

I was pleased when Vickie said, "I rode in the northwest for many years, and we always thought Boyd's was the best. We always looked for places that served their coffee for our coffee breaks." *I can't even find a fault with her there.*

Liz replied, "That's all I need to hear."

I said, "Let's not get ahead of ourselves. I'll contact the company, and they'll have a salesman come to your casino. There are many coffees, so you should try several to determine which best fits your needs. It would make me very proud to know you were serving Boyd's coffee." I laughed and promised them what I said wasn't a sales call.

I told Liz I'd appreciate it if she could make it to Kayti's show, before telling her she was modeling wedding dresses the next afternoon at Bellevue Square. "Honey, I'll be there if you'll tell me the time," she said with excitement in her voice.

I replied, "I'm not sure of the time, but if you can be there at noon, I'll buy lunch. I'll call and get the time." I turned to Tom and said, "I hope you'll come with her."

He replied, "I like pretty girls as much as the next guy." His grin might have been a little much.

Liz nodded and said, "He's always lookin'." She smiled and asked, "Jim, don't you think Vickie is gorgeous tonight?"

"I was just thinking, she's almost too pretty to be a jockey." Vickie told me I better not take her off Charlie, so I said, "You better not get much prettier."

On the way back to the track, Vickie told us she loved both of them and wanted to know how we met. Norm said, "Jim hit an eight spot in Keno, and Tom came down to congratulate him. That started a huge chain of events."

"What kind of events?" she asked.

I answered, "He recognized me from an interview we did after one of Charlie's wins."

She stopped me there and asked, "Then you're saying Charlie's responsible for their friendship too?"

I thought for a few seconds before saying "I'd like to think I could do something without him, but to answer your question, he was."

She said, "What a nice problem to have."

I asked, "Vickie, do you know what I love?" Before she could respond, I said, "I love the way your leg feels against mine."

She turned to Norm and said, "One of these days, I'll call his bluff, and we'll watch him pass out." I hugged her and thanked her for being such a wonderful friend. When we stepped out of the truck, she gave me a nice kiss on the cheek and told me she liked what I said to Liz.

I replied, "**You're a very lovely young lady.**" I was glad we cleared the air, and I was also happy that I could go on flirting with her because she brought back feelings I wasn't sure still existed. Selfishness or not, I didn't wanna lose those feelings again. *I hope I can get my head on straight.*

The next morning, Vickie took Charlie out for a gallop, and as Steve said she would do, she breezed him a quarter. I was pleased at how easily she brought him back to a nice gallop. When she brought him off the track, she said to Steve, "Boss, you've outdone yourself. He's better right now than before the derby. Seattle, get ready because the best horse to ever step foot on this track is in town." It was good to see her having fun, and I loved watching her enjoy her time off. *Will I ever find something I **don't** like about her? If only she wasn't so young.*

I took her aside and asked, "Are you still thinking about putting pressure on Harlan?"

She replied, "That article made me mad, so Harlan has no idea, the pressure he'll be facing."

I told her about the bet I made in Vegas and said, "The odds at the time I made the bet were ten to one, but if Tom can pull some strings, I want some at the odds now. You have a thousand now at ten to one, but if I can get the better odds, you'll get those. I don't wanna hurt Charlie's chances, but the form shows that Harlan folds under extreme pressure."

She said, "Don't worry about Charlie, I promise you, **Harlan will fold!**" I hugged her and told her I'd try to get us better odds. I needed to back away because she felt entirely too good against my body, and she wasn't backing up. That tiny girl was driving me crazy, and it wasn't hard to see that she was enjoying herself. ***Mmmm, dynamite really does come in small packages.***

I called Kayti's cell phone and asked what time the show would start. She told me one thirty and I said, "We have some friends in town that I want you to meet, and Jamie will try to make it."

She told me she was looking forward to seeing everyone, and in her modest way, she said, "I hope I don't fall down."

I promised, "Sweetheart, if you fall, Papa will be there to pick you up." She told me she loved me, and I said, "Me too." *She's always been special.*

We felt bad about leaving Steve behind, but there was no way he'd leave Charlie. We stopped by the bank, and I picked up two cashier's checks made out to Tom. One was the ten thousand that I owed him, and the other was the five thousand I hoped he could bet at the current odds. Norm said, "I might take a couple thousand at those odds."

I replied, "Let's talk to Tom about making the bets." As soon as we saw him, I told him about our plan, and he asked Vickie if she thought she could put pressure on Harlan.

She answered, "As I said to Jim, he has no idea what he's running into. I can't promise that he won't hit the board, but I don't expect him to."

Tom asked, "How much are we talkin'?" I gave him the two checks, and Norm handed him two thousand. Tom said, "I'll bet three to make it an even ten thousand more. After calling, he said, we're locked in at twenty-seven to one."

I whispered, "Vickie, if you're right and can put pressure on him, you have twenty-eight thousand coming."

She smiled and winked before saying "It's in the bag, sweet boy." *She just started calling me that, and I love it.*

They were setting up for the show, so I said, "It begins at one thirty, so we better eat." There was a nice German restaurant inside the mall, and everyone thought it sounded good. The food was fantastic, and two waitresses and a man playing an accordion came around singing German songs. We all had a great time, singing along.

Liz asked me if I had any more ideas for restaurants, before looking at Tom. He said, "I think we can make it work."

We walked out arm in arm, and Vickie said, "I've needed to get away for a long time." We all told her it was nice seeing her so relaxed. *No way could I work seven days a week.*

Liz said, "Come up to the lake anytime, honey, and you'll be treated like a fairy-tale princess." I told her Norm and I would be her honor guard.

Norm made them all laugh when he said "Jim acts like a princess every time we go up." I wished he would talk more and stop saving up for those zingers that were always aimed my way, but I enjoyed them as much as the others did.

It was one fifteen, and they were all set for the show. Tammy looked nervous, and we startled her when we walked up. I asked, "Are they on time?"

She answered, "They are, so you best find some seats."

I said, "Let's try to get an extra seat because Jamie might make it." Just before the show started, Jamie walked in, so I waved her over to the seat we saved for her. I told everyone I'd introduce them after the show. Kayti was the third one out, so I tapped Liz's shoulder and pointed her out. She gave me two thumbs up. There were ten girls, and they each modeled six dresses. To my great disappointment, Kayti didn't fall one time. I wanted so badly to pick her up and tell her she was my little Kayti bug.

After the show, I said to everyone, "Jamie's the morning sportscaster for Comcast Sports, and Kayti's my grandbaby slash model."

Liz said to me, "Sugar, you have some great bloodlines because these girls are beautiful." Both Jamie and Kayti hugged her while telling her she was also beautiful. They all three hugged Vickie after hugging Liz.

I said, "Tom, I worry about women."

He replied, "I hear ya, if I told you I thought you were beautiful, they'd think I was nuts."

I said, "Try it so we can find out."

"Ya, and I'll buy some oceanfront property in Vegas right after that."

I asked Tammy if they were staying the night. They were, so I said, "Let's get you a room."

Tom said, "If they wanna stay downtown, I'll see if they have a room where we're staying." They thought that sounded good, so he called and reserved a room with two queen-size beds.

I asked if everyone had plans for dinner. No one did, so I said, "Let's eat at the Space Needle." Norm said it was his turn to buy. We called and were able to find enough room to accommodate us.

Jamie was on an expense account, so I asked if she could eat there. "Absolutely, in fact, if they'll allow it, we can do our interview from there." Norm gave her the phone number, and they were more than happy to accommodate her.

Kayti couldn't believe a maid would go in and turn down their beds for them. I had to admit; I was impressed the first time it happened to me. The fact was I could only remember one time it did happen to me. We were due at the restaurant at seven, so Jamie left to explain the situation to her camera crew.

While we were waiting for the camera crew to set up, Vickie told me she had been thinking about what I bet on the race before saying "That's a lotta money, Jim."

I explained, "I believe in the risk and reward theory. I'm risking a very small part of my kid's inheritance for a very big reward." I kissed her cheek and said, "The reason it's a small part of their inheritance is Charlie. It all goes back to him, and, sweetie, you fit him like a glove, so you'll make Harlan fold for us." *I love those big blue eyes.*

I must admit; I got pretty excited when I saw love in her eyes before she said, "I love that horse." *That high didn't last long.*

The cameras were set up, but we decided to eat before doing the interview. Everyone ordered steaks, and dinner was great, but the company was even better. Kayti squeezed my arm and said, "Thank you, Papa." I smiled and told her how much I enjoyed her show.

Liz leaned over to her and said in her Southern accent, "Follow your dreams, honey, because you have the real goods." Kayti asked her if she had modeled, and she replied, "Some, but my mama always wanted me in pageants."

Kayti asked, "Would you mind if I ask? What was your biggest pageant win?"

"Not at all honey, that would be Miss Texas."

Kayti was impressed, and I said, "You never told us you were Miss Texas."

We all laughed when she replied, "You didn't ask, sugarplum, and that's not something you run around tellin' people."

"Did you enter the Miss America pageant?" I asked.

She answered, "I was first runner-up, but the old gal that won was as healthy as a horse, so they didn't need me." She grabbed Tom's arm while saying "This is my biggest prize of all." The girls loved that, and if the truth was known, I did too. *That darn chemo is turning me into a little girl.* I looked at Vickie and thought, **No, it's not!**

After dinner, Jamie had the cameraman pan the city through the windows. When he zoomed in on her, she said, "Good evening, this is Jamie Hudson with Comcast Sports. We're in the Space Needle Restaurant to interview the owners and rider of the Kentucky Derby and Belmont Stakes winner Wrong Way North. They're in Seattle to run in the Longacre Mile." Her first question was for Vickie. "Vickie, as the first female in history to win the Kentucky Derby, can you put into words what that means to you?"

Vickie replied, "I've had a long time to think about it, but the answer is still no. It's so far beyond anything I dared to think would happen that I still can't put it into words."

Jamie thought before saying "Some people think the Longacre Mile is a step down, so what would you say to them?"

"No doubt the purse money is much smaller, but it means so much to Norm and Jim that I'll ride as if it was the derby."

"Good answer," Jamie said before going to Norm. "After the bigger wins, why is this race so important to you?"

Norm said, "We're coming home. We wanna win this for ourselves but also for the city of Seattle and the state of Washington. On top of Vickie being the first woman to win the derby, Charlie is the first Washington bred to win the race."

When she turned to me, she said, "The first question is obvious. Where did the name Charlie come from?"

I answered, "Right away we decided we couldn't say a long name like Wrong Way North all the time, so we just picked Charlie out of the air."

"That's cute, and I hope you don't mind me bringing up your heated exchange with the owner of Harlan's Choice. Would you mind commenting on that?"

I replied, "First, he's a fine man, and we apologized to each other for getting upset. We agreed that the love we both have for our horses is what put us on edge. Unless you've owned one of these magnificent animals, it would be impossible to understand how much they mean to us."

After the interview, applause started at one end of the restaurant and worked its way all the way across. A man to our left stood up and said, "I guess I'll be the one to say how much we appreciate you bringing your horse to Seattle. There are many bigger fish to fry, so thank you so much for bringing him to our city."

We all stood up to applaud before I said "That's to the incomparable sports fans, not only from Seattle but the entire state. Please know that we are proud to have always been among those fans." The entire crowd came by to wish us good luck, and they all told us they'd make the race or watch it on television. Many of them recognized Jamie, and a few had her autograph their dinner napkins. I was surprised when a young lady asked Kayti if she was Nurse Gale on one of the Leverage shows. Kayti blushed while telling her she was.

The lady turned to her husband and said, "I told you." She turned back to Kayti and said, "That Elliot is cute."

Kayti replied, "He's very cute and just as nice."

We said "good night" to Jamie on the way out, and I told her we'd see her at the race. I told the girls, Tom, and Liz that we'd see them the next morning.

On the way back to the track, Vickie said, "I meant what I said about riding this race just like I rode in the derby."

Norm said, "What we like best about you is you ride that way every time out." *That might be what he likes best about her but, mmmm, not me.*

She sighed before saying, "Okay, don't make it easy on me. I'm trying to tell you how much you both mean to me."

I put my arm around her while saying "That wasn't so tough, little girl. You know that Norm and I are both head over heels in love with you."

"You're my two favorite guys," she replied.

I said to Norm, "She meant to say 'old guys.'"

Norm replied, "Speak for yourself."

Before we dropped her off, she asked if she could ask a personal question. I looked at Norm, and he nodded. "Have you both always been this crazy?"

I said, "Pretty much." She hugged us and told us she hoped we'd never change.

I whispered, "Have you always been as lovely as you are tonight?"

She smiled and answered, "Pretty much." I was glad our conversation hadn't changed the way we joked with each other. I hoped I'd be able to get my head on straight, but the age issue wasn't going away.

When the sun shines in Seattle, it's as beautiful as any place on earth, and the next day was absolutely gorgeous. We showered and called the girls to tell them we'd come over for breakfast. We didn't call Tom, thinking they might sleep in. The girls were ready when we got there, so we went down to breakfast right away. We could order off the menu or have a waffle buffet, and we all chose the buffet. They made us waffles, and we put assorted fruits on them. The fruit was fresh and delicious. We were just starting to eat when Tom and Liz walked in. "Are you mad?" Liz asked us.

I said, "We didn't wanna wake you, but we're just starting, so please join us." They both chose the waffle bar, so they caught up right away.

As they were sitting down, Liz said, "One thing I know, Jim, **I'm not havin' eggs**." We both laughed before she said to Tom, "This could be a business trip."

She asked me the price, and I said, "I think around ten dollars."

She asked, "What do you think, Tommy?"

"We'll find a spot for it," he answered. I told them they had one almost like it at Caesars, and Liz told me they'd do it anyway.

After breakfast, Tammy and Kayti wanted to go shopping at South Center. I asked if they could find their way to the track, and Tammy told me she had been at the strip mall across the street. I said, "To be safe, be at the backside by three thirty. It's about half a mile past the main entrance, and I'll meet you there."

Tom and Liz wanted to go to the track with us. It was almost noon when we got there, and Steve looked well rested. Vickie was sitting with him, watching Charlie, so I told Steve I'd stay with Charlie if he wanted to go to lunch. Steve, Tom, and Liz went to the café together, and Vickie stayed with Norm and me.

It was sixty degrees, and the sunshine was gorgeous. I said, "The track will be fast today."

Vickie replied, "They always want it fast for Mile Day." I asked her if I had ever told her she was gorgeous, and she whispered, "You mighta mentioned it, sweetie pie." *She'll be mine someday.*

I could feel some nerves creeping in, so I asked, "Vickie, do you get nervous before races?"

She replied, "When I stop gettin' the jitters, I'll stop riding. It helps to keep me alert." I didn't mean to, but I was staring at her, and after a couple of minutes, she asked why I was staring.

She smiled when I answered, "I enjoy looking at you because you have the deepest blue eyes I've ever seen and you're drop-dead gorgeous."

She brushed the back of her right hand along my jaw while saying "You're so sweet." The sexual tension literally hung in the air. *If only I was younger.*

Norm asked when the girls would arrive, and I told him, "Three thirty." He said, "That's a couple hours, so don't forget." I breathed a sigh of relief and was glad he changed the subject. I knew how badly I wanted her, but I wasn't ready to make a commitment, so I hoped she wouldn't find someone. *With the difference in our ages, she wouldn't be interested long, so I'd be setting myself for another heartache. Could she really be interested in me?*

At three thirty, Norm and I were back at the gate, and the girls arrived right on time. On the way back to the barn, Kayti said, "That was quite the applause for Charlie at dinner last night."

I said, "It just shows how good the sports fans are in this area."

When we arrived at the barn, Liz said, "Kayti, you're even more beautiful in the sunlight."

Kayti replied, "Coming from Miss Texas, that's quite a compliment, so thank you very much." Liz surprised all of us when she told her she also thought Elliot was cute.

Tom said, "I could take him."

Kayti said, "He's pretty solid and has had a lot of MMA training." We all laughed when Tom started flailing around and told us he'd get him in a sleeper hold. Both Norm and I thanked him for helping to settle our nerves. He said something about not trying to make us laugh, so we laughed even louder. *I get a kick out of him.*

We were all happy when it was time to walk over with the horse, and in the paddock, he looked like a huge man among boys. He was three to five on the board, and we were in the six hole. Harlan was the two, so I mentioned to Norm, "I love being outside the speed." Harlan was five to two, but I didn't care about the odds; my bet was in Vegas. I told the girls not to bet those odds, and they told me they'd save their money for another race.

When Vickie walked in, she hugged us before Steve legged her up. I told Kayti and Tammy she would wink when they came around, and sure enough, she did. I said, "That always puts me at ease."

The post parade seemed to drag a little, but finally, they were in the gate. "They're running in the Longacre Mile" rang out over the PA system. The two broke like a shot, but Charlie had his head on his hip. "Not a breather, Vickie," I whispered under my breath. She let Harlan slip ahead just enough to hug the rail around the first turn, but going up the backstretch, Charlie pulled alongside and looked him in the eye. Going into the final turn, Harlan hugged the rail, and Charlie was right beside him. Coming out of the turn, I said to Kayti, "Watch this." *Pop, pop,* she hit him twice, and the crowd gasped as Charlie started to pull away. I didn't care about my bet at that moment because I was engrossed in the way Charlie was drawing away. His final margin of victory was nine lengths, and he knocked two-fifths of a second off the track record. I can honestly say, I was sad when I saw that Harlan finished last, but it showed in the form. Before I went into the winner's circle, I walked out and shook Harlan's owner's hand while saying "Harlan will win many races."

He thanked me before saying "He'll never face Charlie again." He very sincerely congratulated me.

Before leading him into the winner's circle, they had Steve walk him around in circles in front of the crowd. Over the PA system, I heard, "Ladies and gentlemen, your Kentucky Derby winner, Belmont Stakes winner, and now, **Longacre Mile winner**, Wrong Way North." There wasn't a seat filled in the place because everyone was standing and clapping for far too long. We could hardly hear a thing while the picture was being taken. Steve told us he wanted to get him to the barn, out of the noise, so he'd skip the interview. The noise level increased when Steve waved to the crowd as he was leading him away. *They do love their sports.*

ESPN led us to a platform, and the interviewer started the interview with Vickie. "What was the difference between today and the last time you faced Harlan's Choice?"

"**Everything**, the pressure you saw today was our plan last time, but we clipped heels with a horse, and everything changed. The other horse is really nice, but no horse on this planet would have survived that pressure."

"You just made a very bold statement," he said before asking "**No horse on the planet?**"

She answered, "Our next start is the Breeder's Cup Classic, and I plan to back up that statement. I love every horse I've ridden, but there's not a horse in the world that compares to Charlie." I loved hearing her say that but hoped it didn't upset Tom. *He knows how excited she is and how much she loves Slim.*

Norm was next. "What do you have to say about that statement?"

He said, "I take the races one at a time, and I'm very happy about today, but I will say, when she's that confident, I've learned to believe her."

I was next, and he said, "I know this has been beaten to death. Is there a special rivalry between you and the owner of Harlan's Choice?"

I said, "Rivalry, absolutely, he has a really good horse as we do, and that'll always make for a rivalry. I wish the country heard us talk after the race. He was a gentleman under extremely tough conditions, and I have nothing but respect for him and his horse."

He went on to Tom and asked him how Slimsfinefood was doing. Tom said, "He's resting, but what I'd like to say is how happy I am for our very good friends. I'd also like to say how good a job Steve and Vickie have done for them and for us."

Walking away from the stand, Kayti said, "I couldn't believe the applause Charlie received."

I replied, "Maybe once in a lifetime a horse like Charlie comes along to very select and fortunate people. He is truly a gift from God. Why were we selected? I couldn't say, but I thank God for him every day. People are always looking for a hero, and believe it or not, Charlie is a hero to more people than you can imagine.

Norm and I would like to take credit for it, but we were just two lucky old guys in the right place at the right time. I'll say it again, he's a wonderful gift from God."

She hugged me and told me she was happy for us. I said, "You'll always be my Kayti bug."

When we got back to the barn, Jamie was there and told us the interview from the Space Needle was such a hit that she thought she would leave it there. She said, "My show Monday morning will be mostly about Charlie." We all hugged her and thanked her before she and her filming crew started back to Portland.

Norm and I walked the girls to their car, and I told them I'd have some money for them when I collect my bet from Vegas. Tammy said, "I heard you talking last night, so if you don't mind me asking, how much did you win?"

"Just over two hundred thousand," I replied.

"How much did you bet?" she asked with a startled look on her face.

I replied, "Fifteen thousand."

"I understand what you were saying about risk and reward now."

I said, "Before Charlie, I wouldn't have bet that much, no matter what the odds. He has given me the money to take these chances, and that's why my horse account keeps growing." We hugged both of them and told them to drive safely. Before walking to the barn, I asked them to tape Jamie's show for me, and they promised they would.

Vickie was at the barn when we walked back. She said, "I really enjoyed meeting your family and seeing Jamie again."

I replied, "They like you very much too." We sat around until late into the night. All five of them were flying out the next morning. Tom and Liz said "good night" before leaving for their motel, and when we walked Vickie to her car, I told her she did a wonderful job. I promised her part of the wager when I received it from Tom. I hugged her while thanking her for being so sweet about our conversation. She told me I meant the world to her before kissing my lips softly. Before saying "good night," I hugged her again and said, "I wish there was some way you could know how good you feel in my arms. You mean the world to me also, beautiful lady."

She whispered, "I'll give you some space." I wasn't sure what she meant by that, and I should have asked. Norm and I went to the barn to wish Steve a good night. We were glad the day was over, and we finally won the Longacre Mile.

Norm said, "That was a great day."

I replied, "If my life was to end tonight, I'd die a happy man."

"Is there something going on with you and Vickie?" he asked.

I replied, "She was delightful when I told her I cared very much for her, but I still had too much love for Linda."

"What'll you do if she finds someone else?" he asked.

"I can tell you honestly, I don't know. I wouldn't like it, but one thing I won't do is take advantage of her until I know I could devote myself to her."

He said, "I love giving you crap, as you well know, but I'm proud to call you my friend right now."

"There's nothing noble about me. I just have too much respect for her to risk hurting her." I smiled when I thought about the hug she gave me. ***Thank God, there's nothing wrong with this old body! She's amazing!***

The next morning, we stopped by the barn, and Charlie was on the walker, having fun. Steve said, "That race took very little out of him, so if we can keep him at this level, he'll be hard to beat in the Breeder's Cup." I asked him how many weeks it was before the race, and his answer was five.

I asked, "What are your plans for him after the race?"

He answered, "Win, lose, or draw, he goes out for six months. He's had a really tough campaign and needs to find out what it's like to just be a horse for a while." I liked the sound of that because we needed the rest as much as he did.

We let Steve take a shower and have breakfast while Norm and I enjoyed some solitude outside Charlie's stall. He asked if I wanted to do anything on our way back to California. I told him I was able to relax well at the beach and wouldn't mind spending a couple of days in Lincoln City.

When Steve returned, he said, "Charlie will be picked up in an hour, and I'll fly out a half hour before him." He had security set up to guard him until he was picked up. The schedule had Steve arriving at Golden Gate an hour ahead of Charlie, and his groom was set to meet Charlie if, for some reason, he should arrive ahead of Steve. *I'm glad Vickie picked Steve to be our trainer. I sure hope she wasn't telling me goodbye because she's tired of waiting. Could I be more confused?*

CHAPTER 13

Some Badly Needed Rest

Heading south after dropping Steve off at the airport, I said, "It sounds like Steve has things under control." Norm was driving, so I called Vickie to tell her we were off on another adventure. I said, "We're two old geezers that are totally in love with our trainer, jockey, and I can't leave out Charlie."

She asked, "Do you have any idea how much I wish I was going with you?"

I told her we'd take her to the lake after the Breeder's Cup and reminded her that Tom promised to make her feel like a princess. I said, "Norm just told me to tell you we both love you."

In a very soft voice, she whispered, "I love you too, both of you." *She's so lovely.*

It was midafternoon when we pulled into Lincoln City, so I suggested that we park the trailer and stay in a nice, oceanfront motel. We pulled into a motel that had two-room suites and paid for two nights. They had a place out back where we could park and plug in. After enjoying a nice dinner, we were back in the room at seven. Our room was on the second floor, and it came with a nice balcony that overlooked the beach. There were two lawn lounges on the balcony, so we each chose one and enjoyed watching the families playing on the beach. The night was warm with a very slight breeze, and I dozed off. Norm woke me at three to go inside. There was a king-size bed in each room, and mine felt like heaven. *Wish Vickie was here.*

It was nine when my eyes opened, and Norm was making the in-room coffee. He agreed with me when I said, "This last year feels like a fairy tale."

After breakfast, we spent most of the day browsing through some shops. We looked at the casino but decided we had been in enough of them for a while. Norm called Steve and learned that he and Charlie got back just fine. We had hot dogs for lunch and decided to have a nice dinner.

When we were back in the room, I was the first one out on the balcony, and I found myself missing Vickie again. I was glad we had some time apart to gather our thoughts because we poured out a lot of emotion to each other. The great thing was we wanted to remain wonderful friends, if nothing more. *I wish I had room for her in my life if she really is interested, but I'm not over Linda.*

Norm joined me on the balcony, and again, he woke me at three to go inside. The king-size bed felt great and allowed me to sleep in. During breakfast, Tom called and told us he had our checks from Vegas, so I said, "We'll be up in a couple days. We're having a wonderful time, relaxing at the beach." He told me he was surprised by how much the races took out of owners, so I replied, "It doesn't get any easier, but what a nice problem to have."

I told Norm that Tom had our checks, and we decided to head back to California. It was midmorning when we reached I-5, and when we were on the road, Norm told me he asked Vickie out a couple of weeks before.

"Did you take her out?" I asked calmly, but I was dying inside.

"She told me she has strong feelings for someone, and I think that someone is you. I wouldn't have tried anything with her if she had gone out with me."

I laughed and said, "Move your mouth without speaking."

"Why do you want me to do that?"

"I want you to open your mouth without lying."

With a little anger in his voice, he said, "I promise, **I won't lie to you!**"

"Tell me truthfully that you haven't already made love to her in your mind."

He took a deep breath and exhaled through his nose before saying "I promised I wouldn't lie to you."

"I'm not going with her, Norm, so it wouldn't be any of my business if you take her out."

He said, "I think you need to wake up." *I wonder if she's been confiding in him and he's trying to help us get together.*

"I really care for her, but I have way too many issues that I'm trying to work through." I was so glad they didn't go out, but it wouldn't be fair for me to hold her back. *How strong are her feelings for me? She's sweet, but she's not perfect, so she'll want a man her own age before long. Life is good, so don't do that to yourself.*

We pulled into the RV park at ten thirty and had everything set up by eleven o'clock. We had stopped on the road long enough to grab burgers, so we went right to bed. Morning seemed to come around way too quickly, and after getting cleaned up, we went to the track.

Steve said, "I took Charlie to the ranch for a week to let him come down a little. I'll bring him and Slim back at the same time." He then said with a big smile, "Breeder's Cup is next." I asked about the filly, and he answered, "She's enjoying her time at the farm, and I think she's grown some." I told him we were going to the Lake to collect our bet and he said, "That was a gutsy bet."

I replied, "The form told me he'd fold under pressure, and I knew Vickie would push him more than he could take."

He said, "That was good handicapping."

"If you dig deep enough, everything is in the past performances, but the problem with the form is it doesn't tell how the horse is feeling the day of the race. That's why favorites only win about a third of the races and why I win betting on the horses you and Vickie give me. Where is Vickie?"

"She took the day off to visit her family because her dad's not in the best of health." *Hope he's okay.*

We called the hotel and told them we were on our way, and the lady said, "Your room is ready, and I'll tell Tom you're on your way."

That sorrowful feeling came over me again as we drove past Donner Pass. Things had been going so well for us that it made me feel even worse for them. I asked Norm if he could imagine how the people felt. He answered, "I don't think anyone could without being there."

"I'd think I couldn't eat human flesh under any condition, but I've never been to the point of starving."

He said, "There were lean times growing up on the farm, but we always had food on the table."

I laughed while saying "There were times when I couldn't go out for burgers with my friends, but I could cook a steak 'most anytime I wanted to. We raised our beef and pork."

"Have you?" he asked me.

"Have I what?"

"You asked if I had mentally made love to Vickie, and now I'm asking you."

"More times than I can count," I answered while seeing her standing right in front of me.

He said, "She's lovely, and I don't want you to miss out."

"If it's meant to be, it'll happen, but not until I can devote myself to her, as I've told you before."

"I won't ask again," he promised. I didn't mind him asking, but the answer wouldn't change until I could get my head on straight. I, too, hoped she wouldn't find someone else. *That's not fair to her.*

We felt at home when we were checking in. The lady we always talked to on the phone checked us in, so I gave her three hundred dollars and told her it was for always treating us so special. After we were in the room, Norm said, "I'm starting to feel as at home here as in our trailer." I asked him how long he wanted to stay, and his answer was "Charlie comes back next week, and I wouldn't mind staying till then."

I said, "We need to explore around the area because that would be too long to just gamble."

Tom must have seen us on his monitor because he was with us as soon as we walked into the casino. He said, "Let's sit down."

I replied, "Give me two minutes to get my Keno numbers because I wouldn't forgive myself if something big came in and I didn't have it."

"You don't know how much we love hearing those words," he said while laughing. I bought my numbers for ten games and went back to where they were sitting. As soon as I sat down, Tom gave me a check for 220,000 dollars.

I said, "I hope this didn't hurt Caesars' bottom line."

He replied, "You wouldn't believe what they made on that wager. After the owner of Harlan said he put fifty thousand on his horse to finish better than fourth, two-thirds of the bets came in that way. The CEO was starting to worry that he might sustain the largest loss the casino had ever taken on one wager, so he was overjoyed when Harlan finished out of the money. It turned out to be the largest profit on any single wager in the history of the casino."

"What was the final handle?" I asked.

He smiled and said, "Two hundred and five million."

I shook my head and said, "We gotta start lookin' for some monkeys."

Tom took us to his food court, and as we walked in, on the left side was a waffle bar. He told us it was going gangbusters before saying "The Boyd salesman called and told us he'll be up next Monday and promised to bring several coffees for us to try."

I said, "When you decide on something, you really move."

"In this business, you have to try to stay a step ahead because, if you're standing still, you're really falling behind."

I said, "Boy, retirement is nice."

"Actually, we're having a lot of fun. Liz is having a ball with the changes." He told us to follow him and took us to a large spot where construction was underway. "This will be the German restaurant, and Liz is in Sacramento, getting uniforms designed right now. She hired a man-and-wife team to play the accordion, and we hope to open in two weeks."

I turned to Norm and said, "That'll give us another reason to come back." I asked Tom if Slim's restaurant was still going strong.

"It hasn't slowed down a bit because the locals love it." He chuckled before saying "They even bet a few bucks when they come in for dinner."

He told us he had to get back to work, and I took great joy in telling him we had to go play. Norm went to play blackjack, and I went to check my keno tickets. I could see there were four games left to play, so I went in search of a slot machine. I remembered that I enjoyed the artist machine, so I found one and sat down. I put a twenty in and started out playing two dollars a spin. After the first spin, a sign came onto the screen, saying "Random Bonus," so I was awarded five free games just for sitting down. The first bonus game produced another five free games. I played in the bonus round for ten minutes, and at the end of bonus play, I was up 310 dollars. "That's a good start to the week," I said out loud. I told myself I'd stop when the machine was down to 250 dollars and started playing three dollars a spin. After an hour, I was up four hundred, so I decided to cash in. I checked my Keno tickets and had ninety-six dollars coming, so I gave the girl six dollars and played the games five more times. I put seventy dollars in my pocket before looking for Norm. *This is fun.*

Norm told me he was down a little, so I gave him a hundred and said, "Play on house money for a while." We decided to play pai gow and were both playing ten on the hand and five on the bonus. After a couple of hands, Norm hit four jacks and won both hands, so they gave him 135 dollars. We ended up playing for three hours, and I lost sixty dollars, but Norm won eighty-five. I can honestly say we didn't care because we had so much fun. It's generally believed that people have the most fun around a craps table, but our table was lively enough to rival any craps table I had seen.

We decided on Slim's for dinner. There wasn't a line, but the place was packed. We both had steaks, and the food and service were fantastic. We saw many pictures that customers had added to the wall, but Charlie and Slim were still front and center. I almost shook hands with the cut-out of Slim on our way out. Norm decided to play a while, and I went up to the room, out of the smoke.

When I woke up the next morning, I realized that I hadn't heard Norm come in. I looked on my nightstand and saw a hundred-dollar chip. *His luck must have improved.* I looked in his room, and he was sleeping. I didn't know what time he came in, so I didn't want to wake him. I turned to walk away, and out of the corner of my eye, I saw a rather large stack of black chips on his nightstand. *His luck must have really improved.* After getting cleaned up, I left the room quietly and checked my Keno games from the previous night. I had nine dollars coming, so I gave the girl four ones and put fifteen dollars with the five to play them five more times. *What a glorious morning.*

I decided to have the waffle bar for breakfast, so I ordered a waffle and covered it with strawberries, for only $7.50. That price included coffee and was a really good breakfast, served in just minutes. It was a win-win because the customers would spend much less time eating and more time in the casino.

After breakfast, I went in search of a unicorn machine and found one that wasn't occupied. I sat down and played on twenty dollars for a half hour. I never did get the machine credits over fifty dollars, but every time it was low, I hit enough to play a while longer. In the end, my twenty dollars was gone, but I had fun and racked up points on my player's card. When I checked my Keno tickets, I was surprised to see 163 dollars show up. I said to the girl, "I must have hit six out of eight twice."

She checked the tickets before saying "Yes, you did." I gave her the three dollars and bought the games ten more times because I enjoyed playing when my numbers were running. I had a change of heart and gave her another twenty before putting the hundred in my pocket. I walked away thinking, *It's nice to share the blessings.*

Norm hadn't gone down yet, so I went outside for a walk. Lindalovestorun went through my mind, as I remembered, in school, Linda was a really fast runner. Girls' sports teams weren't around back then, so her PE teacher wanted her to run against the boys. She was rather shy, so she chose not to. I wasn't the fastest guy in school but maybe in the top 10 percent, and one time I raced her on the road in front of her house. It was all I could do to keep up with her, and if the truth was known, she probably beat me, but I won't tell anyone.

I was so deep in thought that I was startled when my phone rang. It was Norm, so I asked him if he had eaten breakfast. He hadn't, so I told him how much I enjoyed the waffle bar. When he told me he'd try it, I told him I was outside but I would go in and have coffee with him. We sat at a table in the food court for a half hour before I said, "I need to do some banking. Do you know if there's a Chase bank in Reno?" He didn't know, so I called Tom. He told us they had one, so we decided to drive down the mountain.

We turned left out of the hotel and headed toward Reno. I hadn't thought about it, but luckily, we saw a Chase bank in Carson City, and that saved us about a hundred miles. I bought five cashier's checks for a total of eighty-three thousand dollars and put the other 137,000 in my horse account. My balance was really getting up there. I kept checks for Vickie and Steve and sent checks to both daughters and one to Kayti for supporting Charlie in the mile. It felt good to help them, and Caesars was very happy about how the wager turned out.

When we walked back into the casino, I went with great expectation to check my tickets. Numbers start running your way quickly, but just as quickly, they stop. Playing the numbers ten times cost me a total of forty dollars, so I was disappointed that I only had four dollars coming back. I told the girl to keep them and walked away thinking, *You just cashed a winning check for 220,000 dollars, and you're crying over losing forty.* The answer came booming back. *Darn right I am. I'm the kind of guy that, if we play marbles, I won't be happy until I have all your marbles.* I laughed and thought, *I don't wanna offend you, but I do want your marbles.*

We played pai gow until dinnertime, and Norm won a little, but I wasn't as lucky. I was still up a couple of hundreds for the trip, so it wasn't yet time to panic. I decided to buy my tickets ten times and watch the games while we were eating. Norm suggested we go to the buffet and reminded me that I hadn't had my spiders in a while. There was a bit of a line, but we were in no hurry. When we were inside, it was well worth the wait because they had a big pile of crawdads and hot drawn butter. There was no hot and sour soup, so I had a nice salad. We stayed in the dining area for a half hour, and I forgot to watch the Keno games. When I did look at the board, I had two games remaining. I ordered some coffee and sat down as the next-to-last game was starting. I was eating my dessert while keeping one eye on the game, and after one of the tubes was empty, I had three of the odd numbers and two of the even. I couldn't get excited because that was only two dollars, but we still had ten numbers to go. The first number from the other tube was another odd number, so I whispered, "It's time to get excited now." The next four numbers did me no good, but the next was another even number. I told Norm to think number 9. The 9 didn't come, but the 8 did. I said, "**So close!**" He asked what I hit, so I said, "I hit four out of five twice."

"What does four out of five pay?" he asked.

I replied, "Twenty-four dollars."

He said, "You have it twice, so that's forty-eight dollars." He smiled before saying "That's not bad but not exciting."

I replied, "The two together give me eight out of ten, and that's a little exciting."

"How much is it?" he asked.

He was happy for me when I told him it was 1,500 dollars, but he looked puzzled and asked, "Why aren't you more excited?"

I answered, "I'm thinking about what could have been. One more number would have been about nine thousand, and two more would have been twenty-five thousand."

"It seems to me that, in that game, you spend a lotta time thinking about the ones that get away."

"That's the nature of the game," I replied, but I was happy with what I made.

By the time we walked out to the Keno area, the last games had been played. I had a dollar coming from those games, and when the girl ran the tickets through, I made sure the ten spot would be last. The first three tickets added up to sixty-two dollars, and when she put the ten spot in, the screen said winner. She said, "I knew you were the one that hit this." I let her keep the sixty-two dollars and put $1,300 away. I told Norm that paid for my trip, before giving him two hundred. For an instant, I wondered why Vickie hadn't called, but I was excited about the win, so I didn't give it much thought. *She might be losing interest, but it's better it happens now than after we were together.*

I played the Rembrandt machine for a couple of hours and lost a hundred dollars, so it was time to go to bed. Norm was playing three-card poker and told me he'd be up later. When I reached the room, I watched television for a while before drifting off to sleep with my clothes on.

Norm shook me and said, "Sorry to bother you, but you better get in bed." The clock said it was two thirty, and he dropped a hundred-dollar chip on my nightstand, so I asked him what it was for. "Like you say, don't change something that's working."

"How much did you win?" He held up three fingers, so I asked, "Would that be thousand?"

He nodded while saying, "**It would be**." I was happy he was doing well. "Did Vickie call with a horse for us?" he asked.

I answered, "She hasn't, but we'll be here for a while." She had given us one every time we were there, so again I wondered why she hadn't called.

The next morning, I slept until 8:20 a.m., and while I was getting out of bed as quietly as possible, "Good morning" scared the daylights out of me.

After turning halfway around in midair, I said, "I thought you were asleep."

He replied, "Not for the last hour, and that wasn't a bad move for an old guy."

I said, "If you scare me bad enough, I can still move."

"Where are we going today?" he asked.

I suggested, "Let's turn right out of the parking lot and see where it takes us."

"That sounds like a good plan," he said. I asked if he wanted to eat at the waffle bar, and he thought that sounded good. The girl making the waffles was surprised when I gave her a ten-dollar tip on a $7.50 breakfast. Norm looked at me and asked, "Sharing the wealth?" I nodded, so he gave her twenty while saying "More wealth to share."

I said, "Don't forget, you're paying 80 percent of Charlie's bills." He laughed and told me he'd get by. We still couldn't believe how Charlie had turned our lives around, and we still had the filly to look forward to. "Life is good, my friend," I said before we stood up to walk to the pickup. I had a hole in my heart because I missed Vickie terribly. *How could I have allowed myself to get so attached to a woman her age? **Stupid ass!***

Norm was driving when we turned right out onto the road. We were admiring the trees and the glimpses of the lake through the trees, and about three miles down the road, I saw a rather deserted-looking turn to the right. I said, "Turn here, it should end at the Lakeshore." About half a mile in, a young girl ran in front of us, wearing nothing but a smile, as the saying goes. Norm hit the brakes, and I said, "Back in our younger days, she would have been called a streaker." He eased the truck forward into a clearing, and to our surprise, we saw twenty or thirty young people lounging on the beach, completely nude.

Norm said, "That was no streaker, this is a nude beach." None of the sunbathers seemed concerned that we drove up, so he asked, "Would you get out there like that?"

I replied, "Thirty years ago, my body wouldn't have been a joy to look at, and today it would be a crime." We slowly found a place in the clearing where we could turn around and drove back to the hotel. I said, "Now that was the natural beauty I talked about earlier."

Norm replied, "You have three seconds to say you were only talking about the girls, or you sleep in the hall tonight." I just shook my head and didn't think a response was necessary.

When we were inside, we ran into Tom and told him what we saw. He laughed while saying "So you found them."

I asked, "Did you know they were there?"

He answered, "Actually, there are three or four of them up and down the shoreline. You know those glass-bottom boats cruising the lake?" I told him I'd heard about them, and he said, "Not everyone's looking under the boat." He told us he was going to Vegas for a couple of days, but we should stay as long as we wanted to. Norm told him we'd go back the next morning, and Tom replied, "Be sure to look me up when you get back."

We had the waffle bar one more time before checking out. Fall was in the air, so I said, "It's too bad the Donner party couldn't have come through here this time of year."

Norm replied, "They probably planned to, but those covered wagons would have had problems without roads."

I said, "I'm glad we live now. What would we do without cell phones?" He reminded me that we spent the biggest part of our lives without them and computers. *I wonder what it'll be like in twenty years.*

Steve looked surprised when we walked back to the barn and said, "You didn't forget about us."

I gave him his cashier's check for ten thousand dollars while saying "A little bonus."

He asked, "What bonus?"

I replied, "From the bet in Vegas." He thanked me while shaking his head.

I asked him if Vickie was around, and he answered, "I think she's in the café." We walked over and found her talking to a couple of jockeys, so after letting her know we were back, we sat down at a table.

She excused herself and walked over to join us. When she reached our table, I said, "You kept your part of the bargain, so I will."

I handed her the check for twenty-eight thousand dollars, and she whispered, "Jim, I can't accept this."

I said, "If you hadn't applied the pressure you said you would, none of us would have made money."

She replied, "**That's my job!**"

"Yes, it is, and that's a bonus for a job well done. I hope you'll buy yourself something nice. I'm a little upset that you didn't call me with a horse to bet while we were up at the lake," I said in a whisper.

She replied, "I wasn't on anything live enough to call."

I looked deeply into her eyes and said, "I missed talking to you because I love our phone conversations while I'm out of town. I missed you."

She smiled and whispered, "Your phone also dials out, and I missed you too."

I told her I hoped she wasn't pulling away, and she told me I needed some space. "I need your friendship much more than I need space. I **really** missed talking to you, little girl." Again, she told me I could call her. She used her right index finger to wipe a tear from her eye while telling me how much she missed me. I kissed her cheek and told her I hoped she wasn't shutting me out of her life. She promised to never do that. *She's so lovely, but I can't believe I allowed myself to fall for a woman as young and beautiful as she is. Why don't you step out in front of a truck if you enjoy being hurt?*

After hanging around the barn for a while, Norm and I decided to go to the pizza restaurant for dinner. We invited Vickie, but she had plans. We split a medium hawaiian pizza and each had a salad. After dinner, we went to the trailer and sat outside for a couple of hours, enjoying the sultry summer night. Norm said, "That was the first time Vickie hasn't called with a horse for us."

I replied, "She didn't have a good one to give us." *Indeed, my phone does dial out.*

We arrived at the track at seven the next morning, and Steve was busy getting stalls ready for the return of Charlie and Slim. He said, "Time to pick it back up." I asked if he had ever had a horse in the Breeder's Cup, and he answered, "No, but before Charlie, I hadn't been in the derby or Belmont either." With a big smile, he said, "Now I've won both of them, and that's our plan here." I told him I liked his plan before offering to help.

The horses were coming in the next day, and Steve liked to stay ahead, so he said, "You wanted to help, so please put some saddle soap on these." He handed me two saddles and two sets of reins. Norm and I sat close together and did one set each out of one can. After that, we pitched in and helped clean stalls and the shed row. When lunchtime rolled around, we told Steve we were going out to play golf.

We were surprised at how well we hit the ball after so many days off. We laughed and joked all through the round, and Norm ended up 2-over par. I was 3-over. We decided to eat the ribs at the backside café for dinner on our way home.

Again, I wished I could get my head on straight before Vickie found someone. *Just live your life, and let her live hers. If it's meant to be, it'll happen just like the rest of this incredible journey.*

CHAPTER 14

Run for All the Marbles

The next day, we were at the barn when the horses came in and Steve walked them for twenty minutes before putting them in their stalls.

After cleaning some stalls, we went back to the golf course. The days went by quickly as we settled into a nice routine of working at the barn in the mornings and playing golf most afternoons. Steve only worked Charlie twice in the month leading up to the race, and the rest of the time, he galloped him two strong miles. He was as sharp as he could be, but Slim had been off longer, so he required a some more work.

The races were at Churchill, so we knew Charlie liked the track, and we hoped Slim could handle the turf course. It was a week before the races, and both horses were perfect. Either I called Tom or he called me almost every day. Their business was up 8 percent from the previous year, and much of that was food. Every time I talked to him, he raved about all three places they added and told me all three were serving Boyd's coffee. Corporate was looking at the company very strongly, and even though I was retired, it made me feel good to help the company. **The one thing missing from my life was Vickie.** She was keeping to herself more, and I missed her terribly. You really don't know how much you care for someone until they're gone. I felt like I had a hole in my heart, but my problem was I still talked to Linda every day. That may never change, so I was stuck between a rock and a hard spot, as the saying goes. Again, I wondered how I let myself get so attached to such a young woman. It was my fault because I started the flirting, and it was obvious that she wasn't serious about me. I couldn't believe I thought she might be. *I've lived my life, so let her enjoy hers, but I want her in my life, darn it.*

We felt fortunate to find rooms in the Louisville area because the town was packed. I made a reservation for Tom with a forty-eight-hour window to cancel if they couldn't make it. I called him right away, and I was sad to hear they couldn't get away. He said, "With the increased business and it being Breeder's Cup weekend, we can't possibly leave." I understood and promised to root Slim in for them. I called right away to cancel their reservation and told them we would be there for sure.

Steve, Norm, and I were all flying out Tuesday morning, and the horses were set to leave two hours after we did. Steve had a couple of trainer friends who helped him with the last-minute preparations. The horses were set, and so were we. **Where is that music coming from?**

It was my first time to fly into Louisville. There was a lotta flat farmland, and right in front us was an aerial view of the Twin Spires. My mind went back to the derby and how brave Charlie was. I thought, **One more time, big guy!** As soon as we landed, Norm went to get the car. He had reserved one with a GPS so we could find our way around. After our luggage came in, we took Steve to the track so he would beat the horses. We hired twenty-four-hour guards right away, and they were there and had scoped everything out an hour before the horses came in. From that time until the horses were to leave, we would have an armed guard at all times. It was expensive but worth every cent.

Our motel was only five blocks from the track and was a nice, ultramodern motel. We received special rates and found out the only reason we were able to get rooms was we had horses in the races. We checked in and were back at the barn by the time the horses came in. After they backed off the van, Steve put them both on the walker and let them walk for a half hour. Both horses traveled exceptionally well, so it was good to see how Slim had matured under Steve's guidance.

It was 2:00 p.m. and we hadn't eaten lunch, so I told Steve we could take turns going to the café. He said, "You two go, and please bring me back a burger and some fries."

He started to give me some money, but I said, "This time, it's on Charlie." When we walked into the café, we both had flashbacks. **And down the stretch they come** echoed inside my head. Norm asked why I was smiling, so I told him I had some really fond memories. There was a baked chicken special, so we ordered that, plus I ordered a burger and fries to go. I'd pick up the to-go order on our way out.

Steve really put his food away, so I said, "I feel bad, you must have been starving."

"A hazard of the trade, I eat fast because I don't know what might happen the next second," he explained.

I told him I was the same way when I was working on the road, but I had slowed down a little since retirement. I said, "They have statistics on which professions eat the fastest. Would you like to know who was first?"

"Horse trainers?" he asked.

I answered, "I don't know if trainers were in the survey, but of those that were, policemen were number 1, and retail workers, number 2."

He replied, "They both make sense."

I said, "When I was a retail milkman, we started delivering early, and four of us would meet for breakfast at about six a.m., three days a week. We became friends with two policemen that had breakfast at the same time, in the same restaurant. It was unbelievable how many times their meals would be put on the table and a call would come before they could take a bite. They'd say '**Keep it hot**' as they raced out the door, so I can certainly understand them being number 1."

Steve shook his head before saying "If I'm ever on a game show that deals in trivia and that fact wins me a million dollars, I'll buy you a cup of coffee."

I said, "Steve, I'm gonna hold you to that."

At dinnertime, Norm and Steve went to the café and brought me back a burger basket. We didn't go back to our room until ten, and the beautiful Kentucky nights made up for their humid days.

The next morning, we ate the continental breakfast furnished by the motel before going to the track. Steve went to shower and have breakfast as soon as we arrived. Both horses were galloped by the same gallop boy who galloped Charlie up to the derby, and he said, "It's hard to believe, Charlie feels better than he did before the derby." He didn't know Slim but was really impressed with him also. We spent our days helping Steve watch the horses along with the guards. The weather was great, and the forecast was for sunny skies all the way through Saturday. Things were almost going too well, so the fears started to creep in. *What can happen to unright the ship?*

Friday, the filly portion of the Breeder's Cup arrived, and there was much more action around the track, but both horses handled everything like older veterans. Steve took both horses over separately to school them in the paddock, and they both handled the crowds exceedingly well. After both had been schooled, he said, "They're so darn good that it scares me." I remembered Clint Jr. calling it the calm before the storm. My anxiety level was up a little. I used to get nervous running for two-thousand-dollar purses, and we were going for five million. *My goodness, how could anybody be calm running for that purse?*

The forms were in, so I went to the café and purchased one. The Mile was the fifth race, the following day. There were twelve horses in the race, and Slim was number 7. There were two horses inside him that seemed to want the lead. It was good that Slim was outside the speed so Vickie could keep an eye on them. He was fifteen to one in the form and the only three-year-old in the race. The quote by his name said, "Maybe next year." That referred to the fact that it's difficult for a three-year-old to compete against older horses.

Steve said, "He'll be four in a couple months, and I expect him to be very competitive." The Classic was the ninth and last race of the day. There were thirteen horses in the race, and Charlie was number 9. I thought he was a little too far out, but the mile and a quarter had a long run to the first turn, so Steve was sure he could get a good position before the turn. He was five to one in the form. The four horse was a five-year-old that had been racing on the East Coast and had won his last six starts. They were all grade 1s, so his form odds were nine to five. Charlie was the third favorite, and the quote by his name read, "Derby proves he can handle the track but wish he was a year older."

Steve said, "He's old enough, and he should be favored." I liked not being the favorite because, through the years, when we were favored, we seemed to find ways to lose. I smiled as I thought, *That was before Charlie!*

The day went by rather quickly as chalk was winning most of the races, and we were happy when the last race ran. At six thirty, Steve went to dinner, and Norm and I would go when he returned. The horses were very content in their stalls, so Norm said, "It feels like the calm before the storm."

I replied, "Let's pray the storm doesn't come." Even though we had the armed guards, there was much stress. Our purse was five million dollars, and Slim's was two million. I said, "That kind of money can make people crazy." *Darn, I miss Vickie!*

When Steve returned, he said, "Thanks, guys, go eat dinner." We walked to the café and ordered the special. It was chicken alfredo, served with garlic bread, and the meal was great.

We stayed at the barn until two in the morning, and Steve said, "You guys seem nervous."

I replied, "Five million dollars can make you that way."

He tried to explain, "Too much security for anybody to try something, unless he was an idiot."

"Like the guy at the Belmont?" I asked.

He said, "I see your point, but we've done all we can, so we must let faith take us the rest of the way." Him saying that seemed to put me a little more at ease for the moment. He was right; we could only dot our i's and cross our t's so many times. *When Vickie gets here, she'll help me relax.*

We didn't go to bed until two thirty, and I was asleep when my head hit the pillow. I didn't open my eyes until eight thirty the next morning, and the nice thing about sleeping late was the day would go by quicker. After having breakfast, we were at the barn at ten fifteen, and Steve said, "It seems you didn't have trouble sleeping." We apologized before asking if he had taken a shower and had breakfast. He hadn't, so we sent him on his way. It was 11:20 a.m. when he returned, and the races were due to start at noon. We were happy for both horses that there had been no rain.

The favorite won the first race, and a ten-to-one horse won the second. There didn't seem to be any track bias, and the track was lightning fast, having been set up for the special day. When the horses were in the post parade for the fourth race, the horses were called to the holding barn for the fifth. Before Steve walked Slim over, he came to me and squeezed my shoulder while saying "Relax, Jim, this is just another race. Charlie's the best horse, so if I've done my job, he should win."

I said, "Thanks, Steve, I needed that." I said to Norm, "I'll bet Slim in the café and stay with Charlie during his race." I went in and put five hundred to win and place on him.

As soon as the fourth ran, Norm walked to the holding barn so he could walk over with the horse. I could tell from the crowd noise when the horses were walking into the paddock. I wanted to think only about Slim's race, but too many thoughts were running through my mind. *Was Charlie too young at three? Does he belong with these? Could we hurt him by putting him here?* There were so many questions and so many doubts. Why was I being so tormented?

Through my thoughts, I heard, "It's too close to call." That brought me back to my senses. *Who's in the photo?* I wondered. The announcer said, "The photo is between Slimsfinefood, the three-year-old, and the British champion, English

Holiday." The decision seemed to drag on, and the warm sun was beating down on me. I was soooo relaxxxeeed.

"MY SON, WHY ARE YOU TORMENTING YOURSELF SO?" I looked to my left and then to my right. Was someone talking to me? I saw a beam of light coming from above and settle at my feet. I followed the light back up, and a booming voice seemed to come out of it. "FOR THIRTY YEARS, I'VE LET YOU ENJOY RUNNING THESE ANIMALS. I'VE APPRECIATED YOU ALWAYS ASKING THAT THE HORSES RUN THEIR BEST AND COME BACK SAFELY. YOU HAVE NOT ASKED THAT I GET INVOLVED IN THE OUTCOME, AND I WOULDN'T, BUT WHERE HAS THAT FAITH GONE TODAY?" I started to say "But this race is so big." He cut me off. "OH, HOGWASH" came back. "I CREATED THE UNIVERSE, AND YOU THINK THIS RACE IS TOO BIG FOR ME?"

"Jim, Jim, wake up. Are you all right?" Norm asked me.

I shook my head while saying "I must have dozed off. **It was so real!**"

"What was so real?" he asked.

I said, "God was telling me to relax and everything will be fine."

I hadn't noticed that Steve was behind me until he said "Good, maybe you'll listen to him. I've been trying to tell you that all day. You've always had a level head, so why are you so uptight today?"

I answered, "I guess I've been swept up in the enormity of this race."

He said, "I'll say again, I truly believe Charlie is the best horse in the world at this time, and as I've been saying, if I've done my job and we get a good trip, he'll win. Now do as your dream was telling you, and have a little faith."

I said, "It truly is just another race, and money has never been the motivating factor, so I need to relax and have fun."

Steve said, **"Or I could have worded it that way!"** His humor made me laugh for some time. People watching me probably thought I'd lost my mind, but the laughter seemed to be washing the self-inflicted stress out of me.

When I stopped laughing, I said, **"Yes, it's time to have fun!** Who won Slim's race?"

Steve answered, "Slim lost by a slight nose but ran the race of his life. The photo showed him a whisker behind, but the world saw the dawning of a real champion." He said in a low voice, "If you repeat this, I'll deny saying it, but he's not in the same universe as Charlie." I paused for a moment as I realized he used the word *universe*, which I heard in my dream.

I asked Norm if he talked to Tom. He told me he hadn't, so I asked if he would. "Please tell him I stayed at the barn with Charlie."

I asked what Slim paid to place. "Twenty-two forty," he said. That cheered me up a little until I thought about what the whisker loss cost me. *It's like Keno, I can't think about the ones that get away.* Fifty-six hundred wasn't a bad second prize.

I told Steve I was going to the café and asked if he wanted anything, but he told me he was doing fine. Actually, I was going to collect on Slim's place and bet Charlie. They had been posting the odds of the Classic all day, and Charlie was nine to one. I thought, *Nine to one on the nine horse in the ninth race, please don't run ninth.* "I want two separate tickets, two thousand to win on number nine, and on a separate ticket, I'll have twenty-five thousand to win on number nine, please." I had gotten to know the guy punching out the tickets, and he asked if I didn't want place. I shrugged my shoulders and said, "He'll either win or not be there at all." On the way back to the barn, I put the big ticket in my pocket and gave Steve both two-thousand-dollar tickets before asking him to collect one for Vickie.

He said, "You look a little more relaxed. **Wow, why so much?"**

"Sharing the wealth," I said before telling him we were lucky to get the odds we were getting.

"**Now that's the Jim I've come to know,**" he said while smacking my back.

I was glad when the horses were called over for the ninth. I was walking along with them but felt like I was floating. The cheers of the crowd filled the air as the horses walked into the paddock, and I was proud to be walking in with Charlie. I looked at the horses and decided Charlie stood above all of them except the four. He was the favorite that had won six grade 1s in a row, and he looked the part. He was almost snow-white and huge. He had to be close to eighteen hands, and muscles rippled from everywhere. I thought back to when I drove the coffee truck. We were always on a tight schedule, and I was always pushing the speed limit a little, so I was continually looking for patrol cars. They were white, so I referred to them as **the white death,** even though I had several friends in law enforcement. It was a little game I played to pass time behind the wheel. In my game, my eyes would narrow, and I'd look left and right, knowing a patrol car was lurking in the shadows, waiting to pounce. I looked closely at the four and thought, *This is the white death!*

Vickie startled me when she hugged me and said, "Cheer up and comb your hair so you're ready to have your picture taken." She was like an angel, suddenly appearing. It felt good to have her run her fingers through my hair, and that put me a little more at ease. *I should tell her I want her, but I'm too old for her.*

I had never heard Steve give her instructions, but he said, "You know Charlie better than I do, so run your race, but keep a little in reserve because the four **will** be running late."

She smiled and said, "Trust me, boss, it's in the bag." Steve legged her up, and I must have looked nervous because, when she came around, she pointed at my face and then back to her lips. She smiled really big, so she was telling me to cheer up. Then came the wink that I so desperately needed. I realized how much I had missed her the last few weeks, and that wink helped put me at ease. Before leaving the paddock, I said my little prayer, asking that they come back safely. For an instant, I wondered if she might be an angel and God sent her to help me heal. With some of the sexual thoughts I was having about her, I sure hoped not.

Norm looked at me and asked, "Your little prayer?" I nodded, so he said, "Say one for me."

He had no idea what I was talking about when I said "The veil has been rent in two, so **you just did!**" He hardly ever understood me anyway.

I was happy that I'd made my bet because I was able to watch the post parade. Charlie was beautiful, but it really was hard to keep my eyes off the white death. As they walked to the gate, I moved my focus back to Charlie. He acted like it was just another morning gallop, and while some of the horses seemed worked up going into the gate, he walked in and stood like he was back in his stall. "That's class," I whispered, and right then, I loved him more than even I thought possible.

"They're off in the Breeder's Cup Classic" rang out over the crowd noise, and true to form, two speed horses went right to the front. Charlie broke behind them and using his natural speed, Vickie was able to settle him on the rail, two lengths behind the leaders, long before the turn. She didn't ask him at all, so they went around the first turn in that order. Vickie was happy to stay where she was up the backside, and approaching the final turn, she looked under her right arm. Nothing was pressing them, so she stayed on the rail. Coming out of the turn, the two front runners went just wide enough for her to go through. They took the lead in the biggest race in the world, and everything slowed to a crawl. The crowd's noise went away, so I saw people jumping and waving their arms but heard nothing at all.

We're winning the Breeder's Cup Classic, I thought, but out of the corner of my eye, I saw the white death closing like a freight train. Everything was in slow motion, so I could see things as clear as a bell. Vickie hadn't yet hit Charlie, and I was surprised when she pulled his head just slightly to the right. It wasn't enough to make him move but enough that he'd hear the horse coming. I could actually see his right ear rotate to his right. "Why is this race taking so long, and where is the crowd noise? We're gonna get beat," I said out loud. Vickie very calmly reached back and popped him twice, and I couldn't believe it when Charlie's body lowered a little and he found the extra gear that jockeys say the great horses have. The momentum changed, and Charlie was drawing away. "**Where is that finish line?**" I asked out loud. The crowd noise came back, and his winning margin was two lengths, but he had five on them by the clubhouse turn. He truly was, as Vickie and Steve said, the best horse in the world at that time.

I stood in total disbelief, and Norm grabbed my arm while saying "Let's go to the winner's circle." Everything was moving at normal speed, and the noise was deafening.

When Vickie brought him into the winner's circle, she leaned down and said over the crowd noise, **"Nothing in this world was gonna beat him today!"**

I replied, "You've said that all along." She smiled and raised both arms with clenched fists. I didn't think it possible, but the noise reached another level. Through it all, Charlie was totally calm, and I'm sure he was wondering when he would get his oats. Steve had made arrangements for another trainer to take Charlie to the barn so he could attend the postrace interview.

ESPN led us to a platform. A woman was doing the interview, and her first remark was to Vickie. She raised her fist and laughed while saying "**To woman power!**"

Vickie replied, "I said this in an interview a while back, he's all man, and that was all him."

The lady smiled and asked, "Can you put into words what this means to you?"

Vickie thought for a few seconds before saying "There are no words to explain what the horse and this entire team mean to me. Over the past year, they've become family." She excused herself as tears started rolling down her face.

Steve was next. "Were you surprised when Wrong Way North came back on the way he did?"

"I was a little surprised when he didn't hit that gear a little sooner than he did, but I asked Vickie to keep a little in the tank. That'll teach me, she knows the horse better than anybody, so I should just get out of the way and let her do her job. She told the world after the Longacre Mile that, right now, he can beat any horse in the world, and today she backed up her words." He hugged Vickie and thanked her for the faith she had in him and, more importantly, in the horse.

The lady doing the interview said, "One more question, please. What's next?"

"He's had a long year and has earned a rest, so we'll turn him out for six months and let him enjoy being a horse for a while."

"Six months is a long time," she replied before telling us she would miss watching him run.

Steve said, "It is, and well deserved."

Norm had the next question. "What do you think about the six months off?"

Norm said, "Nothing, we pay Steve to think. He has made every decision since getting the horse, and I haven't seen too many bad ones. Like Steve, I think he's earned the rest, and quite frankly, I need the rest as much as he does."

I was last, "Jim, do you have any closing remarks?"

I said, "I agree with Vickie that we've become family, and I'd like to include Tom and Liz, the owners of *Slimsfinefood*, in that family. We're sorry they couldn't make it today, but their horse ran a great race. To go along with the horses, we have the best jockey and trainer we could have. **Thank you, sports fans, for your unwavering support!"**

Charlie was off the walker when I got back to the barn and yes, he was gobbling up his oats.

Steve thanked the other trainer for his help and he said, "It was my pleasure Steve and hopefully you can return the favor someday."

It was dinner time and we were all hungry. Steve didn't want to leave Charlie alone so we had him pick up something at the café and bring it back. I asked Vickie if Steve cashed her ticket for her and she told me he gave it to her, before thanking me. "Thank you for helping me keep my sanity and **I can't believe how much I've missed you.** I hadn't cashed my ticket so I said, "I have to run to the café for a minute." The man at the betting window was able to get me a check and I walked back to the barn with Steve.

We decided to eat at the café. They had a really good stew and salad special. Norm and I had that but Vickie just had the salad. "Your dedication really impresses me. Do you ever eat big meals?" I asked.

"Thanksgiving and Christmas, and even they are small portions. Sometimes you have to suffer a little for the things you love in life and Charlie has made all the years of dieting worth-while."

I hugged her and kissed her cheek before saying, "You're a huge part of our success and we appreciate you so much. You've also brought back my desire to go on living."

She gave me a little peck on the lips before saying "You guys have made my dreams come true."

I whispered, "It's been a long few weeks without you. I can't believe how much I've missed you, and I was so happy to see you in the paddock that I had tears in my eyes. I was afraid they might trickle down my face."

She said, "I saw the tears in your eyes and had to turn away before I cried. I needed my eyes clear, and I don't know of any goggles that protect against water from the inside."

We were laughing when I pulled her face to me for a rather sensual kiss before saying "You don't know how much I've needed that."

Her face was instantly flushed, and she said, "Let me know when you're ready for more than friendship because I missed you more than you'll ever know. I cried myself to sleep every night." I asked her to please give me a little more time, and she promised she would. *Better get my crap together.*

After dinner, we went back to the barn and collapsed into the lawn chairs before one of the guards came over to congratulate us. They were so quiet and professional that we almost forgot they were there. I thanked them for a fine job before, saying, "There will be a gratuity for a job well done." I'd made arrangements with their company to give them each five hundred extra dollars.

Steve told us he was also giving Slim six months off and went on about how great a race he ran. "He'll be a monster next year but not *the* **monster**. I expect the filly to come out running too, so we have an exciting year coming up."

I said, "Like Norm, I'm ready for some time off because this schedule has been tough on an old man." I thought about the kiss I gave Vickie. *Not too old.*

We were all flying out on the same flight at eleven the next morning. The horses would be picked up at eight thirty and would arrive an hour ahead of us, so Steve had made plans for a trainer to take care of them until we arrived.

I asked Norm if he wanted to go see Tom and Liz when we got back, and he replied, "No place I have to be."

Vickie said, "If you have room, I'd like to ride along." We had plenty of room for that little lady. I called to tell Tom we'd be up in a couple of days, and he was happy when I told him Vickie was going with us.

He said, "Charlie never ceases to impress me."

I replied, "Slim is the one that's improving, so next year will be fun."

When I was off the phone, Vickie said, "Slim will never be the horse Charlie is, but he's getting better with every start."

I said, "I'll always love Charlie because, if not for him, none of this would be happening. Please don't ever pull away from me again."

She told me she was sorry before telling me she missed me too. I asked her for just a little more time, and she smiled sweetly while telling me she wasn't going anywhere. I didn't know how far I expected things to go, but knew how much I missed her. *This is getting way too serious because I can't go through that pain again.*

We all went to sleep in the lawn chairs, and the sun woke us up at five thirty the next morning. Norm, Vickie, and I had to go to our rooms to shower and check out.

The flight was perfect going back, and the horses were in their stalls when we arrived. The day was bright, as was the world.

Vickie tickled both of us when she said, "If you boys will move your butts and make room, I'll get in, and we can get going."

She was in the middle, and Norm was driving, so I leaned forward and said to Norm, "This is one adorable lady."

He replied, "**She sure is!**"

I looked at her and said, "We flipped a coin to see who would ravish you on the way up, and **Norm lost**!"

She came out with her beautiful laugh while saying "**As always, *talk, talk, talk*!**"

The End

Well, that's one wager I wouldn't make!

Author's Note: If you've enjoyed this tale, a sequel is planned for the future. Watch for Lindalovestorun Comes of Age.

ABOUT THE AUTHOR

Jim Allen hailed from a small town in Central Washington State. With no desire for college, he entered the workforce and married his high school sweetheart in 1967. Still married to that same beautiful lady, he has retired at age sixty-four.

Jim has a story to tell about Charlie, an uncomparable racehorse, and invites you to come along on book 1 of this remarkable journey. (PS: His wife is not very happy with Vickie, one of the main characters in the story. Read on and find out why.) We hope you will enjoy reading it as much as he enjoyed writing it.

CPSIA information can be obtained
at www.ICGtesting.com
Printed in the USA
FSHW010858240921
84983FS